**She runs until she is directly beneath the moon,
its blue light shining down on her like a guide
to another world.**

She would gladly follow this path of light, if only she knew how.

Her brow furrows as she strains to see through the darkness that separates the trees. Nothing yet, but soon. Once a month, on the full moon, she receives a visitation.

Perhaps she is imagining it all, and her visions are merely a manifestation of her desperation to feel special. If that is the case, then so be it. Her mother loves to remind her of her age, as if it is a reason to stop believing in magic. She rolls her eyes at the thought—yes, she is a grown woman, and is that not magical in itself? To have survived this long, despite the world's penchant for beautiful dead girls? Marigold has grown up surrounded by the poets who propel the narrative—how romantic to die young, unstretched, unsullied, without ever outgrowing the part of the ingenue. But what happens when the girl keeps living, when she ages proudly and defiantly, without abandoning imagination, or stories, or that secret wish to find magic wherever it hides?

Well, then the poets would call her a witch.

The

HONEY
WITCH

SYDNEY J. SHIELDS

REDHOOK

Redhook Books/Orbit
Hachette Book Group
1290 Avenue of the Americas
New York, NY 10104
hachettebookgroup.com

First Edition: May 2024
Simultaneously published in Great Britain by Orbit

Redhook is an imprint of Orbit, a division of Hachette Book Group.
The Redhook name and logo are registered trademarks of Hachette Book Group, Inc.

The publisher is not responsible for websites (or their content) that are not owned by the publisher.

The Hachette Speakers Bureau provides a wide range of authors for speaking events. To find out more, go to hachettespeakersbureau.com or email HachetteSpeakers@hbgusa.com.

Redhook books may be purchased in bulk for business, educational, or promotional use. For information, please contact your local bookseller or the Hachette Book Group Special Markets Department at special.markets@hbgusa.com.

Library of Congress Cataloging-in-Publication Data
Names: Shields, Sydney J., author.
Title: The honey witch / Sydney J. Shields.
Description: First edition. | New York : Redhook, 2024.
Identifiers: LCCN 2023038567 | ISBN 9780316568869 (trade paperback) | ISBN 9780316568883 (ebook)
Subjects: LCGFT: Novels.
Classification: LCC PS3619.H54325 H66 2024 | DDC 813/.6—dc23/eng/20231031
LC record available at https://lccn.loc.gov/2023038567

ISBNs: 9780316568869 (trade paperback), 9780316568883 (ebook)

Printed in the United States of America

CW

7 9 10 8 6

For my grandma Kathy, and for all the impossible girls.

Content Warning

Content warnings include:

- Tattooing/needles
- Burns
- Blood/injuries
- Sex
- House fire
- Bee stings
- Loss of a grandparent
- Death/grief
- Discussions of infertility
- Treatment of miscarriage

Part One

It is the spring of 1831, and Althea Murr celebrates her hundredth birthday alone.

She sits beneath the wisteria tree, her orange cat curled in her lap. The bee-loud glade sings for her, a song worthy of the one hundred years she has lived.

A century of honey, earth, stone, and sky.

Of blood, venom, blooms, and ash.

She thinks of everything that was, and everything that could have been.

The stars peek through the twilit sky, asking her to make a wish, but she has none.

She has no wants, no needs, and no wishes that could be granted in the short time that she has left.

The springtime buds that decorate the earth remind her of childhood when she wanted to grow up to be a flower. She had told her mother, "One day, I will be a rose. And I will plant myself somewhere so beautiful that I will never want to leave."

Her mother laughed. "And what if someone wants to pluck you?"

"That is what the thorns are for," she said.

Since then, she has bloomed, she has thorned, and now she is happily withered. So, instead of granting her a wish, the spirits send her a message. From the sky descends a crow, an omen, a warning—she knows that death is near.

And thus, she has much to do.

Chapter One

Saying no—even thirteen times—is not enough to avoid tonight's ball. On this unfortunately hot spring day, Marigold Claude is trapped between her mother and younger sister, Aster, in a too-tight dress, in a too-small carriage. It's her sister's dress from last season, for Marigold refuses to go to the modiste to get fitted for a new one; an afternoon of being measured and pulled and poked is an absolute nightmare. Her blond hair is pulled up tightly so that her brows can barely move and her eyes look wide with surprise. Her father and her younger brother, Frankie, sit across from them, likely feeling quite lucky to have the luxury of wearing trousers instead of endlessly ruffled dresses. A bead of sweat snakes down the back of her neck, prompting her to open her fan. It's as if the more she moves, the larger the dress becomes. With every flap of her fan, the ruffles expand into a fluffy lavender haze. She is almost sure that she is suffocating, though death by silk might be preferable to the evening ahead.

This ball is the first event since her twenty-first birthday, so now she has a few months to marry before she is deemed an old and insufferable hag. The ride is far too short for her liking, as with any ride to another Bardshire estate. The opulent village was a gift from the prince regent himself; it is the home of favored artists from all over the world, including painters like Marigold's father. Sir Kentworth, a notable composer, is hosting tonight's event as an opportunity to share his latest works.

Though the occasion is more of a way to hold people hostage for the duration of the music, and force them to pretend to enjoy it.

The carriage door flies open upon arrival, the wind stinging Marigold's eyes, and she is the last to exit. Under different circumstances, she would have feigned illness so she did not have to attend, but her younger siblings are an integral part of the program this evening, and Frankie requires her support to manage his nerves before his performance. He's been practicing for weeks, but the melodies of Sir Kentworth's music are so odd that even Frankie—a gifted violinist who has been playing since his hands were big enough to hold the instrument—can hardly manage the tune. Aster will sing Sir Kentworth's latest aria, even though the notes scrape the very top of her range. Since their last rehearsal, Aster has been placed on vocal rest and openly hated every minute, her dramatic body language expressing her frustration in lieu of words. That rehearsal was the first time Marigold saw the twins struggle to use their talents, making her feel slightly better about having none of her own. She's spent her entire life simply waiting for some hidden talent to make itself known. So far, nothing has manifested, meaning she has only the potential to be a wife, and even that is slipping by her with every passing day. Her back is still pressed firmly against the carriage bench. If she remains perfectly still, her family may somehow forget to usher her inside, allowing her to escape the event altogether.

There are countless things she would rather be doing. On a night like this, when the blue moon is full and bursting with light like summer fruit, she wants nothing more than to bathe in the moon water that now floods the riverbanks. She wants to sing poorly with no judgment, wearing nothing but the night sky. And like all nights that are graced by a full moon, she has a secret meeting planned for midnight.

"Marigold, dear, come along," her mother, Lady Claude, calls.

Dammit, she thinks. *Escape attempt number one has failed.*

She huffs as she slides out of the carriage, declining the

proffered hand of the footman at her side. Her feet hit the ground with an impressive thud.

"Do try to find someone's company at least mildly enjoyable tonight," Lady Claude pleads. "You're not getting any younger, you know."

She adjusts her corset as much as she can without breaking a rib and says, "I do not want any company other than my own, and I do not intend on staying a moment longer than required."

Her mother has long tried (and failed) to turn Marigold into a proper Bardshire lady. The woman has introduced her to nearly every person even remotely close to her in age, hoping that someone will convince her that love is a worthy pursuit. So far, they've all been bores. Well, all except one—George Tennyson—but Marigold will not speak of him. He will most certainly be here tonight, and like always, they will avoid each other like the plague. Their courtship was a nightmare, but there is great wisdom to be found in heartbreak. Call it intuition, call it hope, or delusion, but Marigold knows she is not meant to live a life like that of her mother.

Rain whispers in the twilight, waiting for the perfect moment to fall. Dark clouds swirl in the distance, reaching for the maroon sun. This oppressive heat and the black-tinged sky remind her of a summer, almost fifteen years ago now. The summer they'd stopped visiting the only place in the world where she felt normal—her grandmother's cottage.

She'd always loved visiting Innisfree as a child. It was like a postcard, with fields of thick, soft clover to run through, gnarled trees to climb, and wild honeybees to watch tumble lazily over the wildflowers. And best of all, there was her grandmother. Althea was a strange woman, speaking in riddles and rhymes and sharing folktales that made little sense, but it didn't matter. Marigold didn't need the right words to understand that she and her grandmother were the same in whatever they were. She closes her eyes tightly, trying to remember the last summer she'd visited, but it's fuzzy with age.

She had made a friend—a boy her age who was dangerously curious and ferociously bright. He would come in the morning with his mother, and as the ladies sipped their tea, he and Marigold would run among the wildflowers together. She thinks of him often, dreaming of their mud-stained hands intertwined, though she does not remember his name. After what happened that day, she doesn't know if he survived.

She remembers the cottage window—always open, always sunny. Most of the time it could have been a painting, the world behind the glass as vivid as soft pastels. That day, she and her friend were told to stay inside. They snacked on honeycomb and pressed their sticky cheeks to the window, searching for faces in the clouds until the storm consumed the sky and turned the world gray. Her grandmother had run outside and disappeared into the heart of the storm, and the boy tried to grab her hand before he disappeared from her side. She remembers her mother's cold fingers pulling on her wrist, but everything else is blurry and dark.

For years, she has been asking her mother what happened. What was the gray that swallowed the sky? And what happened to the boy who tried to hold on to her hand? Her questions have gone unanswered, and they have never returned to her grandmother's cottage. She still questions if any of these memories are real. But her mother's hand bears the beginnings of a white scar peeking out from a lace glove. The truth is there, hidden in that old wound.

The other attendees spill out of their carriages in all their regalia. They stand tall and taut like they are being carried along by invisible string. Just before they walk inside, her father pulls her into an embrace and whispers in her ear, "Come home before the sun rises, and do not tell a soul about where you are running off to."

He winks, and Marigold smiles. Her father has always been kind enough to aid in her escape by distracting her mother at the right moment.

"I never do," she assures him. It's already too easy for people to make fun of a talentless lady trapped in Bardshire. She and everyone else know that she is not a normal woman. She sometimes wonders if she is even human, often feeling a stronger kinship with mud and rain and roots. Every day, she does her absolute best to play a part—a loving daughter, a supportive sister, a lady of marital quality. But in her heart, she is a creature hidden beneath soft skin and pretty ribbons, and she knows that her grandmother is, too. These are the wild women who run barefoot through the meadow, who teach new songs to the birds, who howl at the moon together. Wild women are their own kind of magic.

She is standing in between her twin siblings when Aster, stunning with her deep blue dress against her pale white skin, is immediately approached by handsome gentlemen. Aster was not meant to come out to society until Marigold, as the oldest, was married. After a time—really, after George—Marigold abandoned all interest in marriage, and the sisters convinced their parents to allow Aster to make her debut early. It was a most unconventional decision, one followed by cruel whispers throughout Bardshire at Marigold's expense, but she has lost the energy for bitterness. She tried love, once. It didn't work, and it is not worth the risk of trying again with someone new. Now Aster is the jewel of the Claude family, and Marigold is simply resigned.

Frankie clings to her side, his hands clammy with preperformance nerves. She flares her fan and waves it in front of his face, calming the redness in his cheeks.

"Thank you, Mari," he says with a shaky voice. She hands him a handkerchief to dry off his sweaty palms.

"You're going to be fine, Frankie. You always are."

He scoffs. "This music is nearly impossible. It was not written for human hands."

"Well, we'll get back at him next time when you have fewer eyes on you," she says with a wink. She and Frankie have always found some way to playfully disrupt events. Snapping a violin string so Frankie won't have to play. Pretending to see a snake in the middle of the dance floor. Stealing an entire tray of cake and eating it in the garden. Anything to escape the self-aggrandizing conversations. She leads Frankie through the crowd while noting the tables lined with sweets and expertly calculates how much she'll be able to eat without any snide remarks. She can probably get away with three—the rest, she'll have to sneak between songs.

The dance floor has been freshly decorated with chalk drawings of new spring flora. The art perfectly matches the floral arrangements throughout the ballroom. Decor of such elaborate design is not common, but Sir Kentworth is known for his flair, and he is exceptionally detail-oriented. His signature style shows in his music as well, though his latest works are growing increasingly baroque, as are his decorations. As they stroll toward the banquet table, Marigold catches the eye of her mother, who is leading a handsome young man toward her. She tries to increase her pace, but the crowd around her is impenetrable. In a matter of seconds, she's trapped in the presence of her mother and the young man while Frankie leaves her alone, set on taking all the good desserts.

Lovely. My freedom is thwarted, once again.

As she turns away from her brother, she flashes a vulgar gesture at him behind her back. Her mother places a hand on each of their shoulders.

"Marigold, this is Thomas Notley," her mother says. She knows this name—Sir Notley was the architect who designed the remodels of the Bardshire estates after they were purchased from the landed gentry. The man in front of her is the famed architect's grandson. They have seen each other many times, across many rooms, but this is their first proper introduction.

Her mother looks up at Mr. Notley. "And this is my beautiful daughter, Marigold Claude."

"It is an honor to be introduced to you, Miss Claude." His smile is bright and earnest as he takes her hand and kisses it.

His cropped hair allows the sharpness of his facial features to be fully admired, while his warm brown skin glows in the yellow light of the ballroom. He is extremely handsome, but like Marigold, he is plagued with a very poor reputation as a dancer. It is likely that not many people will be fighting to add his name to their dance card, despite his good looks.

"The pleasure is mine," she replies with a clenched jaw. It is embarrassing enough to be her age with no prospects or talents, but her mother makes it so much worse with these desperate matchmaking attempts.

"Well, I'll leave you two to dance," her mother says as she pushes them slightly closer together and disappears into the crowd. Marigold glares in the direction that her mother left. Normally, she at least gets one bite of something before she takes to the ballroom floor. "Mr. Notley," she says, "I know not what my mother said to you, but please do not feel obligated to dance with me. I should warn you I have no rhythm."

"Nor do I. My talents are better suited for sitting behind a desk and drawing architectural plans," he says with a smile.

"Then who knows what disaster will take place if we take to the floor together? It may become dangerous for all others involved."

"I disagree, Miss Claude. I believe we'll make a perfect pair."

She often has trouble filling up her dance card, and she must get out of this place as quickly as possible, so she devises a plan to make this work in her favor. Softening her demeanor, she looks up at him through her thick lashes. "All right then, Mr. Notley. Would it be too bold of me to request that you have all my dances tonight?"

He looks stunned, but then a pleased smile inches across his face. This proposition is perfect—she doesn't have to wait for anyone else to ask for a dance or feign interest in multiple stuffy artists all night long. If she can hurry through the obligations of the evening with this gentleman, she'll be able to leave with plenty of time for her own nightly plans. Now, if she can simply pretend to have a good time long enough to get through her dance card...

"I would be honored. Shall we make our way to the floor?"

She pauses, for she absolutely requires a scone while they are still warm and fresh.

"Might we get refreshments first? We have a lot of dancing ahead of us," she says sweetly, and he obliges as he leads them to the table. The luxurious scents of ginger, cinnamon, and cardamom grow stronger as they approach.

"I am guessing you are a fan of sweets?" he says with a bewildered laugh.

She nods as the excitement falls from her face, replaced by embarrassment. "Eating sweets is perhaps my only talent."

"I was not teasing. Please forgive me if it felt as if I were. I am known to have a sweet tooth as well. Shall we select our favorites and share them with each other?" he says politely, and his idea is delightful—less dancing, more eating. The pair find themselves stuffing each other's faces with scones and marmalades and other small nameless cakes that are too tempting to ignore. She removes her glove with her teeth and picks up a small square of honey cake. The white icing is covered in a thick layer of warm honey that drips onto its sides, so it must be eaten quickly.

"Open," she commands, and he almost cannot stop smiling long enough to allow her to feed him, but he does, and she drops the cake into his mouth before taking her fingers to her lips and sucking off the dripping honey.

"That is fantastic," he says with a full mouth, and she laughs as she nods in agreement.

"People always overlook the honey cake because it's messy and impossible to eat with gloves. But that never stops me. I refuse to walk past a tray of honey cakes without tasting them. They have always been my favorite, and the only part of these events that I actually enjoy," she says as she takes another and pops it into her mouth, savoring the sweet golden liquid that coats her lips.

"Miss Claude, you have a little..." he says, gesturing to the

\

corner of her mouth. She tries to wipe where instructed but continuously misses the mark. He finally removes his own glove and wipes away the small bead of honey from her lip. He licks it off of his thumb and smiles.

"There. All better," he says, and she blushes. They maintain eye contact, the heat of his fingers lingering where he touched her face. The two of them are currently breaking a number of etiquette rules, but she doesn't care.

"Well, I recant my earlier statement. It turns out that I am not exceptionally talented at eating sweets either, or I would be able to do so without making a mess of myself," she says, wiping around her mouth to ensure there aren't any lingering crumbs.

They share a genuine laugh, and at this moment, she thinks that maybe marriage wouldn't be the worst fate in the world. Mr. Notley is extremely handsome, comes from an exceptional family, and seems very agreeable, which is an important trait of any person who is going to attempt to fall in love with her.

But something still does not feel right. It would be like painting the walls of her life beige. It would be a safe choice, a comfortable choice that no one could fault her for, but it does mean that every day she would have to sit in her room and look at her beige walls and wonder what could have been if she had painted them bright yellow or pink. What if she had forgone paint entirely? Or better yet, what if there were no walls at all? Only sky, sunlight, salty water, fresh rain, and spring flowers and no one else around to comment on the paint color of the walls. That would be perfect, and that is why it is only a dream.

"What is that?" Marigold asks as she points over Mr. Notley's shoulder at nothing in particular. When he turns, she quickly takes a honey cake and wraps it in a piece of cloth before carefully hiding it in the small reticule purse that hangs from her wrist.

It's not for her, though. It's for her midnight meeting, so she must be sneaky. Mr. Notley turns back around and says, "What? I'm afraid I don't see anything."

She shrugs. "Ah, must have been my imagination. Shall we attempt to dance?"

He smiles as he follows her lead. She takes him in front of the band, where Frankie, Aster, and the other musicians are positioned like statues behind Sir Kentworth as he raises his sparkling conducting baton. Aster's voice fills the room, and though the melody is strange, it seems the vocal rest worked—she sounds undeniably angelic.

"Your brother and sister are extraordinary," Mr. Notley says.

"I hear that often," Marigold says quietly.

She turns her head and pushes through the dance. Mr. Notley is slightly better than she is, and they keep with the beat as best as they can. Focusing on her steps helps her forget the rest of the world for a small moment. The music is demanding—heavy, punctuated beats dictate a complicated dance. The command of the strings and the swift obedience of the dancers fill her with ferocious envy. How unfair that she may always desire but never earn that much control over a room.

A brief intermission follows so that the musicians may rest their overworked hands. People are still filing into the room like ants back from foraging, eager to show off their finds—an artifact that should not be in this country, a new wife wearing the late wife's dress. And then, as if he was waiting for Marigold's eyes to land on the door so that she would have no choice but to witness him, enters George Tennyson: a poet, a prodigy, and the most beautiful monster she has ever known. She has not spoken to him—beyond obligatory pleasantries—in two years, not that he would have given her the chance if she wanted to. He has not even looked at her for more than a few seconds since she was ten and seven and he left her on her knees outside of a ball just like the one they are attending tonight. Bardshire is a small world, so his occasional presence is unavoidable, but she always pretends that he is a ghost when she sees him. A hollow, transparent creature of only the past. Tonight, though, he is too close. She can feel the warmth of him from here. He is so undeniably and mercilessly alive.

He looks at her, intentionally so, surveying her body and settling on her hand intertwined with Mr. Notley's. His cheeks flush red and a devilish grin stretches across his face. His eyes find hers, and she cannot withstand the memories conjured by his gaze. Flashes of promenades and poetry and promises that proved to be empty. He starts walking toward her, and she wishes the floor would open up and swallow her whole. He's smiling, and she surprises herself when she smiles back. Hers is a cautious smile—what if he grants her the closure she has always wanted but never sought? Will he take back the worst of his words? Or could she, with one sharp sentence, ruin him? Words sit heavy on her tongue behind her saccharine smile. He's right in front of her, so happy and so handsome that she almost forgets what made her hate him so. Were they that bad? Could they be good again? His hand is reaching toward her. She takes a breath, moves to reach back, and then realizes too late that his hand is not reaching for her. He sidesteps her. From over her shoulder, she hears, "There you are, my love."

She turns slowly, against her better judgment, to see him kissing Priya Gill's white-gloved hand. The pair moves as one through the crowd and stops in the center. George calls for the attention of the room, and oh God, she knows it before it happens, hears it before he says it, the nightmare is both almost over and only just begun—he proposes to Priya Gill. He does so loudly and with such flair that there are no dry eyes in the room. Everyone else sees a beautiful couple, a grand wedding, another romance for the poets to wax on and on about in their leatherbound journals that apparently everyone takes as law. It's sick, all of it. His gaze locks onto Marigold for one brutal moment, as if to say, "*This could never be you.*"

His hand is wrapped around Priya's, but it's soft. It's not a death grip where he's pulling her back in line or squeezing her knuckles when she says something out of place. There is something prideful about the way he holds on to Priya, and it's maddening. He never loved Marigold like that. It was never soft, never gentle. George is a decade older than her, and during their courtship, he often cited his age as if it meant that he could never be wrong. He was too wise, too well-versed in the nature of people to make an improper judgment. No—George always had to be right, and it killed him every time he was bested by her: a young girl who was only meant to be a muse.

The hold George once had on her was punishing, like he was trying to mold her into a different shape, make it so she took up less space in every room. She blamed his father, high society, social pressures, and the like. Maybe things could have gotten better if they weren't trapped in Bardshire with all eyes on them all the time, if they simply gave up on everything except each other and ran away. She begged for that as he left her. She prayed at his feet like he was a god who might listen if her suffering was compelling enough. He never wanted her, though—not in any true way. He only wanted a bride who would succumb to his violent pursuit of civility.

Congratulations to dear old George. He has all that he wanted and did nothing to deserve it. The men will shake his hand and the women will watch Priya slowly realize that she is trapped, and they will teach her how to pretend that she is not breaking. Marigold, decidedly, will never be broken by him, or anyone, ever again.

The music resumes, and Mr. Notley sweeps her away into a new dance, twirling her until George and his betrothed are out of sight. But she cannot escape the whispers that snake through the room.

"Priya is a much better choice."

"Remember when he was with the Claude girl? What a lark."

"It's too late for her. She will never, ever marry."

She scrunches her nose in a way that makes her look like a lapdog, so says her mother. A bitch, Aster once said before she knew exactly what that word meant. Marigold laughed then— what is so wrong about being a bitch? It is the closest a girl can be to a wolf.

Mr. Notley studies Marigold's face for a moment. "Miss Claude, will you allow me one prying question?"

She squeezes his shoulder as they turn in time with the music. "It seems I am trapped. How can I refuse?"

"How is it that you are not married?"

Marigold flinches. "What makes you think that I should be?"

"You are beautiful and full of life, like springtime," Mr. Notley says.

"And why should those qualities merit promising myself to another? Perhaps there is a reason you cannot marry the spring."

"But I could marry *you.*"

"You speak as if that decision belongs to you alone." Marigold steps on his toes and does not pretend that it is an accident. "I am not married because I have yet to find someone who makes me feel seen."

He steadies himself on his throbbing toes. "You don't believe that I could see you?"

"No. You see only springtime. What happens when I am winter? I will tell you, Mr. Notley. When winter comes"—she leans in close so their noses are almost touching—"you will freeze."

Heat lingers on her lips, and surprisingly, Mr. Notley smiles.

They dance through six songs, enough to fill an entire dance card. Aster makes eye contact with Marigold, her eyes full of apology as they flit between her and George. Marigold bites the inside of her cheek and shakes her head as she makes her final curtsy to Mr. Notley. She begins to walk away from the floor, fighting against an ocean of tears behind her eyes. It gets easier with every step, and so it is decided—she will walk through the whole night if she must, for she will not shed one more tear for that man. He is not worth the energy, and neither is anyone else. As soon as she reaches the door, her elbow is caught, and Mr. Notley pulls her around to face him.

He looks at her as if he thought his hand might pass through her, as if she were only a wish. "Are you leaving, Miss Claude?"

She swallows the last of her sadness. "Yes, I'm afraid all that

dancing has left me feeling quite faint. I must rest," she says
breathlessly, hoping to make her story more believable.

"Might I help you to your carriage, then?"

Her eyes widen, for there is no carriage waiting. She intends
on escaping on foot, through the gardens.

"That will not be necessary. I feel that the fresh air is just
what I need," she says as she attempts to turn back toward the
door.

"Have I done something wrong? I must admit I thought we
were having a lovely time," he says. His words are kind enough,
but nothing he says can change the fact that there is somewhere
else she would rather be. Her skin starts to burn underneath his
unwavering grip.

"My haste has nothing to do with you. I simply have somewhere I must be. Have another honey cake for me," she says as
she yanks her arm away and then shakes his hand firmly in the
same manner that she has seen her father do many times to end a
meeting with a patron that has dragged on for too long. He holds
her hand there, still seeming somewhat dazed and confused at
her rush.

"Is there someone else, Miss Claude? Another man waiting
for you out there?"

She cannot help but laugh wildly. Since George, Mr. Notley is
the only man in Bardshire she has been able to stand speaking to
for more than five minutes, so the idea of having two men who
she would want to spend an evening with is a hilarious joke that
seems to be entirely lost on him.

"There is no other man. I can assure you."

"Then why must you leave me so suddenly? I will not let you
go before I understand."

She lets out a sigh of frustration. "Mr. Notley, I intend to run
out to the meadow barefoot and soak up the blue moonlight. I
intend to sing loudly, to dance freely, maybe even scream if I
wish. I intend to ruin this dress with the mud and the rain. And
if I don't go now, then I will miss the brightest hour of the blue

moon, which only happens once a year. Now, if you will excuse me," she says. She looks back at him as he stares at her with absolute bewilderment.

"You are a wild creature, Miss Claude. I hope to see you again," he calls after her. She waves goodbye and then takes off in a run, knowing that she will not allow herself to be tamed.

Chapter Two

Marigold runs until she trips over a rogue tree root that has curled up out of the earth, and the hem of her dress sinks into the muddy ground. As she kneels in the grass, far away from the rest of the world, she is finally at peace. No suitors, no expectations, no one here but the stars and the trees.

She takes off her shoes and her stockings and lets the grass tickle between her toes. Breathing in the scent of an impending storm, she knows she must hurry if she is to reach the meadow before the first rainfall. She undoes her fanciful updo and lets her hair fall down her back. Her brows sink when the tension is released, and she scrunches her face to wake up the muscles that were pulled tight through the evening. Picking herself up, she gathers her shoes and stockings and the bottom of her dress into her arms and runs again. Her feet have carried her over this path countless times, and now they recognize their surroundings. This feels like home—the wet ground her bed, the breeze her blanket. The trees begin to thin until there are none left, only an open meadow, begging her to center herself inside of it. She runs until she is directly beneath the moon, its blue light shining down on her like a guide to another world. She would gladly follow this path of light, if only she knew how.

Her brow furrows as she strains to see through the darkness that separates the trees. Nothing yet, but soon. Once a month, on the full moon, she receives a visitation.

Perhaps she is imagining it all, and her visions are merely a manifestation of her desperation to feel special. If that is the case, then so be it. Her mother loves to remind her of her age, as if it is a reason to stop believing in magic. She rolls her eyes at the thought—yes, she is a grown woman, and is that not magical in itself? To have survived this long, despite the world's penchant for beautiful dead girls? Marigold has grown up surrounded by the poets who propel the narrative—how romantic to die young, unstretched, unsullied, without ever outgrowing the part of the ingenue. But what happens when the girl keeps living, when she ages proudly and defiantly, without abandoning imagination, or stories, or that secret wish to find magic wherever it hides?

Well, then the poets would call her a witch.

It is better to be lost in a beautiful daydream than trapped in a dim reality. Still, there must be some truth to what she sees, some explanation beyond wistful yearning. This meadow is the only place where she can conjure that feeling of belonging that she once felt during those Innisfree summers before it all went dark.

Like her grandmother, Marigold's heart belongs to the wilder world. It is as if she is an extension of nature, a season of herself—summer, winter, spring, autumn, and Marigold Claude. When they were children, Marigold had hoped Aster or Frankie would understand her strange visions, her undying need to be out in nature, but she has always been alone. Her sister used to tease her and say she was making up magical stories to feel better about not being able to sing. All she knows for sure is that she feels more connected to the characters in her grandmother's folktales than to the people around her because no one else in Bardshire believes in magic.

At her back, between the tallest trees, there is a light blue glow. The light reaches her hair and prompts her to turn around.

"There you are." She smiles as she walks forward. Close enough to tickle her nose is a large butterfly with an aura of bright blue starlight. She pulls the sticky honey cake from the reticule and offers it to the creature. It lands on top of the dessert and uncurls its ribbony tongue to lick the honey from the top. As it eats, its light glows brighter.

"Whatever you are, you sure love honey." This is the creature that Marigold has felt connected to ever since she was a young child. On the nights of full moons, she would feel this relentless call from the woods, and an insatiable desire to answer. The first summer in which they did not travel to Innisfree, she found a way to sneak out of their estate and follow the feeling that tugged at her heart. She met the creature she came to call Lunasia, and ever since, she has thought herself able to speak the language of wild things that no one else can hear.

Tonight, Lunasia seems to flash and buzz with energy. The clouds dance between them, weaving in and out like ribbons between Marigold's shiny blond curls. When Lunasia moves, the clouds move with her and transform into thin wisps of light. Sparks fall around her like lightning bugs. Marigold watches the world glow, and the message seems clear: A new era is dawning. A new life is beginning. Maybe a new love is coming.

This thought sends Marigold into a mild panic as she wonders if the message could mean that she is to be married. Perhaps Mr. Notley may call on her the next morning. They may promenade for all to see. He may ask for her hand in front of the crowd, and in the eyes of everyone else, they will be a perfect pair—of course the worst dancers in Bardshire are meant for each other. She would finally live up to everyone's expectations. To be a wife, and then to become a mother soon after. It all sounds too...stifling. There would be no more running off through the garden at night. She would miss every blue moon from here on out. Every moment of her time would belong to someone else, and she would never again be alone here in the heart of the meadow.

Her mother would be thrilled, of course. There were days after George left her that she thought her mother might have been even more heartbroken than she was. The image of him proposing to Priya flashes in her mind, though it doesn't sting as much as she thought it might. George was right to leave her. They got along fine, sure, but that was not why she cared for him so much. He was widely wanted, with his good looks, remarkable talent, and extravagant wealth. And he *chose* her. He made everyone else be kind to her for the first time. He quieted those who had always teased her. But it didn't last. Soon, he saw her for what she truly was—strange. And when he left her, it confirmed to everyone that she did not belong. She agrees, of course, but what now? What else can she expect for her life? She is growing older. She cannot continue to live with her parents, sneaking into the meadow at night, seemingly working toward absolutely nothing. That will not do—not for Marigold and not for the rest of her family. She must do *something*. And what is there to do for a talentless young lady in Bardshire, other than become a wife?

But this is precisely why she prefers to be alone now. No one would ever understand that the wilder world speaks to her, or how she sees visions in the ripples of the sea, or how she always knows when it is going to storm, days before it happens. She could never explain how she invariably can create the perfect kitchen-made cure to any ailment, or how her dreams have a miraculous way of coming true. No one here could ever believe any magical gifts to be real, and she cannot stand the idea of being called a liar or, worse, a charlatan.

After seeing the message of the stars on this night, Marigold feels the walls rising around her. She senses the sky lowering itself onto her shoulders. She may be leaving Marigold Claude in this meadow and emerging as the soon-to-be Lady Notley. The name feels wrong to even imagine, like stuffing herself into Aster's awful lavender dress from last season.

Rain comes slowly. The first drops fall down Marigold's skin, exploring the soft edges of her body. She dances through the mist until the weight of it compels her to lie down in the grass. She stays in the meadow until the sun begins to reach through the trees in the soft beginning of morning. She imagines the weight of a ring on her finger. It is too heavy, too cold, too tight. Sleep does not come to her—she cannot waste this time with sleep. She wants to savor every second she has to herself. She memorizes the exact shade of blue of the moon. She counts the blades of grass in her hair. She wishes upon the dandelions that pepper the meadow.

And now it is time to return home and face whatever future awaits her there.

She strolls through the rain-soaked woods and walks in time with the rising sun. Lunasia follows Marigold for as long as she can, but she begins to fade toward the edge of the tree line. Her home starts to emerge in the distance, complete with the flourishing gardens featured in her father's paintings, and she sees something that makes her heart sink. The sky above her house burns red. She turns to find Lunasia glowing with that same ominous aura. The rest of the sky remains bright and clear. Another message—this time, Marigold is entirely unsure what it means, but she knows that it is not good. She runs onto the grounds of her home to the small side entrance and sneaks inside, following the distant sound of a heated argument. As she walks through the estate and comes closer to the sound, she recognizes her mother's voice.

"How dare you," her mother says, her words as sharp as a needle. "I am the one who has protected her. I have always protected her, above everything else."

"You speak of this great protection and yet you do not even know where she is right now, Raina," says the voice of an older woman. Marigold stiffens. No one ever calls her mother by her first name, except...

Marigold's grandmother.

With even more care, she tiptoes toward the sitting room with her ear pressed against the door.

"I saved her that day. I did. By myself, without magic," her mother says.

"And since that day, I have worked tirelessly to make Innisfree safe again, but I cannot keep doing it alone. You must let her make her own decision. I gave you a choice. She is owed the same."

"No. There is no choice to be made here. Your life and your world are dangerous. I will not allow you to take her. It's cruel and it's selfish."

"What's cruel and selfish is the fact that you are not willing to let her find her own fate."

"The fate that you speak of is death."

Marigold gasps louder than she meant to. Maybe they didn't hear it? Seconds tick by. She hears her mother's footsteps approaching. It's too late to hide. Her mother opens the door swiftly, finding Marigold crouched behind it, frozen and unsure. She's never been caught sneaking out before. Her father keeps her mother distracted for the evening, and she always comes home before sunrise.

Her mother's brown eyes are bloodshot and puffy, and her blond hair is a tangled mess. She is still in her green gown from the ball, but the shoulders are sagging and the ribbons at the back are coming undone. She pulls Marigold into a punishing embrace.

"Where have you been?"

Marigold peers over her mother's shoulder and meets her grandmother's gaze. Althea is sitting on the plush couch, her small and spotted hands placed neatly in her lap. She smiles, pushing against the tension of the well-earned wrinkles around her mouth. It's been years since they last saw each other, but she never forgot the warmth of her grandmother's face. They have the same eyes—amber brown speckled with gold.

"Answer me," her mother commands, her voice desperate and angry.

"The meadow," she whispers, as if that will be enough to satisfy her mother's raging curiosity.

"What meadow? Were you with someone? Sneaking off with Thomas Notley?"

She scoffs and says, "Sorry to disappoint you, but no. I was... alone."

"Would it have anything to do with the full moon?" Althea says from across the room.

Her mother turns her head and says, "Do not speak to her about such things. I want no more words from you."

"Mother," Marigold gasps. She has never heard her mother speak so rudely, and to her own mother, no less. It is beyond shocking, especially considering that Althea is correct. Marigold turns to her grandmother and says, "How did you know?"

"Because we are the same, you and I," she says as she begins to stand, smoothing out her rose-colored dress. Her mother turns her back to Marigold and extends her arms as if shielding her from Althea.

"Stop this! Stop this at once, Mother. I mean it. You are not to come near my daughter."

"Your daughter is a grown woman. You cannot keep her from her destiny, and you cannot keep her from speaking with me if she wishes to," she says as she leans to the side to meet Marigold's gaze. "And I hope that you do wish to speak, Marigold. It is time for you to know the whole truth. You should have known years ago."

"Marigold, go to your room," her mother says over her shoulder.

"I want to hear what Grandmother has to say."

Her mother's head whips around to face her. She can see the hurt in her mother's eyes, but she is not willing to let anything stand between her and the truth.

Not anymore.

She steps out from behind her mother and hurries to sit beside her grandmother. "I have been kept in the dark my whole life, and it has been killing me. Please, tell me the truth."

"First, tell me where you went. Tell me what you saw," Althea says hurriedly.

"She is not like you, Mother," her mother yells. "She does not see what you see."

With a deep breath, Marigold focuses her gaze on the floor.

"I do see things, and you know that, Mother. I've asked you so many times for so many years to explain it, and you have refused. So, I had to figure things out another way."

Her mother raises her brows. "What is that supposed to mean? What do you think you've figured out?"

"I've been sneaking out once a month to speak with them. Last night was no exception. There is a creature alive in the meadow, and…"

"A spirit? Something that resembles an animal of some kind but clearly isn't?" Althea says plainly, and Marigold searches for words before she responds.

Marigold nods and says, "I also saw something as I came home. Red light spilling from the sky over our estate. It felt like a warning of some kind."

"The second omen," her grandmother says under her breath.

"If this is true," her mother interrupts, "how have you managed to hide it from me?"

She chews on her lower lip for a moment before she decides to tell the truth. There is no use hiding it any longer—not when she's standing before her mother in a mud-stained dress.

"Father knows. He's always known."

Her mother places her hand over her heart. "Impossible. He would never keep that from me. He loves me."

She glares at her. "Love has nothing to do with it. You are no stranger to keeping secrets from people you love."

"Oh, Mari," she says with a wobbly voice. "There is so much you don't know. So much you don't understand. So much pain from which I have spared you!"

"Spared me?" she yells as she stands. "I have been dying here. I have felt completely alone, hopelessly waiting for anyone to make me feel normal. Nothing that you have kept from me could be worse than this."

A tear slips down her mother's face, but she wipes it away quickly. "You are wrong, Marigold. You are not dying here. In fact, staying here is the only thing that has kept you alive."

Confused, she looks between her mother and grandmother, hoping to find some understanding.

Her mother wipes her forehead with the back of her hand and says, "I don't even know where to begin to explain all this. I shouldn't have to." She glares at Althea. "You should never have come here."

"I had to, and you know that, Raina. You also know that Marigold is not a normal girl, and keeping the truth from her is doing more harm than good."

"Oh, please," her mother says as she rolls her eyes and regards Althea with disgust. "You do not care about what is best for her, otherwise you would not be here right now. The last time we saw each other was the worst day of our lives. You almost got my daughter killed!"

Desperate for answers, Marigold interrupts and says, "During the storm? All I remember from that day is watching the world turn black."

"It wasn't a storm. It was an attack," her grandmother says.

"And you were the target," her mother wails. "Your grandmother seems to have forgotten that."

Althea turns to her daughter and says, "As I explained to you as soon as I arrived, Innisfree has been safe for over a decade now."

"But now you need my daughter to risk her life, again, in order to keep it that way? That's not safe, Mother. Far from it."

"Who was trying to kill me?" Marigold interrupts loudly.

Her mother and grandmother stare at each other for a moment before her grandmother says, "Would you like to tell her, or shall I?"

"Do not ask me to relive that day."

Her mother starts to leave the room. She hangs her head for a moment before looking at Marigold. "I have done nothing but protect you. And I do not want to stop protecting you. But if you won't let me, if you don't trust me, there is nothing I can do." Another tear slips. This time, she lets it fall before walking out of the room. Her mother is no stranger to dramatics, but the pain in her eyes looks real and sharp. Marigold is tempted to follow her, but she stops herself. Too many questions have haunted her for too long. And now the answers stand before her.

She sits next to her grandmother and says, "I've missed you so much." Her voice wobbles as her emotions catch her by surprise. She feels like a child again—small, curious, and safe.

"I've missed you more," her grandmother says, and that does it—Marigold surrenders to her tears as she hugs her grandmother tighter than is probably safe for a woman of Althea's age. Her grandmother strokes Marigold's dark blond hair until she catches her breath.

Marigold sits up straight and wipes her face before taking her grandmother's hands in her own. "What happened that day?"

"Our story begins long before that day. Before you, or your mother, or I was ever born. It starts with power, and the endless struggle to keep it."

"What power?"

"We are witches, darling. Every eldest daughter in our lineage is a witch, including you."

Her heart races, beating the breath out of her body. This is it—what she has always felt, always known to be true, that she is not strange or bad or broken as she has been made to feel. New realizations click together in her mind like heavy locks and spindly keys. She places her palm on her chest. "Even Mother?"

"She was. Until she gave up her magic."

Her eyes widen. "Why would she do that? Why would *anyone* ever do such a thing?" She can think of nothing that could make her give it all up, especially not for a life in Bardshire.

"Love," her grandmother says with a resigned smile. "Our line is cursed, Marigold. For us, love and power are opposing forces. We must forsake one for the other."

"So Mother chose love, but you did not?" Wise choice. Love is a burden. It doesn't work for wild women.

Althea has a solemn look about her as she shakes her head. "I did not get a choice. Our line has always been witches, but the curse began fifty years ago with me and the woman who tried to harm you the last time you came to Innisfree."

That sentence heavies the air. Marigold closes her eyes and remembers the storm, now with the knowledge that it was no storm at all. Everything begins to sharpen. She sees the cottage window and recognizes the darkness spilling inside; not clouds, but smoke. Not rain, but ash. Not lightning, but flames. And in the center of it all is not a cyclone—it is a woman with flaming curly red hair.

"Who?" she asks.

"To understand who she is, you must first understand the nature of our power. We're called Honey Witches. Our magic comes from working with the bees to create enchanted honey. We also use flowers, herbs, and spices for our spells. But it is the nature of the universe to have an equal opposite to every force. Fire is the opposite of water. Air is the opposite of earth, and…" she says as she pulls a vial of warm golden honey from her pocket, "the opposite of honey is ash. So where there are Honey Witches, there are…"

She leans in. "Ash Witches?"

"Precisely. And anything that we would utilize, they must burn first before it is of any use to them. So, as you can imagine, Innisfree is of great importance to both of us. It is a land ripe with power and all the ingredients that any witch could ever need, and it is also rich with life." She looks at her hands in her lap, turning them over and counting the age spots like they are annual rings of a tree. "It has granted me over a century."

Marigold's jaw drops as she takes Althea's hand in hers. "How is that possible?"

"It is sacred land. It cares for those who tend to it. There are hundreds of enchanted places like it, tucked in every corner of the world. Honey and Ash Witches are born to protect them. I have only ever used Innisfree's blessings to help and heal others, but my counterpart, Versa, could not say the same. She believed that if we hoarded our power for ourselves, we could use the isle's magic to grant ourselves immortality," Althea says, scowling in disgust.

"And you didn't want that? Why?"

Althea pauses, pinching her brows. "Because it is selfish, Marigold. Ash Witches are meant to clear away the rot of death, to bring warmth to people. Honey Witches tend to new growth in the wake of fire, to help life rise from the ashes. Versa selfishly betrayed all the work we were meant to do together." Althea's knuckles turn white as she tightens her fist. She clenches her jaw. "A life spent on only the pursuit of power is not worthy of eternity. I would not let her take my purpose from me. Not without a fight. And trust that I gave everything I had in order to win." She smiles, though there is something else behind her eyes. A memory, a loss, a sadness of some sort. "That is where the curse began. If she couldn't defeat me, maybe she could outlive my line so that, one day, there would be no one to stop her. She cursed us to never have anyone fall in love with us in an attempt to end us. But it didn't work, of course. I had Raina without love, and then she forsook magic and the curse altogether."

Realization washes over her. "That's why she came that day. To end the line. To end...me." Panic rises in her chest and surges through her blood, causing sharp tingles in her palms and fingertips. No wonder her mother never let her return.

"After Raina's choice, we did not know if her first daughter would have magic. We truly thought it may have ended with her." Althea holds Marigold's cheek and tucks a hair behind her ear. "But here you are, honey-eyed and more powerful than I could have ever imagined."

Her heart warms as she looks into Althea's eyes, but something isn't right. She stands and paces around the room, running her dirty fingers through her hair.

"Why didn't you come here, Grandmother? Fifteen years without a visit, without telling me the truth of what we are."

"Your mother would not permit it, and I respected her wishes. I understood, and still do, why she did not want you to know."

"Then what changed? Why are you here now?"

Althea takes a deep, dry breath and clears her throat as best she can. "I'm dying, darling. I am not strong enough to keep Innisfree on my own. If we are to keep our land and our line, I need you to complete the ritual and join me," she says as she holds the vial of honey toward Marigold with her trembling hand.

She takes the vial and rolls it in her palm. "But what of Versa? She still lives?"

"Versa is weakening as I am, and she will not die quietly. I have seen the omens." She grabs Marigold's wrist and squeezes. "And so have you. She will try to take Innisfree again before her end. But there is only one of her, and she alone is not a match for two witches. I need you to help me keep the isle safe. I have created a veil of protection over Innisfree, but I am no longer strong enough to maintain it on my own. With our power combined, we could make Innisfree safe for centuries."

Marigold places her palm and the vial over her heart. All her life, she wondered what her destiny could be, what talent she could hope to possess. She wondered what that burning power in her heart would lead to, and now everything is beginning to make sense. She may not be a painter or a singer or a violinist, but she is gifted in other ways. For the first time, she has a purpose. She has meaning. She has a future. But with that comes sacrifice.

"If I do this, I can never have a love of my own. How am I to continue the line? How did you come to bear a child?"

"You don't need someone to love you to have a child," Althea says.

"Well then, who is my grandfather?"

Althea stiffens with that same sad look in her eyes as if she is about to say something disappointing. "You don't have one. Your mother was born from my own magic. And if you elect to have a child of your own, you can accomplish it in the same way. Easy as lemon drop pie."

Marigold's jaw falls to the floor. "I could be that powerful? I could create life?"

Her grandmother does not respond while Marigold paces and thinks. It's a lot to take in all at once—the magic, the attack, the sudden and terrifying idea of one day having a child by herself. She finally returns to her grandmother's side and says, "There were others there on the day of the attack. I remember a boy who was my age. What happened to him?"

Althea smiles. "August Owens. He still visits, albeit less than before. His father is a ship carpenter of great skill, and August travels with him to work. But when he's not sailing, he lives in Lenox. It's the town across the lake."

"So he wasn't harmed that day?" Marigold says with relief, and Althea nods.

"And I'm sure he would be thrilled to see you again," Althea says, placing a spotted hand on Marigold's knee. "You belong there, Marigold. You know this to be true."

Marigold smiles but shakes her head. "I don't know if I can leave Aster and Frankie. I'll miss them terribly."

"Once we strengthen the veil together, you may travel as you wish. There is a whole world out there that I would love for you to see," Althea says.

"Mother will never allow this."

"It is your life and it is your choice, Marigold. Completely your choice. Just because she chose a life of love and marriage does not mean you must. I beg you, darling," she says as she grasps Marigold's hands. "Put away all thoughts of anyone else's expectations. Only you have the right to decide your own fate."

A sense of empowerment blooms in her chest like nothing that Marigold has ever felt before. Suddenly before her there is so much freedom, and that is all she has ever wanted.

"I wish I could give you more time to think, but death is too close to wait."

With one deep breath, Marigold's decision is made. "Then let us be quick. I am ready to become a witch."

Chapter Three

What her mother doesn't know won't hurt her.

Well, that's not entirely true. She'll be furious when she finds out that Marigold and Althea did the ritual without speaking to her, but that is a problem for another hour. Now their focus is on sneaking off to Marigold's meadow without a confrontation. Aster is in Marigold's room packing her things for Innisfree. Frankie is leading the way, checking that each room is clear before they enter. Every step is a risk. Every click of a heel, every creak of a stair, could be their undoing. It's not that her mother would be able to stop them completely, but she would do that thing that all mothers do where they stare for a very long time with their brows raised and jaw clenched until they get their way. Marigold has lost to that look many times before—when she tried to stay home from the last ball, when she asked to go back to Innisfree every summer, when she begged to know why her grandmother had disappeared from her life. She does not yet have the confidence to stand up to that look. Most people live their lives in the pursuit of happiness, but she accepted long ago that happiness was out of her reach. So she lived her life in pursuit of her mother's happiness instead but still managed to fall short. No dress or hairstyle or poorly sung lullaby could ever change the fact that Marigold was meant for something more, something magical.

Frankie leads them around a corner, toward the small side exit in the kitchen. "Aster said that if she finds Mother before we've escaped, she'll pretend to faint so she can keep her distracted," he says.

"She is quite theatrical," Althea says.

Marigold laughs and says, "She was born for the stage, in every sense. That's why she's Mother's favorite."

"Hey!" Frankie whines.

"What? Aster is Mother's favorite, and you're Father's favorite, and I'm—"

Suddenly, Frankie collides with a figure standing in the doorway: their father.

"You're what, Marigold?" he says.

The three of them freeze in his presence. No wonder he was so good at helping Marigold sneak out; he's quite the rogue himself, apparently.

"Frankie, Althea, I need a moment alone with my daughter. Both of you, wait in the sitting room." His voice is so stern that no one tries to protest.

"I'm sorry," Althea says before she turns, and he gives an accepting nod with a light smile. He whispers something to Althea—Marigold will always wonder what—and then she is alone with her father.

After a long silence, she whispers, "Please."

"Please, what?"

"Please let me go. Please."

His brow furrows. "Mari, I'm not here to change your mind."

She widens her eyes. "Then why are you here? How did you know we would be doing this?"

"Because I know your grandmother very well, and your siblings, and most of all, I know you. And I know what you've always wanted. That's why I never stopped you before, and I'm not stopping you now."

"But Mother—"

"I know *her*, too. She is only trying to protect you, so much so that she cannot see how it is harming you. Perhaps it is the artist in me, but I've always thought it so romantic to have beauty and creation as your purpose. And that is the life ahead of you, Marigold. I have every confidence in you. Your mother will see that soon, too."

He pulls her into an embrace, and she says, "Thank you, Father." She returns to the sitting room and takes her grandmother's hand, and they leave the estate together.

The journey through the wood feels longer than it ever was, on account of Marigold having to aid her grandmother through the twists and turns of the uneven path.

"Are you sure you want to keep going? I'm confident we can find another suitable spot for the ritual," she says, but Althea refuses to stop, even as her legs tremble.

"Grandmother, please, let's take a break."

"Marigold, at this point, your whining is slowing us more than my legs. I am fine, darling. Onward!"

She rolls her eyes and continues alongside Althea until they finally reach the meadow. The sun is only just peeking over the horizon, waiting patiently to greet the sky. The two women are centered in the meadow, the world around them still as stone.

"Look around and tell me what you see," Althea says as she takes her hands.

"I see trees, streaks of clouds, dew-wet grass, and flowers that have yet to bloom. It's just a meadow."

"Exactly. It is just a meadow. Beautiful, of course, but only a meadow."

She cocks her brow. "Right?"

Althea hands her the crystal vial of honey that she showed her earlier. As Marigold wraps her hand around it, Althea pulls off the lid. The strong, spiced scent of honey fills the air, sweet enough to make her teeth hurt. Inside the vial, tiny flecks of light float throughout the golden liquid, as if they were captured from the sun itself. "Now, close your eyes and drink this. When you open them again, tell me what you see."

She takes the honey potion that will allow her to access her full power. The crystal is cold against her full bottom lip. As she tilts her head back with her eyes closed, the warm honey drips into her mouth, the drops heavy on her tongue. It coats her entire mouth and swims down her throat, landing warm in her belly. Immediately, she feels something surging in her veins—power. It's hot, almost burning underneath her skin.

But it feels good. It feels right. It feels like she was always meant to burn.

When she opens her eyes, the world around her is completely changed. It is the same meadow, her feet still firmly planted in the tall green grass. But all around her, peeking through the leaves, leaping through the flowers, flying through the sky, are the spirits. Not only Lunasia, but dozens more. An entire world lives beyond a veil that has just been lifted.

"The creatures you see now are called the landvættir, and they are spirit guardians of nature."

Marigold extends her hand to Lunasia, who lands on her finger where a gold band would sit if she chose a different fate.

"She is always here," Althea says. "Before, the veil was only thin enough for you to see her during the full moon."

Lunasia's wings are brighter than ever before in the light of the rising sun. Above them are colorful creatures that Marigold does not recognize, turning the sky into a mosaic of flighted beauty. Pastel clouds trail behind them like ribbons. It's amazing. Art, alive. "Are they painting the sunrise?"

"They are. They will paint the sunset as well. It's their job."

"Beautiful," she says, her voice trembling with emotion as she watches a world of beauty unfurl itself to her and welcome her inside.

"How do you feel?"

She wipes a tear that has escaped from her eye, the salt of it stinging her soft skin. She thought perhaps that she would feel heavier in this moment—cursed, trapped, even damned.

But she does not. Her feelings could not be more opposite.

"Whole," she says. "I feel finally whole."

Althea pulls her into a soft embrace, the powdery scent of her hair masking that of the honeyed air for a moment. "You were born for this, darling. Wait until you see Innisfree again after all these years. There are many landvættir there who rely on you to care for them and their home, just as you will rely on them for protection and divination." She pulls back and takes her grand-daughter's hand. "Shall we return to say our goodbyes?"

"Might Lunasia come with us?" As Marigold makes her request, Lunasia leaves her palm and flies behind her.

"She is the spirit guardian of this meadow, Marigold. The same way that you will serve as a guardian of Innisfree."

"I see. So, the goodbyes have already begun."

Althea gives her a sympathetic look. "I'm afraid it will get worse before it gets better, but I can promise you it is worth it."

Marigold smiles. "I believe you."

Chapter Four

Frankie, breathless and drenched in sweat, meets them half-way through the woods on their walk back to the estate.

He places his hands on the top of his head and stands very straight to support the flow of air to his lungs. His blue eyes squint in the morning light. "We have a slight problem."

Marigold scrunches her nose. "Mother?"

"Mother."

The three of them move as quickly as they can to get back to the estate. Once inside, Marigold sees Aster and her father getting scolded by her mother.

"...after I *clearly* said that she should never—"

"Mother," Marigold says. Her mother gasps as she looks up.

"Marigold, tell me you did not do this," she says, rushing over and taking Marigold's face in her hands.

Her mother surveys her, and Marigold can see the moment that her mother realizes it is too late.

A darkness comes over her mother. "How could you?"

"I had to," she says. She does not turn away. She does not look down. She stands tall and proud and certain that she did the right thing for herself.

"And you?" her mother says as she turns her head to Althea like a viper. "You betrayed me. Every person in this room betrayed me."

"You were trying to control a fate that was not yours to decide, Raina," Althea says, taking a step toward her daughter.

"Don't you dare come near me right now, Mother. I mean it. You clearly understood my position on the matter. You knew why I forbid this to happen. And yet, you did it anyway, with no regard for my feelings or Marigold's safety." Her mother steps back, gasping, as if she is drowning in her own words.

"Her safety is the exact reason why I am here, Raina. You think that after I'm gone, if Marigold had no access to her magic, she would stay safe for her entire life? You think that it is a coincidence that your estate has remained hidden from the Ash Witch all these years? No. It was me. It was magic. Always magic."

Her mother's hands turn to fists at her side. "You're lying. I protected her myself."

"I am not. And you know that I am not. You forget, Raina, that you are not powerful like you used to be. You gave it up. That was your choice, and yet you continue to believe that you can protect her from evil on your own," Althea says as she moves into the sitting room toward a gallery wall of Lord Claude's paintings. "The way a protection ritual works—and pay attention, Marigold; consider this the start of your training—is by the use of ancient runes. When the runes are placed, I can channel magic through them." She reaches up to one of the smaller frames and takes it from the wall, turning it around to reveal the back of the canvas where there is an intricate arrow pointing from corner to corner.

Her mother's eyes widen as Althea continues pulling the artwork from the wall.

Runes, on the backs of every single piece.

Raina looks at her husband and says, "All this time, we were in danger, and you said nothing? You worked with her in secret? Why?"

"I tried, my love, and you cannot say that I didn't. Every time we attempted to have the conversation about Marigold, about her magic and future, you panicked. And I understand why! I always understood your fear, but I also saw our daughter wilting, so I did what I thought was best. When Marigold first asked to go

out during a full moon, I wrote to Althea. She wrote me back.
I let Marigold follow her instincts. It seemed like it was best for
everyone, and no one got hurt."

"*I* am hurt. I've been lied to for years, by everyone I thought I
could trust. How do you expect me to heal from this? And what
happens to our daughter now?"

Althea moves toward her daughter and says, "Marigold will
be able to keep herself safe now. She is a powerful witch—"

"My daughter is not a witch!" she screams.

"Yes, I am," Marigold says loudly over them. "I always have
been. And it's my turn to speak." She centers herself in the room.
"I have tried, all my life, to be someone I am not; a lady, an artist, a jewel. I'm sorry I could not be any of those things for you,
but I was never meant to be."

"Mari, all I ever wanted was for you to be safe and happy
and loved. Above all else, loved! And now you've ruined that for
yourself!"

"I have not ruined anything! My life has been a series of
closed doors, but I've found an open window. I hope that you'll
forgive me in time, but it's already done. I am a witch. I'm going
to Innisfree."

The longest silence fills the room, weighing on their shoulders, pressing into the paintings on the floor so that they will be
forever tainted by this moment, this memory.

Frankie sighs loudly and says, "Well, *I* think—"

"Do not speak. I'll deal with you later," their mother interrupts.

Frankie raises his hands above his head like a hostage and
says, "Yes, Mother." Aster tries to hide a laugh under her breath,
but her mother's head whips around to stare her down.

"What was that?"

"Sorry," she says, looking at the floor.

Another silence, somehow worse than the first one. Finally,
her father stands and says, "Marigold, gather your things."

"Now?" She looks at her mother, who can't bear to meet her
gaze.

"Now," her father says.

She grabs Aster by the wrist and tugs her along upstairs. They rush into her room and close the door, grateful for a moment to breathe. As Aster promised, her things are mostly packed in her trunk, though it's clear that Aster was interrupted before she could finish. The two of them move quietly through the room, grabbing tiny trinkets that she cannot leave behind: her diary, her mother's gilded hairbrush that was gifted to Marigold years ago, and her favorite yellow hair ribbon.

"I'm happy for you, and I'm proud of you. But you must write to me as often as you can," Aster says.

"Of course, I will. Think of the adventures we will find after we have time apart. All the stories we will have to share with each other. I'll tell you and Frankie everything. I promise," she says as she embraces her sister.

"You should probably change into something a little less... mine," Aster says, and she laughs as she pulls away. Aster helps her out of the dress and into one of the last dresses waiting in Marigold's wardrobe.

It's yellow—how fitting for a Honey Witch.

"Mother will forgive you soon, you know. She'll miss you too much to stay mad."

Marigold sighs and tenses over the closed trunk. "I hope so."

They carry her trunk back downstairs to find their mother ready to walk out of the room.

"Raina," Althea says. It's the weakest that Marigold has ever heard her voice. "This is the last time we will see each other. Please let it end with love."

Her mother pauses in the doorway and turns her head gently over her shoulder. "I do love you, Mother." She turns to her daughter and says, "And I love you, Marigold. But I can't."

She walks out of the room, leaving everyone in the endless echo of her words.

The rest of the evening is filled with teary goodbyes between Marigold, Frankie, Aster, and her father. She and Althea have promised over and over again that she will write as much as possible, so the goodbye is not quite as painful as it could have been. Beyond that, Althea assures them that it won't be long before Marigold can visit, although Marigold is not so sure how welcome she will be. After seeing that last look on her mother's face, it's nearly impossible to imagine their reconciliation. The last thing that she wants is to further her mother's hurt, so maybe staying away forever is the right thing to do, even though it doesn't feel that way.

To help her remember her home, her father gifts her one of his paintings that depicts the gardens of their estate at the height of spring. After parting hugs and words are exchanged, she and her grandmother fit themselves into their carriage, and the journey to Innisfree begins.

"How long will the travel take, Grandmother?" Marigold asks after hardly any time, indicating her already thinning patience. She's filled with a sense of excitement for her new life, as well as the desperation to be as far away from Bardshire as possible. The estate now feels like a lockbox eagerly left behind, containing all her mistakes and regrets and embarrassing moments that had to happen as she grew up. The problem, though, is that mistakes are not tangible trinkets that can be locked away. They are awfully hard to outrun.

"Once we reach the dock, we will board the ship that will carry us across the sea. It will take the entire day. Then another carriage will bring us to the coast of the lake, and we will take a short boat ride to Innisfree."

"Goodness, Grandmother. I can see why you were put off by the idea of travel," Marigold says.

Althea smiles. "It's not so bad with company."

The carriage ride to the dock is short, and the ship they board is quite luxurious. They have their own suite to themselves, paid for by the generous Lord Claude. Once they have shared a spot of tea and made themselves comfortable, Althea lies down in the perfectly plush bed. The moment is awkward—do they talk about everything that was said between them and her mother? Do they talk at all? Or does it hurt too much to even think about? Marigold can dream of making amends one day, but she cannot even bear to imagine how her grandmother must feel now, knowing that those were the last words she'll ever share with her only daughter. She shifts her weight between her feet, searching for something to say, but Althea beats her to it.

"We both need rest. You were off in your meadow all night. You haven't slept in a whole day," Althea says as she gestures to the second bed in the cabin. She's right—exhaustion weighs Marigold down without mercy. Her knees wobble as she moves to her bed, and she collapses as soon as she is close enough. When her head hits the pillow, she turns to watch Althea, taking comfort in her whistle-like snore. She looks incredibly peaceful and still—it is almost unnatural, like watching a person turn to stone.

Marigold's eyes twitch as she fights to keep them open, but finally, she relents and falls asleep. It is a wonder she stayed awake as long as she did, given the energy that the ritual took from her coupled with the exhaustion that always follows a big argument. She manages to sleep through almost the entirety of the journey, waking only in time to enjoy a few of the amenities of the high-class cabin—a hearty meal, and salty sea air from the privacy of their own balcony.

When the ship docks, the deepest hours of the night are upon them.

"We are here, darling. Come on," Althea says as she moves gracefully toward the door. Marigold struggles to carry her things until members of the household staff come to their aid and follow the two women as they depart the ship. A carriage waits for them at the dock, and Althea wastes no time greeting the driver as their belongings are placed inside.

He is an older gentleman with a remarkably long beard and an eccentric outfit. Bright red suspenders uphold his loose black trousers that are adorned with knee patches. His pale blue eyes are shadowed by a bleached straw hat that he respectfully removes upon seeing Althea approach. His white hair falls around his sunburned face as he smiles widely at the woman in front of him.

"Benny," Althea says sweetly as she struggles to wrap her arms around his neck. He moves to catch her waist and hold her in a gentle embrace.

"Hi, Althea," he says with a gentle rasp in his voice. "How are you feeling, lady?"

"I'm not my best, Benny. I won't lie to you. But I'm very lucky to have my granddaughter Marigold here taking over my work for me," Althea says as she gestures to Marigold, who knows not what to do other than curtsy. Althea and Benny erupt in laughter as she bows her head, so she stands herself up straight immediately. Something about being referred to as only a granddaughter instead of a sister, a friend, or the oldest Claude girl makes her feel much younger than she is. And when a young lady is before her elders, she curtsies.

"She's a proper lady," Althea says to Benny, who extends a hand.

"Pleasure to meet you, Miss Marigold. You can call me Mr. Benny. I'm here to take you both home to Innisfree."

"Pleased to meet you as well, Mr. Benny."

Althea places her frail hand on Benny's shoulder. "Mr. Benny is our neighbor."

She nods in understanding. "Oh, I see! I didn't realize that we had any neighbors."

"Well, I'm not exactly next door, but I have a farm on the coast. I'm never too far away, so if you need anything, give me a shout. If my hearing is still good, I'll come running," he says with a gruff chuckle. After the trunks and bags are put into the carriage, Benny takes his seat on the driver's bench as she and Althea pile in the back.

Marigold immediately leans in close to her grandmother, cupping her hand around her lips and whispering in her ear, "I thought we were cursed so that no one could ever fall in love with us."

Althea gives her a confused look. "We are, darling."

"But, Grandmother," she says as she sneakily points at their driver, "Mr. Benny seems quite...fond of you."

Her grandmother's tired eyes linger on Mr. Benny and she sighs. "Fondness is very different from love. He's a treasured friend," Althea says as her eyes fall back to Marigold, so glassy that she can see the very stars swimming in them. "We work together. The lands by the lake are not often fertile, but I've been using spells to keep his farm thriving for years. In return, we have access to all that he grows. That is the extent of the relationship."

"If you say so," she says, but Althea does not take her joke lightly.

"Marigold, I do not want you to let anything get your hopes up about this curse. In all of my years, through all the known literature regarding our magic, I have found no way to break it. Do not ever let yourself pretend that someone is capable of something impossible."

She nods slowly. This may be the first time that she has felt the weight of the curse, but she resents her grandmother's choice of words. Anyone can be capable of something impossible—as a witch, she must believe that.

Chapter Five

They ride for some time along a dry dirt path, jostling in the back of the carriage. Marigold stares out at the deepening sky, taking in the world without the veil, until Mr. Benny makes a stop. She peers out of the carriage and tightens her grip on her grandmother's hand.

"Althea," Mr. Benny calls, "do you see what I see?"

"My eyes aren't what they used to be," she says.

"We're right by a whole field of bellflowers. Are they still your favorite flower?"

Althea gasps and smiles wide. "Of course! Marigold, let's go pick some. They're beautiful," Althea says as she slides gracefully out of the carriage.

Marigold follows, landing with a thud behind her grandmother. She doesn't recognize the flowers in the field around her. They look to be a cross between a tulip and a peony, ranging between shades of yellow and pink. As Althea steps forward into the field, she extends her arm outward. A striking bird descends from the bright sky and lands on her forearm. The weight of the creature should be too much to bear, but it is not just a bird—it is a spirit. Marigold can tell by the way it moves, and the soft purple glow around it.

"Hello, Dovelyn," Althea says. "Marigold, this is another landvættir."

Marigold walks toward them and runs her hand down the soft

feathered spine of the spirit. "Nice to meet you." She looks to her grandmother and whispers, "Is this how I am meant to speak to spirits?"

Althea laughs. "Speak however you wish. The landvættir do not communicate the way we do. They rely on their empathy and ability to sense true intention. They speak in hopes, dreams, and wishes."

Althea gives Dovelyn a taste of honey from one of the tiny vials that she has on her at all times. Her grandmother also always keeps small jars with her so she has somewhere to put all the delicate ingredients she collects. Marigold takes note of this and considers sewing larger pockets into her dresses so she might one day be exactly like her grandmother, carrying around clinking bottles of hidden treasures. Dovelyn flies from Althea's arm and begins to circle the sky above the field, and something uniquely magical happens: The flowers all begin to glow. They look like candles, or fireflies dancing together in a meadow. She follows her grandmother, entranced by the glow around them.

"How is this possible?" she asks in awe. Her grandmother stops and takes her hand.

"We're Honey Witches, darling. We find beauty where others may not. Spirits guide us to it. We bring marvelous things to life," she says. Marigold sinks to her knees and smells the flowers around her.

"We will use these flowers in many different spells and potions. Their petals house a solution that aids greatly in the process of falling in love," Althea says.

Marigold purses her lips. "When will people stop caring so much about love?"

Her grandmother pauses and shrugs. "When something better comes along, I suppose."

"Like magic?" she says, wiggling her brows up and down.

Althea giggles. "Precisely."

"Well, that's fine. I do not mind making others fall in love. I know it works for some people. I do find new romantics to be quite annoying with all their wooing and swooning, so I'm sure that playing matchmaker for them will remind me why I chose the curse."

"To be clear, we cannot force love upon anyone. Our magic can only lead someone to their true love, and I promise you, that is even more beautiful than finding love for yourself. You will see," Althea says.

"You need not attempt to convince me. I have no regrets and no desire for love." She begins to pick the flowers, and with each snap of a stem, the glowing petals dim until they meet their original colors again.

"I do wish they could keep their glow after being picked, Grandmother. They are so beautiful."

"Think of it like a metaphor of sorts. The Honey Witches are much like the bellflower. We hold this magic inside us, and when we use it, we help people. It comes at a price, but the price is so worth it," Althea says as she bends down to pick flowers alongside her granddaughter.

"I think that is lovely," she says. "It could be rewarding to help someone else find their soulmate. Soulmates are real, right?"

"Of course soulmates are real. Your mother and father are soulmates, in fact," Althea says.

The mention of her mother stings, but at the same time, these are the stories she has always longed to hear. She knows her mother as Lady Claude very well, but she hasn't a clue about the nature of Raina Murr, the once-magical daughter of the Honey Witch. In her mind, those are two vastly different people.

She clears her throat. "How do you know?"

"Who do you think brought them together? After Raina chose to forgo her magic, I used a spell to help lead her to her soulmate. The next thing I knew, your mother felt compelled to travel to Bardshire. The second those two locked eyes, they were in love. It was as quick as the sting of a bee," Althea says with pride.

All children must believe, at least for a small time, that their parents are soulmates. It is nice to be right about that. At least her mother had a very compelling reason for giving up her power; love is one thing, but finding your soulmate is another. "Does she know that your magic brought them together?"

"I think so. On their wedding day, she made a quick comment that only I would catch, but it has stuck with me forever. She said, 'When I saw him for the first time, it was as if I recognized him from another life. Every other life, in fact. He was beside me through them all. We are bound to each other, aren't we?' And I simply nodded to her. She was right, of course. That's how soulmates are. They find each other, life after life," Althea says, though she trails off slightly, as if her mind is beginning to wander somewhere else, her gaze falling back to the carriage.

"So I am assuming that Honey Witches do not have soulmates like that," Marigold says, not that it matters. Even if she did have a soulmate who was destined for her, she would find some way to mess it up. Perhaps it was George and she already ruined it. Oh well, ruining it was worth it—being a witch is so much more fun than being a wife.

"I don't know if I would say that," Althea says. "We have something that finds us, too, life after life, and that is power. We are power, in its truest form."

"I'd choose power in my veins over a ring on my finger any day."

Once Althea and Marigold have picked as many bellflowers as they can possibly carry, the two shuffle back into their carriage and move on. The rest of their journey is filled with the sweet citrusy scent of the flowers, which somehow do not wilt, even after being pulled from their roots. They stop to find little blue fruits from short trees that line the sides of the road. Apparently, they are to be used for both healing and protection spells. Althea spends hours talking Marigold through good and bad omens that she must be able to recognize—crows mean death, honey turning black means that winter will be longer than it should be, and a night without stars means that someone is about to have their heart broken. If a bee flies into the home, an important visitor is coming. When the sun shines through the rain, someone is pregnant. If an ivy leaf with six points is found in the garden, someone is about to fall in love. She commits these to memory as best as she can, but thankfully, there is a massive grimoire waiting for her at the cottage where they are all recorded. That book has been passed through generations of witches, of both Honey and Ash. It can answer anything.

Well, almost anything. But not curses. Evil witches don't like to share what could be their undoing.

They arrive in the early morning in the town of Lenox, which unfolds before Marigold like a familiar blanket. There are warm, sunny seams where the trees meet the clouds, where the sea meets the sky. She remembers this place, though it seems so much smaller than it did when she was a child. The streets are filled with music—a symphony of children laughing, wheels drumming over tiny pebbles, and dozens of harmonic hellos for Althea. Artisans are selling trinkets and baubles along the high street while some offer trades for what they need.

She is quickly overwhelmed by the strong sense of community. She has never lived in a place where it was not considered shameful to ask for something. Bardshire had no spirit of generosity, no neighbors jumping at the chance to lend a cup of sugar. But here, everyone is reaching out their hand. It almost makes Marigold nervous to be surrounded by such goodness. She's always been around people who wouldn't like her anyway, so it never mattered to her how she was perceived. Now she finds herself questioning her own decency. Is she worthy of such treatment? Is she good enough to live among such grace? She is terribly worried that in the painting of this world, she will be a blemish instead of a bloom.

"Are you all right, Marigold?" her grandmother says after noticing her pout.

She shakes her head and smiles as wide as she can. "Oh, fine! Fine, sorry."

"What is it?"

"It's nothing," she says with a sigh. "This place is beautiful. The people are so lovely and warm. I can only hope to earn my keep with them. I worry I could let them down."

Her grandmother places a hand on her knee and says, "They'll love you! Have you forgotten that you already have a friend here?"

She parts her lips. "I do?"

Althea gestures west of the carriage, where a strapping young man is walking toward them alongside two others. He's incredibly tall, with dark brown skin and curly black hair, and his cream linen shirt is tucked poorly into his tight trousers. Marigold watches his approach with confusion until he finally comes close enough to where she can clearly see his round wire glasses, which enlarge his bright brown eyes.

"August, my dear!" Althea says as he helps her descend from the carriage. They are hugging and chatting as Marigold slips out as well to stand beside her grandmother. When Althea and August pull apart, Althea says, "Do you recognize this young lady here?"

Marigold and August eye each other up and down until they're both grinning with recognition. This is the boy who held her hand during the attack-not-storm. The one who helped her make castles out of mud and ribbons out of weeds. The boy she once dared to drink make-believe potions of lake water and browning petals. He is not a child anymore, which shouldn't be surprising, but seeing him now as a man is almost painful, like she half expected him to still be three feet tall and waiting for her with a mouthful of stories. Still, it is enchanting to see what all has grown from the memories she buried here. He's obviously grown quite a bit, now towering over the people at his side—a young blond man with a sunburned face who looks a little like Frankie, and a beautiful red-haired woman who is making it very hard for

Marigold to pay attention to anyone else. She looks to be slightly older than August, or at least she certainly carries herself with more resolve. She has pale white skin that is mostly covered by an overly modest dress that does not fit the summer season at all. The dark green fabric is too heavy for this heat, and her face is noticeably uncomfortable.

"Marigold Claude! My, how many years has it been?" August says, hugging her.

"Fifteen, I think?" she says.

"Fifteen too many," he says as he hugs her. She meets the gaze of the redheaded woman over August's shoulder. The girl forces an awkward smile, curling her raspberry lips so that her nose scrunches, distorting her freckles for a moment. When they separate, August moves to the side and gestures to her.

"Lottie, this is Marigold. We used to play together as children on Innisfree. We would spend entire summers together, joined at the hip."

"Nice to meet you," Lottie says plainly as she tugs a red ringlet behind her ear. She doesn't seem too thrilled to be here, though Marigold can't figure out why. Everyone else she's encountered has been exceptionally welcoming.

"Marigold, this is my best friend, Lottie Burke. She hates just about everyone but me."

"And I only like you sometimes," Lottie replies in a low, monotone voice.

"And this," August says as he puts his arm around the other young man, "is my partner, Edmund."

"A pleasure," Edmund says. He adjusts his ruffled white collar and smooths his hand over his blond beard. His nose is pointy and sloped upward, as if the fates knew exactly how much he would enjoy turning it up at everyone he thought was beneath him. She has seen many young men like this in her life. Bardshire has an annual contest where up-and-coming artists from every country can perform before the royals, and the best will be granted residency. The auditioners were often even more cruel

than those who already lived in Bardshire. They had too much
to prove and it made them arrogant and unkind. Edmund seems
like the type who writes shallow poetry and paints ugly land-
scapes that his family begrudgingly hangs on their wall.

Lottie's green eyes squint upon hearing Edmund's name out
loud. It's clear she does not like him very much, or at the very
least, she doesn't like him with August. Perhaps it's jealousy that
is making Lottie less warm to her. Lottie doesn't seem like the
type to share her best friend—not with Edmund, and certainly
not with Marigold.

The interaction is growing a bit awkward with Lottie's stand-
offishness and Edmund's lack of interest in speaking to anyone
else.

"It's wonderful to meet you all!" Marigold says, bringing her
arms over her stomach and making herself small, hoping she
could disappear from the interaction altogether.

"The three of you should make your way to Innisfree soon,"
Althea chimes in. "Marigold will be taking over my work, and
she could use some company."

"Yes!" August says with a loud clap. "It would have to be
sooner rather than later. I'm to accompany my father in one
month on an extended business trip. We'll be gone for a few
months, but I would absolutely love to return to Innisfree sometime. Wouldn't that be lovely?"

"Hardly," Lottie mumbles under her breath, quiet enough for
Marigold to wonder if that was just her imagination.

Edmund seems equally unenthused, though their reactions do
nothing to deter August's excitement, and Marigold very much
appreciates that about him.

By her quick assessment, August would equally benefit from
spending time together and rekindling their friendship. He
clearly needs more sunny people in his life, and she will desperately need company soon.

As their conversation quiets, a man and a woman rush toward
them, their hands clutching the woman's belly as though their

grip is keeping her intact. The woman's light gray dress is soaked in sweat, and the man is clenching his jaw to keep from shaking. He is tall enough to hide the sun with his frame, but he crouches over so that his face remains close to the woman's.

"Oh, sweet Caoimhe," Althea says, horrified. Her smile falls as she reaches for Caoimhe. Her gaze moves frantically from the woman's eyes to her belly. Althea's hands begin to tremble, and her eyes look as if winter has left them frozen.

"I—" Caoimhe begins, but a low moan overpowers the rest of her words. The man at her side takes a cloth from his back pocket and wipes the sweat from her forehead.

"Caoimhe is pregnant again," the man says.

"But I don't want to be," Caoimhe says through labored breathing. Her whole body tenses until she collapses into his arms. "It will kill me this time."

Marigold gasps and steps back, but Althea glares at her and shakes her head, warning her to keep calm.

Althea waves her hand, commanding August, Lottie, and Edmund to walk away. They take heed, and Marigold is left feeling panicked and lost.

"She's been in pain for days, Althea. And this morning—" the man says, trying to swallow his sobs.

"What happened, Ronan?"

He shakes his head and looks at the sky. "There was so much blood."

Althea nods calmly. She takes Caoimhe's face into her hands and says, "You will not die for this, Caoimhe." Turning to Ronan, she says, "Lift her into the carriage quickly and gently."

As he does as instructed, her grandmother turns to Marigold and says, "I did not intend for you to see something like this so soon, but the world has other plans. You will help me save her."

She shakes her head, not to say that she won't help, but that she *can't* help. "What's happening to her?"

"Her pregnancy is unviable. It has moved to the wrong part of her body, and it is acting as a wound inside of her. We must heal her." Leaving no time for questions, Althea turns to Ronan as he helps her into the carriage. He offers his hand to Marigold, who, dazed, hardly has the wherewithal to take it.

"Now, Marigold!" Althea growls, and she quickly pulls herself together and into the carriage with Ronan right behind her. Mr. Benny yells to his horse, and the carriage takes off like a bullet from the barrel of a gun.

Chapter Six

Caoimhe groans at every bump across the uneven path, and as she turns on her side and curls into her husband, Marigold sees the blood that pools beneath her.

So much blood. It runs like a river through the cracks in the bench, seeping into the pores of the wood. Ronan looks over his wife to the puddle of blood by her side, and he chokes on a gasp.

"Ronan," Althea says sharply. "Stay calm. Keep your eyes on me."

He shakes his head. "Is she going to—?"

"No. Do not even say the word. She is going to live."

Marigold clenches her fists as her eyes dart about the carriage. What can she do to help? What even is there to be done? This world is new, but the stakes are high. She cannot fail now, not when she has given up everything for this, not when another woman's life is at risk. She gathers her skirt into her arms until she gets a grip on her petticoat. With one sharp tug, she tears off the ruffles around the hem. Althea glances at her with her brows raised.

"For the blood," Marigold says. The fabric is white and useless, but it is all that she has to offer. She covers the bench as best she can and sits back in the tense silence that consumes the carriage. They tear through streets lined with a mixture of old white clapboard houses and new redbrick structures like that of the Claude estate. A few Gothic cathedrals scrape the sky with their dark spires. The ground becomes more uneven as they get closer to the water, and the lake's coast comes into view.

Landvættir are still painting streaks of vibrant orange and pink around the golden glow of the rising sun, but there is no time to marvel at the world around her when death looms over them. Ronan carries his wife from the carriage and into a small boat that has ALTHEA painted in blue letters on the side. Marigold follows her grandmother, and Mr. Benny helps them into the boat as well before squeezing between her and the wooden edge. Without a word, Mr. Benny and her grandmother each begin to pull the oars in perfect time with each other. Water splashes over the sides but they do not slow.

She leans forward into her knees, trying to take up less space as they rip through the water. Caoimhe whimpers in Ronan's arms, and his hold on her tightens. His frantic gaze lands on Marigold, and he sees the fear in her eyes. "Why are you looking at me like that?"

She blinks and softens her gaze as she understands her purpose in this moment. Althea will be the one to save Caoimhe— that much is clear. But she can serve as a comfort for Ronan as his entire world cants. She can keep him intact as her grandmother performs a miracle.

"You love her very much," she says. He runs his hand over his face and nods.

"Caoimhe is my angel. I cannot live without her."

Her gaze hardens, feigning certainty. "You won't have to. I promise." Althea quickly pats her on the back as they reach the dock.

Taking in the isle for the first time in years, it's as if her senses are on fire. She is surrounded by beauty and magic but filled with sickening dread. Innisfree is a beautiful haven, with every inch covered in colorful blooms and luscious greenery. Even the bark of the trees seems more vibrant here, with tones leaning closer to red than brown. The song of the birds, the hum of the bees, and Caoimhe's wails of pain create a dissonant cacophony.

Ronan carries Caoimhe out of the boat and onto the dock. Mr.

Benny and Marigold each take Althea's hands to help her onto the dock, and they hurry along the stone path that leads to the cottage. Caoimhe reaches for Althea and pulls her close so her whispers go unheard by everyone else. Althea nods. All rush inside as Marigold trails behind. Before entering, Althea turns to her and says, "Stay here for now."

"But Ronan needs—"

"Stay," Althea echoes before closing the door. Air gusts into her, throwing her slightly off-balance. Having just felt the first pull of her purpose, it takes everything for her not to break down that door and get to Ronan before he shatters. He cannot continue to watch his wife suffer alone. She has no idea what sort of ritual or procedure her grandmother is performing, but it must be shocking if she won't even let her witness it. How will she be able to handle situations like this on her own if she can't train alongside Althea? It's not fair. Standing here, falling back into the throes of self-doubt, helps no one. She is a witch, too. She can help. She deserves a place in that room.

Just as she is building up the courage to barge in, the handle twists. Mr. Benny comes out with his arm around Ronan's shoulders, and he closes the door behind them. In any other circumstances, she would bombard them with questions, but she holds her tongue. If not a source of comfort, she is nothing.

"Althea said everything would be fine in a few hours," Ronan says, though his voice shakes.

Marigold nods, looking up through her lashes. "She is right. She will heal Caoimhe." She places a hand on his shoulder as Mr. Benny moves to pat his back. "You can take comfort in that."

"I'll take comfort in her arms when she is all right again," he says sharply.

Mr. Benny dips his chin. "Have faith, Ronan. Althea never makes a promise that she cannot keep. You know this."

A faint cry comes from inside the house, and Ronan gasps. "I must be with her." He turns to the door, but Mr. Benny holds him in place.

"Ronan, she asked you to leave her for now."

Marigold stills. Why is Althea forbidding anyone else to be part of this? It doesn't make sense unless she fears that Caoimhe won't survive. She shakes her head, disrupting the dark thoughts.

"She is not herself! She doesn't know what she's saying," Ronan cries, ineffectively fighting against Mr. Benny's surprising strength.

"You must respect Caoimhe's decision. She does not want anyone other than Althea in the room right now. Her wishes come first."

There's the answer—it's not Althea separating them. It's Caoimhe. *She* must believe that she will not survive, and she is sparing them all from witnessing her end. At that, Ronan slows until he ceases. He wipes his eyes and says, "I don't understand. Why won't she let me help her now?"

Caoimhe's decision is an act of true love. Even on her deathbed, her final wish is to spare Ronan the lasting image of her passing. Marigold steps closer and says, "You have helped her as much as you can. You cared for her while Althea was away, and you carried her here in your arms. She asks no more of you."

Another cry carries on the wind. Mr. Benny moves to hold on to Ronan, but Ronan doesn't try to run in again. He shudders and says, "If she doesn't want me by her side, I cannot stand here and listen to her scream. I won't be able to stop myself from running to her."

"Come with me, then. We will forage for things that can be used in her aftercare."

He nods, and Mr. Benny steps away from his side. She takes his hand and leads him off the path. She doesn't know this isle any better than he does, but she can pretend. As they walk around the cottage, the sunlight wraps itself around the trees like strings of twinkling lights, and little creatures jump from branch to branch, adding a natural percussion underneath it all.

Innisfree is about ten times bigger than Marigold's meadow. The cottage is surrounded by flower gardens, and the apiary takes up the whole backyard and then some. She hasn't met the bees yet, and to be truthful, she is afraid. The only thing she knows about them is that they sting, and that is the last thing Ronan needs right now. As they walk past it, she counts a total of twelve hives, each five white boxes tall. By her rudimentary calculation, there must be thousands of bees living here. Their buzz hovers over the note of E-flat, creating a meditative hum that calms her and Ronan. His breathing settles into a normal rhythm as they walk. Since she still doesn't know where she's going, she's simply waiting to stumble upon something that looks like a destination.

"How did you and Caoimhe meet?" she asks so he won't notice that she's as good as lost. They weave through the tall trees, pushing branches out of their faces as they walk.

"We grew up together. I've loved her since we were both little kids. I remember pretending to be bad at reading so she would read me stories," he says, followed by a small laugh. He looks up, his blue eyes aglow in the sun. "I would've done anything to get her to talk to me, but she wasn't interested for the longest time."

"You loved her before she loved you?"

He nods. "Everyone loved Caoimhe. Sweet, kind, funny, and smarter than everybody around."

"So how did you get her to choose you?"

"I merely told her the truth. I told her that I'd make it my mission to make her happy. I said that if I wasn't what she wanted, I would make myself become it. I would be soft or strong, funny or serious, a rich man or a farm boy. Anything she wanted. I was willing to defy everything I was for her." He pauses and smiles. "But I didn't have to. She stopped me in the middle of that whole spiel and kissed me because she wanted me as I was, accepted me for who I am. We've been together ever since. Fourteen years. Two kids. A perfect life."

Her heart warms. "Your love story is so beautiful," she says. It's much easier to enjoy love from a distance like this.

He sighs deeply. "As long as she lives, I'll never ask for anything else, never want for more than I have."

"She will live. I know it," she says, and they continue to walk in silence for nearly an hour. The trees finally start to thin, and they find an open meadow filled with wildflowers.

"Here we are!" she says, relieved to have found a place to stop. "We can collect flowers that aid in healing. Lavender, daisies, and goldenrod are all great choices, but you can't go wrong with anything here."

Ronan nods and they move in opposite directions as they work. For every flower Marigold picks, she envisions Caoimhe, perfectly healed and standing alongside her family. Maybe it helps, maybe it does nothing, but it's all she can do. Her fist is full of flowers when she reaches the center of the meadow. There, she finds a small oasis vaguely in the shape of a heart, or a bean for those with weak imaginations. Inside the sparkling clear water is another landvættir—she can tell by the bright glowing aura surrounding it. It's a koi fish with brilliant yellow scales all over its body, and it swims in a constant circle around the pool. She gently eases her fingers into the water, and the koi moves beneath her, allowing her hand to run across its body. The midday sun burns bright above her as she imagines what this place will look like when the blue moon rises in its stead, lending its light to the pool below.

She is enamored with the beauty that surrounds her, so much so that she begins to fear that there will never be enough time to enjoy it all. Even if she were granted an eternity here, she would still leave parts of the isle unexplored. It is at this moment that she perfectly understands why her grandmother never wanted to leave this place, and why she must protect it at all costs.

Somehow, the minutes pass like seconds and the sun starts to fall into the twilight. Ronan takes hold of the flowers as the two of them start walking back toward the cottage. They collide with Mr. Benny at the halfway point.

Breathless, Mr. Benny says, "There you are."

"How is she?" Ronan says.

"She is well," he says, pulling Ronan into a hug, and he immediately weeps into his shoulder.

"She's okay. She's okay," Ronan says through sobs. He pulls back and says, "Can I see her now? Please."

"Go to her. She waits for you at the cottage."

At that, Ronan runs, kicking up dirt behind his every step. Marigold beams up at Mr. Benny. "Thank the heavens that Caoimhe is okay. I was terrified for her, and for their family."

"Thank your grandmother, Miss Marigold. She performed a miracle. I never doubted her for a second, and you shouldn't either. You'll be just as powerful as her very soon."

"I do not know about that. I cannot imagine myself handling today the way she did. It feels impossible right now."

"Well, you only just arrived. Give it time. Nothing is impossible here."

When they reach the cottage, Ronan is carrying Caoimhe in his arms down the stone path, kissing her in between every step. Mr. Benny nods to Marigold and Althea as he follows them and helps them both into the boat.

"How did you do it?" she asks her grandmother once everyone else is too far to hear.

"This is what our magic is made for. When a person's life is at risk, we stop at nothing to save them," Althea says, bringing her trembling hand to her forehead and wiping away the sweat. She remained so calm and strong through the whole ordeal, but now the adrenaline is wearing off, and the pain seems to be hitting her in waves.

"I was worried there, too, Marigold. If we were one day late, Caoimhe would not have survived." She covers her mouth with her hand for a moment as she collects herself. "I hope you can understand now why I did not visit Bardshire. It wasn't only because of your mother's wishes. It was because people needed me." She takes a deep, dry breath and leans against the cottage. "You will be able to travel. I swear it. But never forget your purpose while you are away, and always let it guide you back home."

"I will, Grandmother. I promise."

Althea smiles and stands up as straight as she can, opening her arms for Marigold. "Come here, darling girl." Her grandmother holds her as they watch the boat float into the glittering evening, farther and farther until Mr. Benny's lantern can no longer be seen from the dock.

"You did so well in comforting Ronan. I'm so proud of you."

Marigold sighs into her shoulder. "I felt useless through most of it. I don't know if I will ever be able to do what you did." She pulls back and meets her grandmother's gaze. "I can't believe that your magic is powerful enough to save someone from an affliction so dire."

"*Our* magic, Marigold. You have all the power that I do, and you will have no trouble using it after I train you." She grips her shoulders. "You were made for this. You belong here." Her grandmother takes her hand and ushers her inside for the first time in fifteen years. The door creaks open and leads directly into the kitchen, which is an odd little room filled with much more than typical cookware. The walls are lined with hundreds of jars and vials, all with neatly handwritten labels. On one counter sits a plate full of sweets, but on the other, there is a bowl of black sludge next to an old open book. It smells like rot as she comes closer.

"Is that what you used to heal Caoimhe?"

Althea nods. "Don't get too close to it. You'll make yourself sick. In fact," she says, stepping past her and picking up the bowl, "why don't you head straight to your room? Benny already brought your things inside while you were with Ronan. I'll clean up while you get settled, and we'll explore the rest of the isle tomorrow. I have spent all my energy today."

Taking in the cottage, she can't help but notice all the undone tasks. The walls could use a wash, the floor is decorated with boot prints, and every surface is covered in a layer of dust. Althea hasn't been able to keep this place perfectly clean for some time. "Why don't I clean up for you and you go rest?"

"No, let me. You deserve to start your training in a clean space."

"Grandmother, please let me—"

"Do not think I'm too weak to clean my own kitchen, Mari. Now go on," she says, shooing Marigold out of the kitchen and down the cottage's only hallway. She passes the living room and notes that the green sofa and its pillows desperately need to be fluffed. The rug deserves a decent scrub, and the curtains should be replaced altogether. They're sun-bleached and frayed at the ends. The wood floor of the hallway creaks underneath her step. Her bedroom door is slightly ajar, and she lets herself inside. It has just enough space to feel cozy, yet safe. This room has had more attention recently—new bedding and hardly any dust. She has a beautiful window overlooking the sparkling lake outside, and she can see the beginnings of the apiary. Her bed is large, white, and so very welcoming. Her grandmother has placed a lovely bouquet of marigolds in a vase by her bed that makes the entire room smell like fresh flora.

Marigold starts unpacking her belongings and takes some time to hang her dresses in her wardrobe, which looks to be made of sleek cherrywood. There is a matching vanity with an ornate circular mirror sitting atop it. She witnesses herself for the first time in this new life. Her face looks healthy but quite tired and dull. She starts to undress to then slip on a nightgown, but before she is able to fasten the ribbons into a bow, she crashes into the bed and falls asleep.

Chapter Seven

Her training begins promptly the next morning after a quick breakfast of summer fruit and sharp cheese, both gifts from Mr. Benny's neighboring farm. She and her grandmother stand at the edge of the apiary. While Althea steps through the white garden gate with confidence, Marigold holds herself back, as if waiting for some sort of safety signal.

Althea turns over her shoulder. "Don't be afraid! These bees are your kin now."

"Am I their queen?" she calls back, half-joking.

"No," Althea says without humor. "The queen is a bee that has been fed only royal jelly since birth. She's easy to spot because she's about twice the size of the others. She is the mother of every bee in the colony, while you," she says, taking the arched lid off the top of a hive and pulling out a frame of honey that looks like a stained-glass window, "are simply their keeper. Now, come closer."

Okay. Deep breath. She takes a step forward, tiptoes through the gate, and stands inside the apiary for the first time. The air smells sweet and flowery. A small vibration that tickles her feet with every step. A little hum masks all other chirps and whistles in the air. Some of the bees are gently hovering around their hives, while others are exploring the fruits and flowers nearby. One bee takes a particular interest in her and flies to her hand. At first, she jerks away, but her grandmother's glare scares her into stillness. Lifting her palm, she cautiously allows the bee to rest there as she examines it.

"Will it sting me?" she asks, attempting to hide her nerves as the insect crawls over her skin. It's tickly. She looks closer, noting that the bee is much fuzzier than expected.

"The bees will never harm you. They know what you are by scent, and soon, they will learn to recognize your face the more time that you work with them. Remarkable creatures, really," Althea says as she walks from hive to hive, examining the frames inside. Marigold follows and begins to peer inside them while crouched behind her grandmother. She notices two of them that look completely different from each other on the inside; one is overflowing with thin orange-tinted honey, while the other is heavy with honey so dark that it almost looks black.

"Grandmother, why is this one so dark and different from the others? Is it burnt?"

"You have a sharp eye, Mari. It is made with nectar from blackwell bulbs. And the other one next to it is peach blossom. There are many different honeys in these hives," Althea says.

Her eyes widen. "I didn't even know there were different types." Is that meant to be common knowledge? If so, this is embarrassing.

"Oh yes, there are as many types of honey as there are flowers, and for it to work with our magic, the bees can only retrieve nectar from one type of flower per colony. That is why our relationship with the bees is so important; they make the essential ingredient for every single one of our spells. We tend to them in the winter when the flowers are waiting to bloom. We maintain their homes, their food, and their brood. We grow their favorite plants all over Innisfree, and if they cannot find the flowers they want here, we instruct them on where to go."

"How do we do that? Can I speak with them somehow?"

"Try it," Althea says encouragingly as she scoops up a handful of bees and plops them into Marigold's palm without giving her a chance to object.

Oh God. Okay, no sudden movements. No loud noises. Nothing to disturb the hundreds of venomous insects that are now covering her hand like a glove. Just keep breathing. She raises her hand to eye level and concentrates, hoping to feel something. Strange enough, she does, when she makes eye contact with one bee who stills beneath her gaze. In her own way, through her mind, she tells the bee of the lush harvest of bellflowers that were left in a basket by the front of the cottage. The bee begins to waggle, moving its body in circular motions.

"Is he...dancing?"

"*She*," Althea corrects, "is giving instructions to the others on where to find the flowers. And all the other worker bees—all female, by the way—will follow her directions. Male bees do absolutely nothing but mate and die."

Sure enough, the bees fly off her hand and disappear around the cottage. Her jaw drops in amazement as she moves back to her grandmother's side.

"Excellent job!" Althea pops the lid off of another hive and peeks inside. "Damn," she spits under her breath. "This one is honey bound."

"What does that mean?"

"It means I waited too long to harvest and the hive is overflowing. They do not have room for their brood. If we don't fix this fast," she says, dropping the lid to the ground and reaching for a frame, "they'll swarm and leave us." Her grandmother's arms tremble under the weight of the full frame.

"Let me take that," she says, expecting Althea to shoo her away like she normally does whenever Marigold offers to help. This time, though, her grandmother nods and hands her the frame.

Althea sighs. "I suppose I must admit now that I am too old for this."

"Don't say that." She summons the bravery to reach inside. The bees respect her entrance into their home and do not fight her as she retrieves another frame.

"It's true. I cannot maintain the hives, or the veil of protection. Honestly, I cannot even properly dust inside the cottage anymore. I tried to ignore my body for a long time, but now that you are here, I am reminded of what a witch is supposed to do." She wipes the sweat from her face. "It's simply too much for an old crone like me."

Marigold props the frames against the lavender box on the bottom of the stack and wraps her arms around her grandmother. "Do not speak of yourself this way. You are the strongest person I know, and you do not have to do this alone. Not anymore."

The harvest will begin tomorrow, but for now, Marigold has pulled the heavy frames and replaced them with empty ones. Her priority is to ready the necessary ingredients to renew the veil of protection tonight. While Althea rests on the green couch, Marigold hovers over the ancient grimoire in the kitchen. Her eye catches on a spell for hay fever that requires aster petals. Merely seeing her sister's name causes a slight twinge of pain in her heart. She left so much behind in Bardshire, and so much tension unresolved. If there is a way to make it right, she cannot find it. Perhaps it's better for everyone if she stays far away, at least for now. She brings her mind away from those thoughts and regains her focus in the kitchen. Each page of the book is decorated with splashes and spills from different ingredients and centuries of use. It contains a spell for everything that she could imagine: finding your soulmate, headache cures, fertility control, ensuring a bountiful harvest, and even finding a lost cat. With this book, there is nothing she cannot do.

Except find someone to love her, of course. All of this comes with a price that she has yet to realize how difficult it could be to pay. She continues to flip through the book, noting the wild ingredients she has never heard of, and some that she cannot imagine touching.

"This spell requires frog eyes and the wings of a dragonfly?" she yells out to Althea, her mouth twisting in disgust.

"Some spellwork is less glamorous than others, I'll admit. But look at the soulmate spell. That one is lovely," Althea says.

She flips through the pages and lands on 117—the spell to find your soulmate: lavender honey, lemon seeds, rose petals, and moon water.

"So what happens if we perform this spell on one of us?"

Althea sighs. "A whole lot of disappointment. Trust me, that spell is not the answer to loneliness."

"I see. What do you do to feel less lonely, then?" Marigold asks.

"I got a cat nearly thirty years ago and he's still going strong," Althea says, laughing. "His name is Cindershine. He's around here somewhere, though he is a wild thing. He roams Innisfree as he wishes, but he always comes back eventually."

She gasps. "Thirty years? How is that possible?"

"I told you that Innisfree grants unnaturally long life for its residents. Not just the people."

"Right. I guess I didn't realize how powerful it was." She flips back to the protection ritual and starts pulling out chili powder, cloves, and cinnamon from the cabinets. "If I may ask, do you think that Versa was right? Could you use Innisfree's magic to create immortality?"

The air in the cottage goes cold. Sensing the shift in her grandmother's mood, she immediately regrets asking.

"May I tell you the truth, even if it's frightening?" Althea's voice is low and full of warning. Marigold nods slowly.

"I think it is possible, and that is why she will not give up."

They both go quiet for a moment. Marigold mixes her dry ingredients into a bowl and tops it off with a bit of salt. She pauses. "Would it be so bad if someone found a way for us to live forever?"

Althea stands slowly from the couch and walks toward the kitchen. "Why do you ask?"

She shrugs. "Curiosity," she says, adding blackwell honey to the bowl.

Her grandmother's brow furrows, waiting for a better answer. "It's nothing," Marigold says. "It's too sad to talk about." She keeps her eyes on the bowl, pouring from the jar until the mixture reaches the consistency of thick paint.

"Mari," Althea says, placing a hand on her wrist. "Are you worried about me dying?"

Sighing, she says, "I don't want to lose you. And you certainly deserve eternal life more than she does."

"Eternity is not a gift. It is a punishment. To outlive everyone you know, everyone you love, and everyone who once loved you—" She stops herself and swallows. "One hundred years is more than enough for me."

Marigold places the jar back on the counter. "But I didn't get to spend those hundred years with you." Her voice comes as a whisper. "Even if I did, it still wouldn't be enough. I'll never be ready for you to go."

"Oh, sweet girl," Althea says, patting her hand. "You will be fine without me. In fact, you will thrive."

"I wish I could believe that," she says, sagging her shoulders.

"I promise, Mari. You will see one day. And when I am gone, look for me in the yellow flowers. I'll be there for you, always."

The protection ritual starts with Marigold using the mixture to paint runes in every corner of the cottage. It's the same image that was on the back of her father's paintings—an arrow of sorts, with swirls and shapes along the shaft. The cottage is small: a kitchen with a table that seats four, the sitting room, a short hallway, and three tiny bedrooms. It does not take long to complete her task, and the air feels light and calm by the time she is done. She returns to the kitchen, and Althea stands from the table.

"And now we'll do the same at every corner of the isle," Althea says.

The two of them walk outside, hand in hand. They paint the

rune everywhere—on the hives, in the trees, across stones and petals and dirt. Every corner, every inch. It takes hours to complete, and the exhaustion comes in heavy waves. Her grandmother needs to rest every few minutes, and it is hard to witness. Althea resents her old body, calling herself names and insulting her ability as they go. Marigold's stomach knots when a crow swoops in front of her. An omen of death, a warning of imminent grief. They push onward until they complete the task, and the ritual is nearly complete.

As they walk together, Althea says, "The runes will need to be repainted about three times a year. Honey never goes bad, you see, but it will crystallize and flake away, especially in the winter when the air is dry and cold. Keep an eye on them. Instinct will tell you when the ritual needs repeating, and you will be more than capable of performing it on your own."

Althea then leads her to a glade shaded by a large wisteria tree and stands directly in the middle.

"This is the center of the isle, the very heart of Innisfree. Stand perfectly still, and you can feel it beating beneath you."

Marigold lets out a breath and relaxes every muscle in her body. Her hands rest in her grandmother's grip, and she listens as the isle beats for her.

"Now we channel our magic through the runes," Althea says. "Let it drip from you, from the palms of your hands and the soles of your feet. Visualize the lives of this land that we must protect."

Closing her eyes, she imagines the bees dancing in the sunlight. Pink petals falling in the wind like snow. Tall trees with branches that reach for each other. Whistling melodies of little birds. All the creatures that rely on her to keep them safe.

When she opens her eyes, the glade starts to glow. It's not unlike the field of bellflowers that they visited on their journey, but it's much stronger, and the light feels alive. The glow heightens around them as they continue to chant the spell. As the glimmer touches Marigold's skin, it feels like warm water, like she's moving through liquid gold. The corners of the isle hum in harmony, with a thread of dissonance in between the notes. The glow forms a dome over the entire isle, and shimmering stars fall over them like summer rain. As they chant, the golden light falls faster, harder. It bounces off the branches and splashes in the grass. The dome starts to fade after the entire isle is sun-dappled and safe. The last of the golden light sinks into the earth. The world fades back to darkness, but instead of being ominous, it's a velvety darkness with singsongy winds and waves of lavender in the air. Peace lies against the ground, and the world goes quiet.

Althea hugs Marigold, who feels the wet cheek of her grandmother against her face.

"What's wrong?"

"Happy tears," she says softly. "Proud tears. And tears of relief." She pulls back, her hands still resting on Marigold's shoulders as she says, "We're safe now. Innisfree is safe. And all because of you."

Chapter Eight

The following days bleed into one another, each filled with wonder and magic and spirits and honey. Innisfree is like a dream. A place hidden between here and there, where the lost can stay lost because being found would destroy the mystery of it all, and being lost is so much more romantic. Marigold spends most of her time following the landvættir around the isle, learning their names and their purpose. There is Talaya, an elegant blue snake who guards the apiary and keeps it free of potential predators. Yliza is the koi who guards the oasis. Odessa is a sleek white swan who circles the isle, protecting the coast. Chesha is a mysterious purple catlike spirit who brings warnings of imminent storms. The health of the landvættir is what Marigold may use as an indicator for the overall health of Innisfree. If a guardian seems weak, it is likely that their area of the isle needs some sort of intervention—be it a spell for rain, or lessening temperatures, or an energy-cleansing ritual. When they are all happy and healthy, the isle is constantly aglow with wondrous creatures of love and light.

Althea still handles most of the customer interactions, and Marigold takes notes. Most people do not seem to know exactly why they are here or what they are asking for. Althea is excellent at being a shoulder to lean on for people who need it, and then being able to recommend spells that can help them. Many of the customers are women seeking some sort of cure, refuge, or fertility-control spells. It brings Marigold great joy to know that she can save another woman from being trapped in a life that she does not want, for she was so close to a similar fate. She narrowly escaped the life of a wife and mother, and she will always help another woman do the same. A Honey Witch provides women with choice—something they are all too often denied.

She has also been quick to take over all the strenuous labor that the isle requires: the gardening, the watering, the honey harvesting. From dawn until dusk, she works; her hand covered in soil, her dress soaked with sweat, her lips constantly sticky from tasting the honey that she helps create.

When she is thoroughly exhausted from a hard day of witchwork, she carries her heavy legs back inside. From the back of the cottage comes a strong floral and earthy scent that spices the whole house. She walks alongside her grandmother toward the door until Althea gestures to her to open it. When she does, she is greeted by thousands of hanging flowers of every imaginable color, the scents of the pinks and the blues mixing into a cold lavender mist. There is a massive iron cauldron in the corner filled with a waxy, milky substance. The long dining table is covered in tiny jars filled with crushed petals. The scent, while lovely, is so strong that it makes her eyes itch. She blinks back tears and turns her face toward the hall.

"That's normal. You'll get used to it," Althea says as she pats Marigold on the shoulder and walks inside without a hint of a sniffle. She taps a light finger on the lids of the jars, creating a tinkling rhythm that drums through the room.

"The flowers love music," she says with a smile. It does seem to be true; the flowers seem bolder, brighter, happier when the soft thrum meets their petals. Marigold braves the strong aroma and follows close behind her grandmother, who seems to be a new sun to the greenery around. Althea moves to a wall that is covered with wild vines. She places her palm flat against the leaves and takes a long, deep breath. The space between her hand and the greenery glows bright gold, and as she pulls her hand away, bright purple blooms emerge, tangling new petals with green leaves. It takes her breath away. She moves to sit on a tall stool and braces herself against the table. With her blue dress sleeve, she wipes the sweat from her forehead. "I used to be able to raise entire gardens without breaking a sweat. Now creating a few petals will drain all my energy."

"I didn't know you could make plants grow like that. Can you show me how?"

"It's simple enough to describe. Visualize your intent, imagine the plants growing bountifully before you, and let your magic pour from your open hand so the plants can drink it up. But I must warn you, it will probably take a bit of time to master it completely. When I first became a witch, bringing a bouquet of flowers back to life knocked me out for two days." Once she's caught her breath, Althea stands again and picks the new flowers off the wall, bringing them back to the table.

"What is this room for?"

"Enfleurage," Althea says as she picks up a jar with a soft purple ribbon tied around it. "It's the oldest and best technique to extract the essence of a flower. The scent, the oils, the color—everything a witch needs for a spell." She grabs a tiny jar and goes to the large cauldron, scooping up the milky stuff inside. "This is tallow, but you can use any unscented fat for this. We'll take some of these fresh petals and put them into the jar. Then," she says as she holds up the odd-shaped lid, "this part of the lid presses the petals into the fat, which extracts the essence." As she twists the lid, light purple inky lines bleed from the petals inside. "Replace the petals every other day for a month, and there you have it: floral essence. You'll use it in almost every spell."

Althea hands Marigold the newly filled jar. She twists the lid, allowing the concave insert to twist farther into the jar and smear some of the muddled petals.

"What does it look like when it's done?"

Her grandmother grabs a jar from a different table. The fat

inside this jar has a light pink hue with bright vibrant petals torn throughout. Althea twists off the top, and the powerful scent of summer rose escapes from the jar.

Marigold takes her finger and scoops out a pea-size amount of the essence and smudges it between her fingers. It feels buttery and smooth and smells absolutely divine the more she adjusts to its strength.

"It's a little messy, but it's worth it. A tip for you: Put a smear of it behind your ears, between your breasts, and on the back of your knees for a scent that will follow you anywhere," Althea says as she takes her own small sample and places it where she instructed.

"You are brilliant," Marigold says as she puts the jar back in its place.

"And you are my granddaughter, which makes you brilliant as well."

She smiles, staring at the wall lined with plants. There are a few vines with crunchy brown leaves, and she runs her hand over them. "Can I try to revive these?"

Althea places her hand on her hip. "By all means, but do so sitting down. It's safer that way."

She pulls a stool in front of the wall, and her grandmother holds her shoulders. "Lift your hands. Breathe deep. Visualize their growth and release your magic."

Her palms hover a few centimeters away from the leaves. Eyes closed, she imagines curling vines ripe with soft green leaves. Her fingers tingle and her hands start to heat.

Althea squeezes her shoulders. "Good. Keep breathing."

As her magic pours from her body, her back tenses and her head starts to pound. The muscles in her arms ache and tremble with exhaustion. Her grandmother tightens her grip on her shoulders.

"That's enough, Mari," Althea warns, but Marigold cannot stop it. Her magic keeps pouring, keeps bleeding. Pain rips through her body as sweat drips down her face. Heat building, it feels like the whole room is on fire and her skin is burning up. She falls back against her grandmother, who helps guide her to the cold floor. Her back arches against the ground as she tries to catch her breath. Althea pulls a vial of honey from her pocket and pours it into Marigold's mouth.

"You're okay, Marigold. Breathe and stay calm. Everything is okay."

The honey coats the back of her throat and soothes the burning sensation. Minutes tick by as her breathing calms and her heart settles into another rhythm. Sitting up, she says, "You made that look much easier than it was."

Althea helps her stand. "It will get easier. Practice a little at a time every day and always replenish your strength with honey after you're done. One day, you'll be creating mighty oak trees with a snap of your fingers."

She laughs in disbelief. "You have great confidence in me."

"Yes." Althea smiles. "Yes, I do."

Marigold's first month as a witch nears its end, but she still has much to learn, and much to explore. Time seems to pass differently here—it is not a line or a circle. It moves like a memory, a mirror, a door. There have been moments when Marigold feels too small for her own body, like she should be larger, taking up more space in the world. And then she finds herself shrinking into a child again, mesmerized by the sun and frightened of the dark. But tonight, she feels her own age—her mind yearning for more wisdom, her body reaching for more adventure.

As she catches a glimpse of the moon outside shining down upon the lake, she cannot deny the pull she feels from the water. It reminds her of the last ball she attended, during the blue moon. How she could not wait to escape the night and find her way to her meadow. At that point, she had been so thankful for Mr. Notley that she pondered a life with him, having no idea that her destiny awaited the very next day. On this night, the pull of the lake feels even stronger than the pull of the blue moon. Wearing only her robe, she steps silently out of the cottage and closes the door. She runs down the stone pier and leaves her robe behind as she jumps into the sparkling lake.

The water wraps around Marigold like a lover, and for a moment, she pretends that it is. The current feels like soft arms holding her, rocking her. She lets herself sink until she is hovering equally above the floor of the lake and below its surface. When her breath begins to run out, she gives her scalp a quick scrub before floating back up to the surface. The cold night air brushes up against her face as she pulls herself out of the water and shakes out her hair. Pulling her robe back on, she turns to look at the lake. Out of the corner of her eye, she sees a flicker. It is so small and so fast that it could have been her imagination. When she stares directly at the same spot, there is nothing but the black edge of the coast. But should she turn her head slightly to the side, the flicker appears again. No matter how hard she tries, Marigold cannot catch the flicker with her eyes trained on it. A sour, smoky smell carries on the wind. Dread fills her belly, and she runs up the stone path, through the cottage, and to her grandmother's bedside. Water drips from the edges of her curls onto her grandmother's face.

"Grandmother, something's wrong," she says as she gently shakes Althea awake.

Althea gasps, pushing herself up. Frantic, she wipes her face and examines the wetness on her fingers as if she fears it may be blood. "What happened?"

"I don't know exactly. I just know it's not right. Come see."

She helps Althea out of bed and waits for her to pull on a dressing gown before they walk outside together. Her steps are slow and cautious as she is still learning the twists of the stone path down to the water. As quick as the night will allow, they are there at the edge of the isle, looking deep into the black.

"Do you see it?" Marigold asks.

"See what? What are you speaking of?"

"The flickering thing across the lake," she says desperately, her finger pointing at seemingly nothing. She squints and stretches and bends, trying to fit that strange light back into her vision. It's there, or it *was* there. She is certain. Right? It was there. Across the lake, it was there.

"I swear I saw something, Grandmother. It was this little light, sort of blue and green at the same time. It flickered like a flame. I swear it. Should we take the boat out to investigate?"

"Never go there, Marigold. That's the Hazelwood Forest, and it is as ancient as it is dangerous. Let me look for a moment."

Althea stares for much more than a moment. The steady sound of her grandmother breathing makes her realize the rapidness of her own. She calms herself as best she can while she waits for Althea to make the worry go away with her infinite knowledge. But Althea turns and says, "I see nothing, darling."

Marigold chokes on her gasp. "You don't believe me?"

It feels exactly like when she was a child, when she tried to tell Aster of Lunasia in the meadow. Then she tried to tell Frankie. Then she tried to show them the things she saw. No one else could see, so no one would believe her.

Althea sighs and takes her hand. "I didn't say that. It's likely simply another spirit of the forest."

"What if it's something harmful?"

"What would make you think that?"

"It's just a feeling. You don't think it could be an Ash Witch, do you?"

Althea immediately shakes her head. "No, impossible, Marigold."

"But what if an Ash Witch did try to harm us?" Marigold takes a moment to assess the security of their abode. The doors have weak locks, and the windows are always open. She wonders if she would have time to secure the premises if she spotted an Ash Witch on the pier. Horrific scenarios play out in her mind until her grandmother interrupts her obvious spiral.

"As long as the runes have not been disturbed, she won't be able to come near. Take comfort in knowing that our protection has been renewed. We are completely safe. Let's go back inside," Althea says, and extends her hand to Marigold. They walk up slowly, and Marigold takes every opportunity to twist back around, as if she's trying to sneak up on whatever she saw before. It's still not there. Perhaps it never was.

They spend the entire next day harvesting honey from their hives. It is a lengthy and taxing process that involves a myriad of gadgets and tools, but the work is peaceful, comforting. Althea gives instructions from her seat in the garden, but it comes naturally to Marigold regardless. In one hand, she holds a frame thick with honey, and in another, a blade that she has warmed in the fire of a candle. Once the blade is steaming, she glides it across the honeycomb and melts the beeswax caps that hold the honey inside the striking hexagonal mold. When it drips free, she places the frame into a holder that will catch the honey as it drains. She does this frame by frame from sunrise to sunset. And it is still not enough to finish the task. At the end of the day, she has successfully harvested honey from only one full hive. There are eleven more to go.

It is a challenge, but an enjoyable one. For eleven days, Marigold rises with the sun, has a quick breakfast, and goes to work in the apiary. Her grandmother stays with her the entire time, telling her stories and teaching her the ways of the witch. There almost seems to be a correlation between the honey harvesting and Althea's state of being—the closer the harvest is to being complete, the weaker Althea becomes. But the truth lies unspoken between them. Marigold allows them both to have these days untainted with the knowledge that Althea is slowly slipping away, and soon, she will be gone.

They now sit at the kitchen table, steaming mugs of coffee in hand, trying to recover from another hard week of work. Recovery is cut quite short by a light knock on the door.

Althea takes a long sip of her coffee. "A witch's work is never done," she says as she stands and walks toward the door. The moment she twists the handle, a breathless woman hurls herself into the kitchen.

"He's back," she says as she fights for her breath and braces herself against the table. "He's back, Althea. I just saw him in town."

Marigold stiffens, adrenaline already surging. The panic in this woman's voice reminds her of Caoimhe, and she readies herself to save her life.

"I know exactly what you need," Althea says sagely as she walks back to the counter. The woman nods and collapses into Althea's chair at the table. Her grandmother seems calm, so Marigold relaxes slightly. She watches the woman's gaze move around the room until their eyes meet, and the woman seems to nearly jump out of her skin.

"Goodness! Who are you? When did you get here?" the woman asks.

She sits up straight. "I've been here this entire time."

The woman looks her up and down. Without breaking eye contact, she says, "Althea, I didn't realize you had another customer. I do pray you are not here for the same reason as I am. God knows that's the last thing I need. A pretty thing like you as competition. I'd simply die right here," she whines.

Althea laughs from where she stands at the counter. "Forgive my manners, I'm quite tired. June, this is my granddaughter, Marigold. She'll be taking over my work soon. I can assure you that she has no interest in pursuing your heart's desires."

"Thank God for that," June says. She extends a limp hand to Marigold and says, "June Fairmon, pleased to meet you."

June reminds her a great deal of many ladies back in Bardshire. A demanding presence, a grating voice, and a dramatic flair that accompanies every movement. It's been so long since she has interacted with someone like this that she almost forgets a proper response.

"The pleasure is mine," she manages to say.

"Marigold, come help me over here so I can teach you how to make this. It's extremely important. June, make yourself comfortable as usual."

She stands at her grandmother's side while June moves to their living room and sits on the soft green couch.

"Who is she talking about? Is she in danger?"

"Not at all. She's simply in love with a nice boy named Lachlan Ayles. A sweet ginger lad."

"So what is it that we are making exactly?"

"You'll see soon enough."

Althea begins to gather the beeswax that used to hold the honey that they already harvested. She places it in a small pot and hangs it on the rack above the fireplace. Once it begins to melt, she stirs gently. "Take the mortar and pestle and grind up some of those rose and bellflower petals into the finest powder you can make," she instructs.

She does as she is told and brings the mortar over. Her grandmother drops the powder into the melted wax. "Now bring me some rosemary essence, lavender honey, and some small tins like the ones you saw in the enfleurage room."

She gathers the rest of the necessary tools and ingredients and reports back to her grandmother's side. Althea adds the essence and honey and then removes the pot from the fire with a toweled hand. She brings it over to the counter, though it is not easy for her. The pot is small, but pure cast iron, and Althea is weaker than ever before. This must be incredibly important.

Althea pours the mixture into the enfleurage tins and waits. It takes a few minutes of silence for the substance to harden again into a buttery red balm. Althea picks one up and smiles in approval as she tests the consistency with her fingers.

"It's perfect," she says, and June hurries to her side to admire the product.

"Althea, dare I say you've outdone yourself with this one," she says with a smile.

"It's the bellflower petals. Normally, I only have rose."

Marigold watches them both, still confused as to what she has helped create. It's the same color as Lottie Burke's hair. She shakes her head, resenting how she cannot encounter rich red colors without thinking of Lottie. "What is it?"

"My greatest invention," Althea says. She scoops some of it out into a small dollop on her finger. "My homemade beeswax lipstick."

She slaps her hand on her forehead. "Grandmother! I thought this was some sort of all-powerful love spell!"

Althea nearly chokes with laughter. She applies the balm to her lips and plants a vibrant kiss on Marigold's cheek.

"We don't do love spells. We don't make anything that would interfere with someone's free will. This is merely an enhancement to catch someone's eye."

"I pray that it works," June says as she grabs the tin.

"It will, June. Lachlan won't be able to take his eyes off of you," Althea says. Marigold must use all her willpower not to roll her eyes over June's desperation. It reminds her too much of Bardshire, of the expectation to be perfect, to be impressive, to prioritize attention over everything else. June represents everything she feared for her own life, and she is exceptionally grateful to have found a different outcome. Once June says her polite goodbyes, Marigold can finally let out the laugh that she has been holding throughout the entire visit.

"What's so funny, Mari?"

She gestures to the door as she laughs. "That woman is insufferable."

Althea puts her hands on her hips. "Now why would you say such a thing?"

"Because she..." she says, her laughter falling into silence. "She just...the way she was all...you know..." She mimes primping and playing with her hair. "Ooh, notice me, love me, I'm just a silly girl and I want a silly husband," she mocks.

Althea's hands stay firmly planted on her hips and she does

not laugh at the jokes. Marigold sinks into herself, crossing her arms over her chest. "What? You disagree?"

"I do, actually," Althea says. "I think you're being unkind. June is a nice girl, and just because she is choosing a different life path from you does not give you the right to belittle her. She's not doing anything wrong. She's not hurting anyone. She simply wants a little red lipstick and a nice boy to notice her."

"But shouldn't she want more for her life than that?"

"What any woman wants for herself is not for you to decide. You would do well to remember that."

Chapter Nine

When the harvest is finally complete and the cottage is filled with honey and two exhausted witches, Althea and Marigold relax into their well-earned rest. Marigold has taken over the cooking, and she brings Althea her meals in bed. She often sits in the rocking chair across from Althea and reads to her while they share a bottle of honeyed mead.

Their time together remains cheerful and happy, but Althea looks less and less like herself with each passing day. Her hair has lost its curl. She does not have the energy to make more of her homemade red lipstick, much less put it on. She sleeps more, talks less, and it breaks Marigold's heart. She does everything she can to make her grandmother as comfortable as possible, but it is not enough. While her grandmother sleeps through the days, Marigold starts to realize just how alone she is about to be.

Days pass until Althea wakes with a bit more energy and decides to move to the couch in the living room. Marigold brings over her breakfast, and they watch the sunrise. Soon after, there is a knock at the door. Marigold chews her lip; she has yet to handle a customer interaction completely on her own, and she realizes now that she has no idea what to do. It's the only part of her role that scares her. She's never been great with people, but maybe that only applies to those in Bardshire. Fiddling with her dress, she poses unnaturally in the kitchen, pretending to be confident. Thankfully, Althea is feeling well enough today to help guide the interaction.

"Come in," Althea calls, and a familiar face walks in. Mr. Benny may have trimmed his beard slightly since their last encounter, but it is still well past his chest. He still wears his signature red suspenders, now over a blue striped shirt tucked tightly into his patchwork trousers. He puts a harvest basket full of seasonal vegetables onto the table.

"Benny!" Althea says as she struggles to get up. He rushes over to her and holds her in a gentle embrace.

"Hi, Althea," he says, his tone falling when he sees her in her weakened state. "How are you doing today?"

She gives a soft smile. "Very tired. Marigold will help you now," Althea says. "Mari, here's your very first customer to handle all on your own."

Marigold bounds over to him with excitement. "What seems to be the problem, Mr. Benny?"

"Just had a bit of hay fever; you know how it gets in the late spring. Pollen everywhere all the time. I was hoping you would have some of that miracle potion for this time of year," he says.

"I can whip it up for you right now," she says, cracking open the grimoire and grabbing ingredients. This one is easy—bee pollen, propolis, essence of mint, and black sage honey. "How many jars do you need?"

"I'll take all you have," Mr. Benny says, and Althea gives him a light shove.

"He'll have *one*, Marigold," Althea says as she glares up at her friend, who wears a wicked grin. "She's new, Benny. Don't tease her. For reference, Marigold, one potion is all a person will need. Don't let them overwork you," she warns, and Marigold smiles and nods.

"Well, she has to go through some sort of initiation, doesn't she? I used to always give you a hard time, too," Mr. Benny says to Althea.

"You still give me a hard time, Benny. That never stopped," she replies.

He sighs sweetly. "My, I've been missing you, Althea. I didn't want to interrupt your time with your granddaughter, but... well, you know," Mr. Benny says with a gentle smile. Althea blushes as she holds his gaze.

"Here you are, Mr. Benny," Marigold says as she hands him a vial.

"Thank you kindly, Miss Marigold." He smiles and turns back to Althea. "Is there anything I can do for you, lady?"

Althea looks at the floor for a moment before pulling her shoulders back and nodding. "Yes. Come back tomorrow morning, Benny. Okay? I need you to come back tomorrow."

Benny nods. Their gaze lingers on each other, an entire conversation happening in the silence between them that Marigold cannot decipher. He is turning to walk away when Althea calls his name again. There is a long pause.

"Yes?" Benny says.

"I..." Althea stops herself. She looks at Marigold, then back at Benny. "I wanted to say thank you. I've found myself cherishing happy memories as of late, and you happen to be in many of my favorites."

He smiles softly, his round eyes sparkling in the light that streams through the window. "You know, it's funny," he says with a light laugh. "Maybe it's my age, but I can't clearly remember how we first met. I suppose I'm simply thankful I made a good enough impression for you to let me stay around."

She smiles softly. "You did."

He bows out of the door, and Althea watches him through the window until he is too far to see.

"I love that man," Althea says as she sits back down with a sigh. Marigold's heart sinks as she observes her grandmother now, crumbling into herself on the couch.

"Would you like to head to bed, Grandmother?" she asks, looking for anything to aid in her grandmother's comfort.

"Yes, darling. I should go now before I lose all energy to stand." Althea laughs, but there is truth in her voice. Marigold bears all her weight as they walk into her room. She helps her grandmother into bed, adds another blanket on top of her, and then takes her place in the rocking chair across from the bed. Picking up the book at her side, she removes the bookmark and skims over the page where they left off.

"I will warn you that this is a romance book. This next chapter is quite...descriptive. Shall I skip over it?"

"Don't you dare! That's the best part. Go on," Althea says with a weak motion of her hand, and Marigold laughs loudly.

"You're a deviant," she says.

"I am just a woman with fantastic taste in literature. Now read," Althea commands, and Marigold collects herself as she begins. The two of them giggle until they are blue in the face, and when they reach the end of the book, Marigold leaves to tend to the house. She spends the afternoon tending to the bees, inspecting the hives and checking on the brood nestled within the honeycomb. She brews another batch of the hay fever cure and, after bottling it and cleaning the kitchen, takes her time cooking an elaborate dinner of mushroom stew and bread rolls for her and Althea.

"When do you expect the bees will have made enough honey for another harvest?" she asks.

"I haven't really thought that far ahead, darling," Althea says as a morbid joke that stings Marigold harder than she possibly intended.

"Well, I think it could be soon. I'm amazed at how quickly they replenish."

"They are amazing creatures," Althea agrees as she fights to keep her eyes open. She drifts off for a moment and smiles in her sleep. Marigold counts the seconds between each deep breath until her grandmother jolts herself awake. "Sorry, Mari. I drifted into a dream there."

"What did you dream of? You were smiling."

Her eyes close as she sinks farther into the bed, her voice hardly more than a whisper. "I dreamed of my friends, when we were girls together. When I sleep, I am with them, ageless. We're all barefoot girls with long plaited hair and baby teeth."

"That is so lovely, Grandmother. I should very much like to meet your friends."

"Oh, they are all on the other side now, darling. They are waiting for me."

Silence heavies the air. Marigold picks at her nails and chews the inside of her cheek. "Well, I hope they are patient."

Althea smiles, though her eyes remain closed. "You know, one day, I'll be on the other side waiting for you, too. I'll be there for you, always."

Marigold stands at the side of the bed and hugs her grandmother. "I know you will. In the yellow flowers." Kissing her cheek, she says, "I will let you dream now. I'll see you in the morning."

"Mari…" Althea says, catching her before she leaves the room. "I am so very proud of you. You are the perfect Honey Witch, and I have been so lucky to watch you grow. I love you, darling."

Marigold's heart swells with love that tickles her belly.

"I love you, too, Grandmother. Thank you for all of this. I am so grateful to have seen the beauty you bring to the world, and I am honored that you have taught me to do the same. I know that you have brought me where I need to be."

With that, she goes to her own room, blows out her candle, and tucks herself in. However, sleep does not come. There is a feeling of dread in her chest that burns through the night. Part of her knows that her grandmother is in her final days, but another part of her rejects that reality entirely. It is impossible to imagine the Honey Witch cottage without Althea Murr. It is equally impossible to imagine herself without her grandmother. While she had not often seen her throughout her life, Marigold could always feel her love, and she always felt connected to her. Now she knows why.

What will it feel like when her grandmother passes? She pictures a sudden pain in her side, like a knife burying itself in her ribs. She imagines a tangible bond between them breaking like a bone. Every part of her expects to feel something the very moment that Althea passes. With two people being so similar, and so magically connected, it would seem to be an impossibility to not know when the other passes on.

In the morning, there is nothing in the air that would indicate anything is different or wrong. While sleepiness dulls Marigold's intuition, she takes her time dressing for the day—a white flowing dress and her favorite yellow ribbon in her hair. She makes her way to the kitchen and fixes two cups of coffee before walking over to Althea's door.

For the moment, she feels nothing.

And then, the knowing comes, and she feels everything all at once.

She drops the cups of coffee onto the floor and rushes to her grandmother's side. In the bed, tucked beneath her many yellow blankets, lies Althea Murr, who looks to be finally at peace. While Marigold knew that this day was close, she could not have prepared herself for the sight, and she can't hold back her screams. Her voice echoes so powerfully that it shakes the very trees of the isle. Leaves fall to the ground like teardrops. The time that she spends crying on the floor feels endless, but it feels just as sudden when a pair of strong arms pick her up and pull her into an embrace. A long beard tickles her cheek, and she recognizes the striking red suspenders out of the corner of her eye.

"I remembered," he says, his heavy tears falling onto Marigold's crown.

"Mr. Benny," she whimpers as he holds her hair. Althea told Mr. Benny yesterday that he would need to come back today—her grandmother knew then that her time was almost done, and in this moment, Marigold has never been more grateful to not be alone. She begins to calm down in his arms, but she cannot turn to look at her grandmother again.

"I know not what to do now," she cries.

"I remember everything," Mr. Benny says softly. She does not have the breath to ask what he means. They cry with each other, the strength of their grief holding the sun still so that time did not pass them by. It could have been seconds, it could have been hours, but it did not matter. It was their time to grieve together, and the world would wait for them to catch their breath.

"I spoke with your grandmother before she left to see you," Mr. Benny says, "and she told me that she knew her time was near. She left me with instructions on what to do."

Marigold nods. "Tell me what you need from me."

"Not a thing, Marigold. Go somewhere peaceful, and I will take care of everything the way your grandmother told me she wanted," he says. Marigold wraps her arms around him tightly in another embrace.

"Bless you, Mr. Benny. Thank you," she says as she pulls back to see his sweet smile. She leaves the cottage without looking back.

She walks outside into the apiary, where she is greeted by the sound of bumbling bees and a kaleidoscope of butterflies. Slowly, she walks past each hive and knocks lightly as she whispers the news to them. The bees tumble out of their hive and fly around her body. It's as if the little creatures can sense her grief and want to help her find peace. They lead her back to the oasis, where she lies down on the soft green grass and rests in the presence of a clear, still sky.

Innisfree will weep without Althea, and Marigold doubts that she will be able to fulfill the obligations that her grandmother once did. She has been training for this, of course, but it all still felt far away until this morning. Now she alone is the Honey Witch of Innisfree, and she cannot allow herself to fail. Tears drip down her face and into the grass that frames her. One small bee waddles up her arm and flies to the tip of her nose. It buzzes and tickles until it earns her smile, and then it flies away. She sits up and takes in a deep breath of floral-scented air, and the wind stings her tearstained cheeks. The breeze ripples through the grass and trees, and then it begins to grow in strength. Marigold stands to witness the dancing trees, and suddenly, all around her, yellow flowers start to spring up. In a matter of seconds, the trees are covered in bright yellow blooms, and the petals float lightly in the air like impossible snowflakes in summer. They swirl around Marigold and beckon her to dance, and she spins wildly through the meadow. Every place that she steps earns another yellow flower that blooms as soon as she steps away. The entire meadow becomes a sea of soft yellow, and Marigold knows that her grandmother's presence is here with her.

"If you can hear me," Marigold starts, but the tears find her again. She thinks herself a fool for speaking to the wind, but she stifles her sobs and perseveres regardless.

"If you can hear me, Grandmother, know that I love you and I will not let you down," Marigold says. She waits for a moment until a flower begins to glow at her feet. She smiles, but she leaves the flower unpicked, the glow unharmed. In the light of the setting sun, Marigold and the bees start their journey back to the cottage.

When they arrive, the bees return to their hives, and Marigold meets Mr. Benny sitting on the front steps.

"Hello there, Miss Marigold," he says kindly.

"Hi, Mr. Benny," Marigold replies, unable to hide her nerves. He wastes no time with idle chitchat as he offers her his hand.

"Would you like to see her?" Mr. Benny asks, and Marigold accepts his hand. He leads her around the cottage, to the open yard that sits across from the apiary. There, in the middle of the grass, is a spot of freshly tilled soil adorned with the same yellow flowers that Marigold watched bloom in the meadow moments ago. Beside the spot where Althea is buried, there are heavy copper wind chimes that sing in the breeze. There is no headstone, but there needn't be one. This is the final resting place of Althea Murr—it is something that is sensed, without the aid of a marker. The landvættir all gather behind Marigold, offering their calming presence and promises to keep this ground safe no matter what.

Even if the world were to cave in, they would shield this spot with their sun-bleached bones.

"It's perfect," Marigold whispers.

"I'm glad you like it," Mr. Benny says. He reaches into his pocket and pulls out a ring that Althea wore on days when she wasn't working in the apiary. It's gold with lots of little swirls holding on to tiny emeralds. His hands are trembling.

"She wanted you to have this," he says.

"It's beautiful," she says, placing it on her ring finger. It's a bit dirty and it's too big, but it's perfect. It's the most important thing she owns.

"I'll leave you now, Miss Marigold. I am sorry for your loss. Please forgive me if I take a little longer to return to you. I'll be back soon, but I need some time. I need to make sure I remember it all."

Marigold smiles and nods, understanding the desire to commit every moment with Althea to memory. She intends to take that time as well, to fill her journal with their stories. As Mr. Benny leaves her, she spends the night beside her grandmother's resting place and weeps.

Part Two

It is the winter of 1831, and Marigold Claude celebrates her twenty-second birthday alone.

She fills her day with her favorite things—summer fruit, Earl Grey tea, spell casting, and honeybees. Fresh sunflowers, yellow ribbons, daydreams, and lullabies.

She thinks of the excuse of youth—the thing that makes it okay to be so lost—and how it is slipping through her fingers with every passing year. She ruminates about her last birthday and how much her life has changed. Althea's emerald ring hangs from a silver chain around her neck, reminding her of everything she has and everything she lost.

The honey cake in her hand glistens from the light of the single candle held upright by the icing. One candle for her one wish: to not spend her next birthday alone.

Chapter Ten

M arigold continues her work in the months that pass, picking up right where her grandmother left off like an overture into a melody. She wrote a letter to her father to send word of her grandmother's passing—she did not have the strength to address the letter to her mother. They have not written or communicated in any way since she left Bardshire, and maybe her mother intends to keep it that way. She continued making seasonal brews until she was well stocked, and then she began playing with other curious concoctions. There are few customers at the moment. Mr. Benny says they are trying to give her time to grieve before asking too much of her. This allows her plenty of time to experiment. So far, she has made a spell to keep a fire safely burning through the night and one to make the entire house smell like fresh lemon.

Whenever the rare customer does come, she delivers a perfectly rehearsed monologue about her grandmother's passing. They are kind and caring, but they never linger. Some bring gifts to offer as condolences—pickled vegetables, eclectic teacups, and one man brought a handwoven blue blanket. This day marks four whole months since her grandmother's death. Marigold's grief moves with the seasons. It blooms and rots and shrinks and grows, and just like the winter, it cannot last forever. She becomes more and more confident in her role every day. With Mr. Benny's help, she has been rearranging the cottage to her liking, so there is even more room for guests, should she ever have any. It took her weeks to be able to return to her grandmother's former room, but when she did, it was not the same. Not only did Mr. Benny take care of her grandmother's burial, he also transformed the room into a completely different space. One that held no memories of grief. No remnants of death.

Now it is a library.

The walls are lined with shelves overflowing with Althea's books that were once shoved in random storage spaces throughout the cottage. There are books on almost everything imaginable— some classics, some fairy tales, endless romances, and of course, Althea's journals with spell-stained recipes inside. Her desk sits by the big bright windows. Against the center of a wall, flanked by two white bookshelves, is a new bed about half the size of the old one, made up with fresh linens. Everything is in its perfect place. Althea would have liked the look of it, though she may have complained about the bookshelves. Marigold can hear her now: "*I had my books organized in my own way and I knew where everything was.*"

She finds herself scribbling at her desk when the idea strikes to write another letter home, though she has yet to hear back after the first.

Dear Aster,

I miss you dearly. I think you would quite like it here if you fancy a visit. Grandmother's old room is now a study and a library with a spare bed. I've set up the guest room with new bedding and fresh flowers. Of course, there would be different flowers by the time you got here. What is your favorite flower again?

I know you hate breakfast tea, but might I recommend adding both lavender and honey? You might enjoy it then, and it might soothe your throat should you ever find yourself trapped in one of Sir Kentworth's experimental operas. I've found it to be the perfect drink to calm down after a long day of work. Speaking of work, it is constant here, but it is lovely. I tend to the bees and the butterflies. I feel my magic strengthening with every use. And the customers I meet are always so kind.

Please write back and tell me everything you have been up to back home. Tell me of Frankie's antics and Father's latest paintings. And tell me of Mother. Is she still furious? Do NOT tell her that I asked.

I miss you. I know I already said that, but it is worth repeating.

All my love,
Marigold

She folds the letter and drops it into an envelope before sealing it with a beeswax crest. Mr. Benny will be the one to pick it up and send it off for her. He has been like the grandfather she never had, and she has yet to find the words to thank him for being in her life. He checks on her at least once a week when he brings food from the farm. They often have tea—Earl Grey with lavender syrup—and talk about Althea. Marigold spent years not knowing her grandmother, so hearing stories from someone who knew her feels like making up for the lost time. She would very much like a visit from August, ideally without his unpleasant boyfriend and his wicked redheaded friend. She can understand his infatuation with Edmund enough, for she is no stranger to falling for a self-important man. It is a wonder, though, that someone as kind as August could be such close friends with a woman like Lottie. Perhaps there is more to her than Marigold saw upon their first meeting, but first impressions are usually correct. Lottie is, more likely than not, mean.

A breeze flows through the open window and brings cold air into the cottage. As she walks toward it, she is taken aback by the sudden entrance of a small orange... thing.

No, not a thing—a cat. Not like Chesha, the spirit guardian. A real cat.

Her grandmother mentioned that she had a cat, a magically old cat of thirty years. He has retained most of his color, save for a bit of white around his nose. Now, she must remember its name...

Cindy? Moonshine? Nothing feels quite right, and her memory fails her. The orange cat approaches her and meows loudly when it realizes that she is not Althea.

"Hi, kitty kitty," she says, her voice shaky with nerves. "I'm Marigold. I'm your owner's granddaughter. Oh, well, I guess I am your owner now."

The cat does not respond because it cannot talk, which is a little disappointing. With so many other magical features of this land, it would not be impossible. But alas, the cat merely stares at her until it decides she is at least nice enough to sniff. Slowly, she pets the cat's head, and it nuzzles into her. Now that she is closer, she can see that the cat has a navy blue collar and a name tag.

"Cindershine!"

The cat happily meows at the sound of his own name. She sits in front of him and allows Cindershine to climb into her folded lap and purr as she continues to pet him.

"Aw, I like you, Cindershine. You're a good boy."

After a lengthy process of trial and error, she fashions a makeshift toy to entertain the cat. She spends longer than she intends playing with him, for she did not realize how lonely she has grown, and even this tiny company leaves a great impact. She makes vegetable stew for dinner and shares some with Cindershine as they dine by the fire. Most nights, after dinner, she goes out for a nighttime stroll. This time, Cindershine follows, and the two lightly pad down the snow-covered path and watch the sun melt into the lake. When darkness falls, she witnesses the newly lit stars and waits for messages. The world has been far too quiet as of late. At this point, she even misses the sounds she used to hate.

Slamming carriage doors.

Teaspoons tapping porcelain cups.

Her family calling her by the nickname she despises. What she would give to be Mari, for a moment.

But she is only Marigold, and she is alone.

"You know," she says to nothing and no one except the cat at her side, "I cannot remember the last time I went this long without a proper conversation with someone my own age. The customers are kind but always too quick to leave. At this point, I would settle for simply someone with whom to argue. Or some backtalk from the sky." She stands up on the edge of the dock. "Hello, spirits! Can any of you talk?"

There is a splash from the swan Odessa across the pond, a hiss from Talaya far behind her, and a nuzzle from Cindershine at her side, but there are no words from anyone or anything.

As she turns to go inside, she sees an eerily familiar sight— that small flicker across the lake, deep in the Hazelwood Forest. Her toes curl beneath her. Intuition tells her that something is wrong, but she remembers Althea expressed no need for worry. She returns to the cottage and goes to bed for the evening, hoping that her grandmother was right.

Chapter Eleven

Letters to and from Innisfree take far too long. It took over four weeks to hear back from Frankie, and spring buds are rising from the weakened frost by the time she finally receives word from Aster.

Dear Mari,

I miss you more! Do not argue with me about that, stubborn sister. I see you have forgotten my favorite flower. What else have you forgotten in our time apart? I shall remind you: My name is Aster Claude, I am your favorite sister, and my favorite flower is an azalea.

Regarding what I am up to, I am excited to tell you that I have taken a bit of interest in Mr. Woodrake. We met as Father was giving him a painting lesson. He later asked me to pose for a portrait. It was not the best, but not the worst. Hopefully, his skills will improve throughout our courtship. Maybe you could cast a spell to advance his talents when you visit! It's just a thought. I'm not quite sure what your new abilities entail but know that I am proud of you beyond measure.

I imagine it will be spring by the time you receive this letter. Since you have now been reminded of my

*favorite flower, I expect a pressed azalea with your
response. We all miss you dearly and truly. Frankie
is claiming to be uninterested in any courtship, but
I think he lies. He is having a difficult time finding
a connection with a gentleman, but I can tell that
he longs for love. Father didn't paint for some time
after you left, but he seems to be finding inspiration
again as spring returns. We are eagerly awaiting
your company and the tales of your adventures.*

*All my love,
Aster*

*PS You should write to Mother. She's not furious,
but she has been awfully mopey since "the ordeal."
(That's what we call it now: the ordeal. Mother
didn't like Frankie's use of the term "spooky ritual.")*

From what Marigold remembers, Mr. Woodrake is kind
enough. He is years younger than her, so it's not as though she
has ever spoken to him at length, but she trusts Aster's judgment.
Poor Frankie, though. He has always been a romantic, ever since
he was a child, but he has never courted anyone. He's awfully
picky, but he should be. He's too good for most of the rakes in
Bardshire who pursue heartbreak for the sake of art. Her eyes
are falling over the last sentence when there is a knock at the
door, and she has never been so excited at the sound. Anyone and
anything would be better than pondering her mother. She runs
to the door with the broadest grin she can muster and twists the
handle.

And, because the universe has its own sense of humor, the person standing in her doorway with a red-lipped smile is June
Fairmon. This time, she's with a tall ginger-haired man, so the
lipstick must have worked.

"Oh, hi! Marigold, right?"

"Right," she says, forcing her smile to stay wide. An awkward pause stretches between them until June finally says, "May we come in?"

She laughs softly and motions for them to enter. "Of course, my apologies. And you must be Mr. Ayles," she says to the man on June's arm.

"Yes, I'm Lachlan. How did you know?"

"Call it a witch's intuition," she says in the same cadence that Althea often spoke, and she winks at June behind Lachlan's back.

"Lachlan and I got married! I'm June Ayles now!" June wraps her arms around Lachlan's waist, plants a bright red kiss on his cheek, and brings her hand up to his chin. "Look at my handsome cuddle duck."

"And my perfect little love dove," Lachlan says as he touches his nose to his new wife's. Marigold swallows to ease her nausea as she watches the couple. There was a time when she thought that the most annoying couples all hailed from Bardshire, but the new Mr. and Mrs. Ayles seem to be vying for the title of the most vexatious lovesick pair she has ever met.

"Congratulations," she says. She turns to close the door behind them and relishes the opportunity to roll her eyes.

"Where's Althea?" June asks as she peers into the living room.

The mention of her grandmother's name feels like a sudden pinprick. "Oh, June. You may want to sit down."

June gasps. "Did she—?"

She nods. "About eight months ago, right at the end of the summer."

"Oh, I'm so sorry!" June wails as she wraps Marigold in a hug. She awkwardly returns the embrace and reminds herself that Althea would expect her to be polite.

"Thank you, June. I appreciate it," she says, though her voice is muffled by June's shoulder, into which her face is being smushed. June lets go so quickly that Marigold almost falls onto her chair, and June collapses into Lachlan's arms.

"My love, I am heartbroken by this news. Althea was a saint. A saint among us! What will this world do without the Honey Witch?"

Lachlan holds his wife, strokes her hair, and whispers comforting words in her ear. Something twists in Marigold's stomach as she watches them. It's not jealousy—the last thing she wants is a husband like that. Seeing their interactions makes her all the more grateful that she will never be in the position of being a wife. It looks like they are both putting on a constant performance for each other and the people around them. She cannot imagine a more exhausting task. However, she would not object to having long-term company. A companion. Someone who isn't just a customer. Someone, something, anything to feel a bit less lonely.

"Well, you have me as your Honey Witch now," she says.

June wipes the tears from her face and says, "But can you do all the wondrous things that Althea did? I don't mean to be rude, but Lachlan and I came here with quite an ask."

"June, be kind. We don't want to be turned away by our only hope," Lachlan scolds. While Marigold appreciates his defense of her, she fears that June may be right. She may love being a witch and have a natural inclination toward spellwork, but she is far from an expert. She has worried that every customer can see this and sense her lack of experience, but something about June's immediate assumption that she cannot manage a request inclines her to prove the woman wrong.

"I assure you, I will do all that I can. What do you require?"

Lachlan and June take a deep breath and say in unison, "We want a baby!"

She lifts her brows. "So soon?"

June crosses her arms over her chest. "Well, we've been married for three months now."

"Exactly," she says reflexively, and she hears her grandmother's voice in the back of her head saying that it is not her place to judge others, regardless of how nightmarish their choices

may seem to her. "I mean to say: You want my help so soon?
Surely you would wish to…you know…try on your own?"

Their smiles sink. "We have been," June says, her crossed
arms tightening around her.

"Oh," Marigold says, immediately wishing she could undo the
words she just said. "I'm so sorry; I was being rude and insensi-
tive. I can absolutely help."

June's demeanor softens as Marigold turns to her kitchen and
begins to gather ingredients for a potent fertility spell—acacia
honey, dandelion seeds, cinnamon, rose essence, and basil. She
grinds the dry ingredients into a powder, then adds them to the
wet ingredients in a small jar. She twists the lid onto the jar and
hands the spell to June.

"Put a little bit of this on your belly before bed, and keep
trying."

The couple eagerly accepts the spell and says their polite
goodbyes as they bow out of the door. She watches them through
the window—Lachlan's hand on the small of June's back, the
way their steps are in perfect time with each other, their excited
kisses between every few steps.

Perhaps she is a bit jealous, or maybe this dull ache is something else. Her eyes focus on her reflection in the glass window.
Her face surprises her because she thought she was scowling
this whole time, but she's not—she simply looks sad. Flat eyes,
frowny, frumpy. She should take a bath or at least go for a swim,
but who does she need to freshen up for? Most of the people who
come to her for aid are in far worse shape than this. Customers
and proper company are two different things.

August did visit once before he left. He came by himself a
few months ago in a handcrafted blue boat that he made with
his father. He stayed for tea and expressed his sympathies for
Althea's passing. He spoke of Edmund's poetic pursuits and how
frustrated he has been with Lottie for mocking them, wounding
Edmund's fragile ego. Marigold snickered at that. Maybe that
would be something she and Lottie could one day bond over—a

mutual hatred of bad poetry. Then, a few weeks later, Marigold went into town to see him off on his business trip. She brought a huge basketful of baked goods, a jar of black sage honey for healing, and a bunch of flowers from Innisfree that will never wilt. She saw Edmund there, who was feigning heartbreak and reciting insufferable sonnets about absence making the heart grow fonder and whatnot, but more notably, she saw Lottie. Her red hair looked aglow against the snowy backdrop, and her eyes matched the evergreens. Lottie was made for winter. Marigold could hardly take her eyes off of her, especially as August sailed out of sight. But then, Lottie started acting completely different, and not in a good way.

"I will miss him so much," Marigold said, and Lottie laughed in her face.

"You hardly know him."

Taken aback, she said, "We've known each other since we were children."

"No, you *met* when you were children, and then you stopped knowing each other because you left. You did not miss him for those fifteen years that you were gone, and you do not get to miss him now."

Edmund patted Lottie on the head and looked at Marigold. "The witch of the wood hath poked the fiery beast."

Lottie shoved his hand away. "I do not have to pretend to like either of you while August is gone. I came here to see him off, and I have done so." Without a goodbye, she left them both shivering by the sea.

Marigold replays that interaction over and over in her mind. Everything was fine as they waved goodbye to August, but she made the grave error of touching her shoulder to Lottie's. As soon as she got too close, Lottie made a face as if a monster had overtaken her. Marigold's touch repulsed the woman, which was both hurtful and embarrassing. She cringes when she thinks of it. What did she do that left Lottie so disgusted? Was Lottie simply that rude to everyone, or was Marigold *that* intensely unlikable?

Despite what Lottie said, she does miss August, and quite a bit. His visit to the cottage lasted for hours. They reveled in their nostalgia, finding old memories and making new ones. They have one of those friendships that always picks up where it leaves off, and they will do so once again when he returns. She has no doubts about that. She and August are forever. Unfortunately, the same can be said about August and Lottie, so they'll all have to find a way to get along someday. She has contemplated seeking Lottie out, confronting her until she admits that Marigold is actually quite nice, but that is a bad idea born out of pure loneliness. There is a better solution for that—a spell.

She opens her grimoire until she finds what she is looking for, but there is a significant problem; the spell to cure loneliness requires moonflower honey. It is challenging to create, even for a Honey Witch who can aid the bees in their search. Moonflowers are rare, blooming only in perfect conditions of cool air and a full moon. Even then, the blooms only last a night. The moon is set to be full tonight, so she must find where the moonflowers will bloom before the sun sets; otherwise, she will not be able to inform the bees.

She scours the lake isle. Without their white blooms, moonflower trees look like short, stubby pines that gave up on the idea of being tall. They are not the easiest things to spot, but still, she is having exceptionally bad luck. After hours of searching to no avail, she returns to the cottage, smelling of wet grass and metallic sweat. Heavy with defeat, she explores her spell book for a solution. Twenty pages later, she finds one—a finder's spell, able to locate anything from a lost hair ribbon to creatures that the rest of the world thinks are a myth. Its ingredients are simple: sage, clover honey, bellflower petals, and a white string. She still has more than a bouquet's worth of bellflower from her travels with her grandmother, and she pressed some of them to preserve the memory. In her kitchen, she mixes and muddles together the wet ingredients of the spell, and then she lightly dips the string in the solution until its white threads are rich with the pink dye from the bellflower petals. When the string emerges, she smiles as she holds it to the light.

"Lead me to a moonflower tree," she commands, and the string begins to move. It sways intentionally against the wind in a manner that would be impossible without the magic. She walks in the direction indicated by the string, and it leads her all the way down the stone pier. Her feet balance upon the edge, but the string indicates that the tree is farther away. It must require her to proceed through the lake, but to what end?

Odessa swims past her feet and urges her backward. She trusts the spirit much more than the string, and Odessa is warning her not to leave. In the Hazelwood Forest, the flicker from before remains, though it is stronger now. Marigold can see it directly. A sense of unease floods her body, effectively muting all feelings of loneliness with something much stronger—fear. Marigold returns inside, troubled, and recites her incantation of protection again. She also flips through the grimoire to find any other ingredient that may be useful for protection. With new knowledge, she salts each corner of the house and falls asleep with a sprig of rosemary in her clenched grip.

Chapter Twelve

At the start of her first summer alone, Marigold begins every day by talking to her bees and helping them find new flora to pollinate. She is working on a sunflower garden in an open glade, of which the bees and butterflies are growing quite fond. Recently, she crafted a mnemonic to remember which honeys are best suited for certain spells: lavender for love, clover for clarity, tupelo for truth, peach blossom for protection, black sage for betterment (really, *healing* is the correct word, but she needed something that started with a *B*), and acacia for all else. She spends her afternoons buried in a grimoire, studying. Her goal is to have the entire healing section memorized by this month's end. She wakes with the sun—any later and she would miss her first customers. They tend to come at the crack of dawn or late in the evening, not so much in between. It is a rare treat that someone comes at a reasonable hour. After helping her first customer—a farmer who needed the tip of their finger reattached after an incident with a pocketknife—she then takes a look at her inventory. Her supply of lavender honey is running dangerously low. She slips into a white day dress to head into the apiary because bees do not like dark colors. It reminds them of big predators like bears who want to steal from them.

The bees welcome her happily with loud buzzes, and she greets them with a smile. She pulls a frame heavy with honey from the lavender hives and brings it inside to drain. There is enough honey for about two jars, which is a healthy harvest. When she returns the empty frame to the hive, she stretches beneath the light, allowing her skin to soak up every drop of warm yellow heat.

In the distance, a little blue boat approaches, and her heart soars. She could recognize that little blue boat anywhere. August is home, and finally visiting again. She runs to greet him, her bare feet burning against the stone path.

"August!" she screams from the edge of the dock as she waves her hands in the air.

"Hello, Marigold," he calls from the boat. His voice is a little bit dull, like he's trying to cover up bad news. She helps him tie the boat and step onto the isle.

"Everything all right?" She steadies him with her hand on his shoulder. His chipper facade starts to fade, allowing her to see the ache that lies beyond his surface. Swollen eyes, gaunt cheeks, chapped lips. He shakes his head and says, "Not quite, unfortunately."

"What's the matter?" she asks as they walk together. He's alone, which is odd. She didn't anticipate being his first stop upon his return, and surely Lottie and Edmund would not want to leave his side after being apart for so long. "Where are your faithful companions?"

"Lottie would not be caught dead on a magical isle. She doesn't believe in anything fun," he says with a tired laugh. "And Edmund, well—it seems that he had not the patience to wait for my return. He's moved on."

She gasps so hard that she chokes on the air. "What? You two are no longer together?"

"So it seems. Though he lacked the decency to respond to my letters and tell me." They turn toward the cottage together as she lightly rubs his back.

"I am sorry, August. That's so unfair to you."

"Maybe it is, maybe it isn't. I suppose it was not my place to ask him to wait for me for months. It's not easy to go that long without affection."

"I beg to differ! I have gone nearly five years without affection and I am perfectly fine. Edmund made a promise, and time does not give him permission to break it."

"I suppose that's true," he says solemnly before furrowing his brow. "Wait, did you say five years? What happened five years ago?"

"Didn't your mother ever teach you not to pry?" she says quickly as she opens the door to the cottage and rushes inside.

Following her, he says, "She tried, but that is not in my nature. Prying is my strongest talent."

The door closes behind him and he takes a seat at the table, looking up at her through his thick lashes. "Who broke your heart?"

Sighing, Marigold sits across from him. The breeze from the kitchen window tickles the back of her neck as she brings her hair to the side and fidgets with the ends. "There were a few small heartbreaks when I was young. A girl who never responded to my terribly written love letters, a boy who threw away my sad attempt at a portrait of him. But the real heartbreak, the one that felt like a knife wound, was George. He was my first and only love."

It feels strange to call it love now. It was hardly so grand—it was merely someone else giving her permission to love herself, and then trying to take that away.

"What made you love him?"

"Upon reflection," she says, tucking her hair behind her ear, "I am certain it was less about him and more about enjoying the feeling of being chosen by someone who I thought was better than me. I was infamously strange back home, you see, and he seemed to like that. For a short time, at least. But then he proposed to another girl in front of me right before I came here."

He takes her hand and gives her a sympathetic look. "Was she pretty?"

"Gorgeous."

He scoffs. "That's the worst."

Laughing, she says, "It's perfectly fine. Heartbreak is not always bad. It led me to my purpose here."

"Well, maybe you can help me find some purpose through

this heartbreak of my own. I worry that it will take me a lifetime to heal from losing Edmund unless there's a spell to fix that."

"A spell to mend a broken heart," she says knowingly, and he nods. She flips through her grimoire quickly, though she is nearly certain she remembers the spell perfectly. She had just read it yesterday.

"Give me a few moments and I'll have it ready for you. And again, I'm so sorry to see you like this. I can't even imagine how you must be feeling."

He smiles and shrugs. "Even with a broken heart, I still would rather feel this loss than never have had the love at all."

She flinches, suddenly wobbling under the weight of her curse. She shakes it off and says, "Ah, so you're a hopeless romantic, then?"

"I'm certainly a romantic, and at this time, I do feel quite hopeless," he says with a laugh as he pushes his curly black hair off his forehead.

"Well, I can fix the hopeless part, but I do hope you keep your romanticism." She smiles and starts gathering tools and ingredients.

"Can I help you at all?" He rolls up his blue linen sleeves.

She almost shakes her head before glaring up at the top shelf. That shelf is her nemesis. No shelf has any business being that high. "Could you grab that jar of blue hyacinth petals there for me?"

He barely has to stretch to reach the jar. He hands it to her and returns to his position at the table.

"You're a peach," she says as she sprinkles the petals into her bowl. She grabs black sage honey, orange peels, lavender essence, and the last of her moon water, mixing everything with a hard stone grinder. August laughs softly behind her, and she turns to find him crouched beneath the kitchen table.

"What are you doing down there?"

"Come see," he calls, and she puts her tools down lightly to follow his voice. She joins him beneath the table, where he points to nearly illegible writing on the underside of the wood. It reads:

M + A = Best Friends

There are also stick figure drawings of the two of them, surrounded by unnaturally tall flowers. Or maybe they are supposed to be trees? Or...birds with long legs? It's impossible to tell. The pair erupt in laughter.

"I cannot believe this is still here," he says when he catches his breath.

"I didn't even remember this until now!"

"I think I did the writing and you did the drawing," he says as he traces everything with his finger.

She hides her eyes in her hands and says, "That sounds right. I've always been a terrible artist."

"What are you talking about? Those are the nicest rain clouds I've ever seen," August says through his laughter.

She has tears in her eyes from laughing. "I think they were supposed to be flowers."

"Oh no," he says as he starts to crawl out from under the table. "Then, yes, a terrible artist," he says, extending his hand to her and helping her stand.

She straightens her dress and says, "Thank you for reminding me of that. Do you think there are other poor drawings hidden around here?"

"I'm sure of it. We did everything together when we were young, including vandalism."

She giggles, turning back to her work to complete his spell. "How did you and I come to be? Your family knew my grandmother, I take it."

"Well, the whole town knew Althea. But my mother became very close with your mother and grandmother after she came here desperate to have a child. Your grandmother gave her a spell, and then I was born just a few months after you. So in a way, I owe my life to honey magic," he says, and her heart flutters. She thinks of her grandmother, many years ago, helping the young woman who would eventually mother the boy standing in front of her. Life has such a peculiar way of bringing people together.

Once the mixture forms a grainy wet paste, she needs only one more ingredient to add.

"August, can you make yourself cry?" she asks over her shoulder.

"I can certainly say I have never tried."

"Well, can you give it a try? I need a tear from the broken heart to complete the spell. Or I could stomp on your foot really hard. Or get one of the bees to sting you," she says, though she is only partly joking.

"I see. Let me try."

He widens his eyes and stares at her unblinking for almost a full minute. The pair keep laughing in each other's faces during this staring contest, and the tears finally come. He shuts his eyes tightly and blinks rapidly to recover from the dry burn, and she brings over a tiny teaspoon to scrape the tears from his cheek. She stirs them into the bowl and begins to pour the mixture into a perfect heart-shaped bottle.

"You'll take this home and keep it at your bedside. Put a small amount over your heart before falling asleep."

August eagerly takes the bottle from her and seems to try to stop himself from wrapping her in a hug, but he cannot. He embraces her and spins her around in a complete circle before allowing her feet back on the ground.

"You are my favorite witch in the whole wide world! What do I owe you for this?"

Head spinning, she says, "Happy to be of service. You owe me nothing, but I would appreciate your company more often now that you are back."

"I can promise that. I'll return as often as I can, and hopefully in better spirits after this spell works."

She beams. "I look forward to it, August."

"Farewell, Marigold," he says, bowing out of the door. As he leaves, there is a sinking feeling in her stomach, like she didn't know how badly she wanted him to stay until he was already gone. His tiny boat floats out of view from her vantage point of the window, and she is alone again.

Chapter Thirteen

A long four days pass until August Owens returns to Innisfree, although this time, he is not alone. Sitting in the boat across from him is Lottie Burke, her bright red curls glittering under the sun. August must have dragged her here against her will. As usual, she is pouting and wearing an overly modest black dress.

Marigold takes a long, deep breath, preparing herself for whatever version of Lottie she is about to greet. Lottie was vicious during their last encounter, but August's presence may mitigate that this time. It truly makes no sense—she has been nothing but kind and pleasant to Lottie since they met. She even thought Lottie was beautiful until she revealed her true personality after August departed.

When they reach the isle and begin walking up the stone path, Marigold is overwhelmed with the desire to primp herself in the mirror. She finger combs her hair and smooths out any rogue strands that have escaped her yellow ribbon. She taps homemade rouge across her lips and cheeks and adjusts her yellow dress to flatter her body. And, in accordance with her grandmother's expert advice, she taps rose essence behind her ears and knees and between her breasts for good measure. Upon feeling satisfied with her appearance, she rolls her eyes at herself. Why should she feel obligated to impress a woman who will no doubt find her revolting? A rhythmic knock sounds through the cottage, and she runs to open the door.

"Hello, Marigold," August says.

She had a greeting ready in her mind, but all her words disappear as Lottie comes into view. It's intimidating to be so close to her, as if one wrong move could ignite the air.

"May we come in?" August asks after a time, and she startles out of her trance.

"Of course, you may! My apologies, yes, please come in." She sways out of the doorframe. August walks in, taking Lottie's hand and leading her inside. The two of them stand awkwardly in the kitchen as he stares at her with a devious smirk.

"How might I be of service?" she asks, avoiding eye contact with Lottie to focus on what work needs to be done.

"Well, as you can see," he says, adjusting his collar, "your spell to heal a broken heart has worked tremendously for me. I've never been better!"

She touches her hand over her heart. "Wonderful!"

"It is!" His tone drops when he gestures to Lottie. "But this one does not believe it."

"It's *mythcraft*," Lottie says, scoffing.

"What's *mythcraft*?" Marigold asks, mimicking Lottie's tone.

Lottie rolls her eyes and does not respond.

"It's Lottie's made-up word to describe anything she doesn't believe in," he explains on. "If you haven't already noticed, she isn't exactly a believer."

"I simply don't like charlatans," Lottie corrects as she crosses her arms tightly over her chest.

Marigold clenches her jaw. Since her ritual, this is the first time she has ever encountered someone who did not believe in her magic, and it is the strangest thing. As a child, when her siblings didn't believe her about the things she saw, she would sulk for days with all her choice words tucked tightly behind her pout. But now she feels different and defiant. This woman is a customer who has come to the isle after witnessing her best friend's successful spell. What more proof could she need? And why must she be so decidedly rude? Marigold is a decent judge of character, and she hoped that Lottie would be secretly kind underneath her hard exterior, especially now with Edmund out of the picture.

It's starting to feel like she was wrong this time.

August rubs his temples. "Can you be silent instead of snarky for one small minute, please?"

"If I'm so horrible, why did you drag me here with you?" Lottie says.

"Because you're my best friend, even if you are notoriously sour," August says. "Now, I have argued with Lottie for far too long about this, so I brought her here to see it for herself." He takes another long look around the cottage, admiring the ingredients that line the walls. "What other spells can you cast, if you don't mind me asking?"

"I don't mind at all," she says. Despite Lottie's rudeness, she is beyond thrilled to have more people to talk to, someone else's voice warm in her ear. "All my spells must have good and clear intentions. With those parameters in mind, I can essentially cast anything. Fertility, as you know because of your own mother, beautifying elixirs, a spell to find one's soulmate..."

"Soulmate?" August chimes. "Well, that sounds nice."

"It's one of the more difficult spells, but definitely worth it for those who want to find true love. It's actually the spell that brought my parents together."

August laughs and scrunches his brows. "Who wouldn't want to find true love?"

She shrugs. "Some people are meant for different paths, I suppose."

"Everyone is meant to find love," he says.

She sighs softly—she's not in the mood to argue or disclose her curse, especially in front of the skeptical woman who would likely insult her about it. "Well, would you like that spell?"

"Yes, please!" August says, and Lottie rolls her eyes.

Marigold cannot stand it. She folds her arms over her chest and bores her gaze into Lottie. "Do you have something more you wish to say, Lottie?" She enjoys the feeling of Lottie's name in her mouth more than she expected, but that does nothing to mute her accusative tone.

August snorts as Lottie is visibly taken aback. The woman does not seem like she is typically called out for her rude behavior.

Lottie finally finds her words and says, "Not to you."

August grips Lottie's elbow and pulls her toward the door. "Will you excuse us for one moment?"

Before Marigold can respond, Lottie and August are out the door. August does not close it all the way, so she is mostly privy to their conversation, minus a few words that get lost in the distance between them. She can scarcely see Lottie's face through the crack of the door.

"Lots," August whispers.

"What?" she snaps in the harshest whisper she can muster.

"Why are you being so rude?" he asks.

"I am not," Lottie retorts. She says something else, but it's too quiet. *Something something* Marigold, *something something* mythcraft, *something something* beautiful.

"*Beautiful?*" Marigold whispers to herself as she comes closer to the door midway through August's response.

"...so maybe this is the time to *not* immediately push a nice person away."

Lottie grunts. "What if I don't think she's nice?"

"You're lying. You're doing your lying face."

"I do not have a lying face," she replies.

"You chew on your lip and scrunch up your eyebrows."

Lottie releases her lip from her teeth and relaxes her brows. "Leave me alone, August. I'll support you in whatever you want to do, but I'm not going to believe in it."

Oh yes, you will, Marigold thinks as she steps away from the door just in time for August to open it and come back inside.

"Apologies again, Marigold. You were saying?"

Her smirk is wicked. "I have a proposition for you two."

"Go on," August says.

"I will get to work on your soulmate spell. It will take some time to complete because it requires moon water, and I am unfortunately all out, but lucky for you, the full moon is only one week away."

"That sounds simple enough. Shall we return then to retrieve the completed spell?" he says brightly while Lottie holds her suspicious gaze.

"Well, enter the rest of my proposition; I'll give you your spell, if," she says, stepping toward Lottie, "you give me a chance to convince you that my magic is real."

Lottie immediately laughs. "That won't be possible, Witch."

The title is meant to be an insult, but her heart still warms at the sound. She loves being called a witch. It's by far her most interesting attribute. She stifles that feeling as best she can, determined to maintain her upper hand in the conversation.

"I want you two to stay with me. I want to show you all the possible proof you could witness. And then," she says as she comes even closer, intensity building with every step, "I want to hear you say it."

"Say what?" Lottie says, her voice warm against Marigold's cheek.

"You will admit that you believe in magic, and I'll give the spell to August."

August does not say a word during this entire exchange. It's as if he's never seen anyone challenge Lottie before. Others must find her exceptionally intimidating, maybe even terrifying. But Marigold senses something underneath that cold exterior, and she wants to see it. She wants to know the real Lottie, and find the softness behind her sharp tongue. She is a Honey Witch, after all, and like her grandmother used to say, Honey Witches find beauty where others may not.

Lottie's gaze leaves August and centers on her. She looks her up and down, though she does not seem to relax her demeanor at all. Marigold stands tall and still.

Lottie stops chewing on her lip and says, "This isn't fair."

She almost agrees; normally, she would never withhold a spell from a lonely heart. It is not in her nature to bargain with the fate of others. But something about this woman's absolute rejection of all things magic has sparked her defiance. She feels insulted, embarrassed, and entirely committed to proving herself. Spite is a uniquely powerful motivator.

"If you refuse to have an open mind, it will only be hurting the one person who you seem to actually care about."

There is a long, heavy pause. August nudges Lottie, who is now staring at the kitchen with a look of bewilderment. She steps away from August's side and walks to the window, where the sun reaches through to touch her face. Her bright red curls bring out the green hues of her eyes that seem to glitter in the light. From the first shelf, she picks up a jar labeled LAUGHING SPELL and rolls her eyes again. Marigold knows that Lottie believes none of it and that she has no intentions of changing her mind, but at the very least, Lottie seems like she wants to support August. If anything, it appears as if she would go against her own gut in order to make August happy.

"I'm thinking," Lottie mutters.

August and Marigold both freeze, afraid that any sudden movement from either of them could be what startles Lottie into running away. But she does not run. Instead, she ponders.

"I suppose there is no harm in it," Lottie mutters as she paces around the cottage, again finding herself standing before the sunny window. Marigold comes to her side, and for a moment, they are both lost in the peace of wild things. The misty air weaves itself through the green branches that stretch into the blue expanse above. Heavy fruit hangs from the trees, begging to burst beneath the slightest touch. The surface of the lake shines like diamonds and sapphires.

"Beautiful, isn't it? And there is so much more to see. So much that I can show you if you let me," Marigold says as she rests her palms on the corners of the windowsill and takes a deep breath of sun-warm air.

"It's nice," Lottie replies in a soft whisper that seems to catch her by surprise.

"Let's do it, Lots," August says. "I mean, why not? Marigold, it looks like you have the room and could use the company. And, Lottie . . . Well, we don't have anything better to do. As you said, what's the harm?"

His words are like an answered prayer. Marigold once thought that all she would ever require for happiness would be to fit in somewhere, to be part of something bigger and better than herself. But now that she has that, it is not enough. It may be the case that all she needs—perhaps all she ever needed—are a few good people who will not leave. That will be enough. It has to be enough.

Chapter Fourteen

For the first time since her grandmother's passing, Marigold will not only have customers and Mr. Benny as company, but actual friends staying with her. Well, one friend and one disgruntled guest. They will dine with her during every meal. Walk with her throughout the isle, tending to the wild things around them. She readies the first guest bedroom for August and brings Lottie to the other, which is also her grandmother's old room. She stands before the door, her hand heavy on the handle, but she cannot bring herself to let Lottie into this sacred space until she turns and sees Lottie glaring back at her. Her smile is cold and taunting, like she cannot wait to watch Marigold fail.

That right there, that wicked *I-know-everything* smirk, is the reason she must push forward. A life of being doubted has prepared her for this, and proving this woman wrong will heal decades' worth of insecurity.

So, she smiles back at Lottie—a fake smile with her nose extra scrunched for good measure. She walks into the room and pulls blankets out of the trunk at the foot of the bed to make everything extra comfortable out of spite.

Lottie clears her throat. "May I have a private word with you?" She looks around the room for the first time, taking in what is likely the largest bounty of books she has ever seen.

"Of course," Marigold says, worried that Lottie is about to eviscerate her with words. Lottie seems too distracted by reading the titles of the books to recall what she wanted to speak about. She runs soft fingers across the aged leather, touching the embossed lettering on the spines.

"Lottie?"

"Right. Sorry," she says, pulling herself away from the books. "To be completely honest with you, I simply will not believe in any of this, and I don't intend on changing my mind, but I would do anything for August. We'll play your games while you make the spell. We'll watch you splash around with your silly moon water. But at the end of this, I need you to give him the spell no matter what, and you don't have to worry about me ever bothering you again. Deal?"

A low laugh hums in the back of Marigold's throat. "You will see that it is real. I have no doubts."

Lottie places her hand on her hip. "You are genuinely claiming that you will magically lead him to his soulmate?"

"Yes," she snaps back at the impossible girl before her. Why must Lottie be so obstinate and distrustful? The glares between them are unyielding and sharp—neither one of them is willing to release the other from eye contact.

"You are mad," Lottie finally says. "But it would break August's heart if you let him down, so you better put on a good show. For his sake."

"A show?" she says, insulted almost beyond words. "You think I do this for someone else's entertainment? I stay here, completely alone almost all of the time, with no one to entertain but myself."

"Except when your so-called customers come to sing your infinite praises and spend their hard-earned coin on mythcraft."

Marigold steps forward, her finger pointing at Lottie's heart. "How dare you. I'll have you know that I take no money from anyone. I help everyone who asks."

Lottie leans in closer so that their faces are mere centimeters apart. "You're not helping anyone by giving them false hope."

She pushes back, her chest nearly touching Lottie's. "Nothing about what I do is false. I come from a long line of witches who

have given all that they are and all that they have to this work. You have no idea the sacrifices that I must make to live this life." She accidentally bites her tongue on the last word—that's how mad she is. Through gritted teeth, she says, "But I do it because I have a legacy to fulfill, a family to make proud. I actually help people. You might want to try it sometime," she says as she storms out of the room. August is standing awkwardly in the kitchen after obviously hearing bits and pieces of their exchange. She stands before him, her eyes wide and angry, her fingers and toes tingling with adrenaline.

"What is wrong with her?" she says, her voice mixed with a growl. Her mouth tastes of blood.

"I know," August says. "She's such a skeptic."

"I understand that, but she needn't be so rude about it."

He sighs. "I know it is hard to believe, but underneath that hard exterior, Lottie is a wonderful person with an enormous heart. She is simply very slow to trust others. If you knew all that she has been through, you'd understand. Be patient, and one day, she might let you in."

She nods, though she does not pretend to understand. "August, may I ask, why does it matter to you whether she believes in magic?"

He places a finger on his chin. "I suppose I could ask you the same thing. You are the one who proposed that we remain here until she admits defeat."

She opens her mouth to respond, but the words do not come. She wants to prove herself, yes, but there is something more there, something buried deep. Even she is not entirely sure why she feels such a pull toward the impossible girl. She swallows and says, "I'm merely following your lead. You are the one who brought her here."

He turns, staring out the window. His profile is strong and angular, and his long lashes cast a slight shadow on his cheeks as he squints. The sunlight highlights his strong jaw when he speaks. "She's my best friend, and she needs to believe in something. Give her time to warm up to you. I promise that she will."

She pinches the space between her brows. "I'll hold you to that promise, August Owens."

Day one of attempting to prove her magic involves a thorough tour of the house and an enfleurage demonstration. There are grander things that she can do, but why rush? The sooner she proves herself, the sooner they'll be gone. She can take her time and try to get on Lottie's good side so that the two friends do not disappear forever after all this is done. She begins to cook dinner as the others settle into their rooms.

It may not be the largest meal ever prepared in the history of this kitchen, but it is definitely close. Stew simmers in the pot over the open flame as Marigold opens her spell book and continues to try committing it to memory. It contains descriptions of some of the rarest and most valuable ingredients: snow from winter's first storm, black sand, or a hair from someone of royal blood. She almost understands why Lottie might not be quick to believe any of this. Honey is a miracle in itself; when stored properly, it is the only food in the world that never spoils. There have been legends of honey being buried with the dead as an offering for spirits to guide the soul to the afterlife, and centuries later, the bones are all but dust while the honey is still good and sweet.

She turns the page and finds an unfinished letter to her mother that she used as a bookmark. So far, all it says is:

Dear Mother,

Aster said I should write to you, so if this letter does not find you well, please blame her instead.

What more can she say? Her mother's face was so broken on the night that she did the ritual. Has enough time passed for their relationship to be healed? It's been over a year, but it still feels like it has only been the blink of an eye.

I miss you, she writes.

> *I am so sorry for how things ended the last time we saw each other. I do not know if this will make you feel better or worse, but it's the truth so I am going to tell you: I am where I am meant to be. Never have I felt so sure, so complete, and so happy. I still talk to Grandmother sometimes. Her presence is very strong on the isle. She told me to look for her in yellow flowers, and she meant it.* ~~*If you'd like, you could visit*~~

She crosses out the last line. Her mother made it very clear that she would never come to Innisfree again, so there is no point in bringing it up. It will only make things worse.

> *If you'd like, I could come visit. The isle is healthy and strong. I could spend some time back home. We could talk about everything. Only if you want, of course.*
>
> *I'm sorry.*

> *All my love,*
> *Marigold*

She finishes the letter and stares at the wet ink on the page. Lottie comes out of her room and runs into the kitchen, awakening Marigold from her trance. "Your pot is about to boil over," she says.

Marigold turns bright red. She must look a true fool now, buried in a book of magical oddities, while her soup boils out onto the floor. She runs over to the pot and moves it out of the flame, forgetting to use any sort of barrier between her hands and the hot metal. Once she releases the handles, the pain settles in, and she yelps loudly. Lottie runs over to her and takes her by the wrists.

"Let's go to the water," she says, leading Marigold outside and running down the pier with her wrists in hand. Once they reach the lake, Lottie pulls Marigold's hands into the crystal blue water and comforts her as the coldness stings her burned skin.

"I know it hurts, but it's the best thing for a fresh burn," she says coolly, as if she has extensive experience treating such wounds. Marigold meets her gaze—it's inexplicable, but she has not felt a moment of pain since Lottie took her wrists. All she can feel is Lottie's soft skin on hers. It feels healing, and it's not just the coolness of the water. Something is happening here between their touch, something she hasn't felt since the first time George held her hand. She pulls away swiftly.

"Thank you," she says quietly as she shakes the water from her hands and stands.

Lottie looks up at her from her crouched position, and she gives the softest smile. "I'm good with burns. I could make a healing poultice for you."

Pain pulses in her hand. Really, she can make her own poultice—it would probably be more effective—but Lottie doesn't seem like the type who offers aid often. This is a rare chance to bond. "That would be great. What do you need for it?"

"Aloe and agrimony. You have them in your kitchen."

She pauses. "Were you snooping through my things?"

Lottie nods justly. "Checking for poisons before we eat your food."

Marigold rolls her eyes and the two begin walking back to the house. She outpaces Lottie, careful not to end up at her side. Inside, Lottie makes herself at home in the kitchen and grabs the ingredients she requires. "Bowl?" she asks over her shoulder.

"Cabinet to your right," Marigold says as she approaches the table and watches Lottie work. She's fast—she must have made this poultice a thousand times before. It takes her less than a minute to bring it over and begin caking it onto the burn.

Immediately, the pain lessens and Marigold's skin starts to soothe. It's an impressive concoction. She'll have to write this one down in the grimoire, but with a few modifications. With a drop of black sage honey, this could probably cure burns overnight. And if she added acacia honey, maybe it could get rid of old scars.

"This is amazing," she says as Lottie uses up the last of the poultice. "If I did not know better, I'd think you were a witch as well." She giggles, but Lottie scowls, dropping her hand and jerking the empty bowl off of the table.

"Do not insult me."

"It was a compliment," she assures.

"Not to me," Lottie says, dropping the bowl into a pile of other dirty dishes. "You need to bandage that and leave it on overnight. I would do it for you, but I don't want to earn any more accusations from you." She storms out, walking into August's room and shutting the door behind her.

Breath quickening, heart racing, Marigold can hardly move from her position. It's too easy to scare Lottie away. It's almost funny, but extremely frustrating at the same time. She is slow to find her bandages in a drawer. Cindershine suddenly crawls from beneath the couch and hops onto the counter while she wraps her wound. When she finishes, she scratches the cat behind the ears and sighs.

"I don't know what I'm doing, Cindershine. When she touched my hand, I felt something. But she's positively wicked, and I'm... well, I'm cursed," she says.

Cindershine meows loudly and nuzzles farther into her hand.

"Great advice," she mutters. She returns to her cooking and serves their dinner, giving Lottie the plate that turned out the ugliest. That'll show her.

Chapter Fifteen

The three spend the evening exchanging all the obligatory pleasantries that people are supposed to exchange over dinner. Marigold tells them about her home in Bardshire, her talented family and neighbors, and how she could never quite measure up until she became a witch.

"Bardshire, you say? Is that how you got that original Claude piece hanging in your living room?" Lottie asks.

She is taken aback by Lottie's recognition of her father's work. "Yes. How did you know that is a Claude piece?"

"I'd recognize his style anywhere. He's my favorite painter."

"Lots is quite an artist herself," August says, and smirks.

Lottie purses her lips and says, "I'm no Claude, that's for sure. Did you know him well when you lived there?"

"Quite well," she says through a laugh. "He's my father. That painting is of the gardens in our home."

Lottie drops her fork and it clatters against her plate. "You're kidding."

"I assure you, I am not. Everyone in my family is exceptionally talented except for me."

"Well, that's not true! I bet none of them are as magical as you are," August says, and her heart flutters. There was a time when that was all she ever wanted, to feel like she was talented enough to belong. Now she has that, but at such a cost. Some nights, she lies awake and thinks of her parents, of Aster and Mr. Woodrake,

Ronan and Caoimhe, June and Lachlan, and now August and his future soulmate, and Lottie and whoever her partner might be.

On those nights, she wonders if she got the raw end of the bargain.

She clears her throat. "Perhaps you're right. At times, it is still hard to accept that I have my own abilities. I've been a Honey Witch for a year, and it still feels unreal."

"Wonder why," Lottie says under her breath.

She clenches her fist around her fork. "What is your family like, Lottie?"

Lottie stiffens, and August looks at her with sad eyes. "Lottie is a part of my family," he says. Marigold glances at Lottie, waiting for elaboration, but she says nothing.

"She is definitely my father's favorite," August continues, cutting through the long silence.

"Don't say that," Lottie says. "Your father loves you. He's too afraid to show it sometimes."

"Afraid of what?" August snaps, but Lottie remains composed like they've had this conversation a million times and she knows exactly what to say to ease his aching heart.

"He's afraid of losing you, August. He's afraid that if he loves you too much, too often, and too loudly, you'll disappear. You know that."

Lottie's wisdom and empathy are surprising. Every side Marigold has seen of Lottie so far has been unnecessarily cold, but with August, she is so uniquely gentle. She describes August's father as if she can see to the very core of the man and know his deepest truths. Lottie might be too perceptive for her own good. Can she see past Marigold's walls as well? Is that how she knows to poke at her deepest insecurities?

"Well, that's how all love works," August says. "You can't love anyone without the fear of losing them, without the forethought of grief. There is an inherent loss in love, but that does not mean that love is not worth it."

"That's beautiful," Marigold says. August's words remind

her of her grandmother, and how much she misses her. But it hurts more to imagine a world in which her grandmother did not come to her at the end of her life. They made so many memories together in such a short time—some silly, some beautiful, some heartbreaking.

Althea's passing was peaceful, but Marigold's grief was not. It never is. It is a mistake to think of grief as an absence. It's more of a dark, shadowy thing that sits in constant periphery, always there, always stealing air and making it hard to breathe. It's a demon that she has fought every single day, but it will not leave. Every time she encounters something that she would have once shared with her grandmother—a new recipe, a good book, a bad dream—she sees the face of that grief instead.

But August is right. Even if she knew the pain that would come after Althea's passing, she still would have gone to Innisfree. It was worth it, all of it. Her grief isn't going anywhere, but maybe she can make friends with it. Maybe there are good memories hiding behind it.

Lottie sits awkwardly, uncomfortably, and constantly pulls at her dress, yanking the sleeves around her wrists and the collar up to her chin.

"Well, I am quite full and exhausted," Lottie finally says. "I'll leave you both for the evening and head to bed. See you in the morning," she says through a yawn as she stands and walks lightly down the hall. When Lottie gets to the door, Marigold calls her name, though she is unsure why. Perhaps it is because she has yet to see Lottie from that angle, peering back over her shoulder. The pause between her name and Marigold's next words is far too long.

"I wanted to say thanks for today. For helping me with the burn." She nods stoically in response as she turns away.

"Hey, what about me? Don't I get a good night?" August yells from his place in the kitchen.

"Sure, sure, good night, you big baby," Lottie scolds from behind her door. August laughs and looks at Marigold, who is eyeing him with suspicion. She leans forward to ensure that Lottie's door is closed and whispers, "August, I wanted to ask you something. I don't mean to overstep, so please feel free to leave this unanswered, but I was wondering... Are you only interested in men?"

August laughs. "I don't have any preference when it comes to gender. I love whom I love, without question, and sometimes without logic."

She smiles, having a deep understanding of what he is describing. "So... you and Lottie... have you ever been involved?"

"You and everyone else always wonder about what we are to each other. Lottie is only attracted to women, and our relationship is a little hard to explain."

Marigold starts cleaning up the kitchen, wiping the counter as she says, "As a girl who one day learned that she has magical powers and the ability to communicate with bees, I think I can keep up with 'hard to explain.' Try me."

"Fair enough," August says after a laugh. "I'll let her tell you the story of her life, if she ever decides to open up about it. We do love each other a great deal, always have, always will. But it was clear from the beginning that we were meant to be more like siblings and the truest kind of friends. The ones who never leave," he says.

The ones who never leave. What she would give to be part of such eternity.

"That's beautiful. Friendship is the greatest gift one can give," she says.

"Indeed," August says as he walks over to her side and leans onto the counter, smiling with suspicion. "Why do you ask? Are you interested in her?"

She scoffs dramatically and starts cleaning her mugs. "She *hates* me."

He catches her wrist. "That didn't answer my question."

"Of course I'm not interested in her." She pulls her arm back. "Why would you ask such a thing?"

He shrugs, feigning innocence. "I guess my words fall out sometimes and I cannot control it. That's another trait of mine that only Lottie forgives. I never know when to stop talking."

"It's fine," she says. She tries to put the mugs on the top shelf—that damn top shelf—and he notices her struggling. He comes to her side and takes the mugs from her, smirking as he effortlessly puts them away.

"But Lottie is not courting anyone, in case you are wondering."

"Well, I wasn't wondering about her at all," she lies as she blows out every candle except for one, which she picks up to lead them to their rooms.

"I must say," she continues, "your courage to fall in love even after loss is admirable. I am not entirely sure that love is worth the risk of heartbreak."

He smiles, stretching. They walk down the hallway and reach their respective doors, now diagonal from each other.

"Marigold," August says before going inside. "Love is worth the risk."

Marigold lies awake in her bed, restless. An hour after lying down, Cindershine runs through her open window with Chesha. The two of them pounce onto her, though Cindershine is the only one with any weight. Marigold opens her eyes when Chesha's aura brightens the room beyond even the light of morning. A magical aurora radiates from her, painting the walls and the ceiling with starlight and streaks of green, blue, and lavender. If she squints, she can see wisps of vivid red that match the color of Lottie's hair. Chesha jumps off the bed and dashes to the door, pawing at it to open.

"What's going on, Chesha?"

She continues to paw until Marigold gets up and opens the door. Cindershine and Chesha dart outside and sit directly in front of Lottie's door. Chesha paws again, but when Marigold approaches and places her hand on the handle, Chesha hisses violently.

Marigold pauses, her brow pulled upward in confusion, and then twists the knob. When it clicks, Chesha screeches so loud that she fears it could wake up the entire house—the sound may even travel all the way to Mr. Benny across the lake. She calms down when she remembers that not only is she the only person who can see the spirits, but she is also the only one who can hear them.

She sighs and kneels down to Chesha, offering her a drop of enchanted acacia honey from one of the many vials that she keeps on her person at all times.

"I take it you don't like our skeptical guest?"

Chesha hisses before she takes the honey and nuzzles into Marigold's waiting hand. Cindershine circles around Marigold, scratching his back on her lace nightgown.

Then the door slowly starts to open. Chesha flees faster than a shooting star, leaving Marigold and Cindershine crouched on the floor in front of the door. And Lottie is standing there, wearing nothing but a blanket draped over her shoulders. Quickly, she pinches it tightly at her chest so that her whole body is covered, but it's too dark to see anything regardless.

Marigold promptly stands up, though still cowering slightly beneath the weight of Lottie's glare.

"I'm so sorry. I didn't mean to wake you. Cindershine was pawing at your door and I just came to get him," she says with panic in her voice.

"The pawing didn't wake me up. It was his resounding screech. It didn't even sound like a cat. It sounded like a monster," she says as she fights off a yawn.

Marigold stops. Her jaw drops for a moment, but she picks it up quickly. How could Lottie hear Chesha's scream? It should be completely impossible. It is impossible. It has to be.

And yet, it did happen, and Marigold cannot explain how or why, so all she says is, "I'm so sorry. I'll take him back to the bedroom with me."

Lottie looks at her quizzically, as if she knows that there are more words waiting in the back of Marigold's throat, but she lets it go for now and nods as she turns back to her room.

Marigold breathes a sigh of relief. She carries her cat back to her room and lies in bed with her eyes wide open.

What has she gotten herself into? Who is this wild girl?

Chapter Sixteen

The following few days are nothing but awkward. A few customers come and go, but despite hearing so many testimonials for Marigold's magic, Lottie seems no closer to believing in it. August, on the other hand, is becoming even more entranced by it all. He cannot stop gushing about his potential soulmate, and his excitement has even prompted Marigold to wonder what life would be like with a soulmate of her own. She has caught herself more than once in a daydream with visions of a vague partner by her side, but she never lets the thoughts last for long. That is not the life that she chose. That is not the fate of a cursed witch.

Toward the end of the week, Benny comes by early to drop off fresh blueberries, eggs, and a letter for Marigold. She nearly tears open the envelope with her teeth. She recognizes Frankie's handwriting immediately.

Dear Mari,

We all miss you very much, though I do believe I miss you the most. Compared to you, Aster is a terrible chess opponent, and she is far too busy fawning over Mr. Woodrake to improve her skills. Please DO NOT tell her I said that. The balls have been much less fun without you, and as you know, they were not so fun to begin with.

Can I confide in you, sister? I'm feeling a little behind in life. You have your magic, Aster has her courtship, and I have calluses from years of playing an instrument I do not particularly like. Is this how you felt before you left? It's awful. I am sorry if I ever did anything to make it worse.

Also, Mother received your letter. She smiled when she read it. It's the first time I've seen her smile in a long time. I think she's tried to respond a thousand times, but she always crumples up the parchment and throws it out. Do not worry, though. Aster and I stole them from the bin. I included her most complete letter in this envelope because I think you need to see it.

Do you think you could visit soon? Or perhaps we could both try to convince Mother to let me visit you? Either way, the world is in for chaos when the two of us are reunited. Start scheming.

All my love,
Frankie

She casts his letter aside and reaches into the envelope to find a thoroughly creased letter in her mother's hand.

My dearest daughter,

Thank you for your letter. ~~I should've written to you first.~~ I am sorry it has taken so long to reply. I've been thinking about what to say, but one letter cannot contain all the words that I owe to you. All I wanted was to keep you safe. ~~I realize now that I was wrong.~~ I realize now that I should have been honest with you, ~~but I knew that the truth would make you leave. I am sad~~ I am so happy to hear that you have found such purpose and such peace in your life. I know that ~~mama~~ your grandmother would be so proud. I am relieved to know that you are safe. Losing you was always my biggest fear, ~~but I see that I lost you anyway, and it was my own fault.~~

~~I could visit~~ You could visit whenever you like. We miss you. I miss you. ~~Please~~

~~There are still truths you do not know. There are so many things I need to say. Please.~~

Her fingers tremble against the paper. It's not a letter of forgiveness, but Marigold never expected that. It is, however, a start. A letter of hope. She holds it close to her heart for a moment and rereads the last smudged line.

Still truths you do not know. What more could there be? She tucks her mother's letter into the back of her grimoire and closes it, laying it beside a mixing bowl. Her mind is a mess, and the best way to sort out her thoughts is to do some busy work. Hopefully Lottie and August are hungry because she is about to make the most elaborate breakfast the world has ever seen.

As she pours and stirs, she calculates when she might be able to get away and go see her family. Frankie clearly needs her, so she wants to be there for him more than anything. Well, maybe not more than anything. Her main priority is still to see Lottie admit that magic is real. Then she wants Frankie to be there and help rub Lottie's face in it.

As she goes over the traveling logistics in her head—the tiny boat, the carriage, the big boat, another carriage, and lots of long walks in between—she starts to understand her grandmother's disdain for travel. Beyond that, she does not want to leave the isle. This land has changed her, and it does not want to let her go. And she can't leave until things are resolved with her guests. Can she be in two places at once? Is there a spell for that? It would make this so much easier.

She is flipping through her grimoire again when August joins her in the kitchen. He takes a seat at the table where Frankie's letter is lying open.

"Morning! What's this?" August asks as he picks up the pages.

She pours him a cup of tea. "It's a letter from my brother back home."

He smiles as he reads. "I like the sound of this Frankie. He seems fun."

"You two would get along quite well," she says. Frankie and Aster were babies when they stopped visiting Innisfree, so they never got the chance to meet August properly. "I miss him very much."

"It seems that you two are a lot like Lottie and me."

She flashes a skeptical grin. "Maybe. Though neither of us could rival the sourness of your friend."

"I must apologize on her behalf again. She's normally not quite so rough around the edges," he starts, but then he shakes his head. "Well, that is a lie. But she is extra sensitive around her birthday. It brings up a lot of bad memories for her."

"When is her birthday?"

He slaps his hand over his mouth and groans—he obviously was not supposed to mention this. "It's today, but do not tell her I told you. She hates when people bring it up."

"Why? Birthdays should always be joyous."

"Not for her." He finishes the last of his tea. "She's not even sure if this is her real birthday."

"She doesn't remember?"

Shaking his head, he says, "You must understand, Lottie was on her own at a very young age. It's not only her birthday that she's forgotten—it's everything. When she came to live with us, my parents picked a random day to call her birthday and throw her a party because they couldn't bear the thought of her not having one. My mother made her a cake and they got her a new sketchbook. We started singing to her, and she started crying. Since then, she's been extra bitter around this time of year."

Marigold's heart breaks to think of little Lottie feeling like she didn't even deserve a birthday because it wasn't real. Even though Lottie hasn't been entirely kind to her, she cannot let her suffer through another birthday.

"August, we cannot let her mope in her room all day. We must do something special."

"That is"—August puts a hand on her shoulder—"a terrible idea. One of the worst I've heard."

She pushes his hand away. "I'm serious! It's your job as her best friend to cheer her up, and it's my job as a host and Honey Witch to help you. Now, give me some ideas. What could we do today that she would actually like?"

"I'm warning you, Honey Witch. This could go very, very bad."

"Or," she objects, raising her brows, "it could be amazing, and she might actually smile."

August sighs, then paces, then sighs again before surrendering. "Lottie loves chocolate. The more bitter, the better."

Marigold leaps with excitement toward a drawer full of recipes, and she pulls out one for chocolate cake written in her grandmother's hand.

"August, I need you to go out to the garden and grab some of the tiny edible flowers that we can use for cake decorations. Come back quickly. We've got a lot of baking to do."

By the time Lottie strolls into the kitchen in a new, somehow more prudish dress that swallows her whole, Marigold and August have packed a large basket with the cake, treats, blankets, and other birthday surprises that they intend to present to Lottie during a picnic.

Lottie eyes them both suspiciously. "What is going on here?"

"Lots," August says cautiously, "today is a special day."

She stiffens. "No, it is not."

"Yes, it is," Marigold sings as she skips over to Lottie and stops in front of her. Her instinct is to take Lottie by the hand, but logic stops her from going any closer. "And we are all going on a picnic."

"I am not in the mood for a celebration," she says.

"Who said anything about a celebration? We're just going on a calm, casual picnic. No strings attached."

Lottie does not respond. She glares at August, who cowers behind Marigold.

"I told you she wouldn't like it," August whispers.

"Don't talk about me like I'm not here," Lottie snaps, and then the room is all too quiet. The weight of the basket makes Marigold's arm start to tremble. She and August keep their eyes on Lottie, waiting for what she might say next.

Finally, she sighs and looks down at her feet. "I do not like birthdays."

August's shoulders sink, as if he is already giving up, but Marigold refuses to yield. This picnic is happening even if she has to drag Lottie outside by her annoyingly perfect hair.

"Maybe we can call it something else," she suggests. She hands the picnic basket to August, who can barely hold it, and walks slowly toward Lottie. "There must be a day where people get to celebrate having you in their life."

Lottie almost smiles. "That's silly. And I know that you have no desire to celebrate me coming into your life, Witch. We're not exactly friends."

She flinches. "No, but maybe we could be. And today would be a great time to start. The first annual Lottie Day," she says, hope spilling into her voice.

"Lottie Day? Is that what you propose we call it?" She laughs softly as if she didn't mean to.

August claps. "I love it. It has a nice ring to it. Lottie Day, Lottie Day, Lottie Day. It almost sounds like a song in itself."

"It's perfect," Marigold says. "Now, who is joining me for a Lottie Day picnic?"

"I am!" August says as he drags the picnic basket toward the door. Lottie still does not move, and Marigold extends her hand.

"There's fresh chocolate cake in the basket for you," she says temptingly as she wiggles her fingers. At the mention of chocolate, Lottie finally relents. She rolls her eyes, takes Marigold's waiting hand, and follows them out to the garden.

The sun is warm. The grass is soft. And when she takes a bite of her Lottie Day cake, Lottie Burke actually smiles. Not her usual defiant smile, the kind she wears when she knows she has won a battle of will or wit. A real smile.

"Why are you staring at me like that?" Lottie says to Marigold, her smile faltering.

Her cheeks flush. "I've never seen you smile like that before."

Lottie doesn't say anything, so Marigold says, "It's lovely. Your smile, I mean."

Lottie's spine steels and her eyes go wide. She scrunches her nose like she smells something sour.

Marigold sighs. "Apologies. I know you hate compliments from me."

"It's not that," Lottie says quietly. Marigold and August look at each other, confused. The air is tense and awkward as Lottie wipes a bead of sweat from her forehead. Her breath quickens like she's frightened.

"You okay, Lots?" August says, placing his hand on Lottie's shoulder.

She turns to them and says, "I'm sorry. I do not feel well. I need to lie down." She stands abruptly, holding her stomach, and runs inside.

Marigold stands up and shades her eyes with her hand. "What was that about?"

"I don't know," August says. "But I was surprised she went along with it in the first place, so I'm counting this as a win."

"Everything was fine a moment ago. I don't understand. It should've gone better," she says.

"Well, it could have gone much worse," he counters, standing up and stretching. "We did a good thing, Honey Witch. That is all we can do."

Chapter Seventeen

The next morning, Marigold thinks herself the first to wake, but as she goes outside to see the spirits paint the sunrise, she finds Lottie sitting in the gardens with a sketchbook.

"Hello," she says, her voice startling the pencil out of Lottie's hand.

"Sorry!" she says quickly, raising her hands innocently. "I didn't mean to frighten you. I didn't expect to see you here."

"It's fine," Lottie says as she gathers her things and stands up next to her. "I couldn't sleep, so I was drawing for a little bit. I always draw when I can't sleep."

The grass is dewy and warm as she steps forward. "Can I see some of your work?"

Lottie flips through the pages and shakes her head. "Maybe when I finish this next one. I don't want to show you anything undone."

"All right, then. I will leave you to it," she says as she turns to walk back inside.

"Hey, Marigold?" Lottie says.

She freezes. That is the first time she has heard Lottie say her name. It's melodic, almost haunting, like it could lure her into the sea.

"Yes?"

"Thank you for yesterday," she says, and she smiles again.

"Of course," Marigold says, their eyes locked on each other.

She nearly turns back to go inside, but she pauses. "Can I ask you a question?" Her curiosity regarding the woman has been gnawing at her since she arrived. What is her story? What are her secrets? What more will Marigold discover if Lottie's walls keep coming down?"

"I can't promise an answer, but go ahead."

"Before you met August, what was your life like?"

The woman is taken aback. Sorrow flickers in her bright green eyes. "It was lonely," she finally says. "Very lonely."

Marigold nods in understanding. She was lonely before August came back, too. But there seems to be more to Lottie's loneliness, another layer of hurt beneath it. To her surprise, Lottie continues speaking without her having to press the woman for more information.

"My parents died when I was very young. I was an orphan living on the streets of Lenox, then briefly at an orphanage, and then I met August in school. The two of us became so close so fast, and his parents had always wanted a daughter. So, one day, they asked me to come home with them. And I did." An incredulous smile blooms across her face, as if she still cannot comprehend their kindness. "It was the best day of my life. I'm so lucky to have him."

Marigold basks in the warmth of that smile for as long as she can before she nods. She is actually doing it—she is breaking down the walls of Lottie Burke.

But there is something else happening in her heart. Every time Lottie smiles, every time she stands too close, every time they are alone in a room together, something in the air changes. It feels like having a cool drink on a summer day or a warm fire in the middle of winter, like suddenly everything she needs is right there with her, and she can sink into a sense of peace.

It's a heartbreak waiting to happen. Marigold cannot give in to it.

"He's lucky to have you, too," she says before going back inside to make breakfast.

The table is set for three and includes fresh coffee, scrambled eggs, and pancakes with honey. Lottie, August, and Marigold take their respective seats before it all gets cold.

"Do you eat honey with every meal?" Lottie says in her signature dry tone. August shoots her a look.

"Well, yes," Marigold says with a laugh. "It's the one thing I'll never run out of."

"Do you ever get tired of it?" August chimes in.

"Not at all. You two might think of honey as one flavor, one color, one note. But I know honey to be a magical thing, with so many different variations that it would be impossible to tire of them all in a single lifetime. Would you believe me if I told you that some forms of honey are not even sweet? They can be quite strong and bitter, almost like coffee."

"Imagine trying to sweeten your drink with honey like that. You'd be in for a cruel surprise," Lottie says with a laugh, and Marigold smiles. Lottie is starting to soften around her, although that may not be a good thing. Her heart is precariously placed on her sleeve, and with Lottie warming to her, she fears her heart may leap before she can stop it, and that would be tragic for all of them.

"Are there other types of witches?" August says.

"There are. It's a law of nature that everything has an equal opposite. There are Honey Witches, and then there are Ash Witches."

"What makes them opposites?"

"I believe it comes from the fact that when bees encounter smoke, it inhibits their ability to attack. Burning things until they turn to ash is part of the art of beekeeping for most, though I have the ability to calm them without the aid of anything else. As far as magic is involved, an Ash Witch enchants the remnants of what is burned, while a Honey Witch enchants the honey that is made. There is a long and complicated history involving an

Ash Witch and Innisfree, but I will spare you the details. All you need to know is that she is dangerous, and my protection spells keep her away."

"Wow, it sounds completely real and not at all like a bunch of mythcraft," Lottie says.

Marigold does not acknowledge the insult. She simply sips her coffee and grins. "I want to take you both on a tour to show you how my magic works," she says, her voice dripping with confidence. Today will be the day that Lottie sees the apiary. No one could deny the existence of magic from inside such a magical place.

"Wonderful!" August nearly leaps over to her side. His excitement is infectious; he reminds Marigold of herself when she first came to the isle. Every moment, every inch of the world around was thrilling and perfect—an entire life steeped in magic.

Even Lottie's mood seems to lighten from August's joy as Marigold leads them both outside to the apiary. As the door opens, the pink-stained sun meets their skin. The wind carries the sweet scent of honey and lilac, just above the notes of pine and rain.

"Actually, wait. Lottie, do you have anything else to wear?"

Lottie adjusts her long sleeves and tight collar. "What is wrong with this?"

"Besides the fact that it is summer and you are wearing a dress that is meant for the dead of winter?"

Crossing her arms, she says, "Yes. Besides that."

"The bees do not like dark colors. That black dress will make them think you're a predator." Not that they would be wrong about that.

"Are they going to sting me?" she asks, stepping back slightly.

"You'll be safe as long as you stay close to me," she says as she leads them through the white gate. Hundreds of bees dance around their hives, their buzzes resolving into a soft melody. Marigold walks forward fearlessly, eager to greet them. The bees nuzzle up to her and bumble around like a living aura, a yellow halo around her frame.

"They're attacking!" Lottie yells.

Marigold laughs. "They're not attacking, silly. They're simply saying hello." She extends her hand outward and sends the bees gently in Lottie's direction. Lottie jumps back and stumbles into August, taking them both down to the soft, warm grass. The bees float to the ground and bumble softly around the tangled pair, who have yet to let their guard down for the gentle creatures. Lottie at least pretends she is not afraid, while August's fear is much less subtle. He clings to his shirt collar as a child grips their blanket in the dark.

"They won't sting you. I promise." The bees crowd in her palm.

"How do you know?" August whimpers.

"Because they listen to me, and I have told them not to," she says. The bees begin to fly faster around her, turning their gentle bumble into an angry swarm. She flashes a wicked grin and says, "But don't cross me, August Owens."

She giggles as her friends drop their jaws in response to the bees' performance. August and Lottie find their way to their feet.

"That's incredible," he says, marveling as the bees flit around them like snowflakes. "Hey, little guy," August says as he opens his hand, allowing a bee to land in his palm.

"She's actually a female bee. All worker bees are female."

He examines the tiny insect in his hand. "What do the males do?"

Marigold shrugs. "They don't do much; they merely hope to be the one who is picked to mate with the queen and then they die."

"Harsh," he says as he places a hand over his heart.

"It's the truth. They're called drones."

August takes Lottie's hand, and for a moment when she sees this, Marigold thinks she has been stung. She hasn't, of course. But seeing Lottie hold someone else's hand feels awfully sharp. She averts her gaze, and the feeling passes as she continues forward.

"So, welcome to the apiary. Each hive makes a different kind of honey. I work with the bees and tell them which flowers to pull nectar from, and they return it to the hive. When they release it into the wax, which they shape into hexagons to help stabilize the structure of the honeycomb, they flap their wings to dehydrate the nectar into honey. After I harvest the honey, that hive can make something new." She takes the white wooden lid off the top of one of the boxes and props it up. Reaching in, she peels off a piece of the wax cap that covers the honeycomb, and she lets the honey drip onto her fingers.

"Would you like to try some?" she asks with a motion of her other hand. Lottie stays behind, still skeptical of Marigold's power over the bees. August, however, releases his hand and comes up.

"I'm too scared to put my own hand in the hive," August whispers.

"Here." She dips her finger back into the honey and brings it up to August's lips.

He tastes it and smiles wide. "It tastes like lavender."

"It is, actually," Marigold replies. "It's summer, so we have clover, peach blossom, tupelo, and lavender honey. This honey is made from lavender nectar, and it's primarily used in love spells."

"Of course, it is," Lottie says from her stance in front of the door to the house.

August rolls his eyes at his rude and skeptical friend. "Come try it. Don't be a coward."

Marigold smirks. Unable to resist a challenge, Lottie walks forward, slowly relaxing her shoulders. She stands so close Marigold can smell her: vanilla and sandalwood.

She takes her honeyed fingers out of the hive and holds them up to Lottie's lips. Lottie looks up at her through her heavy brown lashes and smirks. She parts her flushed lips and wraps them around Marigold's two fingers. Her tongue tickles her fingertips, and Marigold acknowledges it with a breathy laugh. Lottie smiles as she slowly pulls her lips away, leaving Marigold's fingers glistening and warm.

She tries to pretend that it feels exactly the same as when she had August's lips wrapped around her fingers, but it does not. Here, with her, there is much more heat.

The two finally break from their trance and fumble with a response.

"Maybe it does taste a little like lavender," Lottie says as she savors the sweetness on her tongue. She leans in closer to Marigold, as if she intends to take her waiting fingers back into her mouth. When she is close enough to taste, she smiles. "Still a bunch of mythcraft, though."

Marigold grimaces. She would like for Lottie to get stung right now, if only to shut her up. Unfortunately, the bees are listening, and one of them takes her idea and runs with it. Or rather, stings with it.

Lottie yelps and slaps her hand over her lip, where a needle-sharp stinger has poked into her skin.

"DAMMIT!" she cries, and Marigold spirals into a panic. It was an accident. Lottie was being so frustrating and negative and rude, especially after the moment they shared then. Or, the moment that she thought they shared. Maybe she imagined the way Lottie's gaze lingered on her. She must have, because she is cursed. Lottie, or anyone else, could never look at her the way that she thought she just saw.

She feels such a fool as she hurries to Lottie to help her. She reaches into the pocket of her dress and pulls out a bottle of royal jelly—a substance made by bees to feed the queen and their babies. It is also a form of magic in itself, and when used by a Honey Witch, it can heal any wound it touches.

"Let me see it."

Lottie is still writhing in pain and refuses to pull her hand away.

Marigold places a soft hand over her wrist and gently strokes her skin with her thumb. "Please, let me," she says. Pain wells in Lottie's eyes as she slowly drops her hand. The stinger has fallen out, and her lip is already swelling. Marigold takes off the lid of the royal jelly and scoops up some of it on her thumb. She then drags the salve across Lottie's swollen skin, over and over again until she is soothed. They breathe in time with each other. Lottie brings her hand back up to her lip and tries to touch her wound, in disbelief that it is already healed. Her fingers brush against Marigold's, and the two share a gentle gasp. Marigold pulls her hand away and puts the royal jelly back in her pocket.

"Better?" she asks, her gaze not leaving Lottie's eyes for a second.

Nodding, she says, "You said that they listen to you and you told them not to sting us."

"Well, yes, but I also said not to cross me," Marigold says with an attempted laugh that comes off ruder than she intends. "And then," she stumbles over her words. "You...you were going on with all your mythcraft nonsense..."

"*My* mythcraft nonsense?" Lottie interrupts.

"Yes, that silly word that you made up. And it frustrated me, and I thought about how I would like you to hush. I didn't realize that the bee would actually act on that thought, and I'm sorry."

Lottie bites her tongue, which must be hard to do with a swollen lip. "At least that one can't sting anyone else," she says.

Marigold's eyes widen. How could she forget about this? Her bees never sting anyone. She has never had to deal with this before. But of course, it remains true that if a bee stings, it loses its stinger and dies. The thought of this poor little honeybee dying on her behalf, and for someone as hateful as Lottie, breaks Marigold's heart. She leaps up from her crouched position in front of Lottie and looks frantically around among the tall grass.

"Help me find her," Marigold commands, panic shaking her voice. August and Lottie approach and begin to follow suit, looking for the tiny yellow body among the sea of grass.

It is August who stumbles upon her and picks her up in his palm. "Here, I've got her."

Marigold runs to him and gently holds the bee in her fist with her eyes closed. She takes a deep breath that stretches out every wrinkle of her lungs, and she centers herself in her own power. She has only ever brought plants and flowers back to life, but she wonders if she can use the same method to save this bee. To bring her back home.

She continues her deep breathing and focuses on the creature in her palm. The magic in the air pours out from the wild things that surround them. The trees, the birds, the roses, the worms. She feels the wild heartbeat of them all as she channels that energy into the bee. Talaya, the snakelike spirit guardian of the apiary, slithers slowly toward her, granting her all the magic she needs. Her energy drains swiftly, as it always does when she utilizes this power, but when she pulls her hands apart, it doesn't work. The bee is still dead, and there is nothing she can do. Her legs wobble with exhaustion.

"I failed her." She can hardly speak. She desperately needs rest.

"It's just a bug," Lottie says.

She clenches her jaw. "You do not understand." Her voice is a weak whisper.

Lottie places her hand on her hip. "We can agree on that."

The two glare at each other until Marigold says, "Entertain yourselves for the day. I'm no longer up to the task." She turns to go back inside.

"Oh, come on. Do not be so dramatic," Lottie calls after her, but she does not turn. Their voices grow quiet as she gets farther away.

Marigold has passed through the gate and is standing at the door to the cottage when she hardly hears Lottie say, "Watch out for that snake."

"Snake? Where?" August yelps.

"Open your eyes. It's right in front of you."

"Stop messing with me! I can't see it!"

Is she talking about Talaya? Can Lottie Burke, somehow, in some way, see the landvættir? If so, it begs the question—what else can this impossible girl do?

Chapter Eighteen

Upon the night of the full moon, Marigold readies a vessel to make moon water. She cleanses it with crystals and wipes it clean with white silk. It rests on her hip, and she carries a white lantern in the other hand. Lottie and August follow close behind.

"Remind me where we're going again?" Lottie asks as she adjusts the tight collar of her black dress.

"We are going to the moon pool. It's a small oasis in the middle of the isle, and the perfect spot to make moon water."

"Why can't you simply fill up the jar with water from the lake?" August asks.

"I could, but it's never quite as potent. We want only the best for your soulmate spell, right?"

"Of course," he says with a playful flip of his curly hair.

When they arrive, Marigold places the lantern on a nearby tree stump and looks for Yliza, the landvættir of the oasis. The bright yellow koi normally greets her eagerly with bubbly kisses beneath the surface of the water, but tonight, she is nowhere to be found.

Still, moon water must be made, and there is no time to waste. As she kneels at the water's edge, she pushes the vessel into the water and allows it to fill to the top. It emerges, filled with fizzy blue water that must sit beneath the moon for the remainder of the night before it is incorporated into any spells. She stands and tries to wipe the dirt away from her knees, but then she has a different idea.

She turns to face Lottie and August. "Would anyone fancy a swim?"

August points at the moon pool below. "In there?"

She nods. "It's deeper than it looks."

That small bit of reassurance is all that August requires. He immediately begins unbuttoning his shirt while Marigold removes her dress and starts unfastening her stay around her ribs.

Lottie scoffs in disbelief. "You're going in that tiny puddle?"

"Aren't you?" August says as he peels his shirt away from his body and drops his trousers to his ankles.

"August, you know I can't." Lottie tries to keep her voice to a whisper so Marigold cannot hear, but the urgency in her tone makes her words impossible to ignore. August glances over at Marigold, who tries to pretend that she is not staring.

"It's dark, Lottie. No one can see anything," August says, his tone reassuring. Lottie still hesitates, but Marigold comes over to her side.

"Do you not know how to swim?" she asks.

August and Lottie look at each other, back at Marigold, then back at each other, holding a silent debate with only their eyes.

"What's going on?" Marigold asks.

Lottie sighs, hugging her ribs. August gives her a sympathetic look and a nod of reassurance.

"I have a certain job..." she says quietly.

Marigold raises a brow. "And this job means you cannot swim?"

"No, but it's a job of which many disapprove. And I don't know you well enough to be sure you'll be kind."

"Well, I'm still unsure of what this has to do with swimming, but as someone who has been ruthlessly mocked by you for my own occupation, I can assure you that I would never do the same to you."

Lottie takes a breath to respond, but she lets it go. She is silent for a few moments, before she finally says, "You're right."

"What?" Marigold and August both say in time with each other. Marigold did not expect Lottie to abandon the fight so quickly.

"I'm sorry, I must have misheard. Did Lottie Burke almost admit to being wrong in her behavior?" August says, and Lottie shoves him nearly into the pool. He catches his balance in time and says, "This is unheard of. Tell me, Lots, what has prompted such an admittance?"

Lottie chews on her lip, the way she always does when she's nervous, and she looks back at Marigold. "I think I trust you," Lottie says, and she begins to undo her heavy dress.

Marigold can barely contain her heart. It throbs in her chest like a new wound. Lottie does not speak. She pulls her arms out of the long sleeves and drops her dress, then her stay, so that she is only in a thin chemise that stops just above her ankles. She stretches her arms out to her side, revealing areas of pinkish skin covered in random black shapes that Marigold cannot quite make out. Immediately, though, she knows that the marks on Lottie's skin are the result of burns. It looks like the wound on her own mother's hand that is always hidden underneath a lacy glove.

"My parents died in a fire when I was young," Lottie starts. Marigold opens her mouth to offer sympathies, but Lottie cuts her off. "Don't cry for me, for I have no memory of it, and I don't know how I made it out alive. I only have scars to prove that it was real."

As she comes closer, she can clearly see the pink and white scars all over Lottie's upper arms. She can also see that the black shapes over them form an elegant, swirling design. They are tattoos, all over her body. Birds, flora, anchors, snakes. Ribbons, Latin, gods, and monsters. Marigold stares in awe. Tattoos are scandalous, even in Bardshire, where people are supposedly more open-minded to any form of art. Even there, they are only for men. For women, tattoos are illegal, punishable by massive fines and possible jail time. She heard a story once about a rebellious daughter of a novelist in Bardshire who fell in love with a sailor boy. The boy had lots of tattoos, as most sailors do, and she asked for one—a letter or a heart or something else perfectly harmless and easy to hide—but her handmaiden saw it one morning while she was helping the daughter dress. When her father heard of this, he took his daughter to a doctor who scrubbed her skin down to the bone with salt and gauze until the tattoo was gone.

"No tattoo artists would provide their services to a girl," Lottie continues, "much less a girl of my age, and the scar tissue is nearly impossible to cover. But I wanted to do it. I had to. I had to reclaim my body and mark it the way I wanted to, not the way that the burns left me." Marigold reaches for Lottie's hand and holds it lightly, lifting her arm toward the moon for a better view. She admires both the tattoos and the scars, as they both tell the story of this impossible girl.

"I'm grateful for the scars. They led me to my purpose, which is art," Lottie says proudly.

"You're so extraordinary, Lottie." The words fall from her mouth before she can catch them, before she realizes what she has confessed. She could not help herself. She thought Lottie was beautiful before, but now she is so much more than beautiful. She is marked with bravery, with artistry, with so many stories. Marigold wants to know them all.

Lottie starts making that pinched, sour face again, the one she makes every time she receives a compliment. She palms her forehead like she has a headache and shakes her head.

"Are you all right?" Marigold asks.

Before Lottie responds, there is a splash behind them as August jumps into the water.

"This is exhilarating!" August screams as he comes up and shakes the water from his hair.

The oasis looks like a pit of glass with jagged edges reaching up toward the moon. When Marigold jumps in, her movement blurs the sharp shards into soft ripples that welcome her inside.

Her hair hovers upon the surface of the water, its bright golden tones piercing through the black of night. It spills down her back as she turns back to regard Lottie, who still stands at the edge with her arms crossed.

"Jump in!" she says, motioning Lottie forward.

"You're both mad," Lottie says, and Marigold splashes her with icy water.

"And you are missing out," Marigold says, pulling herself out of the water to stand by Lottie's side. "Come on!"

She shivers as the cold night air breathes against her body, pebbling her soft skin beneath its touch. Lottie looks down to regard her already wet chemise and giggles under her breath.

"Okay. We fall together?" she asks, offering her hand.

"We fall together," Marigold echoes, taking her waiting hand.

They leap into the air, and Marigold witnesses the moment that Lottie lets go of herself and everything holding her back, and for a moment, the woman is nothing but air and sound. She screams joyously as her body meets the water and she is submerged. Marigold swims down to meet her. Moonlight streams through the inky black water until it is blocked by Lottie's silhouette. A halo of moonlight surrounds her, hugging the sharp contours of her body.

They touch—softly at first, until Lottie pulls her closer. Marigold's fingers fit perfectly around the curves of Lottie's waist. Lottie's hands drift to Marigold's face, and whether she means to or not, she drags her thumb across Marigold's bottom lip. Underwater, they can pretend that this is not intentional, that every touch is by chance alone. Their noses brush, and if they were not close to running out of air, Marigold wonders how much further they could go.

When they come back up, they are both gasping, and not just for want of air. Tension crackles between them.

"Have fun down there?" August jokes. Marigold blushes and Lottie's only response is the sudden shiver that vibrates between her teeth.

"It's summer. How is the water so cold?" Lottie says.

Marigold squeezes her hand, unable to let it go just yet. "We don't have to stay. Whenever you're ready, we'll go inside."

The three of them splash and laugh until exhaustion creeps in. They pull themselves out of the water and grab their piles of clothes before heading back toward the cottage. Marigold leads the way with the dimming lantern in her grip.

As they walk along the coast, Lottie freezes. "Wait," she says.

August turns back to regard her. "What is it, Lots?"

Marigold looks in the direction where Lottie is staring. Her heart stops—the flicker is back, beating like a heart deep within the Hazelwood Forest. The air smells different now. She waits for Lottie to comment on it, to validate that it is real and it is wicked, but she does not. The light is simply playing tricks on her again. She comes closer until the candlelight illuminates Lottie's smirk.

"There is something I have always wanted to do," she says, "and now feels like the perfect time and the perfect place."

Marigold and August share a glance before looking back at her.

"Well, go on, then," August says.

Lottie turns to face the lake. She walks to the very edge where one heavy gust of wind could send her into the water. She takes a deep breath, and she screams without mercy.

Marigold and August leap into each other's arms like scared children. The birds in the nearby trees flee their branches, screeching and squawking in surprise. Curious creatures that were sleeping in the bushes come out to see what has caused such a sound. After a few seconds tick by, Lottie falls into a fit of laughter and turns back to her friends.

"That was *so* freeing!" she says through her giggles.

Honestly, she sounds a bit like she has lost her mind. Marigold and August step back, wary of what Lottie will do next.

"I have never felt so *alive*," she says in a singsongy way, turning the last word into a little melody. "You must try this," she says to August, taking him by the wrists and bringing him to the coast.

"Think of all the bad in the world, all the horrible things you've endured, all the things you know you deserve but do not have. Breathe all of that in, and then scream it out," she says to him frantically, like she can't get the words out fast enough.

He starts to laugh, but she grips his shoulder tightly and says, "Do it!"

Startled, he turns back to the coast, lifts his arms, and screams even louder than Lottie did. The sound makes the water ripple and the branches shake.

"How do you feel?" Lottie asks after he is done. Marigold is curious to know, too.

Like Lottie, he bursts into laughter. "I feel weightless!" he says breathlessly.

Lottie comes up to Marigold and takes her hand. "Your turn, Witch. Think of the life you left behind and let it go."

Falling back, she says, "I am not sure I have a scream like that in me."

Lottie grabs her by the shoulders. "Of course you do! Do not hold yourself back from this moment."

Suddenly, this is too much. Too vulnerable. She shies away. "Perhaps I am trying to maintain a shred of my civility."

"Fuck civility. Fuck whoever invented it," Lottie says, sliding her hand down Marigold's arm and taking her wrist, raising both of their arms toward the sky in triumph. "Tonight, we are shameless." She dips her chin and looks up through her lashes. "Think of your greatest wish that you are still hoping will come true. Think of the redheaded impossible girl who has been admittedly less than kind to you."

Marigold's breath hitches. This feels like the closest she'll get to an apology from Lottie, and she'll take it. She nods, laughing.

"Breathe it in," Lottie continues, "and then scream."

She puts down the lantern in her other hand and follows Lottie to the edge of the water.

Deep breath. She thinks of her protective mother, her gentle father, her chaotic brother and her beautiful sister.

Another breath.

She thinks of George, her broken heart, and her curse.

Another.

Her grandmother. Her grief. All the things that she never got to say.

Another.

She thinks of Lottie. Lottie. Lottie.

She screams with so much emotion and power that her friends must catch her arms to keep her from falling into the lake. She gives all of the air in her lungs to this scream until she chokes on it. August lets go when she finds her balance, but she grips on to Lottie like she is the only thing keeping her from floating away. The muscles in her belly start to tingle, and laughter consumes her.

"How do you feel, Marigold?" Lottie asks, her embrace tightening. They lock eyes, and heat builds between them. Breath quickening, she leans in slightly. Their noses touch. If Marigold did not know better, she would lean in farther and let their lips meet just to see what freedom tastes like. Her chest tightens and her heart races. Realization crashes into her—she cares for Lottie in a way that she's never cared for anyone. She wants to keep Lottie all to herself, stand between her and anything that could ever hurt her. Whatever this feeling is, she can do nothing about it. Not with her curse. Lottie is only a daydream, a wish that can play out night after night when sleep does not come. That will be enough.

That has to be enough.

"Clean," she whispers.

Lottie laughs softly. "Me too."

Voices raw, bodies exhausted, they walk back to the cottage. August enters first, holding the door open for the women. As Marigold is stepping inside, a faint scream carries on the wind. It's rough and angry, sounding more like a battle cry. Leaning back, she listens for it again.

"Did you hear that?" she asks.

"Hear what?" August says.

"I did," Lottie says. "Another scream from far away."

Marigold nods as she takes another step back and places a finger over her lips, asking for silence. She hears it again, though this time, it is more than a scream. It is a word.

A name.

"Marigold."

She and Lottie look at each other.

"Is someone calling for your help?" Lottie asks.

August steps outside and walks past Marigold, cupping his hand around his ear to listen. "What are you two talking about? I don't hear anything."

A chill runs down Marigold's spine. There is something wicked in that forest, and whatever it is, it wants *her.* The voice sounds almost familiar, making it all the more menacing.

"Let's go inside," she says, taking August's hand and pulling him to her side. A witch knows to never answer the darkness when it calls.

Chapter Nineteen

Tonight, for the first time, the curse is heavy. It tugs at Marigold's throat, wells in her eyes, and pinches her soft heart. No one can ever fall in love with her.

No one.

She thinks of Lottie, and how she warmed under the night sky. How they found each other in the pool, no barrier between them except water and want. How badly she wanted to find the courage to kiss her, to be one with her. To be...something impossible together.

August is the first to return, in a fresh sleeping gown and tousled hair. Mead fizzes in three colorful mugs that sit on the raw wood coffee table in front of the plush green couch.

"Well, that was interesting," he says as he sips his mead and looks at her through his dark lashes.

She clears her throat. "It was fun, wasn't it? There's a meadow near our estate that looks positively blue during a full moon. It was always such a gift to get to witness it."

"I would love to see that someday." He falls onto the sofa with a thud. "I must confess, Lottie never lets loose like that. I find her actions to be the most interesting occurrences of the evening." He takes another dramatic sip.

Blushing, she sips her mead to calm her mind. "Why is that?"

"You mean, why doesn't she ever let loose? Or, why is she only letting loose with you?" He smirks, but before she can protest, Lottie's footsteps sound from the hallway. She stands before them and assesses their position, wearing a nightdress that shows off her tattoos.

"What did I miss?" Lottie takes a seat next to Marigold, not August, and grabs her mead. The three of them continue to exchange awkward glances, each trying to have a conversation with someone else using only their eyes. The result is quiet chaos.

Lottie takes a sip. "This is lovely."

"Isn't it?" August says, gulping the rest of it down. "I've enjoyed it so much that I'm afraid I've outpaced you both, and I'm now feeling perfectly tired and relaxed. I shall retire for the evening and leave you two to chat." He stands to walk away and loses his balance slightly from drinking the mead too fast, and Marigold grasps his hand. It is not that she would not enjoy being alone with Lottie—far from it; it is that she knows Lottie cannot feel the same way, and therefore, it is unfair to both of them.

"Do stay," she says, her eyes pleading. August gives her a look of confusion, but he seems to recognize her discomfort.

"Maybe for a little while," he relents as he falls back into his seat. "Anyone up for a game?"

"Oh no, not one of your games." Lottie leans back onto the couch until she faces the ceiling, palming her forehead in frustration. "You know you are the only one who has fun during these."

"That's not true. You're just a sore loser," August says.

"What games are you talking about?" Marigold asks, and August gives a devilish smirk.

"One of my favorites is called Truth or Drink." He stands like a showman before an audience, taking the bottle of mead and refilling his cup. "We ask each other deeply invasive questions, and you can either answer truthfully, or"—he takes a big sip and leans in, whispering—"get very, very drunk."

The mead they're drinking is made from tupelo honey, so it's perfect for the occasion. After a few sips, everyone is much more likely to share their truths. Marigold giggles and says, "Let us begin!"

"Normally, I would object further to this," Lottie says, then sips her drink. "But this drink is divine."

August leans over the table and ruffles Lottie's wet hair. "Planning on drinking a lot, Lots?" He coughs in an attempt to hide a hiccup. "Why are you afraid of the truth?"

"I will bite your hand if you do that again," she says, smoothing out her hair. August chuckles.

"It's true," he says, turning to Marigold. "Lots gets quite bitey when she drinks."

"She's always bitey," Marigold jests.

"I am not!" Lottie says, pushing her shoulder softly. Her hand falls onto Marigold's for a few seconds, and their gazes meet, bleeding into each other like ink on paper. Lottie pulls back, bringing her hand to her forehead as her face contorts. She groans softly and rubs her temples.

August comes around the table and puts a hand on Lottie's back. "Headache already? You've barely had a drink."

"I'm fine. I just need a moment."

"I'll grab some medicine," Marigold says, starting to stand.

Lottie catches her wrist and pulls her back. "No, stay here. I am fine. I promise."

Marigold could melt into the palm of her hand if Lottie would stop pulling it away.

"Then we shall start the game! Marigold, you are the host, so you may ask the first question."

She taps her chin, narrowing her eyes as her gaze moves between the two. Who will she choose? What will she ask? She drinks, exhales sharply, and stands. "Okay, my dearest August, here is your question: Imagine that you are sitting across from a younger version of yourself. Five or six years old, back when we were kids together. You're there, little August is in front of you, and you get to tell him one lesson. One bout of wisdom to help him through all that is to come. What do you say?"

Lottie's eyes widen. "That's a good one."

Marigold is aglow with satisfaction.

August paces and stands in front of the crackling fireplace. After a moment of seemingly thoughtful contemplation, he says, "I think I would tell him that he will never be able to grow a real beard."

Marigold laughs, but Lottie points at him, her arm taut. "You're lying. You have a better answer. I can tell."

He tries to object, but Lottie's intimidating glare breaks him. He groans and says, "Damn you and your strange ability to get inside my head."

"Go on. What would you really say?" Marigold says.

He thinks for a moment, tapping his chin until resting his hand over his heart. "I would tell him that the world is quite nice, but only if you know where to look. Friendships are harder to break than you think, and you will not outgrow the ones that are the most important. Heartbreak is inevitable, but so is healing, so don't be afraid to fall in love freely and often. And..." He pauses.

"You were only supposed to say one," Lottie says.

He plugs his ears. "Shh, I am having a moment of introspection. I think"—he closes his eyes—"I would tell him that the feeling he has when he's alone at night—that burning desire to see the whole wide world and take a bite of it—it never goes away. And I would say that I hope he grows up braver than me. Brave enough to follow that feeling, and do so alone if he must."

His words hit her like a gust of cold wind. Marigold blinks tightly. She knows that feeling well—she was brave enough to follow it all the way to Innisfree, but she did not do it alone. Perhaps she would not have been able to. It's one thing to go on adventures with someone older and wiser guiding the way, but to go out into the great big world alone?

She couldn't do it. She knows, deep in her bones, she couldn't. That's why she hasn't visited her family. She is too afraid to go alone.

August opens his eyes and clears his throat. "That's what I would say."

"What about your travels with your father on business? Does that do anything to scratch that itch?" Marigold asks.

Shaking his head, he says, "It's always the same routes, same ships, same people. And like you said, it's always business." He paces, hands in his hair. "I want to see art. Music! Food! Culture!"

"I think you should," Lottie says, finishing her drink and refilling her cup. "Selfishly, I admit that I hate when you are away. But, because I love you and I know you better than I know myself, I think you should go somewhere. Love someone. Chase something. You can do that, August. I know you can."

He smiles softly, like he knows that it won't happen. "Maybe I will."

"You will," she says.

He sits on the floor across from the couch. "Here's your question, Lots: Why are you so adamant about not believing in magic?"

Oh yes. Marigold would give anything to know the answer to this.

"I choose to drink," she says, downing her cup.

He throws his hands up. "Oh, come now! Why is that so hard to answer?"

She swallows hard. "Because it is sad."

"You can be sad here. It's a good place to be sad," Marigold says, smiling softly.

She gestures to her empty cup. "But I have already drunk. It's against the rules to answer now."

Marigold takes the bottle from the table, refills the cup, and whispers, "We won't tell anyone."

The moment stretches and thins, threatening to disappear until Lottie sighs. "Fine."

Marigold leans in, perfectly silent, barely breathing.

"I do not believe in magic because my mother believed in

magic, and now she's dead. If magic was real, she would be alive, and I would have had a life with her and my father." She picks at her nails, her pointer finger sliding up her hand and tracing a faint scar. "I would have happy memories with them. A story of us that I could share with people. I would have had a real birthday. I imagine my mother would have given me something to cherish—a necklace or a hair ribbon or something—and I would still have it today. And I would fidget with it constantly and say things like, '*Oh, this? My mother gave it to me ages ago*,' and I would smile. But I have none of that. And so, I do not believe in magic."

Marigold has heard, over the years, many people share their disbelief of anything whimsical.

It's all charlatanism, smoke and mirrors.

"Folklore is born only from the mind of a poet. It is all our imagination," George once said.

Those people, their skepticism is born out of the fear that something could be more powerful than what they can create. Lottie, though, she's different. She is not afraid of magic. She is angry with it.

"I understand," Marigold says.

"Do you?"

"I think I do. I think you are allowed to be angry. Perhaps that is the consolation for such a loss—you can be angry forever if you want. No one can ask you to move on from that. It's like asking..." She stumbles over her words, her drink sloshing in her hand. "Oh, I can hardly be coherent. But it's like asking the skies to stop holding rain clouds because they're too heavy. It can't be done. It doesn't matter how hard it is to carry; that grief cannot be let go."

Lottie is frozen still.

Oh, dammit. Did she say the wrong thing? Again? She always says the wrong thing to Lottie. But Lottie does not run or scowl. She smiles, nods softly, and sinks back into the sofa.

"Yes. That's how it is. That is how I grieve."

"You never told me that," August says, reaching across the table and offering his hand to her.

"I never want to seem ungrateful for you or your family or all that you have given me. I love you, but I simply—"

"You do not have to explain," he says, squeezing her hand. "Grief is often too strange and too vast to fit into words."

Lottie nods. Her eyes turn glassy, but she blinks that away.

"Do you have any other family? Did you ever go looking?" Marigold asks.

"My mother instilled a great fear of our family in me." Lottie gulps down her drink. "She said we were made of bad blood, and we could only outrun it if we never looked back," she says sternly, followed by an incredulous laugh. "I don't know why, but I believed her. Besides," she says, leaning her head toward August, "the best family in the world found me. Why would I want for anyone else?"

"Aw, we love you, Lots," August says softly. His words make Lottie's cheeks flush.

Marigold cannot stop herself from saying, "You are good. You have nothing to outrun."

A small gasp escapes Lottie's lips, and she fights against a slight smile. Marigold smiles back.

"Well, that's my answer," Lottie says, clearing her throat. "I think it's your turn to be asked, Marigold."

"Oh, right," she says.

"My question for you is: Why are you alone?"

Her lips part as she straightens her posture. "I'm not alone. I'm here with the two of you."

"You know what I mean. We're guests. Customers. We're not constants in your life."

Each word is a knife wound. A blade to her heart, her stomach, her ribs.

Lottie's gaze does not leave her when she says, "What about when we're gone?"

That sentence is a blade across her throat. She is bleeding

down her dress, into the fabric of the couch, watching it drip onto the floor, *tap tap tapping* like raindrops.

"When you are gone," she says, her voice hardly a whisper, "I will be lonely again."

"What will you do about it?" Lottie asks.

She leans against the couch, nearly bloodless. "Nothing. I can do nothing about it."

"Don't you want someone to share your life with here?"

"It doesn't matter," she says quickly, and Lottie is taken aback. She twists her body, closing herself off from the others.

August leans forward. "Marigold? What is it?"

Her gaze is now fixed on Lottie. "Promise me to keep any comments of disbelief to yourself, else I will forgo my truth and drink instead."

Lottie nods slowly.

"I am cursed so that no one can ever fall in love with me. I will always be alone."

The room goes uncomfortably quiet. Even the fire stops crackling for a moment.

"It's a curse upon all Honey Witches in our family line," she continues. "One that my grandmother was under as well. No one can ever fall in love with me." There is a heavy silence that allows the crickets to sing for what feels like an eternity.

"How could that even work?" Lottie says, slurring slightly.

"It's as simple as it sounds. No one will ever have feelings of true love for me. I will always be alone in that way."

Disbelief flickers in Lottie's narrowing eyes. She opens her mouth to further protest, but August cuts her off as he says, "Oh my, Marigold. That's horrible. Is there a way to break it?"

"No," she says, her jaw clenched. "At the time, I had no qualms with accepting the curse. I wanted to run away from that life, from the balls and the courtships and the life of being a wife. I thought that maybe it was because I was always meant to be a Honey Witch, and my intuition knew that love wasn't for me."

"And do you still think that now?" Lottie asks, quickly and quietly.

She turns so their eyes meet. "Of course." It feels like a lie in her mouth. "It would be a truly sad fate if I were to change my mind, because it is too late. It is far too late for me." She throws the rest of her mead down her throat and refills the mug. Lottie does the same and then reaches for the whole bottle, taking a giant gulp before setting it down and placing her hand to the right of Marigold's. Their fingers are barely touching, until Lottie moves her hand just enough so that they are intertwined.

"I..." Lottie says, and Marigold's head turns sharply toward her.

"Don't believe me? I know," she says curtly.

Her pulse thunders where Lottie's fingers meet hers. Lottie seems to lean closer, her eyes on Marigold's lips, but that must be a drunken loss of balance. Marigold pulls her hand away and pushes her wet hair behind her ear.

"I do not know what to say," Lottie says.

"Then say nothing." She does not wish to talk about it anymore anyway. It hurts. It stings.

August reaches across the table and opens his hand for her. "How can I help you, Marigold? What can I do?"

She sits up, placing her hand in his. "Always be generous with your company, and never stop asking me for help. It is all I can give."

The quiet air grows heavy and blankets over them. The mead is all gone. It is the middle of the night. Marigold is seconds away from crashing into herself, physically and emotionally spent.

August stands and stretches up high. He could touch the ceiling if he really wanted to. "My dearest friends, I am sufficiently drunk and I must go to bed, else I'll be insufferable in the morning."

"More than you already are?" Lottie says, and he shoves her shoulder.

"One day, you are going to meet someone who is a worthy

opponent to your wicked mouth." He looks to Marigold, eyes lingering. She's too tired and too drunk to ask why. When he leaves the room, Lottie and Marigold are alone.

And it is so incredibly awkward. The room is spinning and everything is too hot. She is using the last of her energy to contain her imminent hiccups.

"So..." she says, trying to escape the silence. The word drags on longer than she intended.

"So?" Lottie replies, offering no small talk or pleasantries. She does, however, inch slightly closer to her so their legs are touching.

Marigold almost moves her hand to Lottie's thigh—she cannot help the urge. This woman is a magnet for her touch, but she catches herself and lays her hand back in her own lap.

"So... what did you think about when you screamed your heart out? What were you letting go of?"

Lottie stiffens. "That's what you want to talk about right now?"

"Um..." Marigold says, clearing her throat. "What else should we talk about?"

Their faces are so close. Closer, closer, closer still. Her heart throbs so much that it aches.

"Can I...?" Lottie says, staring at her lips.

Before she has the chance to react, Lottie shuts her eyes tightly and braces her head with her hands. "Agh, dammit."

Marigold pulls back, breathing fast and deep. "Headache again?"

Lottie nods without looking up.

"Will you please let me give you something for it this time?"

Lottie nods again. It must be great pain if she is finally willing to try a magical solution.

She runs to the kitchen and quickly brews a cup of chamomile tea, flavored with lavender and a healthy spoonful of black sage honey. By the time she brings it over, Lottie seems fine.

"I do not understand these headaches. I've never had them before, and they only last for a moment."

"Well, I cannot speak for every headache, but this one is likely because you are drunk."

"We're both drunk."

She hands the cup to Lottie. "We are."

There is a pregnant pause. Lottie starts to reach for her hand. "And we were just..."

"Talking," Marigold interrupts, stiffening her hand at her side. "We were simply talking. And now we are going to bed."

Lottie shifts, then stands. "I suppose we have done enough soul sharing tonight. I'll see you in the morning." She turns to leave, and Marigold's gaze cannot let go of her until she enters her room and closes the door.

Marigold cannot sleep, so she lies still in the small bed of wild-flowers close to her bedroom window. The isle in daytime is always alive with bright green grass and golden sunlight cracking through the sky as if it were made of glass. Even at night, when the moon leaves the sun speechless, the jewel-like stars consume the night. Cindershine is nearby, meowing about something unseen. The air smells of honey and forthcoming rain. She picks a flower by her eye and starts plucking away at the petals.

She loves me not.

She loves me not.

She loves me not.

Plucking petals is a bore when there is only one possible outcome. She tosses the stem and sits up with a sigh. Cindershine's meowing grows stronger, and there is a sudden change in the air. It's souring with scents of salt and smoke, tinted a sickly yellow that licks the corners of the evening. Marigold jumps up and turns to see smoke billowing from the other side of the isle. Cindershine is running away as the smoke grows stronger. She tries to run forward, but her feet do not move. The fire spreads, consuming the edge of the apiary and reaching for the cottage.

It is Versa. It must be.

She has worked to remember the first time the Ash Witch attacked her, but the one thing she could never quite recall, the thing that rested on the tip of her tongue that she could never fully taste, was the fear. What did it feel like to be so close to the flame, to certain death? She can see that day as clearly as a painting in her mind. She sees her grandmother's determination, her mother's terror, and her own vulnerability. How easily she could have been killed that day, how close Innisfree came to absolute destruction. She could see it, but now she feels it—the shock, the heart-stopping dread, the absolute bone-deep knowing that this is where it stops, this is how it ends.

She opens her mouth to scream, but no sound comes out. She is frozen, either by magic or panic, she cannot tell. Too powerless to defend, too weak to even move from her position.

Something heavy collides with her chest. She looks down and sees nothing there, only the grass at her feet, but the weight and warmth on her skin say otherwise. Her arms feel full of lead and she can barely lift them up, but she brings her hands to her chest and feels something soft. Taking a deep breath, she shuts her eyes tightly and tries to scream again. The sound rips through her throat like a creature with claws, and it tastes of blood. When she opens her eyes, the horrors dissipate, and the walls of her room form around her. She is in bed, screaming, with Cindershine in her grip. The world is as it was before she unknowingly fell asleep.

She relaxes her grip on her cat and opens the small window at her side, inhaling deeply—no scent of burning in the air. No yellow smoke billowing through. All is quiet, save for the echo of her scream. Her heartbeat is slowly settling into a normal rhythm. She runs her hands along her bedding, letting the softness remind her that she is safe in her own room. Bad things can't happen to people in comfy beds.

Sounds of movement—rustling in the bushes, splashes in the water, stepping over sticks—drift through the window.

Normally, Marigold would take comfort in this, presuming it to be the music of wild things. But now, after the nightmare, she cannot let the noises go unchecked. Pulling on a dressing gown and lighting a candle, she silently slips through the cottage's front door. The air is calm and clear, but she is not alone—footsteps sound from her left. With her candlelight guiding her path, she approaches slowly, careful to keep her steps quiet. The flame pulses in time with her heart. The glow illuminates the trees, then the beehives, then an open sky. Nothing out of the ordinary—yet. She pushes onward toward the edge of the isle where the fire of her nightmare began.

There, there is movement. A shadow skirting the brink, each step louder than the last as it comes closer. An outline emerges from the shapeless form. It's a person, a woman. The candlelight bounces off her bright red curls and illuminates her sleepy green eyes.

It's Lottie. She walks right past Marigold, moving in a wakeless daze.

"Lottie?" she calls after her, but the woman does not turn. Marigold catches up to her and walks by her side. "Lottie, you're dreaming. You must wake up."

Her words go unheard, and Lottie maintains her stride.

Marigold stands in front of her and says, "Stop!"

Lottie moves to sidestep her, so she grabs her hand, noting that it is warm and sticky. "Wake up!"

Marigold's touch seems to work. Startled awake, Lottie gasps, jerking her hand out of Marigold's grasp and bringing it to her chest. She looks around in a panic, finds the light of the candle, and finally meets her concerned gaze. "What are you doing?" Lottie says.

Marigold's brows pinch together. "I had a nightmare and woke up to strange noises coming from outside. What were you doing out here?"

Lottie shakes her head. "I was having a nightmare, too."

"What did you see?" The candlelight pulses, punctuating the silence.

Lottie eyes the flame and shudders. "Fire."

She inhales sharply through her nose. "Me too." She takes hold of Lottie's hand again. "Why is your hand sticky?"

Lottie pulls back and holds her hand up to her face, spreading her fingers apart over and over again, noticing the tacky pull against her skin. "I don't know." She puts her pointer finger in her mouth, tasting it slowly. "It's honey," she says, confused.

Marigold cants her head. "Were you in the apiary?"

"I guess so," Lottie says while shaking her head. "I truly do not remember."

Again, Marigold reaches for her hand, saying, "Let us return to the cottage. We both deserve rest."

Lottie is staring at her so intently, flitting her gaze between Marigold's eyes and her waiting hand. "I don't know if I can sleep alone." Her voice trembles.

Marigold's spine goes taut. "Oh."

"I'm sorry," Lottie says quickly. "I'll be fine."

"No," Marigold says, unable to withhold her honesty or her desire to stay close. "I won't be able to sleep alone either. So, come with me. Stay with me," she says, bringing her open hand closer. This time, Lottie relents. Her hand sits in Marigold's palm for the first few steps toward the cottage until she pulls away again, shuddering like a fevered child.

"Never mind. I feel like I'm going to be sick," she says sharply as if it is Marigold's fault. Lottie dashes into the cottage by herself, leaving her standing alone in the frigid night air.

The wind blows out her candle, carrying nothing but the hums of innumerable bees.

Chapter Twenty

When Marigold retrieves the moon water from the edge of the oasis in the morning, she sees a dark mass stagnant in the center of the water. From a distance, it looks like a massive dead slug, but as she gets closer, she sees a horrifying truth; it is Yliza, the landvættir of the oasis. Her bright yellow skin has turned midnight blue. Her normally glossy and plump body now looks almost matte and deflated. At first, Marigold thinks she is dead.

Can spirit guardians simply die? It does not make sense. The guardians of Innisfree are immortal—they are not even truly of this world. They sit safely behind the veil, unable to be harmed.

But last night, the moon was full and the veil was thin. Maybe they could have somehow hurt Yliza when they went swimming. It could already be too late. Marigold places her palms in the water, making gentle ripples that grow into waves of movement. The water carries Yliza to her, and she gently rotates the body without pulling her out of the pool.

"Yliza?"

It is the strangest thing; Yliza is alive, her glassy eyes staring straight back at her with no death inside them—only anger. Her round mouth opens to reveal rows of razor-sharp teeth that were not there before. The koi thrashes violently in her arms, desperate to bite. It's as if Yliza has gone through some sort of monstrous transformation. Could it all be from one night of swimming? Something that Marigold has done so many times before? She fishes a vial of acacia honey out of her pocket, pops the cork off, and grabs Yliza again, careful to avoid the teeth. When she is able to force the honey into the koi's mouth, there is an immediate change. Yliza returns to her normal state; her skin loses its inky black tint, the anger in her eyes fades to apathy, and her rows of teeth fall out like seeds.

Marigold makes haste to each of the landvættir guarding the isle. Odessa sits on the coast of the lake, her stark white feathers turned slick black and her long neck bent at an unnatural angle. It looks broken until she comes closer and sees Odessa's glowing eyes, now bloodred, staring back at her.

"What happened to you?"

Odessa lets out a gargled scream. When the landvættir opens her beak to shriek, Marigold is quickly able to get a few drops of honey on her tongue right before she is bitten. The injury is worth it when she sees the black pigment lift from Odessa's feathers, and her eyes fade back to pale lavender. She repeats this process with the remaining spirits—Talaya, the blue snake who had been turned white as bone, and Chesha, the cat who grew new fangs and venomous claws.

What could have happened to them? She has always cared for them, she's never forgotten an offering, and she has never been unkind to the isle. Perhaps they are angry about having more people on the isle than they are used to? But even that does not make sense. There have been plenty of times when her grandmother allowed a customer in need to stay at the cottage for days at a time, and to her knowledge, this never happened to the landvættir.

The only place where she might find an answer is in the giant grimoire that details the history of honey magic. The problem is that the book is over six thousand pages, with very little guidance on what information can be found on what page. The spells at the beginning are indexed—everything else is a guessing game. It will take her years to read and understand the entire

thing cover to cover, but it is the only hope she has for understanding what is happening to the isle that she swore to protect.

After tending to the landvættir, she comes inside with her
moon water ready. She can start her research after she's finished
August's spell, if she can stay calm enough to focus. She fills the
kitchen counter with all the necessary tools and ingredients to
craft it: the fresh-made moon water, the lavender honey straight
from the frame of honeycomb, the lemon seeds from the ripe
fruit in front of the house, the spotted rose petals that feel as soft
as sleep. A heavy mortar and pestle sit empty in their immov-
able spot. She ties her hair into her yellow ribbon and wipes the
already beading sweat from her forehead as she checks over
her spell instructions one last time. Her instinct continues to
tempt her to flip past the spells to start reading the rest of the
grimoire—to not stop until an answer is found regarding the
landvættir's illness.

But for this soulmate spell, everything must be perfect. Flaw-
less. Impossible to deny. A perfect spell is the only way that
Marigold can force Lottie to eat her words, with *mythcraft* being
the first on the menu. Once everything is in place, she goes to
the library, where Lottie and August are entertaining themselves
with a bounty of books.

"Ready to find your soulmate?" she says, and August drops
his book onto the floor and runs breathlessly into the kitchen.
He's so excited that he could be mistaken for a puppy, complete
with panting sounds and a wagging tail. "Is it ready?"

"We haven't even started yet." Marigold laughs. "Take a seat
and watch." She rarely has such an attentive audience when
crafting spells, but she pushes away her anxieties as she focuses
on her work.

She first powders the petals, grinding them into the same
texture that she would use as a pigment in a homemade beeswax lipstick. The powder is transferred to a larger mixing bowl
before she grabs the heavy rectangular frame of honeycomb. She
heats a large serrated knife over the open flame of the nearest

candle sitting in a votive, and she waits until the smallest twirls of steam dance around the blade's sharp edge. The knife glides through the wax that keeps the honey trapped inside the honeycomb, and with one solid swipe, the honey pours like liquid gold. With two hands, she holds the rectangular wooden frame up to the light and lets the sun kiss the honey. She allows some of it to drip into the mixing bowl with the powdered petals, while the rest must be strained from the wax. Carefully, she removes the large pieces of honeycomb from the frame and wraps them in thin cheesecloth. The honey oozes through the thin fabric as she kneads and squeezes the honeycomb over a large bowl. This process takes an eternity until all the honey slowly oozes out and collects in a massive jar that is bigger than her head. The sweet scent warms the entire home, and she cannot help herself; she must taste it, and it is utterly divine—sweet, earthy, with that signature hint of a burn from the magic in the back of her throat. She savors it for a moment before wiping off her sticky fingers and getting back to work.

The honey and the powdered petals mix beautifully, turning into what looks like liquid pink glass. She adds the dried lemon seeds and then a splash of moon water. Once everything is seamlessly mixed, she gently pours the elixir into a vial that is small enough to wear as a charm at the end of a necklace. She corks the bottle, attaches a string, and searches her very soul for the purest intent.

This spell will lead August Owens to his soulmate.

This spell will prove to Lottie Burke that honey magic is real.

This spell will dazzle, amaze, confuse, astound.

As she holds the vial close to her chest, she feels it begin to heat, and she cannot contain her excitement. She holds the vial up by its leather string. She motions to put it on August.

"Oh cute, you made him a necklace. Very powerful myth-craft, indeed."

August makes a disapproving sound. "Could you please let me enjoy this moment, without your remarks? I'm trying to find my soulmate, here."

Lottie rolls her eyes, but she does keep her mouth shut as Marigold loops the necklace around August's neck.

He places his palm over the necklace and presses it to his chest. "Oooooh, it's warm. It's very warm."

"That means it's working," Marigold says.

"It's working a little too well." He carefully positions the necklace to hang over his shirt, rather than beneath his collar where it could burn his chest.

"It's only because it was just activated. Give it a few days and you won't even notice it."

"A few days?" Lottie asks with a sharp tone. "How long is he supposed to wear that thing?"

"Until it leads him to his soulmate."

"Right," Lottie scoffs. "And how long will that take? A million years?"

Lottie's attitude makes it clear that either she got no sleep last night after the nightmare, or she is violently hungover. Possibly both. At this point, Marigold and August seem to both silently agree that they will not be acknowledging her anymore during this conversation.

"How do you feel?" Marigold asks, keeping her eyes glued to August, which is always difficult for her when Lottie is around.

He examines his whole body—he rotates his hand to view both sides, touches his curly black hair, and then runs his hands over his smooth face and holds his hand over his heart, just to the left of the spell. "I don't know. The same? How should I feel?"

"Of course," Lottie murmurs.

"Do you feel compelled to go anywhere? Like you are being pulled in a certain direction?"

August thinks for a moment. He then opens the front door dramatically and stands in the doorway. He licks his pointer finger and holds it to the wind, searching for direction. "Maybe north?"

Lottie erupts in laughter. "Wow, so specific. What a perfect spell you've made, Witch."

She clenches her jaw, because it *is* a perfect spell. It *is* working. Sometimes it needs a moment to acclimate to the wearer. But of course, Lottie will not hear that reasoning. She will not excuse anything. And Marigold has had enough, especially after last night. They had been open to each other, so vulnerable. What happened? Where did that warmth go?

"You know what, Lottie? I think you're jealous."

August turns around to face them both so quickly that he almost loses his balance. Lottie stares, open-mouthed, at her. "Jealous? Of what?"

"You're jealous that August is about to find his soulmate, and then you will be alone. You don't want it to work. Because the minute it leads August to the person he is meant to be with, you won't have him all to yourself."

Lottie wipes a bead of sweat from her forehead. "You are truly delusional."

"Am I? Am I saying something that isn't true, or are you simply too afraid to admit it? You are scared. You are scared of losing him and being left with no one else because you push everyone away. That's why you hated Edmund."

"I hated Edmund because he was a rake."

"A rake who was keeping your best friend away from you."

Lottie tenses her shoulders. Her face grows cold. Her chest heaves as she gathers her words, but Marigold has yet to relent. While August goes to Lottie's side, Marigold turns back to her kitchen and quickly pours the remainder of the spell into another small vial on a leather string. She finds her intentions, says her incantation, and wraps the necklace around Lottie before anyone can protest.

"There. Now you can find your soulmate, too, and maybe we can find some peace away from your company."

"Marigold..." August says, and the world stops. Time stretches itself so that she must sit with the echoes of her words. She watches her cruelty collide with Lottie's skin, seeping into her blood, spearing her pounding heart. Only now does she understand what she has said, and what she has done. She has never felt such sharp, sickening regret. She has equipped Lottie with a spell that will send her away.

Lottie still says nothing, her body is frozen in place, her balance maintained only by August's form beside her. Marigold approaches slowly, afraid that she may get slapped. But still, Lottie does not move, even as she comes within arm's reach. Then she wraps Lottie in an embrace.

The first that they have ever shared. Her arms sit atop Lottie's rigid shoulders, and her hands connect underneath soft red hair.

"I am so sorry, Lottie. I did not mean it."

She feels Lottie start to move, but instead of running away, Lottie does the most unexpected thing—she returns the embrace, her arms tight around Marigold's soft waist.

"You did mean it," Lottie whispers. "But you were right. Again." She pulls away from Marigold, but not completely. Her palms lay flat against Marigold's sides, her fingers flexing in the soft fabric of the dress. She turns to August and says, "I am scared of losing you."

"Oh, Lots," he says as he joins the embrace. "You are never getting rid of me, and I cannot believe you would ever think otherwise."

"A girl can dream," Lottie says with a breathy laugh, her harsh jokes and stone walls already rising up again. She pulls away from the embrace and picks up the vial at the end of her necklace. Marigold mirrors her, grabbing her grandmother's ring that hangs from her neck.

"So, how do you claim that this thing works?" Lottie says.

And the moment is gone. Marigold sighs, wishing she could have held on to it for a little bit longer. When Lottie abandons her callous facade, when she admits her feelings, it is the most beautiful wonder to witness. But it never lasts long.

"The spell essentially weaves itself into your intuition, guiding you to make decisions that lead you where you want to go. In this case, it is to your soulmate. When you feel the pull, you'll know."

"Well, I, for one, cannot wait. And I'm thrilled to be going on this adventure with you, Lots. Who knows? Maybe we'll both fall in love this way."

In this moment, Marigold's heart feels as though it has turned to bone and fallen to the pit of her belly to rot. Her friends are going to fall in love, and it will be beautiful, and so lonely to watch. She realizes now that she has the same fears of which she accused Lottie—she, too, is absolutely terrified of being alone. But she has chosen a life path that ensures she always will be, and it can never be changed.

A knock echoes through the cottage.

"Well, that was fast! Will it be Lottie's soulmate or mine?" August chirps. Marigold smirks and opens the door to reveal Mr. O'Connell, a sweet, middle-aged man with short black hair, constant stubble, and a humble beige cotton shirt untucked from his trousers.

"Hmm," August says, crossing his arms over his chest. "A bit old for me, but I suppose age is but a number!"

She gently places her hand on August's back and guides him to the table. "August, take a seat. Mr. O'Connell, how are you? How is your wife?"

August's eyes go wide. "Oops," he mumbles.

"Oh, we're fine. Howya doing, Marigold?" Mr. O'Connell says, bringing his floppy hat to his chest.

She grins. "Fine myself," she says, stepping out of the doorway to allow him inside. Mr. O'Connell came to see her once or twice after Althea passed away. He brought ripe vegetables and fresh yellow flowers from his garden, which made her wonder if Althea had sent him there from wherever she is watching. It was such a comforting gesture, and she can never say no to new ingredients. She has Mr. Benny, who cares for her and provides her with ingredients from his farm, of course, but he is so old. Mr. O'Connell is decades younger, and the work doesn't hurt him in the same way. He still has the bones for it. Thinking of Mr. Benny working the day away in the hot summer sun makes her feel guilty; she shouldn't allow him to push himself so far. That conversation with him would go nowhere, though. She can envision his exact response in her mind: "*Miss Marigold, you aren't asking anything of me. This is my job. Now let me work how I want to work.*" That man would push himself to the brink of death if he thought that it would help her in any way. She does not know why—she certainly hasn't earned it. Perhaps it is his promise to Althea to take care of her that inspires such devotion, but even then, why would Althea's wishes hold such weight over him, especially after her passing? It would be better, certainly safer, if Mr. Benny went easy on himself, though he never will.

She leads Mr. O'Connell to the empty chair at her kitchen table across from Lottie and August.

She turns to a cabinet to grab a cup. "Hungry? Thirsty?"

"No, thank you, miss. Forgive me for not bringing anything to offer you now. The garden is not well."

She pours him some tea anyway and places it in front of him. He takes a sip and lets the heat of the drink undo some of the tension in his shoulders. "It's burnt."

"The tea?" August asks, confused. Lottie sighs.

Mr. O'Connell shakes his head. "No, the garden. Burned to all but ash."

Interested, Lottie leans in. "A wildfire?"

"Too contained to be a wildfire. My garden borders the Hazelwood Forest, but nothing else was touched by the flames. Not even a slight singe on an overhanging branch. I haven't a clue how it happened."

Marigold takes her seat next to him and across from Lottie. She eyes the soulmate spell around Lottie's neck as tension still stretches between them. Clearing her throat, she says, "That's strange, Mr. O'Connell. When did it happen?"

"Last night. Tried everything I could to put it out, but it just wouldn't die. You'll think I'm bonkers for this one, but I swear water couldn't even touch it. Those flames didn't go out until they finished what they started in my garden."

She stiffens against her chair with every word. It sounds exactly like her nightmare. Lottie fidgets with the hem of her long sleeve.

Marigold pushes herself up from the table. "Give me a moment to gather what I need, and then we will return to your garden together." She nearly invites Lottie to attend so that she may witness the magic she is about to perform. Plant resurrection is no small feat, especially at the scale necessary for a garden of that size. But the nature of this destruction, those undying flames and only ash left in their wake, wouldn't be good for Lottie to see. Telling her story last night and showing her burns was so distressing that it caused nightmares for both of them. Lottie should never have to relive that.

Leaving Lottie and August to entertain themselves, she follows Mr. O'Connell to his small green boat. In a way, it's nice to get away now. August and Lottie are probably talking about their soulmates, about their futures that certainly do not include her in them. She doesn't need to hear any of that.

Mr. O'Connell is a quiet man in general, but he is utterly silent through the entire ride, answering her questions only by nodding or shaking his head. He must be exhausted after trying to fight a fire that would not die.

Her nightmare, Lottie's nightmare, and Mr. O'Connell's garden burning all in the same night? It could be a coincidence, but she is a witch who knows better. There are no accidents.

Not like this.

When they arrive at Mr. O'Connell's garden, it's nothing but a perfect rectangle of dry gray dirt. It's a massive plot, possibly bigger than her cottage.

"This isn't how it looked before," he says. It's the first thing he's said since leaving the isle.

"What has changed?"

"The ash is gone." He leans down and drags his fingers through the dirt. "This was pitch-black when I left. It was completely covered in ash. I swear it."

She inhales deeply through her nose.

The air smells of her nightmare—salt and smoke. Slowly, she understands that this is the scent of ash magic. Leaning down, she runs her fingers across the dirt mixed with the remnants of the ash. Upon contact, it's as if she is transported to a world of only darkness, and she can see nothing but a flickering light in the distance. It looks exactly like the light she has seen in the Hazelwood Forest. In an instant, the light erupts, stunning her vision. She blinks to adjust her eyes and sees a menacing old woman hovering over her, scowling down at her, readying a bolt of fire in a withered, bony hand.

It's Versa. She burned this land, and now she must be somewhere close by with an arsenal of ash.

As the Ash Witch launches the bolt of fire, Marigold closes her eyes and screams, bracing herself for the pain. She feels a pair of strong arms picking her up, and when she opens her eyes, she is back in the garden.

"Marigold, what happened? Your eyes glazed over and you started screaming!"

She holds on to him tightly as she struggles to believe what she is seeing. Is she really here? Truly safe?

"I had a vision," she says, her throat raw from the scream. "I saw the woman who burned your garden." She pulls away from him and hurriedly readies a wealth of ingredients—seeds, honeys, moon water, petals and herbs of every color.

"I need to work quickly to protect you." She paints a rune of protection in the center of the garden so Versa will not be able to reach them. And now the Ash Witch will not be able to touch the garden again.

"Can I help, miss? You deserve to be protected, too."

At first she shakes her head, but then she pauses. "Actually, there is something you can do for me."

Mr. O'Connell leans in, eagerly listening.

"I'm going to do my best to revive and restore the garden," Marigold says, placing her hands on her hips. "I will probably faint once it's done. I wanted to warn you so you don't think I'm dead." She can revive a handful of flowers with only a touch, but for something of this size, she must perform a ritual similar to the one she cast with her grandmother so long ago. She'll craft a honey potion, paint healing runes in the corners of the garden, and use up her energy to bring life back to this land.

He hesitates. "Maybe you shouldn't be doing this, then. It sounds dangerous."

Shaking her head, she says, "Not dangerous. Just exhausting. Promise me that if I do fall unconscious after this, you'll bring me back to Innisfree."

"Marigold..." he says.

"Promise me."

Sighing, he says, "I promise."

"Excellent. Then I shall get on with it."

Marigold wakes up on the soft green couch with Lottie, August, and Mr. O'Connell hovering so closely over her that she can see up their noses.

Mr. O'Connell really needs to trim those hairs.

"She's waking up!" August says too loudly, and she winces.

"Don't scream in her face, boy!" Mr. O'Connell says. It's the loudest she has ever heard him speak.

"Both of you, quiet!" Lottie says. She rests the back of her hand on Marigold's forehead. "How are you feeling?"

She tries to clear her throat, but it's too dry to swallow. "Want to go to bed," she mumbles.

Lottie leans in and wraps her arms around her. "I'll help you up."

August joins, tucking himself under Marigold's arm.

They walk about three steps forward when Lottie's nose scrunches up. "Why do you smell like that?"

"Rude, Lots," August scolds. "Marigold, you smell perfectly normal."

"Don't lie to her, August. She reeks of salt and smoke."

August leans in even closer, taking a big whiff of her. "What are you talking about, Lots? I don't smell anything."

"You must be catching a cold. I could smell her before Mr. O'Connell brought her inside."

"Maybe you're just being mean to her for no reason, as per usual."

Marigold's head drops, and Lottie and August tighten their grip on her as they push forward toward her room.

She struggles to speak. "Can we stop...debating...my... stench?"

"Sorry," Lottie and August say in unison.

"I just...need...sleep."

Eyes closed, she collides, and the world fades to black.

Chapter Twenty-One

A knock wakes Marigold the next day. She slept all the way through morning for the first time in years.

Still in her pink lace nightgown, she hurries out of her room and opens the door with a smile.

"Hello, Miss Marigold," says Mr. Benny.

"Mr. Benny! Come in!"

"Thank you, kindly. I came to deliver this," he says as he hands her an envelope, sealed with a wax emblem displaying her family's crest.

Finally, another letter from home. She takes the letter and presses it to her heart, as if the letter is her dear little siblings whom she can finally pull into a hug after so long apart.

"Thank you for bringing me this. Feel free to help yourself to anything in the kitchen while you're here."

He smiles wide and starts snooping in the kitchen as Marigold tears open the envelope to reveal a letter in her sister's hand.

My dearest sister,

I am thrilled to write to you with such wondrous news. I've accepted a proposal from Mr. Woodrake, and we are to be wed at the end of the month as we have received a special license from the archbishop. I realize that the travel is long and grueling, but you must be in attendance on such a joyous day.

I am also writing to inform you that you will be my maid of honor. In an unconventional twist, I've also decided that Frankie will attend me as well. Mother urged me to simply position Frankie as a groomsman alongside my betrothed (I love saying that. My betrothed. I can hardly believe it.), but Frankie and I insisted. Do begin your travels promptly after receiving this letter. You mustn't be late!

I think about you every day. I am so proud of you, and I cannot wait to hear of your adventures.

All my love,
Aster

Marigold rereads the letter over and over again to be sure. Aster Claude, the girl who had every man's heart held gently in her palm, is getting married. And Marigold was not there when she accepted the proposal. She was not there when Aster realized she was in love.

She missed it. All of it.

"Is everything all right, miss?" Benny asks after her long silence.

Marigold brings her eyes away from the letter and blinks herself back into reality. "My sister is getting married," she says.

"Well, that's lovely," Mr. Benny says.

"And I must leave for Bardshire as soon as possible to attend her wedding."

Mr. Benny clasps his hands together. "Wonderful! I'll take you to the ship myself."

Marigold drops herself into a chair at the kitchen table and sighs, pinching her eyebrows together as she reads the letter again.

"You don't seem excited, miss," Mr. Benny says as he takes the seat across from her.

"No, I am," she assures. "I simply can't picture the Aster that I know getting married, though I know she is more than ready. In my mind, she's still my baby sister. I feel like I've already missed so much. I know I've been here for quite some time, but this is the first time I've truly felt so far away. It hurts more than I thought it would."

Mr. Benny nods. His eyes soften as he takes a deep breath. "I understand. I really do. But that's the beautiful thing about family. No matter how far you go, they are still with you. And when you see them again, it will feel as though you never left. I promise."

She smiles. "I hope so." Gazing down the corridor, she thinks of her friends, who are still sleeping in their beds. "But now I must leave them. And I don't know if I'm ready for that either."

"You know you'll see them again when we return. Take the rest of the day to prepare for the travels and say goodbye. I'll return in the evening and we'll go."

Marigold nods. As the logistical plans come together, she falls deeper into her emotions. She is overwhelmed with gratitude for Mr. Benny, not only because he will be taking her to her family, but because he comforts her when she needs it the most. She wraps her arms around him tightly.

"Thank you. Thank you for everything you have done and everything that you are." She pulls away and touches her grandmother's ring that hangs from her neck. "Thank you."

He says his parting words and leaves Marigold in the house, waiting for her friends to wake up. She pens a letter to her brother, though she will likely see him before it arrives.

Dear Frankie,

Well, she has done it. Aster Claude has found a rake and turned him into a gentleman. I could not

*be prouder. If her wedding is to be our first reunion
since I came to Innisfree, we must plan accord-
ingly. How might we disrupt Bardshire? There
must be some scandalous rumors surrounding my
sudden departure. Shall we indulge them?*

*My head is racing. I must admit, it is going to be
very difficult for me to leave the isle now. Believe it
or not, I actually have some friends here, and I am
quite enjoying the company. Of course, no company compares to yours, but I'm fond of these new
companions all the same. I will tell you everything
of my adventures soon.*

All my love,
Marigold

To distract herself from the impending partings, Marigold
casts another protection spell on the house and makes her rounds
through the isle to offer honey to the landvættir and strengthen the
protection wards. She gives them each a massive dose of honey,
larger than she has ever given before. It is the only way she knows
to keep them healthy, and they'll need to be sustained during
her trip to Bardshire. She then whips up an enormous spread for
breakfast. Eggs, spiced sausages that were made by Mr. Benny,
warm honey cakes, and freshly squeezed orange juice. When
Marigold is thoroughly exhausted and covered in flour, Lottie is
the first to rise and come into the kitchen. She wipes her eyes and
stretches her arms toward the ceiling until her back cracks.

"Morning," she says through a yawn.

Marigold attempts to wipe the flour from her face to no avail.
"Morning," she says without turning to greet her.

Lottie cocks a brow as she walks closer to her. "Everything
okay?"

She continues to whisk dry ingredients in a bowl, sending
more loose flour into the air and onto her person. "Yes, fine."

Lottie stands behind her, silent as a wish, until her chin could almost rest upon Marigold's shoulder. "You sure?"

Startled by her closeness, Marigold nearly drops the bowl from her hand. Her sudden movement still sends the whisk flying through the air, decorating both of them in flour as they slip on the floor together.

The commotion stirs August awake, and he comes running out of his room. He tries to catch his breath and steady himself as he observes the scene before him: Marigold and Lottie on the kitchen floor, covered in flour, holding on to each other. "What's going on?"

Lottie pulls herself up first and dusts off the flour before offering a hand to Marigold. "That's a question for the witch."

She takes her hand and stands. "Let's discuss over breakfast. I've been cooking for hours to try to take my mind off of things." She begins assembling plates piled high with sweet and savory treats, and the three of them take their respective seats at the table.

"Don't leave us waiting any longer," August says. "What's on your mind?"

"My sister is getting married in Bardshire, and I am to be her maid of honor."

Lottie takes a massive bite of her triple stack of pancakes and nods. "Sounds lovely," she says, unenthused.

August forces himself to swallow before he's finished chewing. "Don't be rude."

Lottie gives him an annoyed glance and continues eating.

"The wedding is on the first day of autumn," Marigold continues, "so in order to be there in time, I must leave tonight."

August and Lottie both put down their utensils and glance at each other before returning their gaze to her.

"Do you have to go?" Lottie asks.

"To my sister's wedding? Yes. I have to go." Her tone is harsher than she intended.

"You seem upset about it, like it's the last thing you want to do," Lottie says.

Marigold sinks farther back into her chair. "It is."

"Why?" Lottie asks.

"Because I do not want to leave you..." Marigold says before she remembers herself and fights for her composure. "Or August. I don't want our visit to be over."

The two stare at each other, unsure of what to say next. It is August, as always, who interrupts the silence. "But what of the spell?"

"You don't need me anymore for it to work. You'll be able to return home, and you," she says as she places her hand on Lottie's shoulder, "will finally find your soulmate, too. God help them."

The three of them share a soft laugh, but it is swiftly muted by the heartbreak of impending separation.

"So this is it, then? This is our last day together," Lottie says.

Marigold sighs and pushes back the tears already welling in her eyes. "I suppose so."

"Wait," August says, and Lottie and Marigold turn to meet his gaze. "I think I'm getting that feeling."

Lottie sighs. "You don't have to announce it, August. Just go to the privy."

August shoves her playfully and says, "You know what I'm talking about. The spell. I'm getting that pull telling me to go somewhere."

"And where is that?" Lottie asks.

August flashes a devious grin. "Bardshire."

Marigold's heart quickens. "August, don't tease me right now. Do you truly feel it?"

"I really, truly do. It's almost impossible to describe. It's almost like—"

"Almost like you don't really feel anything?" Lottie mumbles with her mouth full.

"No, I'm serious," he says as he places a hand over his heart. "It feels almost frightening."

"Like an itch?" Marigold asks.

"More like a bite, maybe," he says as he scratches the spot where the necklace sits.

Marigold throws her arms over August and cheers. "It's working! See, I told you! And now you'll come to Bardshire!"

August pulls Lottie into an embrace. "And so will you, Lots. Our adventure has only just begun!"

Lottie tries to fight her way out of the group hug, but it is no use. They only wrap their arms tighter. "You know we cannot afford tickets on the ship," she protests.

"I'm paying for both of you. Please, come," Marigold says.

"It will be so fun, Lots. Please come on this adventure with us. You'll always regret it if you don't."

"I'll show you all the worthwhile sites. And you can meet my father! You can even take his art class!" Marigold says.

Lottie chews on her lip and tries to pretend she is not smiling. Her gaze flits between August and Marigold. "You two aren't going to let me say no, are you?"

Marigold smirks and August laughs in response. "I'm afraid you're stuck with us, Lots," he says.

Lottie sighs, though there is a hint of excitement in her voice. "Fine. I guess we're all going to Bardshire."

Part Three

It is the start of autumn, and the ash is still warm. Still fresh. Still smells of what it once was.

Althea Murr is long gone. Her granddaughter is delicate and afraid. Everything is deliciously wrong. Ash magic bleeds from the dark runes that live deep in the Hazelwood Forest. And the will-o'-the-wisp, the specter that keeps Versa's black heart beating while she waits to return to Innisfree, is awake. Beckoning.

Flickering.

It can sense that its creator is close.

Chapter Twenty-Two

When Mr. Benny arrives at the Honey Witch house that evening, he finds two eager passengers waiting for him at the dock, and one slightly less eager passenger behind them.

"Is there room for two more?"

"Always room for friends," Mr. Benny says with his soft and crooked smile.

Marigold feels much more anxiety than she cares to admit. Innisfree is her true home now, and she hates to leave it when the spirit guardians are going through such a strange metamorphosis, but she has no choice. It has been more than a year since she saw her family last. She has already missed too much. She promised Aster and Frankie that she would come, that she would be there for them, that they would still have their sister.

She cannot break that promise—now—or ever.

Beyond that, it is time to see her mother again. To speak, to share, and hopefully, to reconcile.

The small boat drifts through the night without a word from anyone. The sky above them is a clear, velvety blue that looks soft enough to touch. There is tension radiating off them, and poor Mr. Benny seemingly has no idea how to react. He is a particularly chatty person and clearly struggles to sit in silence for too long.

He clears his throat. "Lovely weather, isn't it?"

"Indeed!" August says, eager to have someone who hates the

quiet as much as he does. "It has been a lovely summer, hasn't it, ladies?"

Lottie does not respond, and neither does Marigold.

Has it been lovely? No, largely, this has been a cruel summer. She has missed her sister's proposal, the landvættir are inexplicably ill, and now she has developed feelings for a girl who defies everything that her world is supposed to be.

Overall, the magic is worth it. This life is worth it—but she would not be herself if she did not allow for time to pout. Who made this rule that people cannot have everything that they want, all at once? She would love nothing more than to write them a strongly worded letter detailing her displeasure.

"Are you looking forward to your sister's wedding, Miss Marigold?" Mr. Benny asks.

"Yes. Though I must admit, I am exceptionally relieved to not be going back to Bardshire alone." When she turns, she finds Lottie's gaze there waiting for her.

"We couldn't let you do that, Mari," August says as he reaches across the bench and places his hand on top of her knee. She stiffens at the mention of her old familial nickname. She has not heard it since she left home, and it makes her heart burn. She tries to hide it quickly, not wanting to make her friends more uncomfortable than they probably already are in a too-small boat on a journey to somewhere that they've never been, and likely would never have had any reason to go otherwise. Unfortunately, Lottie is particularly perceptive.

"I don't think she likes that nickname, August," Lottie whispers.

"It's not that." She sighs. "That's what my family calls me. I used to hate it, but now that I haven't heard it in a while, I just realized how much I miss it."

"Well then, we shall call you that more, Mari," August replies as he relaxes back into the bench.

"*Mari* is really pretty," Lottie says.

"So is *Lottie*." She smiles. There is a sweet pause in the boat before August finds the wherewithal to destroy it.

He nudges Marigold and gives her a devious smirk. "Are we still only talking about nicknames, you two?"

"Of course," she says, straightening her spine.

"Well, I want one, too. What about *Auggie*? Auggie, Lottie, and Mari," August says.

"Perfect," Marigold says.

Once they reach the coast, they leave the little boat and pile into Mr. Benny's carriage. As they transfer their belongings, Lottie starts frantically digging through her bag. Her breathing heavies and her hands begin to shake as she continues searching for something that is not there.

"Lots?" August says.

She puts her hands on the top of her head and tries to calm her breathing. "I forgot my book."

August immediately starts searching through her bag while Lottie paces around the carriage. "There's no way," he says. His entire arm is swallowed by the bag. "It has to be in here."

"It's not!" Lottie yells.

"I'm still looking," he assures her, but the hope is leaving his voice.

Marigold walks over to Lottie and follows her as she paces. "What book?"

"It's silly," she says, though she can barely get the words to come through her panic. "It's a small book of nursery rhymes, but it's the only thing I have from my real parents. I never go anywhere without it."

"I am sure we will find it," Marigold says as she reflexively takes Lottie's hand to comfort her. To her surprise, Lottie does not pull her hand away.

August approaches slowly with his head hanging. "I'm sorry, Lots. It's not here. You must have left it back at Marigold's."

Lottie tightens her grip around Marigold's fingers as if she will never let them go. "How could I have done that? How could I have been so foolish?"

He shrugs. "I don't know. Your mind has seemed a bit"—he stares at Lottie's hand that is still wrapped around Marigold's fingers—"preoccupied lately."

She finally drops Marigold's hand. "Be serious, August."

"I am," he says. "You've been distracted."

"August," she snaps. "Stop. Talking."

He nearly speaks, but he stops himself when he catches Marigold's gaze.

She turns to Lottie and says, "Do you want to go back to get it?"

Lottie chews her lip and thinks for a moment, but she says, "No. Let's keep going."

"Are you sure?" August says.

Lottie nods. "I'll be okay. I don't need a silly book to keep me safe."

"That's right," August says as he pulls her into an embrace. "You have me." He opens one arm and invites Marigold into the hug. "And you have Mari."

She approaches slowly before weaving her arms around her friends. "You do have me," she says into Lottie's neck. The three of them separate and regather their belongings. Once they are all safely seated, Mr. Benny drives them farther into the night.

The carriage ride to the port is shorter than Marigold remembers. They arrive as the sun creeps into the sea, and their ship comes into view when they get close to the dock. It is the same one that carried her from Bardshire when she left. It's all the same, just as she last saw it. They say their thanks and goodbyes to Mr. Benny as he starts his return. Everything feels more real when his carriage is out of sight. Before, she could pretend they were all simply going into town, picking up baubles and coming back to the cottage. But now he's gone, and the only place to go is aboard the ship. This ruthless anxiety from leaving the isle will all be worth it when she sees her family.

Right?

Her foot catches on the dock before she steps onto the ship, and she wonders if it is a sign, wonders if she should turn back now and go back to the only place that has ever felt like home. Lottie and August step past her, boarding the ship and waiting for her to come along. So much of her does not want to follow, but she does. She must. Crew members carry their belongings behind them and lead them to their rooms. August is reluctant to stay alone, but Marigold reminds him that they are high society travelers now, and high society members of any kind are very strict. Boys stay in their own rooms, away from the girls without a chaperone.

Of course, it is not entirely devastating to have a full night alone with Lottie. The night after they all swam in the moon pool was fun, but it was just an evening of silly stories and games. This is different.

The walls of their room are decorated with damask wallpaper and brass sconces. There are two small beds across from each other, each with a small nightstand at their side. A velvet chaise sits next to the door that leads to their private balcony.

Lottie seems absolutely exhausted, which does not bode well for the evening. The woman is sour at the best of times, but she is lethal when she is tired. Without a word, she begins removing her modest black dress that hides her scars and tattoos. When she starts to remove her chemise, Marigold stops her with a gasp.

"What are you doing?"

"Getting ready for bed," Lottie says, her tone indicating that she does not understand Marigold's surprise.

"And you must undress completely for that?"

Lottie shrugs. "It's not like I have anything to hide now. You saw everything when we swam in that moon pool."

"Not everything," she protests. Her blush warms her cheek.

"It's burning hot. I can't sleep in this heap of fabric," Lottie says as she wrestles with her skirt. "Close your eyes if you're so squeamish." She tosses the chemise over her head and falls into bed on her front, leaving Marigold no time to avert her gaze. Her pale skin looks impossibly soft under the golden glow of candlelight.

"You don't have any tattoos on your back," Marigold says.

"Well, I can't exactly reach back there, can I?"

"Right. I forgot you do them all yourself. You're very talented."

Lottie laughs into her pillow like she does not believe a word she hears. "Am I?"

"I think so."

"I think," Lottie groans as she rolls over, keeping the blankets pressed to her front while looking up at her, "that you are merely trying to be polite, Mari. Tattoos aren't for everyone, and that's okay."

"Why would you think that I couldn't like tattoos?"

"Because you can barely look at my body right now without wincing. Or is that because of my scars?"

Marigold clenches her jaw tightly, so hard that her teeth could turn to powder beneath the weight of her bite. It's true that she won't look at Lottie's body, but not because of the scars or tattoos. She fears that if she looks too long, if she wants too much, she will break her own heart.

Lottie is not hers to admire.

Lottie is not hers to love.

Lottie is not hers at all.

And yet, she cannot stop herself from saying, "I think you are amazing."

At that, Lottie smiles. "For what?"

"For everything. Your talent, your skill, your ability to turn pain into something beautiful. You are an amazing person, Lottie. Even if you are always sour."

The two of them sit in a warm silence for a moment until Marigold sits on the edge of Lottie's bed. "You, your scars, and your tattoos are perfect as they are."

Lottie chews on her lip. "Why are you being so kind?"

"I'm merely telling you what I think."

Lottie sighs, expelling her nerves before she speaks. "I want to show you my favorite tattoo."

"Show me," she says before she can stop herself. This is what she has always wanted from Lottie—a chance to see her, *really* see her, and the art that makes up her person.

Lottie stands from the bed, allowing her body to be exposed to the candlelight. She keeps one arm over her breasts, and she extends her other arm to Marigold, bringing her in closer. There are black tattoos that cover her thighs, hips, and stomach. Flowers, faces, and more Latin phrases. Lottie says nothing as Marigold's eyes wander over her entire body, every scarred and inked inch touched by her gaze.

She stares for a long time. Too long. Pointing to a string of Latin across her rib cage, she asks, "What does this one mean?"

Lottie brings her hand in closer, letting it brush against the tattoo. She traces the tiny letters with her soft trembling fingers.

Vita brevis, ars aeternus

"Life is short, art is forever," Lottie says.

"And this one is your favorite?" Her voice is a dry whisper. Lottie shakes her head and takes Marigold's hand from her ribs to the space below her breasts. In this place sits a delicate arrow. She drops her other arm that was concealing her chest, letting the candlelight illuminate her entire body. Marigold gasps as she moves her head quickly, but Lottie brings a hand to her cheek and directs her gaze back down. She tucks Marigold's hair behind her ear, letting her nails drag softly through her wavy blond hair. With her other hand, she wraps her fingers around Marigold's hand and traces the lines of her sternum tattoo.

"This one is my favorite. And it's the first I ever did. I love it."

Every detail is perfect; the lines are smooth and solid. There is an intricate pattern of swirls and shapes surrounding the arrow. The longer she stares, she realizes that this arrow bears a striking similarity to the rune that she paints in the corners of the cottage during a protection spell. The same one on the back of her father's paintings. It could be chance, but she is all too clever to believe in happenstance over fate.

"Mari?" Lottie says, bringing her attention back up to her eyes.

210   Sydney J. Shields

Her blood is striking through her veins like lightning. "What made you want this one?" she asks as she flattens her palm over it, letting her fingers brush against the sides of Lottie's breasts.

Lottie's breath hitches. "Remember how I said I don't remember much of my parents? And I don't remember the fire? Well, I remember this," she says, keeping Marigold's hand on the ink. "I don't know where it came from, but this image is my first-ever memory. When I try to think of my childhood and what my life was like before the fire, this is all I can see."

Marigold's eyes widen, and her lips part in shock. Lottie said her mother believed in magic. She never said that her mother tried to *use* it. Clearly, she does not know what this rune means. Marigold cannot take her eyes away from the tattoo. What is hidden away in the back of Lottie's mind? What memories of hers hold the key to understanding this? Somehow, Lottie has been able to see the landvættir upon the isle. She has a tattoo to protect her, though she does not know what it means. And most of all, Marigold is beginning to care for her in a way that she shouldn't, in a way that she never expected, and if she did not know it to be impossible, she would think that Lottie cares for her as well.

"What are you thinking?"

Marigold places her hand in the space between her breasts. "I want one."

Lottie raises a brow. "You want what?"

"I want a tattoo. I want a tattoo of a bee in that same spot. I'll pay any price."

Lottie laughs so hard that she brings both of her hands up to her mouth. "You are joking."

"I…" She stumbles over her words as she pretends to still only be looking at Lottie's tattoo. "I think I am serious. Can we do it now? Before I get too scared?"

Lottie looks her up and down and ponders, her smirk widening into a grin. "Okay. Undress, Witch."

Chapter Twenty-Three

This idea is absurd. It's spontaneous, dangerous, and a bunch of other things that she cannot think of right now because if she thinks about it any longer, she will lose the courage to do it. Lottie dons her chemise again and starts readying her supplies on the nightstand in their suite. Marigold pulls the chaise closer to a sconce with a little light. She then unties the ribbons of her light pink dress until it loosens from her form and falls to the ground. Her stay is more difficult to undo, but she manages to slide it off before Lottie approaches.

"And this," Lottie says as she playfully plucks the straps of Marigold's chemise, and her fingernail scratches her shoulder, sending shivers down her entire body.

"I'm nervous."

"Don't be nervous, Mari. The pain isn't nearly as bad as you might think."

"No, I'm not scared of the pain. I'm scared of you seeing me...like this. Seeing all of me...you know..." She motions to her chest, and Lottie laughs.

"You're hardly the first naked woman I've seen."

Blushing, she says, "But you are the first I've seen, and the first whom I'll let see me. And it doesn't help that you're so—"

"So sour?" Lottie interrupts coldly.

She shakes her head and looks down, playing with her necklace. "I was going to say beautiful."

Lottie stiffens at the sudden compliment. "I'm beautiful?"

Her eyes stay on the floor. "The most beautiful girl I've ever seen."

There is a long, silent pause—too long for comfort. Her mind is racing. What did she just say? What on earth is she thinking? She has made a proper fool of herself now.

"I'm sorry, I should not—"

Lottie interrupts her by pulling her into a tight embrace. Their hearts are pounding into each other.

"I feel the same way about you," Lottie says softly into her ear.

Shocked, she tries to pull away, but Lottie doesn't let her. She keeps her tightly in her arms, pressed against her chest.

"You do?" Marigold whispers in disbelief. This was the last thing she expected to hear from anyone, much less Lottie Burke. Being here, being called beautiful, being with the girl who makes her feel something she has never felt so strongly before— it could change things. It could change many impossible things.

"Yes," Lottie says. She runs her hand up Marigold's spine in a soft line until she reaches the top hem of her chemise. Her finger skims the seam, gently touching her skin. She reaches the point of the chemise where the strap meets the bodice, and she pushes it off of Marigold's shoulder. "I want you to let me see you."

When Lottie pulls away, her gaze is wild and hungry. Marigold nearly loses her balance, but she straightens herself quickly. She pulls her chemise over her head and lies down on the chaise, clothed in nothing but cold air and candlelight. Her entire body tightens as she tries to position herself in whatever way might be most flattering. Lottie's eyes roam over her, and her seductive smile grows with every step. She wraps her hands around Marigold's wrists and pulls them upward.

"Rest your arms over your head," Lottie instructs, her tone sharp and warm. Marigold obeys, pulling the skin around her ribs taut. Lottie grabs a wet cloth in one hand to clean the area before the tattoo begins. Marigold sucks in a sharp breath as the cold, wet fabric touches her. Her skin pebbles as Lottie drags it across her sternum. Their eyes lock as Lottie's knuckles graze the underside of her breasts, and the air heats between them.

"Is this okay?"

Marigold nods fervently.

When Lottie finishes, she takes the wet cloth away and grabs a new sharp needle along with a vial of black ink. Hovering over Marigold, she dips the tip of the needle into the ink and takes a breath.

"Be very, very still. And don't distract me more than you already are."

Marigold says nothing—how could she? Her curse and her heart are at war with each other. She knows the nature of her curse—no romantic love of any kind. So, what is all this? Lust? Her imagination? A really, *really* good dream?

The needle pierces Marigold's skin for the first time, and she lets out the slightest whimper.

Lottie moans, her voice hungry. "Don't do that to me, Witch."

"But it hurts."

"It will hurt a lot more if you move. Here," Lottie says as she takes the yellow ribbon out of Marigold's hair, letting her blond curls fall around her shoulders. She places the ribbon against Marigold's lips and says, "Bite on this."

Her lips part, and Lottie uses two fingers to place the ribbon between Marigold's teeth.

"Good girl." Lottie continues with the tattoo, going seamlessly back and forth from the ink to the skin.

She is almost too mesmerized by her rhythm to feel the pain. Almost—but not enough. She definitely still feels the pain. Over and over and over again. Tiny little stings that seem to never end. Every few minutes, she gets a few seconds of peace, and then the needle comes back and it hurts worse than she remembered.

But it's a great distraction from the throbbing between her legs. She aches to touch herself there like she does when she's alone at night.

Lottie takes the smallest moment to reach up to Marigold's forehead and caress her cheek. "You're doing so well for me."

Marigold bites down hard on the ribbon and lets out a real moan.

"Easy, tiger. Almost done." An eternity of pinpricks later, Lottie pulls herself away from her and grabs another wet cloth. With the cloth hovering above the tattoo, she says, "It's going to be very sensitive at first, so do not spit that ribbon out yet."

As soon as the fabric touches her skin, pain shoots through her body and she growls.

"Okay, okay. We're all done."

Marigold fights to catch her breath as Lottie picks up a small mirror from the desk. "Take a look."

She pulls the ribbon from her mouth and takes the mirror from Lottie's hand, angling it toward herself. In the diamond between her breasts sits a small bee, no bigger than a pocket watch. She tries to touch it, but Lottie catches her wrist.

"I wouldn't do that if I were you. I'm going to wrap it up in a moment. I just wanted to know if you like it."

Marigold searches for words. It is beautiful, even better than she could have imagined. It's small, sweet, and perfect. Lottie's talent is otherworldly—better and more impressive than anything she ever saw in Bardshire. She would hug Lottie if her skin was not so tender.

"It's absolutely stunning, Lottie. How much?"

"Consider it a trade for this," she says as she gestures to the spell tied around her neck. Lottie starts wrapping a bandage around her ribs to protect the tattoo, and Marigold says, "Are you telling me that you might actually believe in my magic?"

Lottie pulls the bandage tight and Marigold winces. "Those were not my words. But perhaps I don't mind the idea of a soulmate."

"You've changed your tune quite a bit, Lottie Burke. You are getting dangerously close to admitting you were wrong."

Lottie hands Marigold her chemise. "I didn't say I believe in magic, and I definitely do not believe in any of that nonsense about you being cursed."

"Believe me, I wish that part were not true." She pulls her chemise over her head.

"It's not true, Marigold."

Can she pretend that Lottie is right for a moment? Where would that lead? Maybe giving in to this lust wouldn't destroy her in the end. Or maybe it would, but it could be worth it. She approaches Lottie and stands before her. "And how do you know?"

"Because..." she says as she tucks a blond curl behind Marigold's ear. "Just look at yourself. How could someone not fall in love with you?"

The two of them stare into each other, the candlelight vibrating between them. Marigold adjusts her chemise and touches her hand to her burning cheek. "Do not say things like that to me when you know them not to be true."

"Mari, I mean it. I'm—" Her face suddenly loses all color, and she clasps her hand over her mouth, gagging. "Oh no, I'm going to be sick." She hastens to their private balcony and retches over the side.

Marigold cannot stand the sight or sound of vomiting, so she keeps her distance. "You should have told me you're the type to get seasick. I would have brought something to help you," she says as starts cleaning up Lottie's things.

Lottie, bracing herself on the railing, yells, "I never get seasick," followed immediately by violent heaves.

"I find that hard to believe considering what I am witnessing."

When Lottie starts to quiet, Marigold approaches with a glass of water and a vial of black sage honey. "Honey first, then water. It's not a perfect cure, but it will help."

Lottie clearly doesn't have the energy to fight or object, so she takes her medicine quietly. She lets out a breath of frustration. "I do not know what is happening to me. Headaches, nausea, tension. I have these random bouts of pure misery that I've never experienced before."

"You've been in a new environment for days. You're away

from your normal comforts. You've been drinking. And now you're on a very fast ship. It's all perfectly normal."

Crossing her arms over her chest, she says, "You are not hearing me. I am telling you that this is not normal."

"Then, what do you think the problem is?" She places her hand on her hip.

Lottie wipes her mouth with her forearm. "I do not know, but I am going to figure it out."

Marigold hovers for a moment until the air is too thick to breathe, the tension too heavy to stand. She goes to her bed across the room from Lottie's and lies on her back. Lottie blows out the candles, blanketing the room in perfect darkness. She goes to lie down and steadies her breathing quickly. Marigold thinks that Lottie is asleep until she hears her voice from across the room.

"Glad you like your tattoo."

She turns her body to face Lottie's bed, though she cannot see her through the darkness. "Thank you for giving it to me."

"Happy to," Lottie says.

"Glad you like your spell."

Lottie snorts. "It's not working. I haven't felt anything remotely similar to the feeling that you and August describe."

She sighs. "Give it time." She sounds certain enough, though she does find this concerning. Lottie should have felt something by now, surely. There is not a reasonable explanation for her magic not working. Unless... Lottie doesn't have a soulmate.

But that cannot be possible. Everyone, except a Honey Witch, has to have a soulmate. Even Lottie Burke, who hates everyone around her. Someone is her soulmate. But where are they? And if the spell won't work, how will she find them?

"Mari?"

"Yes?"

"I meant what I said."

"About what?"

Lottie smiles so that you can hear it in her voice. "You're so gorgeous."

She doesn't know how else to respond other than with the truth. "So are you." The moment she says it, shame creeps over her body. If she keeps allowing herself to acknowledge her feelings, or worse, act upon them, she will torture herself. Lust is not enough.

She clears her throat. "Lottie?"

"Yes?"

"We shouldn't get too close."

"What does that mean?"

"I mean, I am cursed. And I do not want to get hurt. So we should just... maintain a respectful distance."

Lottie sits up and releases a breath. "What is a respectful distance?"

"You know," Marigold says as she waves her hands around in an attempt to illustrate her point. "Me here, you there... respectfully."

"Respectfully, I do not think that is what you really want," Lottie says.

"Well, *respectfully*, you do not know me better than I know myself."

"*Respectfully*, I think I do."

Marigold huffs. "*Respectfully*, I am done with this conversation. Good night."

Lottie lets out a breath, but she does not continue the argument. There is nothing more to say.

Chapter Twenty-Four

The morning light is soft through the window of the ship. August is the first up, awakening Marigold and Lottie as he pounds on their door. The two simultaneously leap out of bed in a panic at the banging.

"Rise and shine, ladies." His voice is muffled through the heavy door. "We're pulling into port."

They rush to dress, but as Marigold tries to put on her stay, she yelps out in pain and drops it to the ground.

"Oh, Witch," Lottie says. "That tattoo is going to be sore for a few days."

She looks around—surely, something here might serve as a soft barrier between her rubbed-raw skin and her clothing. Or maybe she has something that could take away the pain altogether.

"What do you think would happen if I put royal jelly over it? That's the salve I used when your lip got stung." She starts to dig through her things, searching for the little jar.

"I think you might actually have a miracle product for tattoo artists there. Let's try it. I need to change the wrapping anyway."

She pulls the jar from a pile of dresses and twists off the lid. She turns away from Lottie as she takes off her chemise and starts undoing the wrapping around her. Suddenly, there is a tug on the bandage from behind, and she feels Lottie's warmth against her back.

"Let me," she says, her voice tickling Marigold's neck. She pauses. "Unless, of course, this would not be 'maintaining a respectful distance,' as you so call it."

Marigold stiffens. "I'm sorry. I'm only trying to do what I think is right."

"Well, what about what I think?" Lottie wraps her arms around Marigold from behind and pulls away the bandages until the tattoo is revealed. "Turn around."

She is wary of letting Lottie see her like this again in the light of day. Lottie called her beautiful only when the darkness shielded her features so much that she could appear to be someone else. Still, she turns.

Slowly.

Lottie's hands hover on her waist, and her eyes fall to Marigold's tattoo. She smiles. "You heal quickly."

"Well, I am a magical witch," she says with a smirk, and Lottie lets out a low laugh.

"Sure you are," she says, her hands burning against Marigold's hips.

Entranced, Marigold loses her grip on the salve and it falls to the ground. The clattering sound pulls Lottie's attention, and her hands, away from Marigold. She kneels to pick up the salve quickly and says, "Sorry about that. Got distracted by my own craftsmanship."

"Right." She laughs awkwardly.

On her knees in front of Marigold, Lottie takes two fingers and dips them into the salve before rubbing it gently into Marigold's sore skin. Marigold cringes at the touch, until Lottie says, "Breathe for me. You're doing well."

Marigold takes a deep breath and tries to exhale all her confusion and worry at once.

Her fears of what could be happening to the spirits of Innisfree.

Her deepening feelings and desires for a girl who could never love her back.

Her stress regarding her sister's wedding that is mere days away.

She tries to let it all go, but it clings to her insides like hardened wax along a taper's edge.

Lottie finishes applying the salve and adds a new layer of bandages around Marigold's waist to keep her tattoo covered. Marigold begins putting her clothes back on and attempts to slip into the stay again. It's not nearly as painful this time as she tightens the ribbons. It still stings, but it's more than bearable. She slides her dress on, and Lottie fastens it at the back.

Lottie's fingers brush up against the smooth skin of her neck, but she does not linger there. Marigold ties her hair in her signature ribbon and helps Lottie into her own dress. It is one she hasn't worn before—blue as the autumn sea, and carefully covering all her tattoos with intricate lace designs. When she is caught staring, Marigold blushes.

"You look nice."

Lottie laughs. "I try. It's not every day you meet a royal family."

"We're not exactly royal, Lottie."

"Your father is as close to royalty as I'll ever meet."

"Well, that's not entirely true. There will be lots of people just as famous as him at the wedding."

Lottie stops. "And I am going to the wedding?"

"Of course you are. Why would you think otherwise?"

"I assumed we would simply wait at your estate during the event," Lottie says. Her breathing starts to quicken, and her mouth gets dry. Marigold can scarcely believe what she is witnessing— Lottie Burke is scared.

"I've never been to a wedding before," Lottie confesses. "I don't know how to dance or speak properly. I'll make a fool out of myself. I'll embarrass you in front of your family, in front of everyone."

"Lottie, I promise you it will be fine. It will be lovely and you'll have a great time." She takes Lottie's hands in hers. "I will not ever leave your side. Respectfully, of course."

Lottie laughs softly. "Promise?"

"I swear it."

Lottie pulls her into a tight embrace. August bangs on the door again, frightening them out of each other's arms. "Ladies, let's go. We've got soulmates to find!"

They gather the rest of their things and finally open the door. Staff are there to carry their things off the ship and escort them to their carriage that is waiting at the end of the dock. The three of them squeeze onto the carriage bench—Marigold, Lottie, then August—and begin the ride to Bardshire.

The estate has changed so much, and yet it is exactly the same. They ride alongside the wrought iron gate that matches the detailing on the balconies. The redbrick of their home is decorated with ivy, and the windows are open and trimmed with white shutters. Autumn has grown over the garden, summer green bleeding from the leaves until they turn gold. Red-tinted trees line the path that leads up to the steps of the estate. Decorators, chefs, and handmaidens are all scattering throughout the grounds readying the place for the wedding.

When they round the path to the front of the house, the carriage stops in front of the steps and a footman opens the door. Marigold freezes.

She cannot do it.

Despite how badly she has missed her family, she cannot face everything she left behind.

"Miss?" the footman says as he waits for her hand.

She picks up her hand from her lap, and it is trembling.

"Mari?" Lottie says. "Are you ready?"

Her bottom lip quivers. "I have not seen them in so long. I do not know what to expect."

"They are going to be thrilled to see you! I recall reading your brother's last letter to you. I know that, at the very least, he will be ecstatic," August says, and she nods, though it hardly calms her nerves.

"No matter what happens," Lottie says, offering her hand, "you will not face it alone. We fall together, remember?"

Her heart melts. When did Lottie become a source of comfort for her? Did it happen slowly, or just now, all at once? She smiles, taking Lottie's hand. "We fall together."

They exit the carriage and walk up the steps. Her anxiety starts to fade as the familiar sights all come into view: the arched marble frieze above the entrance, the gilded handle of the door, the rich scent of dark chocolate as soon as they walk inside.

She expected it all to feel more like a trap—this place she barely escaped from and was foolish enough to return to. But it doesn't, and somehow, that makes it hurt more. It was easy to be away from here when she convinced herself that it would be a nightmare, that they wouldn't even want her to return despite what was said in their letters. Now that she's here, it feels like a home she has neglected for far too long.

She must make up for that.

Lottie has not let go of her hand once. Her hold tightens with every step they take. Thousands of flowers decorate the grand staircase. The household staff gushes over her return in every room, but she has yet to run into a member of her family. Marigold's heart thunders, and her breathing turns into panting as she continues through the massive estate. Who will she see first?

Please, God, do not let it be Mother.

Lottie pauses and brings her other hand to her forehead. "Not now," she mumbles, groaning.

"Another headache, Lots?" August says. "They're becoming nonstop. I'm beginning to get very worried about you."

Lottie drops her hand and turns away, rubbing her temples and taking deep breaths. A few seconds pass and she regains her composure. Slowly, she turns back to Marigold and stares at her with great intensity. Her eyes are bright and wide open, and her lips part slightly, aghast at something. "I think I may know what is causing them."

"What?" August asks.

Before she can respond, Aster, dressed in a cloud of white, rounds the corner and collides with Marigold. Lottie and August step back, giving them space.

"Mari!" she cries as she grabs her sister in a steel embrace. She smells like apples and azaleas. She's older, marked by her sharpened jawline and light brown hair down to her waist. Oh, sweet Aster, she is so perfect and lovely and she is *here*. It is not a dream or a wish or a lie. The two of them sing with happy tears as they hold each other for the first time in so long.

"You are so, so late," Aster scolds, all while keeping Marigold in her unyielding embrace. Aster is right. Marigold should have visited long ago, after Althea passed and before she got so lonely. Here, in Aster's arms, she cannot recall what held her back for so long.

"But I am here now," she says.

Aster pulls her head from Marigold's shoulder and stares at her, taking in all that has changed since they last saw each other. "Thank you. I couldn't do this without you."

She wipes a tear from her cheek. "I would not let you."

Aster presses her forehead against hers. "Shall we go find Frankie?"

"What about Frankie?" Frankie says as he rounds the corner, tossing an apple up into the air and catching it over and over. When he sees Marigold, the apple drops to the ground and bounces like a croquet ball.

"Oh my, Mari!" He runs to her, picking her up and spinning her until she feels sick. He is much stronger than before, and he has grown an extraordinary amount, although he still is not as tall as August. When her feet hit the ground, she loses her balance and stabilizes herself on Frankie's shoulders. She then takes his face in her hands. There is stubble there for the first time. His cheeks have lost their youth, granting him exceptionally sharp cheekbones and their father's jawline. He's so grown-up. Did he always grow this much in a year? Or was he saving up his age, keeping it in a bottle just to drink it down the moment she left?

"I missed you so much," she manages to say. She steps back,

taking in the full view of her siblings. "How dare you both grow up so much without me."

"You've changed more than both of us combined," Aster says, moving her gaze to August and Lottie. "And you have lost all your good manners. You must introduce us to your companions!"

Marigold motions to bring them forward, noticing that August's gaze is locked on Frankie. He walks up to him slowly, as if in a trance.

"Aster, Frankie, this is my friend August Owens."

"August Owens," Frankie repeats back. There is a certain heaviness in the air, as if fate has come to pass in this very room.

"A pleasure to meet you," August says, eyes wide and burning.

"A pleasure to make your acquaintance as well, Mr. Owens. And who might you be?" Aster asks as she turns to Lottie. Lottie makes her way to Marigold's side immediately, urgently, as if she could not spend another moment out of her reach.

"This is Lottie Burke," Marigold says, and Lottie's eyes are ablaze with panic. She fiddles with her skirt, as if she should— what, curtsy? Shake hands? But Aster gracefully bows her head in a friendly nod, and Lottie quickly follows suit.

"Nice to meet you," she says.

"You as well," Aster says, her knowing gaze flickering between them.

Marigold blushes. "Let me get my friends settled and then I'll find you. Frankie, why don't you show August to his room? He's staying in the blue room next to yours."

"I'd be delighted," he says, extending his hand to him. August is quick to take it, and the two round the corner and their footsteps sound up the stairs.

When she is certain they are out of earshot, Marigold tells Aster, "I believe I may have made my first love match. August asked for a spell to find his soulmate, and it compelled him to come with me to Bardshire. I think I know why."

Lottie's eyes widen. "You think that Frankie is August's soulmate?"

"Did you see the way they looked at each other then? This could be it."

"Oh, how wonderful! Mari, you should have seen him on the day of the proposal. Moping everywhere like a sad little puppy." She places the back of her hand on her forehead and does a terrible impression of Frankie, saying, "Oh, I'll never find anyone; don't rub your love in my face; why couldn't I be the one with the love curse and the marvelous magic?"

She and Lottie both stiffen at the mention of the curse. Lottie nudges her slightly, one of those *I-must-speak-with-you* nudges that no one else can detect.

"Aster, excuse us as I show Miss Burke to her room. I'll return swiftly. Oh, and"—she leans in, whispering—"where is Mother?"

"She and Father are out picking up a few things for the wedding. They will return soon."

"Right."

Aster cants her head. "Do not get all panicky like you tend to do. She will be happy to see you. I promise."

With a deep breath, she nods and takes Lottie's hand, leading her up the stairs to her room. She opens the white door to reveal red damask walls and a luxurious golden bed, a desk that matches, and a gilded oval mirror in the corner. The gold curtains pool on the parquet wood floor. Members of the household staff follow, carrying Lottie's belongings and arranging them neatly in the room. Lottie chews her lip, clearly anxious and aching for a moment alone with Marigold.

Likely because the woman regrets coming here. It's all too much, too far, too fanciful and different for her. She'll ask Marigold for the first carriage back to the ship, and she'll disappear. When the staff leaves, Marigold braces herself for heartbreak.

Lottie starts pacing back and forth and pinching her brows.

"What is it?" she asks.

"I have a theory," she says, still pacing. She rubs her hand along her forehead.

"About the headaches?"

"Yes, all of it. The headaches. The nausea. The sudden bouts of rage, or 'sourness' as you love to call it," she says, punctuating every word with dramatic hand motions. "I may be wrong. But I must test it." She walks up to Marigold and cups her cheek. "Do you trust me, Witch?"

Her breath hitches as she nods.

"I must warn you, this will not involve a respectful distance. Is that okay?"

She nods again, her heart racing.

"Okay." Lottie leaves one hand on her cheek and threads the other through her hair. She leans in, brushing her nose against Marigold's softly. Then Lottie kisses her.

It's delicate, desperate, it's the universe meeting itself for the first time. It is everything and still not enough. Marigold reaches up and touches Lottie's face. The woman's skin is too soft, like a kitten or a flower or some other thing that is too easily killed. Their kiss deepens, and she pushes Lottie's sleeve off of her shoulder, caressing her collarbone and feeling the first of her scars. It ignites a protective instinct within Marigold. She will do anything to keep Lottie safe. Anything to make sure that Lottie never gets hurt again. She wants to bite her, swallow her, keep her hidden behind her heart so no one else can touch her.

Suddenly, Lottie pulls away, and it feels like a blade being ripped from a wound. The woman falls back on the bed, her body convulsing violently, her eyes rolling back until only the whites are visible. She's gasping for air and choking on it. Blood streams from her nose and her skin turns white as bone.

Marigold races to her side, pulling her up to a sitting position and grabbing her chin. "Lottie? Lottie, what's happening?"

Lottie's eyes are wild and glassy as they find her. She tries to speak, but no sound comes.

"What do you need? I'll do anything." She starts to stand, intent on finding honey to help her, but Lottie does not let her go. Marigold holds her, rocking her back and forth until her breathing starts to calm and her body is barely shaking. It feels like they have been there for hours, maybe days.

"Fuck," Lottie finally whimpers, bringing a trembling hand to her face and wiping the blood from her lip. "It is real."

"What's real?"

Exhaustion is creeping over Lottie. She slowly sinks into the bed, curling into herself.

"Everything." Her eyes cannot stay open any longer. With the very last of her energy, she says, "Your magic. Your curse. It is real."

Chapter Twenty-Five

She spends an hour watching Lottie's every breath, counting the seconds between them. Lottie's suffering is the work of the curse. It must be. When they come together, when their hearts collide, she gets sick. It all starts to make sense now, almost perfectly, minus a few missing pieces. When she is confident that Lottie is safe and recovering, Marigold silently steps out of the room. She tiptoes down the hall and walks into her own room to find her mother waiting there on the bed.

They lock eyes. Should she speak?

No, her mother should speak first. She is the one who never truly responded to her letter. She exhales, drops her shoulders, and waits. Her mother stands, approaching slowly, her steps cutting through the silence.

"Hello, Mari, darling," her mother says. She almost reaches for Marigold's hand but pauses. "I have missed you so much," she says through broken sobs, and Marigold cannot hold back anymore. In her mother's arms, she collapses.

"I've missed you more." Her head is buried in her mother's shoulder. "I'm so, so sorry for how I left."

"So am I," her mother says, stroking her hair. "I never should've hidden anything from you. I should have told you the truth from the beginning. I should've…" She pulls back and holds Marigold's arms. "I should have done *everything* differently, Marigold."

"I'm starting to feel the same way." She buries her face in her hands. Her mother wraps her arms around her and leads them both to the edge of the bed.

She releases a shaky breath. "Frankie sent me your unfinished letter."

Her mother looks surprised, but then she sighs. "I should have expected nothing less from him. And in truth, I should have sent one in the first place."

"I wish you did."

Her mother strokes her cheek and wipes away her tears. "Which letter did he send? I started many."

"The one that said that there are still truths I do not know."

Her mother nods and takes off her glove, revealing the scars across her hand. "This burn is from that day. From that witch who tried to kill you."

Marigold traces the burn scar with her finger.

"I'll never forget seeing this unnatural bolt of pure fire coming for you. Your little legs couldn't move fast enough. You froze there in front of the window, and I had to pull you out. I didn't even feel the pain when it happened, but I looked down at my hand to see nothing but blood and bone." Her lip trembles as she looks at Marigold's face. "That could've been you. It terrifies me to this day. That vision that my imagination created. You, and blood, and bone."

"But you saved me," she says with hardly any air left in her lungs.

"That's all I ever wanted to do. Save you from her. Marigold, that day awakened something in me. A rage I never knew I could possess. In that moment, I would have forgone everything I had in order to keep you safe. I asked your grandmother then if I could change my mind, give up my love so I could have my magic again and fight for you."

Perhaps she recognizes that protective rage—she felt it with Lottie as they kissed, like she would burn the world and everyone in it if it meant keeping her safe.

"You would have given up Father?"

She winces. "If it meant keeping you safe, yes. I would've given anything. Even my own life." Rage flickers in her mother's eyes. "I wanted to kill that woman. I wanted to rip her apart. And it killed me to know that I had given up the power I needed in order to do so." Shaking her head, she continues, "Don't misunderstand me, I love your father with all that I am. He is my soulmate. But you, you are our *child*. You and your siblings are our entire world. We love you in an entirely different way that words cannot express, and we would both give all that we have in order to protect you."

"I love you both so much. That's why it hurt to leave. It hurt to write. It hurt knowing that I had gone against all that you had done for me."

Her mother smiles. "No more of that. I am so proud of you. You did what was right for you."

She shakes her head. "I do not know if I did."

"Why?"

"I met someone." Her lip trembles. "Someone who cannot love me the way I want them to, and it's my fault."

"Is this the man you brought here with you?"

"No, it's—" She pauses. "How did you know I brought anyone with me?"

Her mother gives her a knowing look. In unison, they say, "Aster and Frankie."

Of course.

"It's not August," she continues. "It's the woman. Her name is Lottie. At first, I thought it merely lust, but now—" She stops herself. "Forgive me, I should not talk of such matters with you."

"Oh, nonsense. I do have three children, you know. I am no stranger to this."

She clears her throat. "Somehow, the woman is resistant to the curse. Not entirely immune, but able to withstand it to an extent."

"I don't know if that's possible, Mari," her mother says slowly with pity in her eyes.

Marigold crosses her arms. "I would agree with you if she hadn't just kissed me."

Mouth agape, her mother says, "Well, that changes things."

Her mother stands and looks around, as if to ensure that no one is listening. Force of habit from living among such notorious gossips for so long. "Maybe the fairy tales are right."

Marigold perks up. Her ears twitch like a cat's. "What do you mean?"

"You know how they all end. Perhaps any curse can be broken by true love."

"Lottie doesn't *love* me," she says with an incredulous laugh, followed by a sharp pain in her chest. It hurts to have said it aloud.

Her mother shrugs. "Maybe not yet. But if what you say is true, if she can resist the curse and acts as though she cares for you, then maybe there is hope. She's already doing what we thought was impossible. Who knows what could happen next?"

Breaking the curse is a thrilling thought, but one met with many logical objections. Her head is spinning wildly, her pulse quickening so much so that her vision blurs. "I think Grandmother would warn against this kind of talk. She was very adamant that the curse was unbreakable."

"Your grandmother would want you to be happy. She would want you to follow your heart. And if there was a possibility that you could break this damned curse," she says, touching Althea's emerald ring that Marigold wears as a necklace, "she would want you to try."

Perhaps her mother would think differently if she knew what happened when she and Lottie got too close. It wasn't safe. But maybe it was worth it.

Wrapping her arms around her mother, she says, "Thank you, Mother. For everything. And for loving me, even when I didn't deserve it."

"You always deserve love, Mari. Always."

Marigold quietly enters Lottie's room, careful not to disturb her in case she is still sleeping. Luckily, she is awake, and she rushes to Marigold's side as soon as the door closes behind her.

"There you are," she says with relief. "I have been pacing for what feels like an eternity, but I know this place is a maze so I did not dare venture out. We have much to discuss."

"Indeed, we do," Marigold says. "The curse—"

"I have it all figured out," Lottie interrupts. "I have feelings for you. I believe I have had them since the first time I saw you, because that is when all this started." She speaks of her feelings academically like she is discussing an equation. "You got out of the carriage with your grandmother, and your face...it made me feel..."

Lottie pauses, waving her hands around like she is riffling through the air in search of the right word. Marigold's very soul is on fire.

"Made you feel what?" Enchanted, perhaps? That is how Marigold felt.

"Nauseous," Lottie finally says with a massive grin. "Absolutely disgusted. I could have been sick right then and there all over your dress."

She crosses her arms, deflated. "How lovely of you to say."

"No, this is good, Mari!" Lottie takes her hands.

"It is good that my face makes you physically ill?" she asks, brows raised.

Lottie's lips press into a thin line. "It is not your face, you impossible girl. It is your curse. That is what it has been all along. When I try to act on my feelings, it is immediately followed by pain and the smell of salt and smoke. I know now that scent means magic. I could recognize it anywhere." She is nearly leaping with excitement as she speaks.

"That's not how it's supposed to be," Marigold says, throwing her arms up in frustration. "You shouldn't be able to feel anything for me at all. Are you certain it's not simply lust?"

Defensively, Lottie says, "It's more than that. I know it." She reaches for Marigold's hand, sending shivers up her spine.

"It makes no sense," Marigold says, palming her forehead in confusion. "It's as if you are defying the curse, and it's punishing you for it."

"What else is there to understand? It simply doesn't affect me the way you thought it would, and that's a good thing."

"But why you? How are you resistant to it?" Her mind wanders to the night she saw Lottie's tattoo on her sternum—the rune of protection. Could that be it?

Lottie interrupts her thoughts and says, "Don't you see, Marigold? Now that we know what causes it, perhaps we can outsmart it."

"How might that work? We draw the curtains and blow out all the candles so that it cannot see us in the darkness?" she chides. "We cannot hide from this."

"I know that. But you see, every time we try, we get a little bit further. Before, I could not look at your face without feeling like death. And now I am holding your hand and my head is only throbbing slightly!" She squeezes her hand and leans in. "Let us try, Marigold. Let us see how far we can go."

"Lottie, that is so dangerous. I will not risk your safety. You did not see what I saw. You, lying on the bed, convulsing like you were being strangled. Your body looked broken."

"It is my body to break if I so wish! Please, Mari. Please do not deny me. I want to try. For you." She wraps her arm around her waist. "For this."

She looks deep into Lottie's green eyes as if she is trying to read a book while the pages are turning too fast. She takes a breath and touches Lottie's hand at her waist.

"I cannot deny you. But will you allow us to wait until our return to Innisfree? I don't want the curse to hurt you here when I don't have all that I may need to heal you. It scares me." Beyond that, Innisfree needs to be healed first. If the isle continues weakening, they could be vulnerable to an Ash Witch attack. She could lose everything and be forced to come back to Bardshire, powerless and alone.

"I'm not scared," Lottie says, tightening her arms around Marigold. "I'm yours."

As a light gasp escapes Marigold's lips, a bell rings throughout the estate to signal dinner. She blinks, letting Lottie's words echo in her mind. Squeezing Lottie's hand that rests on her waist, she says, "And I am yours."

Chapter Twenty-Six

The table has someone at every seat; the Lord and Lady Claude sit at opposite ends. Frankie, August, and Mr. Woodrake sit along one side, while Marigold, Lottie, and Aster sit along the other.

"It's so lovely to have you all here," Marigold's mother says.

"A toast," her father says as he stands and raises his glass. "To my lovely daughter and her betrothed. May life award you years of happiness and peace. And," he continues, turning to Marigold, "a toast to Marigold's first return to Bardshire, and her new lovely friends. Thank you all for being here to celebrate with our family. We welcome you."

Everyone raises their glasses and sips softly. It takes Lottie only a moment to catch on and replicate the movement. August seems to be acclimating quickly, and Marigold imagines that Frankie must have given him a lesson or two in high society behavior during their time together. She regrets that she did not do the same for Lottie, as this dinner will be very involved. At least six courses: a soup, a fish, and four entrées. And, of course, puddings. It would not be a Claude dinner without puddings.

"Father," Marigold says, turning to him. "I should mention that Miss Burke is a fan of your work."

Her father beams and clasps his hands together. "I am beyond honored to hear that."

"She is quite an artist herself," August chimes.

"Really? What is your medium of choice, Miss Burke?"

Lottie freezes and looks at Marigold, panic in her eyes. She takes a deep breath and clears her throat. "I have a few mediums I enjoy, but I am working on improving my skills with simple charcoal and paper."

"Wonderful! Drawing with charcoal is deceptively difficult, wouldn't you agree?"

"Very much," Lottie says.

"I would love to see your work during your visit. Maybe you can teach me a thing or two. Would that suit you? Perhaps sometime tomorrow?"

Lottie exhales softly, as if in disbelief. "I would be honored, though I can't imagine I will be able to teach you anything."

"Nonsense," Lord Claude says. "We're both artists in our own right, and I have as much to learn from you as you could learn from me. I'm quite excited!"

"As am I," Lottie says, and Marigold gives her an encouraging nod.

The first course comes, and everyone grabs the proper utensil to enjoy the piping-hot butternut squash bisque—except for Lottie. She stares at the array of forks and spoons and knives before her, and her eyes look almost glassy. Aster leans over and whispers, "Start from the outside and work your way inward as the new courses come." Marigold catches Aster's eye quickly and she smiles in thanks.

There is mild conversation over the soup—the weather, the wedding, the plans for the days leading up to it. Aster and Mr. Woodrake sought out a special license that would allow them to wed at the Claude estate rather than the church. The church is fine enough, but very few places can rival the beauty of their own garden.

The soup is taken away and replaced with a delicate fish as Aster babbles on and on about her dress.

"You'll have to go to the modiste first thing tomorrow for a fitting, Marigold," Aster says. Marigold almost protests, but this is her sister's wedding. She must have a new dress that actually fits properly, and she can't wear one of the casual dresses that she has been living in while on the isle. So she simply nods and shoves a huge bite into her mouth.

"You will go as well, Lottie. The modiste will make you a new gown for the occasion. I'm thinking emerald green with black lace. You will look lovely."

She nearly chokes on her fish. Lottie cannot have a fitting with the modiste without revealing all of her tattoos.

Oh no. She forgot, until this moment, that she now has a tattoo to hide as well. They look at each other with wide eyes, unsure of what to do. Both of them absolutely require a dress for the event, but they have an important secret to hide from the most notorious gossip in town. Wary of leaving the silence for too long, Marigold says, "Lovely."

She leans close to Lottie and whispers, "We'll figure something out. Don't worry."

Lottie does not look fully relieved yet, but the next course comes before any further conversation about it can continue.

"Marigold," Frankie says, "I intend to show your friend August the pleasure gardens tomorrow evening. Would you and Lottie like to join?"

"Pleasure gardens?" Lottie asks.

She nods. "They're sort of like parks, only with more entertainment. There's a garden maze, gorgeous statues, and many other surprises."

"And tomorrow is the masquerade," Frankie says.

She stiffens. "Is it? I forgot about that." She did always enjoy the masquerade and its delicious proximity to trouble—not that she ever did anything scandalous. It was simply a thrill to know that around any corner could be an adventure with a masked stranger. After she and George ended, she'd always hoped she might find someone who interested her, but she never did.

Until now.

Bringing Lottie to the masquerade sounds like a dream, but

with her curse still intact, it could be a nightmare. Who knows what they might get up to with champagne in their blood and masks hiding their truths? If they go too far too fast, Lottie could wind up seizing in the middle of a waltz.

"This will be your first masquerade, right, Frankie?" Aster says.

"Yes, and I'm sure it will be the best one yet for us all." He looks at August, his gaze unmistakably excited for what is to come.

"Will you two be joining us?" Marigold asks Aster and Mr. Woodrake, but Aster shakes her head.

"I'm afraid we will be far too busy. But you all should go," she says with her words aimed toward Lottie. "You'll love it."

The following courses come and go—rich savory meats, hearty fresh vegetables, and decadent sauces that decorate the plates. The tablecloth is removed and replaced with heaps of puddings. Servers pile up everyone's dishes with a little bit of everything. Marigold and Frankie are the first to dive in, neither able to resist a dessert for long.

"You haven't changed at all, Marigold," her mother says, laughing, and then she looks to Lottie. "I want to thank you personally, Miss Burke, for keeping my daughter company. You as well, Mr. Owens. We are very grateful for you both."

August smiles. "It is we who should be thanking you. We are so lucky to be surrounded by so much love."

"Yes, thank you very much," Lottie says, but Lady Claude waves it away.

"You owe me no thanks. Please allow our family to care for you all as long as you would like to stay."

Marigold smiles softly. She had not forgotten how lovely her family is, but it is always nice to be reminded that one has kindhearted people in their corner. After every crumb of dessert has been devoured, everyone moves to the sitting room to enjoy some entertainment.

Aster plays a sweet song on the piano, and she then sings a lovely duet with her betrothed. Then Frankie makes a cruel suggestion.

"Why don't you sing for us, sister?"

Marigold glares at him, but her father seizes the conversation. "Oh, please do, darling. We have missed your singing voice so much."

"I'm quite tired, Father."

"Just one song?" he says.

She sighs. She cannot say no to him, no matter how much she detests singing in front of people. She sits beside her sister in front of the piano as Aster plays a soft ballad. Her voice fills the room, falling from note to note until the melody finishes.

No one claps. They all simply stare. She sees August and Lottie looking at each other with great concern. She stands and walks back over to Lottie.

"You're not very good at that, are you?" Lottie says, intending to whisper but failing to do so. The entire room hears her comment, and Frankie is the first to erupt in laughter.

"Stop it!" Lady Claude says to her son, but even she cannot help but laugh.

"Dear sister, it remains true that you are the worst singer of Bardshire, and possibly the entire country," Frankie continues.

She pouts until even she must laugh a little. "I don't know why you always make me sing, then."

"Because it is so funny," Aster says. Mr. Woodrake sits snickering beside her, fighting with everything he has to stay polite.

"Come now, everyone, quiet down. There is nothing wrong with my daughter's singing," Lord Claude says, but his smirk says otherwise. "She just always chooses to scream along with the music instead."

The entire room bursts into a cacophony of laughter, some more musical than others. There are a few more minutes of small talk and pleasantries before everyone excuses themselves for the evening.

Marigold, Lottie, and August all find themselves alone in their rooms, nearly collapsing into their beds. The exhaustion from the travel is heavy, and there is no more energy to fight or argue or plan.

Chapter Twenty-Seven

When Marigold wakes up the next morning, she dresses faster than she ever has before and hastens to Lottie's room to get them both prepared for the modiste. She slowly opens the door and pokes her head inside.

"Lottie?"

No answer.

She walks in to find the bed empty and seemingly untouched. Did Lottie run away? She opens the curtains to let in more light and investigates the room. Lottie's things are still here—that's a relief.

"Lottie? Hello?" she asks one last time before leaving the room and closing the door behind her. As she descends the stairs, she finds her mother, Aster, and Mr. Woodrake having tea in the sitting room.

"Good morning, darling," her mother says.

"Morning," she says hurriedly. "Have any of you seen Lottie? We need to get to the modiste."

"I don't believe so," says Aster.

Marigold groans. "All right, thank you anyway." She turns to her sister's betrothed. "A pleasure to see you again, Mr. Woodrake. I'm thrilled to welcome you into our family."

"Thank you so much, miss. Though it seems that we will not be seeing too much of each other. Where is it that you live again? Some island?"

Aster shakes her head. "It's hard to explain, darling. Just let her go."

Marigold nods in understanding—of course, he does not know of Innisfree, nor does he know of her magic. She suspects that Mr. Woodrake would be kind and intrigued by it, but it is best to keep matters as this contained to those who have proven their trust. Who knows what would happen if Bardshire learned that the Claude girl was a witch? Luckily, she will never have to find out. She will return to Innisfree as soon as she can, ensuring that everyone who needs her help may have it.

She walks to August's room and knocks on the door. He opens it enthusiastically, but his smile falls when he sees it is only Marigold.

She laughs. "Hoping for someone else? My brother, perhaps?"

"Maybe," he mumbles.

She giggles and says, "Do you happen to know where Lottie is?"

"Come now, Mari. You know her well enough to guess."

"I don't think so," she says, but August insists, leaning against the doorframe and looking up through his lashes.

"Lottie always struggles to sleep in a new bed. And what does Lottie do when she can't sleep?"

She ponders before she says, "She draws."

"And where does Lottie like to go while she draws?"

"Outside?"

"And who is her favorite artist who paints the gardens of his home, which happen to be the same gardens that are currently outside her bedroom window?"

"Of course," she says, palming her forehead. "She's in the gardens."

"There you go," August says.

Marigold runs down the stairs, through the door, and into the gardens, where she finds Lottie sitting against an apple tree sketching the world around her. To her surprise, beside Lottie is her father, peering over Lottie's shoulder and attempting to draw in a sketchbook of his own.

"Good morning, you two," she says.

"Hello, darling!" her father says. "I must say, Miss Burke here is an exceptional talent."

Marigold tilts her head to the side as she stares at her with admiration. "She is, isn't she?"

"Stop it," Lottie says as she laughs softly and tucks a wild red lock behind her ear.

"We shall not! You have a gift that needs to be celebrated!" Lord Claude says.

Lottie smiles and looks up at him. "I cannot even begin to tell you what an honor it is to hear that from you. Thank you, truly."

"The honor is mine," he replies as he walks to his daughter's side and gives her a hug. "I shall be in my study practicing some of the new techniques I've learned this morning if anyone should require my presence." Once he walks up the stairs and into their home, Marigold turns to Lottie and says, "You must allow me to see your sketchbook now."

"It's not finished yet."

"You said that last time!" Marigold takes the sketchbook out of Lottie's hand. "I'm afraid I can wait no longer."

Lottie is fast, but not fast enough. Marigold clutches the book to her chest and runs out of the garden with Lottie trailing behind.

"Give that back!"

Marigold narrowly escapes out the gardens and runs through the trees. "I will if you can catch me!"

Lottie hesitates, unaware of the new surroundings, but pushes forward. She is only a few steps behind Marigold, but she cannot seem to get a grip on her. When she gets the slightest grasp on her elbow, Marigold elegantly twists herself out of it and continues to run away. But Lottie doesn't tire and Marigold must resort to other tactics of escape. She takes sharp turns until the two seem to be waltzing through the trees together. Even still, she slips through Lottie's fingers like summer air, weaving between the tall trees before they taper into an open meadow.

Here, Marigold stops. She had no intention of leading Lottie

to her meadow, a place that she intended on keeping secret—
sacred, even—for her and her grandmother alone.

Frozen still, with the sketchbook held to her chest, Marigold
feels entirely exposed. Lottie takes advantage of her state and
snatches the book out of her hands. She begins to run through
the field before realizing that Marigold is not chasing her back.

Lottie tries to catch her breath. "Are you quite well?"

She stares back at her with wide eyes but says nothing.

"Mari," she says, her tone taking a serious turn. "What is it?"

"I didn't mean to bring you out here."

Lottie looks around at the meadow before her, taking in the
beauty of it all. She moves closer to Marigold, keeping her sketchbook close, as if she suspects this is all a clever ruse that Marigold
is playing just to take the book again. "Where is here, exactly?"

Her jaw feathers and her eyes shut tightly for a moment. "This
is where my grandmother and I performed my ritual to become a
witch. This is the last place she saw before we left."

"Oh, Mari, I'm sorry…"

"It's my fault," she interrupts. "I was being silly with all that
nonsense, taking your sketchbook."

Lottie looks upon the field, then back at Marigold, who is lost
in the vision of the wildflowers swaying in the wind. She then
opens the book, the thick parchment making the most satisfy-
ing crinkle. She pulls a piece of charcoal from the pocket of the
book and begins to draw.

At the sound of coal scratching on paper, Marigold glances at
her. "What are you doing?"

"Don't move," she says.

"What?"

"Shh. Don't speak."

Marigold stands in silence, listening to the wind carry the
sound of scribbling charcoal on dry parchment. She finds a
moment of peace, of calm, of stillness. They have the entire
world waiting on tenterhooks for what they might do next.

"Almost done," Lottie says. Marigold remains perfectly still—a trait she mastered sitting for many portraits. When Aster was first learning the art of the brush, she would always practice on Marigold. Every time she would move, Aster would threaten to splash her with paint-stained water and ruin her dress. She followed through with it once, peppering splashes of bright blue across Marigold's new white gown. Their mother did not allow Aster to paint again for an entire season, and her artistic skill never truly recovered. She is as good at painting as Marigold is at singing—that is to say, not very.

"And, finished," Lottie says as she turns the book around. "This is the face you make when you speak of your grandmother."

Marigold stares at herself on the paper, thinned into a graphite line of every truth she had been trying to hide. She sees her own eyes for the first time, swelling with love and light, with memories and dreams. This drawing is a reminder to her that this is the girl her grandmother would want her to be—happy.

"You're smiling," Lottie says, and Marigold touches her own cheek.

"I didn't realize," she says.

Lottie's eyes soften. "I know it is certainly not the best portrait of yourself you've ever gotten, what with you being a Bardshire lass and all. But I feel like it was a moment worth capturing. A moment with her," she says.

Marigold looks back at the open meadow and feels the embrace of the air.

Yes, a moment with her. Althea is here now, in the yellow flowers.

"Lottie, it is by far the best artwork I've ever possessed." Lottie shakes her head, but Marigold insists. "You have true talent." She starts to flip through the book but stops herself. "May I look through it?"

Lottie contemplates for a moment before surrendering. "Yes, but I have a confession to make first."

Marigold nods and Lottie stutters through her response. "This may not be the first time I've drawn you."

Marigold turns red as a summer rose. Slowly, she flips through the pages of the book, working from the back to the front.

There is a drawing of her in her kitchen, wearing her patterned apron and yellow ribbon in her hair.

There is another of her playing with Cindershine in the living room. Another of her in the apiary, surrounded by a halo of bees.

Then, there are drawings of Innisfree. The trees, the birds, the night sky with striking constellations.

Then, the spirits—Odessa, Talaya, Chesha, Yliza.

"You drew the spirits," Marigold says, her voice soft with surprise.

Eyes wide, Lottie says, "I thought they were merely strange animals native to the isle."

"They're called landvættir, and they protect the isle. Somehow, you can see them."

Lottie takes her sketchbook back. "Am I not supposed to?"

Marigold shakes her head. "They live beyond the veil. Perhaps it's exceptionally thin on Innisfree, and you are quite perceptive. Still, it's strange." It's equally strange to witness Lottie react with calm curiosity toward anything magic. Normally, the woman would've been rolling her eyes the entire time.

"Well, I'm happy I can see them. They're lovely to draw," Lottie says.

"You captured them perfectly. You are such an incredible artist, Lottie. I've never seen anything so perfect."

Lottie blushes, unable to handle so many compliments. "Shall we return? God knows what August will get up to if he is left alone too long."

"Right, of course."

With a final parting glance at the meadow, Marigold leads Lottie back to the house. Before they go inside, Lottie stops.

"What was your grandmother's name? I only know her as the Honey Witch, but she was so much more than that, wasn't she?"

Marigold sighs, smiling. "Her name was Althea."

"Beautiful," Lottie says.

"She was." She looks at the ground, and right at her feet, there is an omen. An ivy leaf with six points; someone is about to fall in love.

Chapter Twenty-Eight

The carriage ride through Bardshire is smooth and sunny. There are tall, colorful shops selling anything imaginable, and the air smells of too many horses. Marigold points out various sites to Lottie and tells her the most salacious stories of the people they pass by.

"That is Lady Covington," she says, pointing to an older woman in a bright orange gown and a very dramatic feathered hat. "She's been married three times, as her husbands kept mysteriously dying."

"She's a killer?"

"We'll never know for sure. But now she's extraordinarily wealthy and enjoying her fourth marriage—this time, with a woman. See?"

Another woman in a bright teal dress comes beside Lady Covington and takes her by the arm. They wear each other proudly as they stroll through the streets.

"They make a beautiful couple. If she is a husband killer, I cannot say I blame her."

Marigold jokingly flicks her fan against Lottie's hand. "Now, Miss Burke. We cannot condone murder."

"But it's so romantic, Miss Claude." She lays the back of her hand against her forehead and pretends to swoon. She exaggerates a breathless voice when she says, "All is fair in love and war. The poets say so."

"I've met enough poets to know that they are all afraid of a real fight." She keeps her eyes peeled for George. He must be around here somewhere, parading his wife.

Shaking her head, she says, "As you can see, this whole place is rife with gossips—"

"Yourself included," Lottie adds.

She giggles and bumps Lottie with her shoulder. "Oh, I haven't gossiped in so long. Allow me to indulge! They make it too easy with their love affairs and gambling debts and the like. But as I was saying, there are many gossips, and word travels fast. We must be careful keeping our tattoos hidden."

"We could bribe the modiste to keep it a secret," Lottie suggests.

"A bribe may only make it more scandalous."

"Well, what do you suggest?"

"I think mine will be easy enough to hide beneath my stay, but for you, we will simply insist that she take your measurements over your dress. She will press us for information, I assure you. Give her nothing."

"What would she do if she saw?" Lottie swallows hard.

"Do not even think of it. She will not see a thing."

The driver stops the carriage and opens the door, helping them descend. The modiste shop is blessedly empty. Madame Genevieve eagerly greets them both at the door.

"Miss Claude, so lovely to see you! My, how long it has been. Where did you run off to?"

"I am here now," she says, dodging her question.

The modiste welcomes them inside. "I have been working on your dress for some time now based on your former measurements. I increased them slightly, per your sister's request, but I am eager to fit it perfectly for you." She turns quickly and pulls the dress out of a pristine protective bag. It is a beautiful shade of dark orange, exactly like that of autumn leaves and peach blossom honey.

"That's lovely." She takes the dress and motions to Lottie.

"Madame, this is Miss Burke. She will also require a dress for the wedding, and perhaps another for the evening ahead."

"Splendid! Lovely to meet you, Miss Burke. From where do you hail?"

Lottie looks at Marigold, who gives the slightest shake of her head. "A small town far from here. Most have not heard of it."

Even that is too much information.

"Ah, is that where you met Miss Claude? That is where the two of you are living? A town so small that you will not speak of it?" The modiste smirks, likely thinking of how she will narrativize this tiny tidbit of information to entertain the town. Perhaps something like *"The talentless Claude girl has been forced away to a nameless village far away from her family. Oh yes, very sad indeed, but would you not have done the same if you were her parents? The girl never belonged here. They knew that as well as any. I believe they did her a favor."*

Lottie stammers as a response. Marigold swoops in and says, "We met some time ago. Pardon me, I must change. Do not speak of anything interesting without me!" she says, a warning to the both of them. In the changing room, she fights to escape her current dress so that she may pull on the new one. It's been so long since she wore anything with such frill. Her favorite dresses now are hardly grander than the chemise she wears underneath. Her gown for the wedding has lace and appliqués and tiny jewels scattered over the whole thing. She cannot reach all the buttons on the back. She emerges and stands on the pedestal in the center of the shop. The gilded oval mirror before her allows her to see every inch of herself, and she is more pleased than she expected. The dress is nearly perfect, with only a small bit of slack in the waist. Madame Genevieve leaves to retrieve her pins while Lottie walks up and starts buttoning the dress, her fingers playfully skimming Marigold's skin.

"What do you think?" she says, looking down at Lottie.

Lottie stares at her all over, her gaze burning. "I think you look perfect." She looks up through her lashes and parts her lips to say something else, but Madame Genevieve returns to her side before Lottie can speak further.

"As for you, Miss Burke," she says as she pins Marigold's dress, "there are limitations as to what I can provide on such short notice. Go and undress quickly so that I may take your measurements and assess what I can offer."

Marigold turns, getting herself poked in the rib with a tiny needle. She yelps before saying, "Shall we save time by simply taking her measurements now with her clothes still on? We are all in quite a rush, are we not?"

"Nonsense. There is always time for proper measurements." Madame Genevieve gestures to the changing room. "Miss Burke, please."

Quickly, Marigold steps off the pedestal and walks to the many dress forms toward the back of the shop. There are a few dresses that should do well to cover Lottie's tattoos—a white one with red appliqué, a solid black one with intricate opaque lace sleeves, and an emerald green gown made of heavy satin.

"Are these complete, Madame? Lottie can choose from these." She motions for Lottie to come to her side and softly explains the details of the gowns.

"She must still be fitted properly," Madame Genevieve calls after a few moments. "I will not have my designs worn incorrectly."

"Of course." She takes Lottie's two choices off the dress forms. The modiste moves swiftly over to help her, ensuring that Marigold does not damage the garments with her lack of delicacy.

Marigold hands the dresses to Lottie. "She may take them into the changing room and try them on, and you can fit them to her form then. Yes?"

Sighing, Madame Genevieve says, "Of course, miss."

The first that Lottie tries on is the emerald green. When she steps out, time stops moving. Her beauty is lethal. She looks to be floating as she moves through the shop and steps up on the pedestal.

She sees herself in the mirror and runs her hand along the fine fabric. Tugging at the sleeves and the collar, she says, "I worry that this is too much."

The modiste hurries over. "I beg your pardon?"

"It's perfect," Marigold interjects before Madame Genevieve gets too defensive. "It hardly requires much alteration. Wear this one to the wedding."

Lottie turns and looks over her shoulder to see the back of the dress in the mirror. "Do you think it will look good next to yours?" She's asking about much more than color coordination. She's asking if she will be left alone at the wedding, or if Marigold will keep her word and stay by her side.

"You will look perfect next to me."

Lottie smiles, relieved. The modiste pins a few places before ushering Lottie back into the changing room to try on the second dress.

"I cannot do much to this dress before the masquerade tonight. If it does not fit, we will have to find a different garment. I have some lovely gowns from the summer season, and they—"

"I am sure that this one will work," Marigold interrupts.

"It is a bit tight," Lottie calls. "I am doing my best."

The modiste turns sharply on her heels and walks toward other gowns, pulling a light blue dress with short puffy sleeves and butterfly appliqués. "Why don't we try this one? It will look perfect with your red hair, Miss Burke."

"That is truly unnecessary," Marigold says, rushing to barricade the entrance to Lottie's changing room. But she is not fast enough. She is a few steps away when Madame Genevieve opens the curtain and reveals Lottie, halfway into the dress, with her chest and shoulders exposed.

Lottie's jaw drops as she wraps her arms around herself.

"Oh, my word!" Madame Genevieve's eyes roam over Lottie's body. Marigold steps in between them and closes the curtain.

"You saw *nothing*," she says sharply, leaning in close to Madame Genevieve and baring her teeth. "You will alter the dresses and you will say nothing to anyone. Understood?"

Her smirk is devilish. "Oh, but, Miss Claude, I must. I cannot aid in covering a crime."

She steps even closer, puffing up her chest. "Your eyes are playing tricks on you, Madame. It must be your age. You saw nothing but lace decorating her skin."

The modiste narrows her eyes and purses her lips. "I saw a girl with sailor markings whom I have no reason to protect."

Her grimace deepens. "What can we do to change that?"

Madame's smirk widens into a wicked grin. "I do believe I have yet to share with you my amended pricing. The cost of dresses has gone up significantly since you left."

She should have expected no less than blackmail from this woman. "How much?"

"Forty pounds," she says.

Marigold swallows hard. That's twice the amount it should cost for these four dresses.

"Each," she continues.

She gasps. "You are mad."

"That is nothing compared to the fine for such a crime."

She is right, and Marigold is livid with both the modiste and herself. She failed to protect Lottie, and now she must pay the price.

Through gritted teeth, she says, "It seems I have no choice but to accept."

"Excellent. You will pay before you leave, and you may have them picked up in a few hours' time." She extends her open palm. "It has been so lovely doing business with you, Miss Claude."

In any other circumstances, a handmaiden would have been sent to retrieve their dresses. But this time, Marigold goes alone. She walks into the shop silently, holding a slice of fresh honey cake on a small porcelain plate. The honey is peach blossom from her own apiary, along with a few other ingredients that, when combined, create a perfectly vicious spell.

"Miss Claude, I did not expect you. I assure you, you need not worry." She dangles her heavy change purse and drops it onto the counter. "I will respect our arrangement."

"I came to apologize for my behavior earlier," she says. "I brought you a piece of the wedding cake to make amends. It is from the finest patisserie in all of Bardshire."

"Oh, you kind girl. I knew you would come to understand that I was doing you a favor." She takes the cake, and Marigold hands her a small fork.

"Do let me know if you like it. Your opinion is most important."

"Indeed," she says, taking a large bite. She chews for a moment and moans softly. "It is wonderful! And this honey, I have never tasted anything like this! It's so—" Suddenly, she drops the plate and grabs the sides of her head. Her face contorts in pain.

Marigold smiles, feigning innocence. "Are you all right, Madame?"

The modiste groans, stumbling. She braces herself against the counter, where Marigold's dress boxes sit. She looks up slowly. Her eyes are milky white and her expression is dazed.

"Miss Claude..." she says through heavy breathing. "My, I haven't seen you in over a year." The woman blinks rapidly and fans herself. "Forgive me, I seem to be a bit faint. Have you come to be fitted for your sister's wedding?"

Marigold beams. The spell worked perfectly. The woman's memory of the day is destroyed.

"I am here to pick it up, Madame," she says, taking the boxes from the counter. "We spoke of it just now, don't you recall?"

"I..." She looks down at the cake on the floor. "Where did this come from?"

"I am not sure. It was there as I entered. I presumed you had not the time to clean it up."

Confused, the modiste rubs her temples. "My deepest apologies, miss. I must be exhausted from making all these gowns recently."

Madame Genevieve starts toward the back of the shop where a chaise sits against the wall. The woman is truly out of her mind if she cannot manage any prying questions about Marigold's return.

"Not a problem. Now, I must pay you. May I?" she calls, gesturing to the change purse on the counter.

"Oh, yes, it is five pounds," the woman says, lying down on the chaise and resting her hands over her eyes. Her head must be throbbing.

"Perfect," Marigold says, taking back the money that was extorted from her earlier. She is not a thief—she leaves the amount that the dresses should have cost. Everything else is evidence, and she cannot have Madame Genevieve wondering why there is an extra sum in her purse.

"Thank you for your work, Madame. I am off." She steps out the door, poking her head back inside for a moment to say, "Do rest well."

Chapter Twenty-Nine

The four of them sit comfortably in a carriage and ride toward the masquerade.

"We look amazing," August says, wearing tight trousers and a sage green and gold corset vest over a proper white shirt with a soft lace ruff. He dons his gold mask and hides the ribbons in his curly hair. Beside him, Frankie is wearing a perfectly tailored vest of an expensive blue fabric with a shimmering pattern throughout. He leaves his black coat unbuttoned, and his mask matches the vest and accentuates his blue eyes.

Marigold has a masquerade gown she wore a few years ago that she still fits into. It's almost better fitting now that she fills it out. Her breasts press against the top, making them look even fuller than they are, and her waist is cinched tightly in the corset that she wore over the dress. It is a deep red with orange and gold throughout, and the matching mask is complete with designs of dancing flames. The true jewel of the evening is Lottie with her black satin dress, complete with thick lace that covers her arms and collars her neck. Her green eyes look unmistakably feline behind her intricate mask.

She reaches up to Lottie's face, her red satin gloves smooth against her cheek. "You are bewitching."

Lottie laughs. "I should be saying that to you." Her voice is shaky.

"Nervous?"

She takes Lottie's hand and whispers to only her, "I will not leave your side. In truth, I will not be able to."

This year's theme is apparent upon arrival: le cirque des étoiles, the circus of stars.

Striped tents line the gardens. Bright balloons and ribbons and silks decorate every inch of the grounds. Glittering sculptures of stars and other celestial bodies, all made by Bardshire's finest, hang from the trees. There are acrobatic dancers, the clown laureate, and a mischievous fortune teller with a dark deck of cards.

Frankie extends his hand. "August, come with me. Let us explore and leave the ladies to their own adventure."

"Lead the way," August says, and then Lottie and Marigold are left alone, surrounded by a group of people who do not know who they are. Lottie gets many lingering glances and wanting stares. She looks wicked, seductive, and hungry.

But her eyes are only on Marigold.

"Do you want to know your fortune?" Marigold asks.

Lottie rolls her eyes. "No."

"Well, I want to know mine." She walks confidently to the fortune teller and sits down in front of her, handing her a coin. "One reading, please."

The fortune teller smiles, but her eyes remain wide and round. She stares for a little too long with a fixed, menacing expression that freezes Marigold in place.

"Of course, miss. Pick a deck." The fortune teller places two decks of cards in front of her; one is light blue and decorated with some sort of ancient runes, while the other is black with bright oil paintings of enchanting flowers. Marigold hesitates to reach for a deck but eventually finds the courage to tap on the card with a painting of an orange lily on top. "This one."

"Wise choice," the fortune teller says as her sharp teeth catch the end of the word and drag it out into a long hiss. Marigold shifts in her seat as she feels something threatening radiating off the sinister woman before her.

"I bet you say that to everyone," Lottie mumbles under her

breath. It seems that the fortune teller does not hear her, or perhaps does not care what she has to say. Her eyes are pinned on Marigold like tiny needles. She shuffles her cards and then turns over one, revealing the three of swords.

"I see a struggling heart. Perhaps you are waiting on a proposal, or a confession of love that you fear will never come."

Marigold wraps her arms tightly around her body. "Oh."

Lottie's silk-gloved hand slides onto her shoulder, occasionally stroking the side of her throat. "It's not real, Mari."

The fortune teller proceeds to turn over another card—the nine of wands. "But you refuse to give up. You do not fear your broken heart. You defy it." She turns over a new card and gasps at the picture: the tower. "There is a danger growing. A burgeoning darkness. A great battle will come, and it will require dire sacrifices." The final card is revealed, and even Lottie gasps with recognition of this one. It is Death. The fortune teller smiles and runs her tongue over her teeth, as if she is savoring the taste of this moment.

"What does this mean? Am I to die?"

She shrugs. "Maybe. Maybe not. This card merely symbolizes the death of an era that does not serve you anymore. There will be change. There will be reformation. Then, if you play your hand correctly, there will be resurrection."

"I see," she says, though the words do nothing to calm her beating heart. Lottie pulls her out of the chair and holds her chin with one hand.

"Calm down, Mari. It's a circus act, not a curse."

"I thought you believed in magic now."

"I believe in yours. Not this."

For the first time, Marigold is glad for Lottie's skepticism. She does not want to believe the reading. Not tonight.

"You're right. Let's dance."

Lottie stiffens slightly, but she pushes past her discomfort. "You must teach me."

"Do not fret; I am a terrible dancer. There will be no judgment from me."

She can feel the eyes of the fortune teller upon them as they walk away, but she does not look back. Something in her core tells her to keep walking away without so much as a glance over her shoulder. She keeps her gaze on the impossible girl at her side.

There is a striped tent in the center of the gardens with light streaming out from the point at the top. As they enter, it's as if the entire world stops to look at them. She pulls Lottie to her side possessively, and they are almost immediately swept away in a mass of moving people. The enticing sound of a string quartet carries their feet through a sensual waltz.

Marigold holds Lottie's hand and puts the other on the bend of her waist. "Follow my feet, Miss Burke. I'll lead."

Their bodies are pressed together, every movement in perfect time with each other. Lottie has a few stumbles, but Marigold holds her tightly and continues leading her across the floor. Together, they are fire and wind, desire and grace, seduction and fear. Marigold spins Lottie outward but keeps a strong hold on her hand, prompting her to twirl back into her arms. As Lottie moves, the skirt of her dress flares around them like a cloud of smoke. When she is pressed back against Marigold's chest, Lottie brings her hand upward and strokes Marigold's cheek. Her fingers trail farther down, all along the outline of her jaw, down her exposed throat, and off her collarbone. Their masks scrape as they keep their faces close and sway into each other's bodies. Other masked dancers circle around them, unable to pull their gaze away. When Lottie notices all the eyes on them, she smirks.

"We've gathered some attention, Mari."

This is usually the point where she loses control of her feet and makes a mess of the rest of the dance. She has a moment of fear and panic when she sees the still onlookers around them, but she pushes it away.

"I don't care. I only see you."

"Just you and me," Lottie says as she surprises Marigold by seamlessly taking the lead in their dance and waltzing them both around the open circle in the middle of the floor. Lottie places her hands against the small of Marigold's back and dips her low, her blond hair almost touching the floor. Lottie presses a feather-light kiss to the bending point of her neck. She then brings Marigold upright and spins her to the center of the floor, chasing behind. When they reconnect, Marigold braces her hands on Lottie's waist and picks her up. They spin gracefully to the sound of roaring applause from their audience. The sounds of the violin begin to shrink, and they part at the end of the song with a curtsy to each other. Their chests heave against their tight gowns as their eyes remain locked.

Marigold's deep breathing scratches her dry throat. "May I grab you a glass of champagne?" she asks.

Lottie nods. "Hurry back to me."

With a squeeze of her hand, Marigold steps away to find a server carrying a tray of champagne flutes. As she turns, the swaying crowd disorients her. She searches the crowd frantically until she spots Lottie again and can breathe a sigh of relief.

A man in a white marbled mask steps in her way and blocks Lottie from her vision.

"Who is this exquisite creature?" he says loudly. Lottie's only response is a scoff, which he does not take kindly.

"Are you going to make me fight for your affection?" he says as he approaches and grabs Lottie's face. "Because I will fight, if need be." The moment his hand rises, Marigold all but leaps into action as she runs to them. Her hands are on his wrists; her anger strains her voice.

"Get your hands off her." She throws his wrist out of her grip hard enough to make him stumble. Her body shields Lottie from the man, braced as if she is ready to take a bullet if she has to.

"Come now, I only ask for a little fun."

She recognizes this voice. She still hears it in her nightmares. The man behind the mask is George Tennyson. Her gaze moves to his left hand—no ring. He did not marry Priya.

"What happened with your betrothal, George? Did she realize

she was too good for you?" She knows she's breaking a cardinal rule of the masquerade by identifying him and using his name, but she doesn't care.

Taken aback, he says, "How dare you—" His eyes narrow, then glimmer with recognition. "I know that dress. My, my, Mari. When did you return?"

She grimaces. "That is not your concern."

"I disagree. From my understanding, my proposal was the reason you left."

She cannot help but laugh. "You misunderstand. I left for something far more important than you."

Lottie takes her hand and glares at George. "Leave my girl alone."

My girl. Marigold's whole body ignites with passion.

George laughs. "I have no interest in her. I am here to dance with you."

"She is mine," Marigold growls in a voice too angry to sound like her own. Even she is unaware of what is coming over her. Never has she felt so enraged, so defensive, and so protective of another person. Energy buzzes and clicks at her fingertips. A mild wind encircles them—something that should be impossible inside the tent. There is a deafening crash of thunder above them, as if the sky is colliding with itself, snapping the clouds like brittle bones. The entire tent gasps at the sudden sound. She stands perfectly still, solid as a spire, and her magic pours out from her in a way she has never experienced before. Her imagination runs wild with visions of George getting struck by lightning, of the entire crowd being consumed by hungry wind. Torrential rain pours from the opening of the tent, and she grins. George's eyes grow wide with fear as he turns, running into the hectic crowd until he disappears.

Lottie grabs Marigold's waist. "Mari, is this your doing?"

"I will not let anyone touch you," she growls.

"He's gone now. You must stop. People will know this is unnatural if it grows any further. It's not safe!"

Lottie is right, but she can't stop. She doesn't know how.

"Mari, please," she whimpers. "I'm scared of storms."

She freezes, feeling the terror radiating from Lottie's body. She wrestles with her rage and swallows her murderous desires. The rain slows, but it doesn't stop. As she starts coming to her senses, she feels disgusted with herself. How could she lose herself so much? How could she give in to such bloodlust? What would Althea say if she could see her now?

With all her might, she starts pulling her magic back into herself. It feels like trying to move a mountain with only ribbon and twine. Her limbs shake as magic floods her blood. She's drowning in it. She can't see, can't breathe, can't move. No matter how hard she tries, she cannot force the air back into her lungs. Blackness pools at the edges of her vision and her knees give out, but Lottie does not let her fall. The wind and thunder quiet, and a tense silence consumes the room until the people begin chattering anxiously around them. The string quartet awkwardly resumes the music, and people slowly start moving again.

Adrenaline pushes through her blood after the shock of her magic starts to wear off. She works to stand up on her own, pulling her weight from Lottie's arms.

"How did you do that?"

"I do not know," she manages to say. She has never performed such a feat, and her grandmother never spoke of an ability like this—creating a storm from nothing. She was so close to losing control of it. If Lottie had not held her there and kept her grounded, there would have been irrevocable destruction. "Are you all right?"

Lottie's lip trembles as she takes Marigold's face into her hands. "No one has ever fought for me like that before."

"I cannot help myself. My need for you makes me wicked." She presses her forehead to hers. "I would do anything to keep you safe, Lottie. Anything."

Lottie looks at her lips. "We need to run away. I need to be alone with you."

"I know a place," she says, taking her hand and racing through the crowd.

They run hand in hand out of the tent, each holding up their skirts to move faster through the garden. They nearly fly through the entrance of the hedge maze, leaves and branches scraping against their exposed skin.

Marigold does not care.

All she sees is Lottie Burke. All she feels is absolute, unyielding desire.

For Lottie's kiss, she would forsake all else. For her love, she would undo legacies.

They pause for breath at a dead end. Sweat and humid air caress their skin. They are each braced against a hedge wall for balance and steadiness, but they cannot hold themselves back from each other.

"So many times, you have left me aching with want, Mari. I have thought of you every night since we met," Lottie says breathlessly.

Marigold bites her lip as it trembles. "You have defied all that I know. I am starved for you." She moves to stand an inch away from her face, caging Lottie in her arms against the hedge.

"I am going to close my eyes, and when I do, I want you to kiss me. I want to see if the curse will have mercy on me if I am not the one to act first."

"I will try. But you must tell me if it hurts you the very second it starts. Do you promise?"

"I promise."

The tension between them is tangible, able to be held and licked and savored. Lottie closes her eyes and parts her lips slightly. Marigold grips Lottie's hands as if they are the only things that might keep her tethered to this world. She pulls Lottie close, takes her face in her hands, and kisses her. It feels like they are weightless, frozen in time. They move like they are underwater again, back in the moon pool. Lottie's tongue dips into Marigold's mouth for the first time as their hands roam over each other's bodies. Their fingers thread through each other's hair. Their passion drags them both to the ground where she straddles Lottie. Her kiss moves from Lottie's lips to her neck, to the swell of her breasts. Lottie's hands push upward underneath Marigold's dress until she reaches her hips. They are completely lost in each other, until Lottie's body goes completely rigid beneath her. Startled, Marigold climbs off her and moves to her side.

With her back arched, Lottie gasps for air, her hands clawing at her throat as if trying to break free from a merciless grip. "Cannot... breathe..." she says between gasps.

Marigold searches her pockets for a vial of honey, any honey— lavender, tupelo, black sage, whatever she grabs first. She holds Lottie still by her chin and pours it into Lottie's mouth. This is exactly why she wanted to wait until they returned to Innisfree. What if this honey isn't enough?

"Why didn't you tell me to stop?" she asks, panicking.

Lottie swallows the honey, and her heart rate begins to calm. A few intense minutes tick by, and her lips start to move. Her words punctuate her labored breathing. "I... did not... want... to stop." Her trembling hand finds Marigold's. "I... still... want... you."

Her heart swells so much that it could consume her, could rid her of all logic, but she fights against it. Her selfish heart is putting Lottie in danger. "You impossible girl, you cannot—"

Thunder cracks and booms above them. The air sours with the scent of dark magic. Shadowy swirling clouds consume the sky above like those that she summoned a moment ago against George. And then it's the attack-not-storm all over again. It's the summer of sixteen years ago. Marigold sees everything all at once, clearer than on the day it happened.

Her grandmother fought Versa in the center of the isle. Her

mother's hand was skinned clean, bleeding all over her body. She was soaked to the bone in her mother's blood as Mr. Benny picked her up, held her tiny body to his chest and whispered desperate prayers for her to live.

"Mama!" her mother screamed to Althea.

"Go, Raina! Now!"

Then they were in a carriage—she was sitting next to little August. They huddled into each other, crying silently, as if they knew that they were supposed to be hiding. August's mother was putting pressure on her mother's hand. Mr. Benny was driving. The carriage was moving so fast. It was bumpy. Her mother's blood kept splattering on the walls. It got in her eyes and it burned.

"You're going to be all right," Mr. Benny kept calling from the driver's seat. "You're going to be all right."

He was crying. They were all crying.

Because they weren't going to be all right.

August's mother had a jar of honey. She was fumbling with it, trying to get it to open, but her mother pushed it away.

"It's too late," her mother said. Marigold knew then that her mother was going to die. She pulled herself out of August's little arms, stood up and wobbled on her short legs in the bumpy carriage. Her mother closed her eyes, surrendering to the loss of blood. August's mother cried over her and cursed the world. Marigold found the jar of honey, fought against the blood on the lid that made it slippery, and got it open. She scooped it out with her fist, slathered it onto her mother's wounds, and breathed.

Eyes closed, she pictured their last happy day. Bumblebees and sweet pies. Her grandmother's silly stories. Mud potions with August. Her mother, beautiful and whole, sipping tea in the garden. The world was beautiful. Her grandmother was not fighting. Her mother was not dying. And she was just a child who wanted everything to be good again.

And when she opened her eyes, it was good. Her mother's bones were no longer exposed. Her breathing had steadied. She was asleep, but she was not dead. She was not even dying. And it was good.

How did she perform such a feat at six years old without ever performing the ritual to access her full power? What could have given her such strength, and why was the same storm happening again now?

Suddenly, Marigold is back in the present. A ring of fire surrounds her and Lottie, trapping them in each other's arms.

"What's happening?" Lottie says breathlessly as she presses herself into Marigold's body. Another impossibly loud crack of thunder. The flames start to rise and lick the hem of their dresses. Marigold wraps one arm tightly around Lottie's waist and helps her stand, while she reaches her other hand up toward the sky. She instinctively curls her fingers into a fist, bringing the clouds closer. Lottie whimpers as the storm closes in on them, but then the rain comes. The clouds cry over them, soaking their gowns and putting out the mysterious flames.

When the flames die down, Marigold releases her fist, and the clouds dissipate as suddenly as they appeared. She and Lottie find their breath together as they stare into each other's eyes.

"Are you okay?"

Lottie nods. "What is happening?"

"I wish I could better explain. Something is strengthening my power beyond what I can control."

Lottie moves her hand to hold the back of Marigold's neck. She brings their noses together and says, "Must we stop now?"

Bewildered, she says, "After all that, you still do not want to stop? Lottie, if we keep going..." She runs her fingers through her hair and shakes her head. "It will destroy us both."

"Isn't it worth it?"

Marigold laughs, either in disbelief or excitement—even she is not sure. All she is sure of is that she doesn't want to stop. She wants to be with Lottie, even if it means the rest of the world will burn away. It's selfish, dangerous, but most of all, irresistible.

"You are worth everything I have," she says as she leads

Lottie farther into the maze, fighting her way through unexpected bends and corners until she can find the center. She needs to be alone with this girl, and they need a place where no one else will find them. There is no better hiding spot than the heart of a dark and twisted maze. Her legs tremble with exhaustion as she continues to run with Lottie, hand in hand. The sound of the fountain that marks the center of the maze trickles behind the hedge.

As soon as they turn this corner, the world will change. She pulls Lottie around the edge, ready to tear off her dress with her teeth if she must, but something catches her eye as soon as they stand in front of the fountain.

It appears they were not the only ones with the instinct to find secrecy in the maze's heart.

Sitting on the rim of the fountain, with undone vests and masks cast aside, are Frankie and August, entangled in a wild kiss.

The sight of them pulls her out of this ridiculous daydream. She and Lottie will never be able to kiss like that again—not without Lottie suffering through more unimaginable pain. Despite Lottie's willingness to brave that, Marigold cannot let her. It's her job, her heart's purpose, to keep Lottie safe, even if she is the most dangerous thing in the world for Lottie.

She takes a deep breath, thankful that seeing Frankie and August has brought her back to her senses.

"Hello there," she says, startling the men so much that they both fall back into the fountain.

Marigold and Lottie cannot help but laugh. The way they both flail around in the water trying to stand themselves up is even funnier than the performance from the clown laureate when they first arrived.

When Frankie and August finally step out of the fountain and stand before them, they're embarrassed and soaked through.

"We were just—" Frankie says, but he cannot find an excuse. He looks to August for help.

"Kissing!" August blurts out. Frankie slaps his palm to his forehead.

"What?" August says. "It's okay. We're soulmates."

Frankie blushes, but he nods and stands next to August. "Just tell them everything, why don't you?"

"Well, they saw us, love."

"It's true, we did see you," Marigold says through her smile.

"Saw a lot more than we ever needed to see," Lottie echoes. August gives her a knowing look.

"Caught without a chaperone in the maze garden, entangled in a passionate kiss? How scandalous, Frankie Claude. What will the papers have to say about you?" she teases.

"And what were you two heralds of virtue planning on doing out here? I know why Frankie and I are soaking wet, but what's your excuse?" August asks breathlessly.

Marigold and Lottie look at each other with wide eyes. They both stumble over their responses and excuses, wringing out the rain from their hair, and August laughs. "That's what I thought."

"Wait," Frankie says. "You two?" He points to Marigold and Lottie. "But what about"—he leans over to Marigold and ineffectively whispers—"what about the curse?"

Marigold grits her teeth. "You're right. I don't know what I was thinking."

And then, it's over.

The night, and all its potential, all its promise, all its danger, is done. This can never happen again. Frankie and August wrestle with their vests and don their masks. The reality of the world clicks back into place as the four of them find their way out of the maze in silence. There is already a carriage waiting to take them home, and they pile in, exhausted and thoroughly bruised.

Chapter Thirty

M arigold should be celebrating; she just helped her best friend and her brother come together. Her sister is getting married tomorrow. Lottie Burke has admitted her feelings and her belief in magic.

But all she feels is anger.

She is surrounded by so much love, and yet she cannot have any of it for herself.

It is a cruel trade, a heart for power; she is left questioning whether any of it was worth it.

Of course, if she had not become a witch, she never would have met Lottie in the first place. Is it better to have loved alone than never to have loved at all?

The quiet estate welcomes them home, and they each go up to their respective rooms. August and Frankie elect to keep their own rooms for the night, happy to take it slow. They are soulmates, after all. They have a lifetime together ahead of them. There is no need to rush, to run, to hide. She is extraordinarily happy for them, and wildly jealous. She can hardly stand to look at Lottie without thinking of their last words before they stumbled upon August and Frankie.

I am starved for you.

I did not want to stop.

I still want you.

Want—the word is bitter in the back of her throat. Lottie wants her. She aches for her. She lusts after her.

But she cannot love Marigold without destroying herself.

The two women are standing outside their respective doors, backs turned to each other.

"Mari," Lottie whispers.

"What?"

"Do you think you'll ever be able to break your curse?"

She sighs. The answer is no—tonight's disaster proved that they can't come that close without causing terrible destruction—but she can't bring herself to say it. "I'm not sure. Rest well for the wedding tomorrow, and then we shall figure it out." Marigold pushes through her door before Lottie can respond, and she throws herself onto her bed, weeping wildly.

She gives herself a few moments to grieve, to mourn the love she will never have. Lottie is in the room next door, and it takes every bit of her strength to not rip through the wall just to be by her side. Tonight was the only time she would allow herself to pretend that a kiss between them could mean more than a moment, and now it is over. There is a sharp hopelessness in the pit of her belly that tells her she will never have another night like this.

And now that she is positive her soulmate spell works, it is only a matter of time before Lottie is pulled away to someone else.

Someone whom she can truly love.

Though she does not understand why it could be taking so long. The effects of the spell should have started by now. Why is August already with his soulmate, but Lottie has not felt a singular pull in any direction?

She distracts herself with the book spread open across her bed. Her tears threaten to splash the pages. This book has answered all her questions so far; a history of spirit guardians, the magic of resurrection—it must have something in it that explains what happened back at le cirque des étoiles.

Did she truly summon that storm and then cast it aside? Without a spell or incantation of any kind? And the flames—where did they come from?

She flips toward the back of the book, hoping for any helpful information. This section of the book deals more with how Honey and Ash Witches work together. An interesting passage catches Marigold's eye—what happens when ash magic is close by? Their energies feed off of each other—air and flame, life and destruction. Proximity increases both of their strengths. An Ash Witch can control the flames and rock, while the Honey Witch can control both air and water. So, she may not have been controlling the weather so much as pushing the air around them and pulling the water from the clouds.

But it wasn't simply a storm. There were wicked flames surrounding them. Does that mean that an Ash Witch was near? Or was it simply the ash magic of the curse rearing its head at their kiss? Her head is spinning as she replays the events of the evening in her mind.

She thinks back to her ailing landvættir who await her return to the isle. Could their transformations be an Ash Witch's doing as well?

It must be.

They weren't sick—they had been poisoned. And it is only the beginning. She saw it in her tarot reading and feels it now in the pit of her belly. Something dark is coming, or perhaps it already lies in wait. Her blood is thick with fear and regret from the entire evening. She put her heart, her life, and Lottie's safety at risk. Now she wants nothing more than to return to Innisfree, but despite how terrified she is for the fate of herself and her isle, she cannot leave yet. She could never do that to Aster, no matter how badly she wants to run away. Regardless of whether tonight's destruction was because of the Ash Witch or the curse, she must protect her family from both.

She darts to her bags and spreads her tools across her bed. With a vial of peach blossom honey in her hand, she retrieves cloves, salt, and chili powder from the kitchen to create a protection spell to try to ward off Versa. It takes nearly an hour to reach each corner of the expansive estate and paint that protective arrow, now doubling the number of runes hidden throughout the house and on the backs of her father's paintings. The work calms her, bringing her from a state of panic to one of exhaustion by the time she finishes and comes back to her room. Tears prick her eyes as she finally starts to remove her costume, layer by layer, until only her chemise is left. She removes that, too, and then tugs at the bandages around her torso that protect her tattoo. As she pulls, the bandage rubs against her still-raw skin, but she does not stop.

She welcomes the pain. It is the only distraction, and it hurts less than the truth she has seen on this night. When her skin is exposed, she touches the small bee that sits below the swell of her breasts. Her greatest fear is that this may be all she will ever have of Lottie Burke, but it is not only a fear—it is a promised fate.

She vows now to herself in the mirror to build up her walls, to no longer be flesh and blood, but a girl of ice and stone. She cannot be weak again. She will not give in again.

Chapter Thirty-One

The day starts with a bang. The sound echoes from the kitchen, and screams follow. Marigold's lady's maid, Helena, bounds through her bedroom door and nearly shakes her awake. Her mind is cloudy, but a surge of adrenaline floods her body.

The grimoire is still open next to her, but she has no time to ponder everything she learned last night or continue more research this morning.

"Miss Claude! We must start dressing you at once!"

Marigold stretches her arms upward, and Helena seizes the opportunity to grab her wrists and pull her out of bed.

"Why the haste, Helena?"

"It is your sister's wedding day, for goodness' sake!"

She sits Marigold in a chair in front of her vanity and starts combing her hair. Another bang sounds from downstairs.

"What on earth is going on down there?"

"They are preparing a massive spread for after the ceremony, and there was a small incident at the crack of dawn that changed the schedule a bit."

Her blood runs cold. "What happened?" She did everything she could possibly do to keep her family safe, but unease still floods her body.

Helena leans in, whispering words of a scandal. "Let's just say that the cake was ready last night, and this morning, it was not. So now they are finishing a new one."

Marigold gasps. "Someone knocked over the cake? Who?"

"I heard from the butler that there were two giggling young boys riffling through the kitchen for a midnight snack. And things may have gotten physical."

"A fight?"

Helena blushes. "Not exactly."

She ponders until the information clicks in her mind—August and Frankie, of course. They must have been much more caught up in their budding relationship than they admitted last night when they took to their separate rooms. Marigold laughs, as she cannot entirely blame them. She is the one who brought them together, and if she were lucky enough to find her soulmate, she imagines that she would behave the same.

A sudden sharp pain makes her wince; a broken heart?

No, it is only Helena, violently combing tangles out of her hair with unyielding strength.

"I'd like you to leave at least some hair still attached to my head, Helena."

Helena makes a disapproving face. "Well, I'd like for you to have brushed your hair out of its style from last night. Wishes do not always come true."

"You are right about that," she says, shifting in her seat.

"Goodness, how did it become so tangled?"

She grits her teeth as she remembers the kiss from last night, when Lottie had her blond curls in her fist, when Marigold got to hold the bend of Lottie's waist—for the smallest moment, they were one, and it was as beautiful as it was dangerous.

Helena is finally able to twirl Marigold's hair into a fashionable updo adorned with small pearls. She stands to begin dressing in her elaborate gown that has been fitted perfectly to her form.

"Have you seen Aster this morning? How is she feeling?"

"Oh, she is nervous. But she is also thrilled, and she looks marvelous. An absolute jewel, that girl."

Smiling, she says, "She is. I cannot wait to see her."

"Well, stand still and let me dress you so we can get you out of here as soon as possible."

Marigold tries to hold her tongue to allow Helena her focus, but she cannot resist more questions. "Have you dressed Miss Burke yet?"

Helena pulls her corset tight so that it knocks the breath out of her. "She declined, miss."

She whirls around. "She did what?"

"When I woke her this morning, she politely stated that she was too ill to attend the event."

Is it the effect of the curse again, or is Lottie trying to avoid her after everything that happened last night?

"Let's hurry, Helena."

"What do you think I've been doing here, miss?"

Helena finishes dressing her as quickly as possible. She hurries to Lottie's door, pushing inside. Lottie sits in her chemise at her vanity, brushing out her hair. She gasps at Marigold's entry.

"You are meant to knock. You of all people should know that," she says, her tone cold and dry.

"And you are meant to be dressed by now," she says as she approaches. She stands behind Lottie, only able to see their faces in the reflection of the gold mirror on the vanity. There is a sadness in both of their eyes that they pretend not to notice.

"I need you with me today," Marigold says. Her hand cautiously sits on Lottie's shoulder, and Lottie stiffens beneath its weight.

"You do not need me for anything."

"That's not true and you know it," Marigold says as she squeezes Lottie's shoulder.

Lottie sighs and places her hand on top of Marigold's. "After last night, I feel as if I know nothing. Everything I thought was true has turned out to be wrong. Magic is real. Your curse is real. There is something between us, and I cannot hold on to it no matter how hard I try." Her lip quivers as if she is trying not to cry. "I wish I could fix it."

"I do, too," Marigold says. There is much more to be said and explained, but she does not want to disturb Lottie further. Now is the time to be strong and selfless, for Aster's sake.

"I know. And I do not want to make you feel worse on your sister's wedding day, so leave me here." She stands and faces Marigold, her eyes wide and glassy. "Let me do this for you."

"If you want to do anything for me, you will allow Helena to help you dress quickly and you will come with me. I want you there." She reaches to hold her hand again but stops herself.

It is not right. It is not fair.

Her hand hangs heavy and empty at her side. "Please."

Lottie chews her lip, but she nods. "Okay, Mari. For you."

The ceremony between Aster and Mr. Woodrake takes place in the gardens of the Claude estate. The greenery is tinged with autumn, providing a warm honey-colored glow throughout the venue. Some chairs have been set up to face an arch that has been decorated with peach flowers and burgundy ribbons. A violinist and harpist play soft, joyful tunes that float delicately through the light breeze.

Mr. Woodrake stands at the arch, his family and friends sitting in the seats closest to him. He is the son of a great novelist, so his family has talent and wealth that rival that of the Claudes. On paper, Aster Claude and Mr. Woodrake make an excellent match. But as Aster rounds the corner, holding on to the arm of her father, it is clear that there is much more between her and her betrothed than titles or wealth.

There is true, undying love.

From her position at the arch, next to Frankie and across from Mr. Woodrake, Marigold can see the love in his eyes as he watches his bride approach. He mouths something to Aster that Marigold cannot quite read, but Aster smiles in response. Perhaps it was a compliment, or an inside joke, or some other joyful phrase that one can share with the person they love.

The officiant begins the ceremony as Aster and Mr. Woodrake stand hand in hand in front of the arch. Aster recites her vows through her happy tears.

As the two exchange vows, Marigold's eyes drift over the onlookers. She sees Mr. Woodrake's family, her own parents, and many famed Bardshire residents. But her gaze stops on the beautiful Lottie Burke. Their eyes meet, both welling with tears, until Lottie looks away. She would give anything to hold Lottie right now, to kiss her without causing her any pain, to give her the love that she deserves.

The ceremony commences as Aster places a golden ring on his finger, and he does the same for her. The two seal their vows with a kiss and are met with roaring applause. The newlyweds must immediately follow the officiant to write their marriage lines, but Aster hugs her sister first.

"I love you, sister. Thank you for being here with me."

"I love you, too, Lady Woodrake."

Aster squeals at the use of her new title, and she runs back to her new husband's side as they follow the officiant. The rest of the guests are ushered inside the manor and seated at a comically large dining table that is covered with the largest breakfast spread that the world has ever seen. August and Frankie sit directly across from Lottie and Marigold as they all begin eating.

"That was a beautiful ceremony," Lottie says. It comes as a bit of a shock; Lottie usually relies on August to make small talk and pleasantries.

"It truly was," August says in response, happy to run with the conversation that his best friend started.

Frankie leans over to August. "It makes me wonder what our wedding will look like one day."

August cannot help but smile, while Lottie and Marigold look completely stunned.

"You proposed?" Marigold asks her brother.

"You're engaged?" Lottie asks.

Frankie shakes his head. "Not officially, no." He sips his

orange juice and looks at August, who is anxiously touching his collar.

August clears his throat. "Well, we are soulmates. What else could one expect?"

"But being engaged would mean you are already starting a whole new life together. Don't you have much more to figure out before you start wedding planning?" Lottie asks him, and he nods.

"Exactly. Which is why we are not officially engaged yet," August says.

There is a pregnant pause between them all. Marigold is happy, of course, as are Frankie and August.

But Lottie looks terrified. She puts down her cutlery and sips her water until the glass is empty. The moment it is refilled by a server, she drinks it down again.

"Do you have anything stronger?" Lottie asks the server.

"Lots..." August warns.

"What?" she snaps.

"This is a happy time."

She takes a deep breath. "You are right. You are very right, and I am happy you both have found each other."

"Thank you, Lottie. I am so glad to hear you say that," Frankie says. The four of them resume their breakfasts quietly for a moment, but there is a question waiting on the tip of Marigold's tongue.

"So will you return with us to Innisfree, brother?"

Frankie looks up with only his eyes, which then glance over to August.

"You don't have to," Marigold says. "But I thought it would be nice to extend the invitation so that you two do not have to be apart."

Frankie says nothing. He allows August to handle the next part of the conversation.

"Frankie is not coming to Innisfree, but we are not going to be apart." He looks at Lottie, who is the first to realize what he is saying.

"You're staying here with him, aren't you?"

August's cheeks flush. "We're going on a trip. *The* trip, Lottie. The one I've always dreamed of. We're going to see the world, listen to the most beautiful music, eat the most delicious food, and dance with strangers."

Lottie says nothing, but Marigold can feel the panic radiating off her. Lottie has always acted tough, but that was because she had August. She did not need anyone else to like her as long as she had her best friend by her side, but now she is losing him. Yet Marigold knows that Lottie cannot resent him for it. It's likely that the woman would do the same thing if her own soulmate spell would actually work.

Lottie fakes a smile. "That's so wonderful, August."

"It is?" August asks, his voice filled with pure relief.

"We will return to Innisfree in a few months before we're off again!" Frankie adds.

Lottie keeps her gaze low. "Where will home be for you, though?"

"Well, I think it makes the most sense for us to reside in Bardshire"—Frankie looks at August—"right?"

"We'll figure that out when the time comes," August says, eyes locked on Lottie. "Nothing is for certain yet."

Lottie nods, but she says nothing else. If she tries to utter one more word, Marigold can tell that she will start crying, and she cannot have that. Not in front of him, not in front of all these people. She would grab Lottie's hand if she thought she could offer her comfort without causing her pain. Her mother stands in the doorway chatting with other ladies about the lovely ceremony. When Marigold sees their conversation grow quiet, she stands from the table.

"Pardon me, I'm going to congratulate my mother on orchestrating such a wonderful event," she says. She makes her way to Lady Claude's side and hugs her tightly.

"This was perfect. Aster is so happy."

"Oh, I am so glad," her mother says in her ear. "And I am so grateful that you came."

"I am, too. I would not have missed such an important day."

Her mother smiles and cups Marigold's cheek. "You look tired, darling. Did you get enough rest?"

Shaking her head, she says, "Apologies, Mother. Something happened last night. I spent hours adding more runes of protection about the estate to ease my anxieties."

Her mother's face contorts as she takes Marigold's hand and leads her out of the room to a small sunroom, closing the door behind them. "What happened?"

With a deep breath, she says, "Last night, something made my magic surge out of control. I started summoning a storm and flames erupted around us."

Her mother's eyes darken. "Do you know what caused it?"

Marigold keeps her gaze to the floor. "I read in the grimoire that it could mean that ash magic was close by, but now I think it's another symptom of the curse. There is something I didn't tell you before. When Lottie and I get too close, it's like the curse punishes her. And last night was the harshest punishment yet."

"Were you close to Lottie when it occurred?"

Marigold blushes. "Very close. Too close. In the maze garden."

Lady Claude gives her a knowing look. "That is so dangerous, Marigold. You should not risk your safety like that, or Lottie's for that matter!"

"I didn't mean to! That's never happened before."

Her mother closes her eyes tightly and places her hand on her own heart. "Please promise me you will not take a risk like that again. That woman could be your undoing if you are not careful."

She envisions Lottie in her mind. They have a long ride back to Innisfree in the morning, and now August will not be with them. When they're completely alone, will she be able to hold herself back?

"I promise," she says, hoping that she will be able to keep it.

The rest of the morning blurs in the background. The

newlyweds cut their cake and try the smallest piece, and then they are off for a glorious honeymoon. Lottie and August take time for themselves, away from everyone and everything else. Their goodbye will not be easy. It might even be harder than Marigold's own goodbyes that she must make to her family. Her poor parents—everyone is leaving all at once. Aster is off on her honeymoon. Frankie will be adventuring with August. And Marigold will be back on Innisfree, fighting to keep her heart intact.

Chapter Thirty-Two

It has been said that one cannot ache more than they love, that love is all-consuming and more powerful than anything else. Marigold finds that to be completely untrue. It seems all she does is ache and wallow and wish that things were different. She feels all too similar to the way she did before she became a Honey Witch; she feels trapped.

And once again, there is nothing that she can do.

She stands at the bottom of the steps, waiting to get into the carriage behind her.

"My darling, we will miss you again so much," her mother says.

She bites her lip. "I will miss you more."

"Can you not stay, then?"

Marigold shakes her head. "Innisfree needs me." She does not give any more details, careful not to worry her already anxious mother. The only thing delaying her is Lottie, who should already be at the carriage.

"At least you'll be back for another wedding soon," her father says. "Frankie and August are so taken with each other. It's every man's dream to see his children fall so deeply in love."

Fall so deeply in love—something that Marigold will never do. She turns cold. "Right."

Her father realizes his words struck a nerve with Marigold, so he does not speak further. He simply hugs his daughter and says a silent prayer that she will find her own happiness again.

She begins to worry that Lottie has run off somewhere, that she's hidden herself in August's bag so she doesn't have to leave him. She should be here by now.

"Where is she?" Marigold mumbles to herself. "We're going to miss the ship."

Her mother chimes in and says, "You're already late, Mari. All the more reason to stay a little longer!"

A few more minutes pass, and Marigold is sure that they will not reach the ship in time if they do not leave this instant. And she cannot spare another day away from Innisfree—not when the landvættir had been so mysteriously ill right before she left.

Just when she is about to give up, Lottie comes bounding down the stairs.

"Apologies for being late. I had to say goodbye to August one more time." Her face is red and puffy. She is not even attempting to hide the fact that she has been crying.

"It's all right," she says, but Lottie is already barreling into the carriage, as if she cannot bear to stay one more moment, lest she feel compelled to run right back into the manor and say her goodbyes to her best friend all over again. Marigold darts into the carriage and sits next to Lottie, closing the carriage door behind them. The journey begins as the setting sun fades behind them.

"I'm sure the time will pass quickly and they will join us on the isle again in no time. August will miss you and his family too much to stay gone for too long," Marigold says.

Lottie does not speak. She processes everything in silence, leaving Marigold to wonder wildly about what she might be thinking.

Does she have any regrets?

Does she hate Marigold for casting the spell that took August away from her?

Is she still frightened of the storm Marigold summoned?

The rest of the ride is silent, save for the threatening whispers of thunder in the distance.

As they depart the carriage and make haste toward the dock, they watch in horror as their ship to home drifts off into the foggy night. They are too late, and the carriage that would take them back to the Claude estate for the night is now gone as well. A mist of rain falls around them and begins to grow into a storm. Not one of Marigold's doing—a real storm that will consume the night and all who are left exposed to it.

Lottie holds a flat hand above her eyes to maintain her vision in the rain. "What do we do now?"

"There's an inn over there, but it's very small. I don't know if they'll have room."

Lottie takes Marigold by the hand and starts to run. Mud flings upward as her feet collide with the ground, dirtying the hem of her dress. Lottie does not seem to care—it's as if she does not even notice.

She does not stop her, nor does she ever let go of her hand. Lottie is terrified of storms, and even though Marigold does not yet know why, she would never make Lottie stop and stand in fear. She knows better than most—sometimes being still can feel worse than death.

The inn comes into view and Lottie does not slow. She hurries inside, taking Marigold in with her, bringing them both to the ground in a pile of loosened ribbons and soaked chiffon.

"Sorry," Lottie says quietly as she picks herself up from the floor, offering Marigold a helping hand.

"It's fine," she says, careful not to cause Lottie any embarrassment over her fear. She turns to the innkeeper. "Do you have two rooms?"

He flips through the large book in front of him and looks up with his brows raised. "Unfortunately, I only have one room."

"That's fine," she says, and Lottie looks at her with widened eyes, as if to say, "*Is it?*"

Marigold responds with a stoic nod—truthfully, it worries her deeply to have to take any more time away from Innisfree. She has no idea how the landvættir are faring without her, and every moment that she is not with them is terrifying. But there is nothing else she can do, and she needs to protect Lottie from the storm. The innkeeper hands her a key as she gives him the money for the room. They go up the stairs, their shoes squelching beneath every step.

Her hair drips relentlessly down her body. Her dress molds to her form, leaving her shivering in the autumn air that drifts through the corridor. She finds the door to their room and opens it quickly, revealing the horrifying truth: Not only is there just the one room, with a broken window that the wind whistles through, but there is only one small bed as well. She looks at Lottie, but Lottie does not react at all. She simply walks into the room without a word and waits for Marigold to follow.

When the door closes behind them, she leans against it and finally takes a deep breath, while Lottie stares at the rain through the cracked window.

"Are you okay?" she asks.

Lottie shakes her head. "No. You know I hate storms."

She walks around the room, lighting the candles, and it comes to life with a warm yellow glow. Standing by the candle closest to Lottie, she says, "Is that all?"

Lottie bites her lip. "I miss August already. A lot. I feel so alone when he is gone."

Marigold approaches her slowly, cautiously, as if not to frighten her away. "But you're not alone. You know that, right?" When Lottie doesn't turn away immediately, Marigold walks closer. "I am here with you."

There is a hint of a smile tucked in the corner of Lottie's mouth, but it falls too quickly for Marigold to memorize all the beautiful details.

"I'll find a way to pay you back for the room," Lottie says, trying to change the subject as fast as possible.

"Don't," she says. "I have no need for it."

"I don't want to be indebted to anyone."

"You are not indebted to me, Lottie. I want to take care of you."

Lottie's mouth twitches as she fights against her frown. "I have never known myself to be anything but a burden. Even to August and his family. Do you think they wanted to take in an aimless orphan? Another mouth to feed who was not one of their own? They are good people, and the closest thing to a family that I will ever have, but I do not truly belong with them." She sits down in the wooden rocking chair in the corner and begins to cry. "And now that August is with his soulmate, he won't be living with his parents any longer. I can't expect them to continue to care for me when he's not even there. I am not theirs. I am no one's. *I* am no one. I am nothing and no one and I do not belong anywhere."

Marigold kneels before Lottie and pulls her hands from her face.

You belong with me, she thinks, but she does not say it, for she knows that it is not wholly true. For the first time, she thinks that she and Lottie may share a fate: They belong to no one.

They are alone.

Damn it all, why can't they be alone together?

She curses the world, just as the world has cursed her. She knows not what to say to this beautiful, broken girl in front of her. There is no comfort that she can offer, no peace that she may give.

"You are everything that I cannot have," Marigold says, which is the closest thing to the truth that she can confess without anyone getting hurt. Her hands are still wrapped around Lottie's. She had not realized how tightly she was holding on until now, but she does not let go, and Lottie does not pull away.

Lottie's eyes darken. "Shall we go to bed?" Her voice is barely more than a whisper.

Marigold shakes her head. "You take the bed. I'll take a pillow and a blanket to the floor." Marigold tries to stand and pull her hands away from Lottie, but Lottie does not let her. She tightens her grip around her hands, prompting Marigold to look back at her.

"Marigold."

"Lottie?"

"Come to bed," she says. She rises, Marigold's hands still tightly woven between hers. "Come to bed with me."

Chapter Thirty-Three

Their rain-soaked clothes are draped over the rocking chairs to dry by the fire, leaving Marigold and Lottie in their undergarments. This, of course, is not the first time that Marigold has been in a state of undress in front of Lottie.

But this time feels very different.

Marigold's heart pounds in her chest so much that it hurts, as if it is bruising her bones.

Lottie is lying next to her in the soft, warm bed. Her scent of vanilla and sandalwood tangles with that of fresh rain, and her red curls are spilling over the pillows, close enough to tickle Marigold's cheek. She breathes her in, savoring the warmth of her. The softness. Lottie Burke—the real, soft, vulnerable girl who only wants to be loved, even though she will not admit it.

What she would give in order to be able to give Lottie the thing she has always wanted. What she would give to be that girl, to belong to Lottie Burke in every way that one person can belong to another.

She would give anything.

"Is your heart beating really fast?" Lottie whispers.

"Yes," Marigold replies.

Lottie takes a sharp breath. "My heart is beating really fast, too."

Her hand drifts closer to Lottie. They breathe in time with each other, their bodies falling into the shared rhythm. Lightning flashes against the window, and Lottie shivers.

"Why are you so afraid of storms?" Marigold asks.

"Must we talk about it?"

"No. But I am here to listen if you need me."

She hesitates, then sighs. "It reminds me of when I was little. There was a period after the fire and before the orphanage when I was stuck on the streets. It would rain, and the rain would ruin everything. Whether it was a dirty piece of bread I could find in someone's trash, or a tattered blanket that was already barely staying together." She clutches the blankets on the bed and pulls them closer to her chin. "When it rained, I had nothing to protect myself and what few possessions I retained. Most of my worst memories are of the rain. And now, whenever it storms, I have to get out. I have to run and save myself. Otherwise, it feels like I'm drowning."

Marigold turns to look at Lottie, who is staring at the ceiling. "How old were you when your parents died?"

"I was six."

"I'm so sorry, Lottie. Did you ever learn the truth of them? Of who they were, or what caused the fire that took their lives?"

"No," she says sharply, closing her lips over the word before the sound fully escapes. Marigold goes rigid beside Lottie, too afraid of saying the wrong thing to continue. As if realizing her own harshness, Lottie sighs and turns to face her. Her brows soften apologetically.

"I do remember something. I remembered after I showed you my first tattoo. The arrow."

"Really?"

"Yes. I remember seeing that image in my home. All over the walls, sketched out like mad musings. My mother did them. When I think of the fire, I see those arrows on the wall, unscathed. Everything else around me, even my parents, became ash. Somehow, only the arrows and I survived."

Her blood runs cold as she listens to Lottie's memory. "I need to tell you something about that arrow."

Lottie props up slightly and leans in close to listen.

"It's not a random drawing. It's a rune of protection. It's all over my cottage, too."

"It's magic?"

She nods, and Lottie's jaw drops. "You recognized it when I showed it to you. I know you did. Why didn't you say anything?" "Would you have believed me then if I told you it was magic? Or would you have called it mythcraft?"

Lottie sighs and lies back down, glaring at the ceiling once more. "So, what are you saying, then? That my mother was a witch like you?"

"No," she says quickly, then shrugs. "I don't know. I can't explain how she would have known about the protection rune, but I'm trying to figure it out. I've been reading all I can. I'm searching for answers for you."

"Don't. They are gone, and no amount of knowledge is going to bring them back. If you want to put those books to good use, find an answer that will break your curse."

"I've searched for that, too. All I want is to touch you without hurting you."

Lottie's hand moves gently against Marigold's thigh, up and down, waiting for her to reciprocate. Marigold pulls away from her under the sheets and turns over. She presses her cheek into the pillow, rage burning in her cheeks. It is breaking her, moment by moment, bone by bone, to know that loving Lottie and keeping her safe are two opposing forces. She has to pick one, and she already knows the answer.

Lottie moves closer, touching her lips to Marigold's ear. "I have another theory to test."

The warmth of Lottie's voice sends waves of insatiable desire through her body. Her intuition pulls her closer. Her heart thunders in her chest; her lips tremble as she fights to control herself against the strength of her desires. "Tell me."

"Do you touch yourself, Witch? Do you let your fingers roam over those aching parts of you when you're all alone?"

She nods slowly, and Lottie grins. "Show me."

Marigold's eyes widen. Clearing her throat, she says, "Lottie, I cannot—"

The woman throws the covers off herself and moves to the end of the bed. In the subtle glow of the candle, Lottie looks positively inhuman in the best way. She could be made of stars.

"I'll show you how I touch myself if you do the same."

Marigold can hardly breathe as Lottie leans back, parting her legs and cupping her breast with one hand. Her eyes flutter closed. "I'll imagine that this is your hand. You're trailing your fingers down my body. You're tracing my tattoos. I can feel your breath against my skin."

Marigold is throbbing with need, aching for touch. Her own hand moves underneath the covers. She drags her nails across herself until she reaches down between her legs and moans.

"Show me," Lottie says.

She obeys, tossing the covers to the floor and parting her legs. The cold air meets her wet center. A low moan hums in the back of Lottie's throat.

"Good girl. Pretend your hand is mine. Tell me what you would have me do to you," Lottie says, circling the apex of her thighs.

Heart racing, Marigold says, "I would beg you to tease me like this." She rubs along the inside of her thigh, skimming the seam of her center as she moves to the other thigh. "And you would have me shaking before you finally gave in." Her hand settles in between her legs and two fingers dip into herself. Lottie echoes, moving her own hand to her center and moaning at her touch.

"Say my name."

She moves her fingers in and out, whimpering, "Lottie."

Lottie leans back farther, taking her other hand to her breast and pinching her nipple. "I love my name in your mouth, Marigold."

"I love..." she says, stopping herself. She won't say it. She will not ruin this moment with a love confession that will not be returned.

"I love imagining your mouth on me," she says instead.

"Mhmmm," Lottie moans, sitting up and staring at Marigold's center.

She pulls out her fingers, watching them glisten in the candlelight.

"I bet you taste so sweet. Like honey," Lottie says.

Marigold brings her own fingers up to her mouth, tasting herself. She smirks as Lottie's moan turns into a growl. Her fingers move back between her thighs and circle the most sensitive spot. Her entire body is buzzing. Every inch of her skin feels so sensitive, like the slightest touch could send her over the edge.

"Lottie..." she whimpers.

"Yes, Marigold. Say my name. Say it," she commands, thrusting her fingers in and out of herself.

Pleasure rips through her entire body, forcing her to fold in on herself so that she can hold on to this feeling for as long as she can. She imagines that she is moaning Lottie's name into her mouth, gripping Lottie's wrist and keeping her hand in that perfect spot until the end of time. Every muscle in her body starts to let go of the tension that she has carried for so long. She is completely weightless and undone. Her eyes close as she sinks into the aftermath of such immense bliss.

This can be enough. Lottie doesn't have to love her. She can love Lottie enough for the both of them if they can keep doing this every night. This is all she needs.

Fighting for air, she says, "Lottie?"

She doesn't respond, but if Marigold does not say what she is feeling at this very moment, she will lose all her courage. "I think," she continues, "I think I love you. You don't have to say anything. I know you don't feel the same. But I'm too weak to keep myself from saying it right now."

Lottie says nothing.

"I'm sorry. Did I ruin the moment for us? I'm so sorry."

Again, she says nothing. Marigold opens her eyes and pulls herself up.

Lottie lies on the edge of the bed, unmoving.

Marigold crawls over to her and grabs her by the chin, tilting her head toward the light.

Her eyes are open, but her stare is vacant. Blood streams from her nose all the way down to her neck. Her chest is still. No breath, no pulse.

Lottie is dead.

The curse killed her.

Chapter Thirty-Four

M arigold's entire body is completely numb. If she stops to think, if she crumbles under the weight of what she has done, the guilt will kill her, too. There must be something that can undo this.

She brings Lottie to the floor and presses her hand over her heart. Instinct tells her to use the same magic that she uses to revive plants. Concentrating on her breathing, she closes her eyes and visualizes her intent. She imagines all their best moments—the day Lottie helped her heal her burn, Lottie Day, swimming in the moon pool, the night of her tattoo, their first kiss in Bardshire, their passionate dance at the masquerade. But every good thing was followed by terror—the nightmares, Lottie's excruciating pain, the storms, the flames. Marigold is sick with guilt. How could she even think that this night would end any differently? She cannot have such goodness. After all the suffering she has allowed Lottie to endure, she does not deserve it.

She opens her eyes, and nothing has changed. Lottie is cold and unmoving. Her magic is failing her, and she is failing the girl she loves. Gripping Lottie's jaw, she forces her mouth open and starts breathing air into her lungs. Her tears spill onto Lottie's cheeks. Nothing is working.

She rushes to her bag and pulls out every ingredient she brought with her—all types of honey, royal jelly, essences, herbs, and moon water. Every second counts as she mixes everything together. With her trembling finger, she paints healing runes over every bend and curve of Lottie's body and calls upon her magic again. Her hopes fall as she lays her hands on Lottie's still heart. It may be too late to save her. It may not have been possible in the first place. Eyes closed, heart racing, she gives all her energy to this moment. Leaning down, she continues to breathe life back into Lottie. Her muscles tighten and strain so much so that it feels like they could snap her bones. Air leaves her lungs. The metallic taste of blood spills into her dry mouth, and Marigold's body shakes violently. The flames of all the candles in the room erupt to dangerous heights. The glass of the oil lamps and the windows explode into snow-like fractures.

Head spinning, Marigold pulls back and stares into Lottie's vacant eyes. No change. Seconds away from losing consciousness, she has nothing left to give. She told Lottie at the masquerade that if they kept fighting against the curse, it would destroy them both.

She was right.

She collapses next to Lottie, her hand still flat over the woman's quiet heart.

"Please," she mouths, for she has no voice left. She fights to keep her eyes open, but she cannot. There is a loud buzzing sound in her ear that makes her hands and fingers tingle. She forces one eye open to see a massive swarm of bees flying in through the broken window. They are not her bees—she could recognize them anywhere, even in such a state. No, these are wild bees that she has never seen before.

"Help," she whimpers. She doesn't know what she is asking for, but they fly down to where her hand sits on Lottie's chest. Slowly, she slides her hand away and lets it fall to the floor. The bees crawl over Lottie, gathering over each of the runes. In an instant, they sting her all at once. As their venom courses through Lottie's veins, mixing with Marigold's magic that was poured into her blood, Lottie's body starts warming rapidly beside her. The last thing Marigold sees before her body gives out is life flexing in Lottie's neck over and over again until it grows into a pulse.

"Marigold?"

Lottie's voice warms her ear, and she tries to move.

"Don't," Lottie says. "Just lie still. Everything is okay. You've been asleep for two days, but you are fine."

Eyes closed, she reaches for Lottie and feels her fingers thread through hers.

"You're alive," she whispers.

"So are you," Lottie says, her voice wavering.

"How?" she says, her eyes fluttering open. She's still on the floor and a blanket is covering her. Lottie sits up beside her wearing her chemise. There are stingers splintering in her swollen skin. Broken glass and dead bees litter the ground. And Lottie, oh thank the fates, Lottie is alive. Everything comes crashing into Marigold—the fear, the desperation to save her, the infinite guilt when it seemed like she had failed. She runs her hands over the hollow bodies of the bees. They're cold and feel like they are made of paper.

She tries to swallow. It feels like every breath she takes is spiked with needles. "The bees saved you."

Shaking her head, Lottie says, "You saved me, Mari."

"I didn't. I couldn't." She chokes on her words as she tries to sit up, but Lottie gently lowers her back down.

"Don't try to move. You need to rest."

"I killed you, Lottie." As soon as the words leave her mouth, panic sets in. The guilt starts eating her alive, gnawing through her stomach and clawing its way through her entire body. It wraps around her throat, choking her as she wails, "I killed you." Pushing against Lottie's hands, she forces herself to sit up. Her hands wrap around her throat as she fights to breathe. "I killed you," she repeats over and over again.

"You did not! Marigold, I am alive and well. Whatever happened to me was not your fault, and it's over now. See?" She takes Marigold's hand and presses it to her heart.

Beat. Beat. Beat. It is so beautiful and so impossible that it brings her to tears.

"You did not kill me. You did nothing wrong." Lottie pulls her into an embrace, and she sobs into her red curls. Even now, she is so disgusted by her own selfishness. Lottie went to the brink of death, and yet Lottie is the one who is comforting her now. She does not deserve such kindness. She deserves to be eaten by her guilt, to rot and die in its stomach.

She deserves to be alone.

So, it is decided. When they return home, she will send Lottie away, and she will never see her again. It is the only way to keep her safe. She turns her head to the broken window and looks at the sky—a night without stars. An omen of heartbreak.

The rest of their travels are silent, but not because of Lottie. As they sail on the morning ship home, she does her best to get Marigold talking again—quips about the food being too salty, the weather starting to turn from autumn to winter, a few questions about her magic. Nothing works.

Marigold slowly builds a wall between them, pulling herself away from Lottie as much as she can. If she were to leave her heart open, it would only cause more pain in what she knows she must do next. It sickens her to the marrow of her bones, knowing that she must push her love away. At one point, she leaves Lottie alone on the ship as she paces the different decks, pondering what she is going to say when they return. Every word tastes sour on her tongue. By the time the ship arrives, nearly ten hours later under a twilit sky, Marigold has no better idea of what will happen next.

Benny is not there to greet her this time, as she had no way of communicating their change in schedules. They must take a different carriage to Benny's house and then pray he is still awake to lend them his boat.

When the carriage doors shut, Lottie grabs Marigold's face and touches their foreheads together.

"Why won't you speak to me?" Her green eyes are glassy with sadness and worry. Her eyes search Marigold's face for any explanation. "Where did you go, Mari?"

It takes too long for Marigold to pull her gaze away, and Lottie knows that there is something on the tip of her tongue.

"Tell me what you are thinking."

"I feel sick," she finally says.

"What kind of sick?" Lottie asks as she gently releases her grip on Marigold's chin. She slowly brings Marigold's head to her lap and strokes her hair. "Just rest. We'll be there soon."

Lottie holds Marigold like that for the rest of the ride, until they arrive just outside of Mr. Benny's cottage on the coast. They gather their things and stretch their legs before knocking on the door.

When Mr. Benny opens the door, it is clear he has not slept. He takes a moment to confirm what his eyes are seeing, and then he wraps Marigold in a relieved embrace.

"You are three days late," he breathes. "I was so worried."

"I'm so sorry, Benny," Marigold says, her voice already heavy with impending tears.

"I had no idea if you were coming back, or what state you would be in when you got here. My mind went to the worst places."

"I'm okay. Everything is going to be okay."

He shakes his head. "Something is wrong on the isle, Miss Marigold. I saw smoke billowing from it last night. I should've gone to help, but I couldn't leave here in case you needed me upon return."

"What?" she yells.

"I do not know what we're about to walk into," he says.

Another disaster. Another tragedy that is all her fault. Another reason that she deserves the worst that life can give.

"Whatever it is, I will not leave your side. We'll fix it together," Lottie says. Her words rip Marigold into pieces because the truth is that this is the last time they will ever see each other.

This is where it ends.

Chapter Thirty-Five

As the boat swims through the lake, a thick, opaque fog surrounds them. Marigold can see nothing through it except a familiar flickering light, now stronger than ever.

"Is that a will-o'-the-wisp?" Mr. Benny says.

"You see it, too?" Marigold says, horrified.

"Of course. It's shining clear as day."

"What is a will-o'-the-wisp?" Lottie asks.

"It's sometimes called a ghost light. It's an old superstition," Mr. Benny says.

Marigold and Lottie both stare, waiting for him to continue.

"Well, it's an old folktale, really. Supposedly it is an omen of something sinister or strange. But it's silly."

Marigold looks at Lottie. "Do you see it, too?"

"That flickering light? Yes, of course I see it."

Marigold is already on the verge of panic. That will-o'-the-wisp has been casting its threatening glow ever since her arrival. Her grandmother thought it was another landvættir, but Althea never saw it for herself. She did not know what it was, but Marigold felt it in her bones from the beginning. Now that the will-o'-the-wisp is strong enough for even Lottie and Mr. Benny to see, it is far beyond an omen—it is a threat.

The boat emerges from the wet white fog once it reaches the dock of Innisfree.

Someone else has been there. Marigold senses the disruption, the invasion. She stiffens in her seat, rigid beside Lottie. Odessa, the swan landvættir, has reverted to her sickly state, and Marigold blames herself entirely. It is not as if she could have stayed here instead of going to Bardshire, but if Lottie were not with her, she would have been here to protect it when whatever Mr. Benny saw occurred.

And Lottie would not have been with her if Marigold had just let her go in the very beginning, the way she should have done. The landvættir were obviously too weak to protect the isle on their own fully. But what of the protection wards? Why weren't they enough to stop this?

The air is sour and tinted green with the smell of ash and death. As she pulls herself off the boat, all the horror before her becomes real.

Cindershine runs to meet them at the coast, screeching in horror as he beckons them to follow. While Marigold stands frozen, Lottie rushes to her side. Marigold looks past her to Mr. Benny, who has just emerged from the boat. As he walks, he pauses. A thought comes to him, slamming into his head like a hammer to an iron nail. He gasps. "Her grave."

It is all he needs to say to send Marigold into a panic. Her grandmother's grave, left alone and exposed to her greatest enemy. She drops every belonging, and she runs.

Up the stone path.

Through the flower gardens.

To the apiary behind the Honey Witch cottage.

Her dress is sullied with the dirt and blood that speckle the ground. The moist air burrows through her dress and slimes her skin underneath, but she does not slow. She must get to Althea.

The hives do not peer over from a gentle vantage point, waiting to greet her. She sees no white boxes, no drips of fresh honey, no bees bumbling like dandelion wishes.

She sees the ruins of what it once was.

All of the hives—destroyed. Empty. Burned.

All of the bees—dead. Their tiny bodies litter the ground like bullet shells after a battle. Talaya, the landvættir of the apiary, looks even worse than she did on the day that Marigold first discovered the sickness. Talaya is barely able to move, her body withered to nothing but scales and bone. Versa is the only threat who could have caused such damage. What other enemy exists? Who else would be able to harm the landvættir? Still, the Ash Witch should not have been able to penetrate the protection wards. It's impossible.

The copper wind chimes at Althea's graveside lay on the ground, snapped in half like twigs. Marigold walks forward, her legs shaking beneath her anger. Her knees collide with the splintered wood and honey-sodden grass where a hive used to be. She runs to her grandmother's graveside and weeps.

"I have brought this upon myself. It's all my fault." She wipes her tears with sticky fingers. There is a hand on her shoulder now, but it is not enough to pull her from the agony in her mind. She has never felt such a deep sense of failure. Someone is speaking to her, but the sounds fall over her like the fog above the lake.

"I should have been here to protect them. I knew they were weak, and I left anyway," she cries again until the hand on her shoulder tenses into a strong grasp.

"Was it the Ash Witch? How could she do this?" Lottie says.

"My protection wards were not strong enough. My return was late, and it cost us everything."

"It's not your fault. There was nothing you could have done," Lottie says.

She looks up at her. "There is something I could have done. And I should have done it a long time ago."

Chapter Thirty-Six

Now is the time for Marigold to break her own heart. Shatter her own world even further than it already has been. Protect herself and her isle from any more damage. She looks at Lottie one last time, taking in every detail.

The gold flecks in the center of her wintergreen eyes.

The string of freckles across her nose that look like newly bloomed dandelions.

Wild red curls that touch her face softly, lovingly, the way Marigold cannot.

She takes a breath and shuts her eyes, unwilling to witness Lottie's face as she speaks.

"I need you to go."

Lottie almost laughs in surprise. "What?"

Marigold hears the sadness in her voice, but she cannot stop. "Go, Lottie."

Lottie stumbles for a response until she says, "Okay. I can give you some time alone, and then we'll figure this out."

Her entire body tenses; her muscles tighten like new violin strings. "No. I need you to leave the isle. I need you to leave and not come back." She finally opens her eyes and sees Lottie before her, breaking slowly, word by word.

"Why?"

Because I am desperately in love with you and I feel my heart bleeding out every time I look into your eyes. Because I feel like

I am suffocating every time I think of how my curse broke you. Because right now I would rather be dead than say the things I'm saying to you, but I don't have a choice.

She says none of her truths.

Marigold gestures to the destruction around them. "Because it's not safe here for you."

Lottie shakes her head. "I don't need safe. I need you."

"*I* am not safe for you. My curse has already killed you once. It will do it again, and I cannot protect you."

Lottie says nothing, but she does not move.

"Please, Lottie, I am begging you to leave. What more can I say?" Her frustration builds and buzzes within her fists.

"Say you don't want me," Lottie says.

She almost laughs in her face. "What?"

"Say you don't want me, and I will leave," she says, her voice even more defiant.

She searches for words. "I . . ."

"You can't," Lottie interrupts. "You can't say it because it's not true. You want me."

"Stop it." Marigold's hands cover her face, but Lottie pulls them away.

"Admit it."

"Admit what? That I am hopelessly in love with you? Is that what you want to hear? Fine! I am! But my love will kill you if we let it, so you must leave. I cannot live with myself if you get hurt again."

"I cannot live with myself if I leave you now. Look around you! You need me now more than ever."

Marigold sobs and screams until the two sounds merge into one trembling voice. "Please. Go."

Lottie reaches for her hand. "After the night at the inn, I thought we could be—"

Marigold pulls away. "You're wrong. We were both wrong. We are nothing."

Lottie doesn't move, and Marigold erupts, her rage clouding

above her. She calls to her magic and raises her hands, bringing a storm above them. Thunder cracks, lightning strikes, and harsh rain begins to fall, but only over the isle. The lake itself is calm. August's blue boat awaits under the dry, cold sun.

Lottie's panic rises, her chest rapidly rising and falling. "What are you doing?"

Marigold closes her palm, pulling the rain to the earth even harder than before. "Pushing you away."

"Mari..." Lottie says, her fear of the storm softening her voice.

"Get out of the rain, Lottie."

Lottie cannot stand it. She readies her stance, primed to run. "I cannot forgive you for this."

"I will never ask you to."

Lottie runs to the blue boat, far enough away that Marigold can no longer make out the details of her face. She is but a speck of wild red, leaving the isle for the very last time.

And Marigold is alone, the way she always should have been. She turns away, unable to watch Lottie fade into nothing. She walks back to the apiary to be with the rest of the broken things. She is one of them now. Lying in the grass, she closes her eyes and focuses on the raindrops hammering into her skin. Her grandmother's resting place is by her side.

"I'm sorry," she says. The rain taps against her teeth as she speaks. "I'm so sorry, Grandmother."

She rolls over, resting her hand over the grass, but as she moves, she sees something that makes her stomach turn.

There it is, in the smallest corner of the apiary, the one place that she was careless enough to miss before she left—only half of a protection rune. The rest of it has been wiped away. The other wards kept Versa off the isle, but even this small disturbance was enough to let ash magic rain down upon the land.

Someone had to come to the isle to do that.

Someone else let Versa in.

Part Four

It is the winter of 1832, and Lottie Burke has not seen the sun in days. Her room is made of darkness. Her wrists are heavy in chains. She cannot recall the taste of clean air. Her lungs are stained with ash. There is power in her veins, a dark magic that she refuses to accept no matter how much torture she endures for saying no. Fate calls her back to Innisfree.

She will return, and soon, but she will not be alone.

Chapter Thirty-Seven

Marigold does not know where Lottie went, nor does she allow herself to wonder in the month that passes.

Though she does wonder if time is passing at all. She has always heard that time heals everything, but if that is the case, how is she still so broken? Where are these healing hands of time, if not here, stitching her wounds? She feels as if she has been left to suffer, to bleed, but she does not allow herself to believe that the pain is undeserved.

She did this.

To herself.

To Lottie.

To the isle.

She's able to distract herself from it all during the day. She exhausts herself by strengthening the protection wards and healing the landvættir, providing bountiful offerings twice a day. This is the only way she has been able to keep them even remotely healthy, but she is almost out of honey, and her apiary is still destroyed. Soon, she will have to make a choice—give the honey to the land-vættir or maintain her protection wards upon the isle. In the cold winter air, she works tirelessly to rebuild the apiary so that she may call upon wild bees to make Innisfree their new home. Hopefully, she can finish before her honey, and her magic, runs out.

Mr. Benny comes to help a few days a week, and he is always a comforting presence, but he is very old and cannot work the way he used to. He gives great instructions on which tools to use, how to cut the wood, and he's always happy to paint. He asks her how she is feeling, and she always lies. What more can she do?

There have been no additional attacks from the Ash Witch yet, but it is not over. The will-o'-the-wisp's warning still flickers in the forest. She knows that she must still be afraid and prepared for any sudden horrors that may come. But the landvættir kept Versa from overtaking Innisfree before, and now that they are seemingly back to their full health, they should be better equipped to defend their home.

At night, she is consumed with reading as much as she can of the grimoire, denying herself sleep until it forces her under. Customers have all been warded off by Mr. Benny. Marigold cannot bring herself to care. She is too tired, too broken to heal anyone else.

When she does try to go to bed at a reasonable hour, she cannot escape the thoughts of Lottie. It is absolute torture, lying there awake and alone.

The guilt is overwhelming, heavy, and seemingly endless. She is sickened with the feeling that she has made the world worse. She feels the jagged edge of every promise she has broken, every person she has hurt, and all the landvættir she let down. Night after night, she cries herself into a panic. Even Cindershine can no longer stand to stay in her room at night. The screams keep him awake. She curls into herself on the bed, praying that she can make herself small enough to disappear forever.

She finds herself screaming Lottie's name over and over again, as if it were an incantation that could bring her back. Her grandmother warned her of this pain, this loneliness, but she never knew it would be like this. She has become a hollow, heartbroken girl who grieves the love she never truly had, and there is nothing she can do to change that.

There never was.

Another month has passed, and the hives are almost all rebuilt. Marigold sands the last one to get ready for Mr. Benny's bright purple paint. She knows that he is far more exhausted than he is willing to admit, and she has always wondered about his unwavering dedication to helping her, and to her grandmother, before she died.

"Mr. Benny, can I ask you a question?" Her voice feels rough against her throat, like the sandpaper scraping the wooden hives. Benny nearly drops his brush out of surprise. She has barely spoken a word since Lottie left, let alone initiated a conversation.

"Go ahead, miss."

"Why are you still taking care of me?"

"Because you are a sweet girl who does not deserve to be alone. And because I promised your grandmother, long before you ever came to the isle, that I would protect you until my last breath."

"What made you want to make such a promise to her?"

He walks over to Althea's grave and puts his hand over his heart. "I loved her, Miss Marigold. I loved your grandmother."

"But the curse—"

"Before the curse. And then during the curse, but in another way. A part of me knew that I loved her, but something inexplicable, something undefinable, was missing. I always felt like I was waiting for it to fall into place, and I never understood why it didn't. Until she died." Tears well in his eyes and stream down his wrinkled face. Marigold comes to his side and places a hand on his shoulder.

"When I found you on the floor of her room when she died, I remembered. That was the moment I remembered everything. Marigold—" he says, but the words fall beneath his sobs.

"What did you remember, Mr. Benny? Please tell me."

He can hardly find his voice. He sits down in the grass, curling his old knees into himself until he can breathe again. She sits with him, holding him for what feels like years.

"Althea and I were soulmates," he finally says to the waking stars. "There was a time when we had a life together. But when she was cursed, so was I. I lost all memory of what we were. We lost the life we were supposed to have. And when she died, I felt it. The crash of my memories and my love that had been waiting there, waiting for her, for fifty years. I finally understood why I could never love anyone else."

He wipes his face and wraps his arm around Marigold's shoulder, pulling her closer.

"Her ring that you now wear around your neck was her engagement ring. I made it for her."

Her hand moves to the ring as tears sting her eyes. "Oh, Mr. Benny, I am so, so sorry. Why didn't you tell me then?"

"Because it would have been too cruel to you. I couldn't look into your eyes and tell you that you could have a soulmate out there who could never love you back. And selfishly, I couldn't bring myself to say it, to tell you the reason why Althea and I were both so lonely. People think of loneliness as a feeling, but it's a presence. It's a living thing that takes the shape of the company you wish you had. For me, loneliness grew into the shape of her, but I didn't recognize it until it was too late. That is the true cruelty of your curse, Marigold. No one can fall in love with you, not even your own soulmate, who remains incapable of loving someone else. So, two people end up alone, and only one of them truly understands why."

This changes everything. She always thought that Honey Witches were destined to be alone, that she did not even have a soulmate. But now she knows it's not true, and maybe if she can find a way to break this damned curse, she can fix everything.

Marigold leans into his hold so that her head is on his chest. "What was it like before the curse, back when you were both in love?"

His low voice vibrates against her cheek. "She was magnificent and terrifying in the best way. She was stronger than me, smarter than me, and better than me in every way, but she would pretend that she wasn't just to protect my pride. She was the moon and I was the sea, and we were always reaching for each other. I don't think that pull ever truly went away."

"I don't think so, either. I saw it between you two from the moment I arrived. She never stopped loving you, Mr. Benny. It was always in her heart, and in her eyes."

A sharp breath escapes him and morphs into a desperate laugh. "Can I tell you the moment when I knew she was the one?"

"Share all the moments with me. I want to know everything."

He smiles as his gaze drifts into the distance. "It was the first snow of winter. There was a snowflake that had stuck to her cheek. I went to move it, but she pushed my hand away. 'Leave it,' she said. 'Use it as a guide if you ever find the courage to kiss my cheek.' I had no idea what to do, so I laughed. I thought I ruined my chances right there, but then she smiled."

"Then what?"

"Well, I'll tell you this—that day, I learned that both snowflakes and witches can melt beneath a kiss. And I knew that she was my soulmate. Always, but not forever. I know now that those are two different things."

"Neither of you deserved such pain, but you still cared for her. You buried her. And now you care for me. You are the closest thing to a grandfather that I have ever known. As far as I am concerned, that is what you are to me."

"Oh, sweet Marigold," he says. "You do not know what it means to me to hear that." He stands to face her and wipes the tears from her cheeks. "To have you as my family. To protect you as my granddaughter. Nothing could ever mean more to me."

"Then, as my grandfather, can you help me? I have to make this right. I must avenge the love we both lost."

He nods. "Althea would be so proud of you right now, Mari. So very proud."

With Mr. Benny helping her, Marigold pulls a few other interesting ancient texts from the shelves that line the library he built.
They each take a comfortable chair inside, a steaming mug of
strong coffee in hand, and they read.

For hours, and hours, and hours.

Days upon days of doing nothing but reading and never letting a book leave their hands. They search for something, anything that would allow her to defeat the Ash Witch once and for
all, save the isle, and break this curse.

"I found something," he says, breaking a silence that has
stretched on for days. He raises a small book toward her. "Take
a look."

Marigold takes it from his hands and sits on the floor beside
him. It's a tattered children's book with strange drawings and
singsongy poems.

"This must be Lottie's book that she left here."

"I know," Mr. Benny says, and her eyes widen as she reads.

> *Ash of rose and lemon seeds*
> *Make a man admit his deeds*

She turns the page.

> *Ash of oak and locks of hair*
> *An enemy will soon despair*

Again, she turns the page.

> *Ash of bones and ivy vines*
> *Bring another back to life*

Marigold chews the words as she reads them. "These aren't
children's rhymes." She looks up at Mr. Benny. "These are spells.
This is ash magic."

"I think you're right," he says, but Marigold hardly hears him.

She flips through the book over and over again. "But why would Lottie have this? I do not understand."

"Miss Marigold..." Mr. Benny says cautiously.

"No." She slams the book shut and casts it aside. "Lottie cannot be an Ash Witch. She would not have been able to step onto the isle."

"There is no other explanation," Mr. Benny says.

"There must be. It's not Lottie. It cannot be Lottie. She was with me the entire time that we were in Bardshire. She couldn't have done this."

She says this, willing herself to believe it—but she knows that Lottie is connected to this.

"I refuse to accept that Lottie would ever have anything to do with the destruction. She is not evil. I will not believe it."

He gives her a knowing look. "Who do you think disturbed the rune in the apiary?"

Bewildered, she says, "When would she have done—?" She stops herself, remembering the night that she found Lottie wandering around the isle. They were both having nightmares of fire. She woke her up. Lottie didn't remember how she got out there, but her hands were sticky with honey.

That's what Lottie was doing in her sleep. She let Versa in.

Everything comes together in her mind—how Lottie could see the landvættir. How she could smell the ash magic. The bad blood that Lottie's mother tried so hard to outrun. They were running from Versa.

Lottie shares the Ash Witch's blood. That's why she was able to resist the curse and fight against it. She is a descendant of the witch who created it. And if Versa was already close, where might Lottie have gone when she left? Who might have found her?

"Mr. Benny, I think Lottie is in trouble. Versa must have found her and used her to get to Innisfree. And after I sent her away, I fear"—she chokes on her words, swallowing her tears—"I fear I may have led her to ruin." Panic rises in her chest as she paces the library. "I must kill Versa to save Lottie from her. I have to take down the protection wards and let the Ash Witch come." She is terrified, not only for Lottie's life and her own, but for the fate of the isle. This is no longer only about the curse—this is about defending a Honey Witch's entire purpose.

Mr. Benny sighs before he stands and offers her a hand. "Come on."

"Where are we going?"

"You're going to brew up a lot of spells with the last of your honey. You'll need them to fight off this wicked witch."

Chapter Thirty-Eight

When she has made every possible defensive spell that her grimoire holds, she painstakingly removes every rune of protection from each corner of the isle. Let Versa come—let her come, and let her die.

Marigold's abilities have strengthened immeasurably in the past few months as she had been unknowingly spending so much time steeping in Ash Witch poison. She has perfected her control of wind and rain, air and water. She can control the movement of the lake. She can shift the direction of the breeze. And when pushed, she can appear to summon a storm—though it pains her to think about using that power again after she used it to intentionally hurt Lottie and drive her away.

There are sudden pangs in her chest when she encounters anything that reminds her of Lottie. It has been hard enough to spend so much time in the library where Lottie stayed during her time here. She nearly lost all composure when she saw Lottie's favorite mug still sitting on the bedside table. If she thought she knew how it felt to miss someone, she was wrong. It's different from grief—not worse, but not any easier.

When she retires to her room after a long day of learning and crafting the new spells that she and Mr. Benny discovered in the library, she finds herself completely incapable of sleep. Her bed feels impossibly cold, and positively miserable. Underneath the covers, she closes her eyes and reaches out her hand, pretending that she is back in the bed at the inn with Lottie. She keeps reaching, waiting for the back of Lottie's hand to touch hers. She lets herself pretend that she feels a weight on the other side of the bed, that she is not alone, that she has nothing to fear, but it is all a lie.

She has everything to fear, and everything to lose. She sits up as her panic rises in her chest. When she turns her head, her vision collides with her reflection, and she truly witnesses her state for the first time since she returned. Her body looks weak and pale. Her plump cheeks have sunken in, and her eyes are ringed with dark red circles. There are teeth marks on her lips from biting them so much. Her hair is dulled and unwashed. But perhaps the most significant difference is in her eyes—they are dull, verging on lifeless. She sees herself, in all her failures, and all her mortality, and she weeps.

Death has never felt so close.

Love has never felt so far.

In case she loses a fight with the Ash Witch, and in case she loses her life, she finds a pen and paper and writes her goodbyes to anyone who may find them. Her last words are to Lottie:

My dearest Lottie,

I know not what to say except this—my heart left with you. I would be a fool to dream that this letter could ever reach you, but I cannot die with these words unsaid, even in this small way. I once believed that I was made for a life without love, but you have inspired defiance in me. I love you. All of my wants fall into the shape of you. If you ever forgive me, will you find me in another life? I will be there waiting for you.

All my love,
Mari

In her dreams, she sees the end, and all its ribbons untied. She dreams of herself trapped in a swirling storm of wind and ash, fighting its way into her very lungs as she screams. She hears a voice calling her name, but she sees nothing as her vision is filled with endless smoke. Her mouth forms the name—*Lottie*—but there is no sound. She tries to run toward the voice, but her legs cannot move. Suddenly, she is sinking into the earth below, and there is no one to pull her out. Every omen that she has learned, she witnesses here. Every landvættir is at her side, sinking with her into ultimate destruction. When she has sunk down to Hell's very edge, she finally sees the silhouette of her enemy looming over her.

Then Marigold wakes, and the knowing comes. Today is the day the Ash Witch will arrive. Anticipation burns in her throat and bubbles in her blood. She rushes to the library where Mr. Benny is sleeping, and she shakes him awake.

"Mr. Benny, I need you to go home."

"What?" he says through a yawn. "Are you okay, Miss Marigold?"

"The Ash Witch is coming. It's not safe for you here."

He sits up immediately. "I am not leaving you here alone."

"You have to. Please, Mr. Benny. I will not be able to live with myself if you get hurt."

He places a hand on her shoulder. "I will not be able to live with myself if I do not stay and protect you."

"Mr. Benny, you are not going to be able to keep your promise to my grandmother if you allow yourself to be killed now. I must do this alone. Please. We do not have much time."

Tears well in his eyes, but he nods. "I hate this, Miss Marigold. It makes me sick to know that you will be in danger and I can do nothing to stop it."

"But you have done everything in your power to make sure I survive. You have done your part. I am forever grateful for you."

"My granddaughter," he says softly. "I am so grateful for you, too."

When he is ready, they walk to the dock together, and he sails into the fog.

Now Marigold must wait.

She is hungry for a battle.

Chapter Thirty-Nine

The air hums with tension. The landvættir vibrate with rage. But Marigold is no longer afraid—she has been waiting for this, for an opportunity to fight for her freedom by any means necessary. All of her pain and losses have brought her to this moment. She is both a witch and a warrior.

As she stands close to the dock with an array of different spells and potions all fastened around her body in a makeshift harness, a black boat emerges from the snowy fog. It comes closer, carrying flames that are whipping in the wind.

No, not flames—bright red hair. The boat reaches the dock and a hideous old woman steps out, standing a few feet away from her.

Beside Versa stands Lottie, chained by the wrists and thoroughly bruised. Her clothes are tattered and covered with powdery ash. The ends of her hair are singed, and her skin is wounded with countless cuts and burns.

"Marigold," Versa taunts. Her breathy, ragged voice drags out the vowels. It's the same voice that Marigold heard on the night that they went swimming. The harsh features of the witch become clear as she comes closer. Her old skin is pale and paper-thin with inky black veins spidering over her body.

Her widened gaze moves to Lottie, who will not meet her eyes. She knew the Ash Witch would be horrific, but the sight of Lottie in such a state of pain—knowing that she sent her away—breaks her heart into pieces.

"Get away from her."

"She is my blood. My granddaughter. I will do with her as I wish." Versa strokes Lottie's hair as if she were a dog. Lottie winces every time the witch's hand rises. Marigold's fist shakes with rage. She reaches back slowly, wrapping her fingers around a healing honey.

"She is my heart. If you want to live, you will let her go and you will leave this land."

Versa laughs behind her thin, tight smile. "This"—she waves her arm over the land, her tattered black sleeve whipping against the wind—"is mine." Pulling on the chain around Lottie's wrists, she drags her forward. "It is ours." She grins, though it does not reach her eyes. It's one of those smiles from a nightmare, from a monster watching through the small crack in the wardrobe. The witch, her crazed smile unmoving, takes a deep breath and shrieks. It's inhuman, like metal screeching against metal. The cottage windows all shatter at the same time, and slowly, the lake starts to bubble up.

It's boiling.

Versa raises her hands, pulling Lottie's chains up with her so her arms are forcibly stretched out. "Look how this land listens to me. It will restore me," she says, weeping with madness. She steps forward.

"Do not come any closer," Marigold shouts over the wind, but Versa pays her no mind. She keeps walking, pulling Lottie alongside her.

"The last time I was here was the day I lost you," she says to Lottie. "Your wretched mother refused to help me reclaim this land that should have always been ours. She paid her price, her and your weak excuse of a father. But you, my little Lottie, you are a survivor like your grandmother. You fled that fire because you were stronger than them. You were born to take what is ours. This cottage. This land. Eternal life. We will have it all."

Marigold snarls, summoning thunder and lightning to crash above her. "Innisfree belongs to me."

"You lost it the minute that Lottie let my magic back in. All it took was one bad dream."

Lottie is visibly shaking with sickness and rage. "Mari, I didn't know..." she cries, but Versa raises her hand, and Lottie's words get stuck in her throat. Every time she tries to speak, Versa's magic tightens around her neck, and Lottie's words turn into chokes. Marigold starts to run to her, but Versa's other hand rises. The hard earth beneath Marigold's feet turns to sticky mud that slows her to a stop.

Versa's magic loosens against Lottie's throat, and her gaze snaps to Marigold. "Look," she says, reaching out and bearing her wrist. She drags her long yellow fingernail down a black vein of her arm. "Ash can keep you from dying, but—" Her skin parts, but there is no blood. There is only powdery ash that peppers the wind. "—it cannot keep you *alive*. Don't you see? Your grandmother forced me to do this to myself. I want my life back. Only Innisfree can give me that, and it can grant me that forever."

"Do not speak of my grandmother," Marigold snaps. "You have burned yourself from the inside. It is too late for you."

Versa grabs Lottie by the chin and presses her cheeks together. She has the same red hair as Lottie, though it tapers into darkened and burnt ends. Her eyes are a similar shade of green, but more wicked. "My granddaughter will continue my legacy, and she will use this land to restore me."

"You could not keep Innisfree alive long enough to save yourself. Your magic would destroy it."

"So then you will stay. Your magic will keep this land alive for us, and you can have Lottie. If she completes the ritual, I will lift the curse. All she has to do"—she turns, grabbing Lottie by the hair and throwing her to the ground—"is say yes. I have not been able to get it through her little head." Versa smirks up at Marigold. "Maybe you can change her mind."

The words splinter off Versa's tongue, their sharp snaps echoing in Marigold's ears.

"Unless, of course," Versa continues, "you do not love her.

You tortured her, you know. For weeks, she burned for you, and you never came. I would hear her calling for you, screaming your name in the night." She turns to Lottie. "Why didn't she come for you?"

Lottie is allowed to speak for the first time, her voice broken, her words rehearsed. "Marigold does not love me."

"Good, pet. Say it again."

"Marigold does not love me."

"Who is the only person who loves you?"

Lottie does not respond, and Versa raises her hand as if she is about to slap her across the face. Lottie winces and says, "My grandmother."

"Exactly." She turns back to Marigold with a wicked smile. "At least she knows the truth now."

"Lottie, that's not true," Marigold says as she fights back tears.

"Isn't it?" Versa says.

"No."

"Then prove it to her, right here and now. Make her perform the ritual. Then I give you Lottie, and you give me Innisfree."

It is now that Marigold must decide what love is worth. Could it be worth giving up everything? She sees the pain in Lottie's eyes. She cannot even begin to imagine what Lottie has been put through since they parted, and it is all her fault. There are no words and no immediate actions that could make up for the pain that she allowed. It will take the rest of her days to earn Lottie's heart and her forgiveness, and even then, she is not sure if she will deserve it.

But she wants that more than anything.

More than absolutely anything and everything, she loves Lottie Burke. The agreement is on the tip of her tongue, but before she answers, she remembers her grandmother's words. She remembers that it is never her place to decide someone else's fate.

"I will not take your choice away from you, Lottie. You decide."

"What?" Lottie whispers.

"If you want to do the ritual, I will give it all up for you. But I will not decide your fate. Because..." She chokes on her impending tears. "I love you."

Heavy tears fall from Lottie's face, though she does not return those sacred words. With the curse in place, she cannot. She must decide.

Lottie stares at Versa, vicious venom pouring out of her gaze, until she turns back to Marigold.

Lottie shakes her head. "I can't. I can't bear to watch you lose Innisfree for me." She turns to Versa. "And I will never be like you."

Once she has made her decision, there are no more deals to consider, no trades to offer.

Marigold wants vengeance.

She wants blood.

The wind gathers around her; the clouds are ripped in two as the rain bleeds from them. She lunges for Versa and rips Lottie's chains out of her frail hands. Her fist collides with the witch's face, knocking her to the ground. She hovers over Versa as a storm burgeons at her command.

Versa smiles up at her with black ash staining her teeth. "You are going to regret that."

Chapter Forty

In an instant, Versa is on her feet, and Marigold is sent flying backward as a clump of earth collides with her chest and knocks the air from her lungs.

"I made you a very kind offer," Versa growls. She positions herself so Marigold is blocked from getting to Lottie. "And this is how you repay me?" Fire rages in her palms. "You are exactly like my daughter, and like Lottie—thankless and rotten to the core." She throws a ball of fire toward Marigold and barely misses her face, burning her shoulder instead. "You two deserve each other. It's such a shame you will not live to have her." The other bolt of fire comes flying toward Marigold's face, but she rolls out of the way just in time. Air swirls around her, forming a moving shield as she steps toward Versa again. The wind spins outward like a whip and slashes Versa's paper-thin skin across her face. Ash falls from the wound in a diagonal line, from her temple to her jaw, resembling the form of a monstrous black mask. Versa licks the ash clean from her mouth and growls.

She crushes a vial of ash in her fist and utters a wicked incantation as she throws it toward Marigold.

It pierces through the wind that protects her, and when she uses her arms to shield her face from the attack, the ash leaves her with harsh white burns. She screams and listens to Versa's wretched laughter carry over the wind. She falls to her knees in pain, searching her instincts for what to do next. She reaches for a healing elixir in her pocket and takes it quickly as Versa readies another attack.

But Versa's attention has strayed from Marigold as something collides with the back of her head. She falls to her knees in pain, Mr. Benny standing behind her with an old shovel in his hand.

Of course he didn't leave when Marigold told him to. He said he would protect her until his last breath, and he meant it.

"Run, Mr. Benny! Run!"

He doesn't. He stands there, bracing himself as Versa stands and faces him. Her attack is instant and deadly. She turns, grinning wickedly back at Marigold. She steps out of the way slowly, taunting Marigold with her last violent deed.

Benny is dead. She sees it before she feels it. He lies there, his body bent into an unnatural shape, crushed into a heap of his own blood and bones. His red suspenders tangle with his limbs like he is prey caught in a spider's web. There is no time to rush to his side. Marigold cannot heal him. The closest thing she had to a grandfather is gone. She turns away, unable to stare at his body any longer. Her ears are ringing loudly, and the world moves in slow, blurred motion. Grief wells up inside her, stretching out her insides and threatening to pull her apart, but she swallows it down. There is no other choice. A monstrous rage comes alive in her belly, fueled by her grief, spite, and bloodlust.

Versa conjures a fire that immediately swallows the trees at her back. It continues to grow and feed off the air that Marigold is commanding until it takes on a life of its own. A raging wildfire begins to rip its way through Innisfree, destroying everything in its path. It is already dangerously close to the cottage—soon it will devour the abode.

Then it will take the apiary.

Then Althea's grave.

Then everything else.

In response to the fire, the landvættir emerge from their posts and hurry to Marigold, who is in desperate need of aid. To Marigold's utter shock, they all become aglow with powerful magic that blinds both her and Versa. They erupt in a burst of bright gold, and when it fades, they have all taken a new form.

Such is the nature of landvættir—they take the form that best allows them to protect what they have pledged to guard.

The enchanted animals are now giant horned monsters of rage and ruin, with leathered skin to protect them from blades, and ravenous fangs ready to tear their enemy apart. They stand in line with Marigold, their commander, as she calls to the water of the lake and brings forth a giant wave that bends over the very top of the wildfire. The water comes crashing down upon the trees, drowning every last flame before the isle is entirely consumed. As she keeps her focus on controlling the water, the landvættir are after Versa.

But the witch does not back down.

Even as they attack her, biting through her delicate skin, snapping her old bones, she is smiling. When one of them throws Versa into a pile of her own ash, she laughs wildly.

"I poisoned you all once. I will do it again," she swears as she flings her ash into their faces. Marigold watches in horror as their eyes gloss over into milky white spheres.

"Attack her," Versa commands, and the landvættir turn to Marigold with promises of pain in their eyes.

"No," she cries as she is still trying to control the water. If she breaks focus, the fire may not be extinguished, or the water could flood the entire isle. She holds her position as long as she can, and then she drops her arms and only prays that she has done enough. The landvættir grab her, each holding one of her limbs with a punishing grasp. They betray themselves as they are forced to bow to Versa's command. They bring her before the Ash Witch and pin her to the ground, where Lottie is weighed down by her chains. The earth beneath them starts to crack, creating a deep chasm where the stone path used to be. Marigold is held hovering over the edge, and Lottie is just out of reach, now covered by the clouded smoke.

"Is this how you dreamed it would end for you?" Versa screams.

It is. This is her nightmare, only worse because Lottie is suffering right next to her and there is nothing she can do.

The landvættir push her face down farther into the chasm. "Look at your fate, foolish girl. Look at the grave you have made for yourself and the girl you claimed to love."

Marigold sobs in agony. Versa's ash swarms all around her, and it breaks her very soul. Every ember is a fragment of Innisfree that has been destroyed. She was not strong enough to stop it, and now she is not strong enough to save it. The wildfire reignites, making a wealth of endless ash that ensures Versa's victory.

This is where it stops. This is how it ends. People do not often dream of dying, but they should. They should dream of a warm supper at a big table where every seat is full, then lying in their bed made of fresh linens, and the final page of a book that they will read before blowing out a candle for the last time. They should dream of being old and soft and blissfully tired, of having made so many memories that their heart cannot hold any more, of being ready to walk away from their body and into a world of stars. That is what death should be—not this. Not this shock, this unspent grief, this infinite pain consuming the last of her. She can hardly see Lottie through the smoke that is thick enough to feel of heavy fabric, but that may be for the best. Lottie does not deserve the pain of watching her die. Versa stands over Marigold with a bolt of fire hovering in her hand.

"Stop!" Lottie screams, throwing herself in between Marigold and Versa. "I'll do anything you ask if you let her live."

Marigold tries to say no, but no sound comes out. She shakes her head, blood sloshing in her ears. The wildfire rages behind them.

"*Don't*," she whispers, but Lottie does not hear.

Immediately, Versa retracts her magic back into herself, eliminating the gray-green glow from the air. "I knew you would break for her."

Lottie tilts her chin so that the light brushes her feathered jaw. "So did I."

"This is the offer: You accept your magic and join me. Innisfree is ours, forever. Marigold can live if and only if she obeys my command. She will keep the isle alive for us. Otherwise, she dies."

Lottie looks down at her with glassy eyes. "I cannot let you die without knowing how it feels to finally love you the way I know I am meant to." Turning back to Versa, she says, "I accept. Do what you must."

Chapter Forty-One

The landvættir remain trapped in their monstrous forms, poisoned with ash. Chesha keeps her unwavering grip locked on Marigold. Her wrists are probably broken by now, but her body is starting to go numb. She had to use the rest of her energy to put out Versa's wildfire—once a fire that big has started, even an Ash Witch will lose control. Summoning a rainstorm was the only way to stop it. She's now held under the wisteria tree, barely able to stand, watching her world fall apart. Odessa and Talaya take all that is left of her honey and dump it into the lake so that Marigold will have to maintain the isle using only the magic in her blood. Exhausting herself like that, with no honey to restore her, will keep her weak—too weak to fight back.

The Ash Witch ritual is a dark mirror to what Marigold performed with Althea. The tip of Versa's finger ignites, and she presses the flame onto Lottie's waiting palm. Lottie winces as the witch presses the sharp point of her long fingernail into her skin until she draws blood. As it pools in her hand, it starts to bubble and boil against the flame, and Lottie screams. Her knees buckle beneath her and she falls to the ground, but Versa keeps a firm grasp on her hand.

"Power is pain. We burn for it," Versa bellows. Lottie claws at her throat with her other hand until suddenly, she ceases. Her eyes frantically take in the world around her. Can she see the beauty that Marigold sees? Or is there a hidden darkness making itself known to her? Versa utters something under her breath, and her eyes glow as the air grows warm around them. Marigold's skin is burning up as it feels like her blood is boiling in her veins.

"What are you doing to her?" Lottie screams, but Versa gives no response. Marigold is then hovering just above the ground, gasping for air. Her heart feels like it could explode inside her and tear her body to pieces. Black smoke spills out of her mouth as she falls back onto the ground, the impact forcing the rest of the air from her body. As she lies there, unmoving, she feels a weightlessness that she has not felt since before accepting her magic.

The curse is broken. Turning her head slowly, she meets Lottie's eyes that are filled with worry. Marigold can see the moment her heart gives way to all the love that has been waiting there for so long. Lottie tries to pull away, but Versa will not let her go.

"*I love you,*" she mouths to Marigold.

Marigold struggles against Chesha's grasp, unable to break free, unable to get to Lottie's side. "I love you," she shouts.

Versa laughs. "Look at what love has made you both." She picks Lottie up by her hair and walks her over to Marigold. "So weak," she says, flinging her forward. She clings to Marigold, hugging her waist tightly. "It was always going to end this way, Honey Witch. Your grandmother knew that, too. The only way to win is if you have not a heart to lose."

She starts walking toward the cottage. "Come, pet. Help me reclaim our home."

"What about Marigold?"

"She will stay outside like the insect that she is."

Marigold doesn't have the strength to fight. Chesha's grip on her is already bruising her. If she pulls too hard, the landvættir will crush her bones.

"Go, Lottie. I'll be fine here."

Lottie tightens her arms around her. "I cannot let you—"

"Pet. Come!" Versa commands.

"Please," Marigold says. "Neither one of us needs to suffer more tonight. Follow her. It will be okay. I love you so much."

"I love you," Lottie says, reaching up to her face. "I just started loving you the way I want to. I can't leave you."

"She is not going anywhere. She'll be working through the night to create flora for us to burn." Versa pulls Lottie off her and grabs Marigold by the throat. "Isn't that right, Honey Witch? When we wake up, there will be gardens waiting for us. There will be dire consequences, if not. Who knows who will reap the worst of my punishments? You, or my pet?"

With that, her twisted fingers thread back into Lottie's hair and tug her away. They close the door, and Marigold is alone.

Fearful of what punishment could await either one of them, she works through the night, exhausting all her magic and energy to regrow the beauty that was burned. Roses, oak trees, bloodred berries, rows of lavender, and ivy vines. Chesha's grip never wavers in strength and does not yield. Through it all, she thinks of Lottie. In her wildest dreams, they are far away from this. They kiss in the mornings and Marigold brings her tea in bed. They can hardly escape each other's arms. The moon rises early just to watch them dance. There is no ash, no curse, no pain. They have all that they have ever truly wanted—love. Unconditional, all-encompassing, damn-near-suffocating love. She wants all of it, too much of it. She would let herself drown in it. That would be the perfect little death.

When morning comes, it is not Lottie who wakes her. It's Versa and the smell of sour smoke. The gardens that she healed through the night are on fire.

Crack.

Snap.

Gone.

Versa kicks her in the ribs. "Get up. Do it again."

Breathless, she says, "Where is Lottie?"

"Training. She will not see you until she is strong enough to kill you if she must."

Horrific visions flash in her mind of Versa poisoning Lottie against her. Lottie's words from the battle echo in her ears: "Marigold does not love me." That's what Versa forced her to say. What if she starts to believe it?

It goes on like this for three days. Everything she creates, Versa destroys. On the third day, when she has had no food or water or honey to replenish her magic, she breaks. Her blood feels too thin in her veins. Her bones are her heaviest burden. Every breath is a reminder that all this pain is earned. Lottie felt this every time they kissed. Every time they got too close. Every time Marigold pushed her too far.

She does not scream. She does not cry. She sits with her punishment, makes friends with it, pours it a cup of tea sweetened with her blood. That is her only choice.

That night, Lottie comes to her with food and water. Chesha stands guard, one hand still firm on Marigold's wrist.

"I am so sorry I couldn't come to you earlier," Lottie says, kneeling beside her. "Her magic trapped us all inside. She's been forcing me and the other landvættir to try to heal her."

"How... did you... get out?" she asks between ragged breaths.

"I have been studying. I learned how to undo her spell."

She brings a cup to Marigold's cracked lips, and the water is so cold it feels like it's shredding her mouth. She spits it out.

"You must drink, my love."

She nods, letting Lottie bring the cup back to her lips. She forces herself to swallow.

"My... love..." she says.

"You must understand, Marigold. I took this power for us. I am going to find a way to end her myself. I'll burn that house from the inside if I have to. Give me a little time."

It's no use. Lottie will not be able to defeat Versa in whatever short amount of time Marigold has left of this life.

Without honey, she is nothing.

"Let me go, Lottie. You must think of yourself. You have to survive her without me."

"I cannot, Marigold. You are the other half of me." She reaches into the bodice of her dress and pulls out her soulmate spell. It glows as she brings it close. "You are my soulmate."

She tries to gasp, but the air shreds her dry throat. "What?"

"I felt it the moment the ritual was complete. It was you all along." She kisses her softly, wary of hurting her, but Marigold does not care. She forces herself to sit up and take Lottie's perfect face into her free hand.

"You're mine," she says, weeping.

"I'm yours. And I will not let you die here."

Their kiss deepens, breathing life back into her. She tastes Lottie's magic as it mixes with her own—this warm, sweet ash. Still entangled in the kiss, she reaches for the soulmate spell around Lottie's neck. It's warm in her hand. She runs her fingers along the glass, feeling the curves and points of the heart shape.

Lemon seeds.

Rose petals.

Moon water.

And honey. Sweet, soft lavender honey.

"Lottie, the spell," she whispers. "It's honey."

Lottie pulls back, nodding. "Of course."

"No, you are not hearing me, my love. It's *honey*."

Confused, Lottie tries to give her more water, but she pushes it away with the back of her hand and tightens her grip on the spell. "Lottie, we can use this to give a honey offering to Chesha and free her from Versa's control. I'll be free. Then we can destroy Versa together."

Lottie gasps, wrapping her hand around Marigold's as she holds the spell in her palm. "You are brilliant." She kisses her cheek. "You are perfect." Then kisses her forehead. "You are the reason we are going to be free."

Their lips find each other, and they melt like harsh winter

under a ruthless sun. This is love. This is the secret that everyone is searching for. This is the warmth in the bones, that sleepy-sweet feeling in the muscle. This is the moment between a dream and the morning, where such goodness feels so real but impossible to hold.

And yet, here she is, holding on to it. Holding on to her.

Her hand flexes and moves to Lottie's hair.

"Does it hurt?" she asks.

Lottie smiles against her kiss. "Not anymore."

Lottie strengthens Marigold every night, and Versa is none the wiser. She sneaks out during the smallest hours, bringing food and water and a heart full of love. Marigold can feel it working within her—muscles stitching back together, bones clicking into place. They start planning their attack. Marigold is too weak for battle, and without honey, she's useless. Lottie's magic, while strong, is too unstable. She can hardly manage it, and Versa refuses to teach her anything that would allow Lottie to fight back. It was Lottie who came up with the most perfect plan, one that allowed for such poetic vengeance.

Tonight is the night. In the morning, they will be free.

As the moon reaches its highest point, Lottie sneaks out of the door with the Honey Witch's grimoire in her hands. That was the only thing that Marigold asks to be saved. Everything else can burn. Lottie lays the book at the base of the wisteria tree and kisses Marigold deeply, as if it is the first and the last time she will get to do it.

"Are you ready?" she asks when she pulls away, pulling the soulmate spell from her neck and handing it to Marigold.

"Yes," she says, pulling out the tiny cork with her teeth. She stands and lightly runs her finger across Chesha's white-knuckle grip.

"Chesha, my sweet girl, I'm going to save you."

Chesha does not acknowledge her. She remains cold and still

like a statue. Lottie takes a deep breath, then lunges for Chesha's throat and drags her to the ground. The landvættir thrashes violently, pulling Marigold around as if she were weightless. Her head collides with the gnarled roots of the nearby tree, but before the pain can set in, Chesha flings her to the other side and smashes her back against the earth. Something cracks. Pain shoots through her neck and chest.

"I cannot hold her!" Lottie says.

Gritting her teeth, swallowing down the worst of her pain, Marigold pulls herself up. The soulmate spell is broken in her hand, and glittery shards of glass burrow deep into her palm. Her fingers find the part of the bottle that is most intact. With all the fight in her body, she brings her hand to Chesha's mouth and pours the honey inside.

It is instant. The milky haze leaves Chesha's eyes, and they light up when she sees Marigold. Her grip releases. There are bone-deep black bruises and broken blood vessels in its wake. Lottie pulls her away from Chesha, but the landvættir does not move.

In Chesha's eyes, there is such profound apology, such deep sorrow. Marigold smiles up at her. There will be no grudge held here.

"I'm free," she whispers, as if she cannot believe it. If she says it too loud, will some cruel fate chain her up again? She keeps this freedom close to her chest, nurturing it with quick, desperate breaths. Her pain is extreme, but she has to push through it. There will be time to heal in the morning.

"Chesha, guard the door. If Versa tries to escape, do not let her." Chesha nods, moving silently to her post.

"We must be quick," Lottie says, kissing her fast and pulling her toward the back of the cottage. They crouch below the window of the enfleurage room, still shattered from Versa's battle cries. Inside, there is the large cauldron filled to the brim with tallow. That is the key. If they can get it hot enough to catch fire, the cottage, and everything in it, will burn. Marigold will feed the oil fire with wind and spread it with water. Lottie will keep it burning with her magic no matter how much Versa tries to fight it.

Versa will die the same way that she killed Lottie's parents.

Lottie raises her palm. Dark tendrils of magic unfurl from her hand and reach into the room. Marigold keeps her hand on Lottie's shoulder and encourages her to keep going. It's not easy for her to control her magic yet, but they have no other choice. As the cauldron heats, the tallow melts into a yellow-tinted liquid. Marigold calls to the smallest slivers of magic that remain to try to make the plants in the room grow enough to reach the tallow. They need to be touching it when it catches fire if this plan is going to work. Her eyes close. Her body shakes. It feels like her insides are being ripped through her mouth as her magic moves into the room and threads through the veins of the plants. The leaves start to rustle and the flower buds open, but she's not strong enough to grow them to the height she needs. Sweat pours down her face and burns in her eyes.

"I cannot do it," she says through her teeth.

"You have to, my love. We're so close," Lottie says.

Breathing deeply, she pushes even harder. Her knees buckle beneath her. The bones in her wrist that Chesha fractured start to crack into pieces. Blood drips from her nose, her ears, and her mouth.

And it is not enough. The plants hardly grow at all. The vines are nowhere near the cauldron.

"I have to go inside," she says.

"You can't," Lottie says. "She'll hear you. It's too dangerous."

"We don't have a choice. The tallow burning on its own will not be enough to burn the entire cottage. The plants must catch fire, too."

"Then let me do it," Lottie says.

"No. I will not run the risk of your magic accidentally starting a fire while you are inside. You stay far away from this."

"Mari, I—"

"Just let me. You have been burned enough. Please."

Lottie tries to protest further, but Marigold silences her with a kiss.

"I'll be quick," she promises as she fights against the burning pain in her wrist and pulls herself through the window. Shards of cold glass scrape her skin. Her feet hit the ground with a thud, and she balances herself against the wall. She allows herself three seconds to breathe it all in, and another three to say goodbye.

Her grandmother's favorite room.

The happy memories they made here.

The cottage where she found magic, love, heartbreak, and grief. This is how it ends.

Quickly, she breaks away dry branches from the wall and dips them into the tallow before tossing them onto the floor. She does this repeatedly, covering the floor with saturated petals and leaves.

The handle of the door twists.

The hinges start to creak.

With all her strength, she shoves the hot cauldron over, pouring the rest of the tallow onto the floor and burning her palms so much so that the skin sticks to the iron.

Versa flings the door open. "What are you doing?" she shrieks. She takes a step forward and the tallow squelches beneath her. Enraged, she lunges for Marigold, who is just out of reach. Versa falls onto her stomach and chokes as the impact knocks the breath out of her.

"Do it!" she yells to Lottie. "Now!"

"You need to get out first!" Lottie screams.

"There's no time! Start it!"

"You have to get out," she sobs. Arms outstretched, palms open, she starts to summon her magic, holding it back until Marigold escapes.

Versa howls as she pulls herself across the floor by her arms. She slips in the oil every time she tries to stand. She meets Marigold's gaze with death in her eyes. Her wicked face contorts into that familiar crazed smile, and she summons a bolt of fire in her palm.

"If I burn, you burn with me," she growls as she throws it onto the floor. The flames move like water, smooth and merciless, and the entire room ignites in seconds. The smell of salt and smoke burns Marigold's nose. Thick black smoke makes it impossible to see.

"Mari!" Lottie screams from outside. She tries to follow the sound of her voice.

"Lottie," she yells with the last of the breath in her lungs before the smoke takes hold.

Marigold's tallow-soaked dress catches fire as she reaches the window. The flames feel like knives slicing through her feet. She fights for air as she claws her way out. Her arms reach out the window, and Lottie rushes to her with a look of horror across her face.

"Get away," she yells, but Lottie doesn't listen. She takes Marigold's bloody hands and starts pulling her out, but Versa grabs her by the ankles. Looking back, Marigold sees that the Ash Witch's body is consumed by flame. Glowing embers stick to her face and eat away at her skin like maggots.

"Burn with me!" she shrieks, and the whole cottage shakes. Pieces of the ceiling start to fall. A wooden beam lands on Versa's legs, crushing them flat. The witch's head snaps back, and her hair ignites. Marigold kicks her in the jaw, feeling the bone split beneath her heel. Lottie pulls the rest of her body from the window. The remnants of the broken window stab into her legs. The skirt of her dress is still burning, and she cannot stand. Lottie starts dragging her body far away, screaming something Marigold cannot make out. It feels like her limbs are being torn off her. Her lungs are heavy with thick smoke. Her mouth drips with hot blood. She keeps her eyes on the flames, though blackness creeps into the edges of her vision.

There it goes.

Her home.

Her grandmother's home.

Her favorite place in this world. The cottage groans and creaks as it gives way to the flame, as if it, too, is screaming out in pain.

Versa's fingers are curled over the windowsill until they burn away. The last thing she sees is the cottage crumbling into nothing but ash.

Chapter Forty-Two

M arigold wakes in a field of yellow flowers. She lies still in the soft petals as the pink light of the sunset warms her skin. The wind tangles with the sweet song of the birds. As she stands, her body is unusually light and she feels no pain. Her skin is not burned, and her bones are not broken. Her white dress is no longer stained with ash and blood. Everything is calm and beautiful in an uncanny way. Why don't the flowers move in the wind? Why are the wispy clouds so stagnant? It's too still, too placid. It cannot be the real world.

She clears her throat. "Hello?" She touches her neck. How is her voice so smooth and effortless? She stretches her hands before her—no cuts, no calluses, not even a speck of dirt under her nails. Palming her forehead, she runs her fingers through her hair. It feels clean and it's tied up with her favorite yellow ribbon. She walks forward. The yellow flowers part before her with every step. From behind, she hears a voice say, "Hello, Mari."

She knows that voice, and it's not possible. That voice has been dead for more than a year. But as she turns, she sees her grandmother Althea standing in a flowing white dress, her gray hair perfectly pinned and bright red rouge across her lips.

"Grandmother?" she whimpers. The reality of this world starts to set in. She's dead. That's what this is. She was killed. She waits for the panic to set in, for her heart to beat against her bones, and for her limbs to start tingling, but it doesn't happen.

Perhaps that is not possible here. What is there to fear, here, when the worst has already happened?

"Come here, darling girl," Althea says, running to her faster than her knees should allow.

She falls into her grandmother's arms. "I missed you so much. I don't have the words for this moment," she says.

"You need not speak, Mari. Just rest. I am so proud of you."

"I lost," she says, weeping. "I failed you."

"You did not fail me. You are the most magnificent Honey Witch the world has ever seen."

"How can you say that when I am here?"

She pulls back, gripping Marigold's shoulders. "It is not over. You get to decide if you want to stay here with me, or if you want to try again."

Wiping her face, she says, "I can go back? How?"

"I'll show you."

She hesitates. "But I just got you back. I can't leave you alone here."

Althea beams. "I am not alone. I have my soulmate with me."

"Mr. Benny?" She grips her grandmother's hands.

"My Benny," she says, looking over Marigold's shoulder.

She turns, and there he is, tall and unbroken. His beard is neatly trimmed and his bright red suspenders look brand-new. He takes off his straw hat and holds it over his heart.

"Hello, Miss Marigold."

She runs to him and throws her arms around him. "You're here," she sobs into his shoulder. Althea walks up behind them and embraces them both. She finds her grandmother's hand and holds it tightly. "My family. I cannot believe I'm seeing you both again."

"I told you I would be here waiting for you," Althea says, her voice trembling.

She pulls away and watches her grandmother and Mr. Benny fit perfectly into each other's arms. Two soulmates, finally together the way the fates intended them to be. The way that she and Lottie could be if she went back.

"If I go back, will you still be waiting for me here one day?"

"Always," Althea says.

"We will never leave you, granddaughter. We promise," Mr. Benny says.

She smiles, nodding. "Thank you. I love you both so much, but I need to go back. I have to be with Lottie."

Her grandmother slips out of Mr. Benny's arms and comes to her side. "Lie down. I'll help guide you home."

She lies on her back and looks at the sky, steadying her breathing before returning to her broken body.

"Grandmother, how did you know when it was time for you to go? And how did you stop yourself from coming back?"

"I knew it was time when I was the only thing standing in the way of the rest of your life. When you get older, people want to take care of you, and that's so lovely and comforting for a time. But eventually, you get so old and so sick that all people can *do* is take care of you. They cannot move on. They cannot live their own lives. If you love them, you must leave them. So, I did." She cups Marigold's cheek and wipes the tears with her thumb. "And my, Marigold, how you bloomed. You were so astonishing. I cannot wait to watch the rest of your life flourish."

She smiles, placing her hand atop Althea's. "I will not let you down."

"Darling, you never could."

She closes her eyes and listens to the low hum of her grandmother's voice, feeling herself drift away.

"Mari, please." Lottie's voice sounds from a faraway place. She lets that voice lead her home.

Pain. Blinding pain. Her body is made of suffering.

"Mari, wake up. We just got our lives back. You cannot leave me now!" Lottie cries over her. She's telling her hand to move, to reach up to Lottie and touch her face, but her body isn't listening.

I'm alive, she screams in her head, but her lips will not move. She takes the deepest breath she can. It burns her ribs.

"You're breathing. Oh, thank the fates, you are alive. Please keep breathing, my love. I'm going to fix you. Please do not stop breathing."

She nods, or at least, she tries to.

"Do not move," Lottie says.

She strains to open her eyes. Lottie, covered in ash and sweat, starts raking warm ash from the ground and placing it on Marigold's body. The woman flattens her palms on Marigold's chest and starts whispering something. The ground around her starts to heat. Her entire body shakes and her bones rattle in her skin.

Lottie leans down and kisses her forehead. "You'll be perfect again. Hold on for me."

Her muscles tighten and snap into place. Her splintered bones come back together. Sweat drenches her dress and covers her entire body. She feels a slight tingle—it starts in her shoulder, this ball of everything bad and hard and sticky. It rips through her, tiny spindly fingers reaching for the worst of her until it lands with a thud in her stomach. And there it grows, this twisted mass of guilt and grief and pain and teeth.

Lottie holds her face. "Stay with me, Mari. It's almost over."

She cannot stop screaming. Black smoke spills out of her mouth, making it impossible to take another breath. Choking, she forces herself to sit up and retches the ash out of her lungs. A dark mass falls into her lap with a thud and skitters away like a spider. Lottie crushes it with her fist, powdering it into the earth.

Marigold's hands cannot stop roaming her own body—is she here? Is she whole? She breathes, and it doesn't hurt anymore.

And Lottie, her soulmate, her Ash Witch, loves her.

"Mari?"

That voice, her name in Lottie's mouth, is the sound that pulls her from death itself. It's too perfect. She reaches for Lottie and holds her with such force, not allowing so much as wind to come between them.

"You saved me," she says.

"I love you," Lottie replies, and her eyes well with tears. "Oh, let me say that again. I love you. I. Love. You," she says, kissing her between every word. "I can say it without pain. I can kiss you without fear. I can love you as hard as I want to."

"I love you, too. I will always love you, my impossible girl."

Part Five

It is the end of winter, and Mr. Benny forever rests beside his soulmate. The apiary is alive with new bees, and their honey is ready for the first harvest.

Frankie and August have returned to help rebuild the cottage, but tonight, they rest.

Marigold and Lottie sit beneath the wisteria tree with snowflakes melting between their kisses. Stars shine bright above them, and they have only one wish. Fates—grant them a daughter of honey and ash, a girl with star-shaped freckles and strawberry blond hair. A perfect family in a perfect home where no one ever celebrates birthdays alone.

Acknowledgments

We can't outrun death, but we can rewrite it. When I started this book, I set out to write a better death for my grandma Kathy. She used to tell me countless stories, and she is the reason I now write my own. I am honored to be her granddaughter.

I owe endless gratitude to the people who helped turn this story into a book. First, to my agent, the magical Mollie Glick. Your belief in me has changed my life. I hope you know I still giggle and squeal after our every exchange because I am so thrilled to work with you. You inspire me to create without fear.

Thank you to my US editor, Brit Hvide, for your expert editorial guidance and enthusiasm. I remember a time before I started writing this book when I encountered your videos for the first time. I dreamed of working with you one day, and I still cannot believe that you made that dream come true. Thank you also to my UK editor, Nadia Saward, for your warm and witchy imagination that helped bring Innisfree to life. Thank you to my dear friend and sensitivity reader Joey Timmons for your insightful notes and constant support. The entire team at Orbit/Redhook has blown me away, and I am so lucky to work with all of you. Thank you all for creating the perfect home for me and my books.

I am truly blessed to have so many author friends in my life who pick me up when I'm down and send little treats when I am in desperate need of sugar. To Breanne Randall, my strawberry girl and stardust fairy, thank you for being a constant light in my life. To S. T. Gibson, I will forever be your fangirl and I am so honored to be your friend. To Lauren T. Davila for being there for the highest highs and the lowest lows without ever letting go of my hand. To R. J. Valldeperas for your kindness, enthusiasm, and bright orange energy. To Megan Jauregui Eccles, who helped me polish my query and gave me confidence when I had none. To my agent siblings, Kasey LeBlanc (my whole heart and guiding light) and Deborah Crossland (my author mom who has accepted me as her middle child). To Morgan Forté, Keturah Maree, and our hilarious group chat that keeps us all somewhat sane. To Kendall Annette for always being ready to scream with me at a moment's notice.

Thank you to Ted Dennard of Savannah Bee Company, who taught me all that I know about bees and honey. To Nikki Moss for being the best sounding board for all my ideas and also for being an incredible friend. To Danie Gustafson, my kindred soul who believed in my writing before anyone else and stood by me through everything. To Liz Burton and Kayleigh Wright—thank you for being lifelong friends and thus teaching me to write heartwarming friendships that rival our own. To my parents, who push me to pursue my dreams and always accept me for who I am. Thank you to my wonderful family for the unwavering enthusiasm. And to Will, my partner and my person, you make me believe in magic. Thank you for everything.

Any expression of gratitude would be incomplete if I failed to thank all the readers who have supported this book and cheered me on. Thank you for letting me tell this story.

Meet the Author

Will F. H. Jones

SYDNEY J. SHIELDS is a swamp creature who evolved to hold a pen. She is a magna cum laude graduate of Columbus State University, where she majored in communication. She currently lives in Savannah, Georgia, with her partner and their dog. You can find her across social media @SydneyJShields, or her website, sydneyjshields.com.

if you enjoyed
THE HONEY WITCH
look out for

A LETTER TO THE
LUMINOUS DEEP

The Sunken Archive: Book One

by

Sylvie Cathrall

A beautiful discovery outside the window of her underwater home prompts the reclusive E. to begin a correspondence with renowned scholar Henerey Clel. The letters they share are filled with passion, at first for their mutual interests, and then, inevitably, for each other.

Together, they uncover a mystery from the unknown depths, destined to transform the underwater world they both equally fear and love. But by no

mere coincidence, a seaquake destroys E.'s home,
and she and Henerey vanish.

A year later, E.'s sister, Sophy, and Henerey's brother,
Vyerin, are left to solve the mystery, piecing together the
letters, sketches and field notes left behind—and learn
what their siblings' disappearance might mean for life as
they know it.

Chapter 1

LETTER FROM E. CIDNOSIN TO HENEREY CLEL, YEAR 1002

Dear Scholar Clel,

Instead of reading further, I hope you will return this letter to its envelope or, better yet, crumple it into an abstract shape that might look quite at home on a coral reef.

I become exceedingly anxious around strangers, you see, and I dared only write this note after convincing myself that you would never read it. It is only now – when I can picture you disposing of these pages in some appropriately dramatic fashion – that I may continue my message without succumbing to Trepidation.

You do not know me at all, Scholar Clel, but after reading your most recent publication (as well as the four preceding it), I feel as though you have become a dear friend. I only wish a human companion ever brought me as much intellectual bliss as *Your Natural History Companion* does!

Surely you receive letters of this nature from eager readers all the time, though, so I will depart from flattery and approach the more pressing

Sylvie Cathrall

subject that inspired me to risk writing to you in
the first place. As a Scholar of Classification, might
you assist me from afar with an inquiry of relative
import?

A few tides ago, I encountered a species unlike
any I have ever seen. Lacking a name for such
creatures, I dubbed them "Elongated Fish". They
cannot be Subtle Pipefish, as they do not possess
needle-like "noses" and far surpass the approxi-
mate measurements you offered in your Appendix.
(My Fish are also decidedly Unsubtle.) During my
observation of the Fish, I noted the following additional traits: they are remarkably quick in the water,
possibly crepuscular or nocturnal, and territorial to
a fault.

Allow me to elaborate, if I may.

Yesterday, I sat by my window, watching glim-
mers of sunset from the surface dye the drop-off
waters a stately purple. I do this sometimes when I
feel most at odds with my Brain, you see, and find
it quite effective. I was all alone – my sister Sophy
recently departed on the Ridge expedition – though
because you are also a Scholar, I assume you know
about that expedition all too well – my apologies –
and it was then that I witnessed a most unusual
scene starring the Elongated Fish. Their colouring
was a kind of magenta speckled with silver, but
stretched almost transparent – like strands of hair
about to break. Most bizarrely, their bulbous green
eyes sat flat on the very tops of their heads rather
than protruding in profile. From tip to tail, each
measured longer than our house is tall.

O – my apologies again – I hoped to avoid bor-
ing you with biography, but I suppose the preceding paragraph might confuse you since you do not

know where I live. You may have heard of the late, renowned Architect, Scholar Amiele Cidnosin – she who developed the first underwater dwelling, located a few hundred fathoms off-coast from your own Boundless Campus and colloquially called the "Deep House", Well, she was my mother, and I colloquially call it "home". While I am not a Scholar myself (and pray that you will forgive my boldness in writing to someone of your Academic prestige), perhaps you have encountered my esteemed sister Scholar Sophy Cidnosin (from the School of Observation at Boundless – o, I mentioned her just a few sentences ago, did I not?) or my (rather less) esteemed brother Apprentice Scholar Arvist Cidnosin. (Yes, our mother defied the typical Boundless custom and gave us what she deemed "Scholarly Virtue Names" – which we all promptly despised and altered. "Sophy" is short for Philosophy and "Arvist" (somehow) for Artistry. I dare not tell you *my* given name.)

Now you understand that I am uniquely privileged when it comes to observing marine life in its natural habitat.

I first noticed only one creature: a solitary ribbon lost in looping sojourns around the window. When she (?) first darted past my window I felt my heart vibrate. Her eyes rolled around in perfect circles as she executed repeated stalks – perhaps not quite grasping the presence of the glass that disqualified me as potential prey. (The sharks who frequent the waters just outside my chamber long since learned to ignore me.)

Some amount of time later – I found it hard to keep track of the hour – I marvelled at the moonbeams illuminating the Elongated Fish as she continued watching me. After ages of stillness, she flinched, folding and opening like a concertina. I assumed I startled her with my stirring until I spied an even larger creature pulsing its way around the house. As this second Elongated Fish sped closer, "my" Fish dashed towards the interloper, swirling into a furious helix. They wove around each other, tighter than thread. Tails choked necks and fins found wounds. I watched with rapt horror as they fell into the abyss below the drop-off together. Neither returned.

Now, considering your diverse experiences "in the field", as it were, I suspect you will not find this encounter especially impressive – and I confess that my Elongated Fish can hardly compete with the Exceptional Squid Skirmish my family witnessed at the Deep House in Year 991 – but the novelty of these unfamiliar creatures struck me. I adore how each "Epilogue" of your books invites readers to stop by your Laboratory Anchorage at Boundless Campus to share news of unusual sightings with you, but circumstances prevent me from coming in person. Still, I would be most grateful if you would consider assessing my account of these creatures from afar.

That is, of course, assuming you did not do as I asked by destroying this letter without even reading it.

Sincerely,
E. Cidnosin

P.S. Allow me to apologise for the rudimentary sketch of the Elongated Fish that I enclosed. Please attribute any unforgivable errors to my non-existent professional training.

LETTER FROM SOPHY CIDNORGHE TO VYERIN CLEL, YEAR 1003

Dear Captain Clel,

Forgive this unexpected intrusion from your former "acquaintance-through-grief" – otherwise known as me, Sophy Cidnosin (well, Cidnorghe now, technically – as my wife and I are newly wed, we combined our family names in accordance with Boundless Campus custom).

If it helps, I also go by "E.'s sister".

When you and I met for the first (and final) time – just after Henerey and E.'s disappearance – I promised "to keep in touch" in that vague, non-committal way that one so often does. Well, I come at last, a year later, to make that promise less empty. I do not wish to resurrect painful memories for you; rather, I hope that the contents of this package will provide some comfort.

After I lost E., I tasked myself with putting my sister's belongings in order as a distraction. Even after the Deep House's destruction, E.'s safe-box – a funny, waterproof little thing designed by our mother – survived intact, tucked into a crack in the coral bed. When the salvagers presented me with the safe-box just days after the explosion, I wasted no time (nor spared any expense) in hiring a locksmith to open it. I expected to find the box stuffed with drawings, rare books, curious shells, and perhaps a family photograph or two. Imagine

my surprise when I discovered that my excessively
introverted sister kept a cache of countless letters,
the bulk of them dating from the period just before
her disappearance – and sent by your brother.

I am a researcher by profession, Captain Clel.
When I face a problem, I investigate all evidence
and form a hypothesis. But it seems that my logical
self vanished when E. did.

I did not ignore the safe-box entirely during
those early days. I was not so far gone. I sorted
through the box's contents, arranging the letters
into neat stacks on my desk for safekeeping. (Oddly
enough, it was at this point that I found that day-
book of Henerey's I gave you when we met last year.
Why, I wonder, would he store it in the safe-box
and not take it with him?) Yet every time I thought
about opening even a single letter, I felt half-sick.

My guilty conscience tormented me for tides as
I resisted the urge to read E.'s personal documents.
I considered destroying the papers that serve as
her only physical remains – cramming them into a
crucible in my wife's laboratory, donating them to
my brother in the guise of "mixed-media art supplies", or sailing out to the vast trench in the sea
that marks the site where our family home once
stood and sending the letters to meet their maker.
I suspect my sister may have preferred any of these
more destructive options. She was quite a private
soul. But, dear Captain Clel, I must confess that
tragedy has equipped me with a new propensity for
selfishness. I can ignore the lure of the letters no
longer, even if that makes me a traitor to my own
sister.

A few tides ago, then, I pledged to construct an
archive of E.'s existence – which is to say that I have

started looking through the letters at last. I realised, however, that my "records" have limitations. I may read only what E. received from others, not her own words (excluding those she sent to myself and our brother Arvist, of course, which I already possess). With the exception of this enclosed draft of her first letter to Henerey (which I intentionally placed before my letter in the package so as to pique your interest with mystery), I do not know anything about what she said to him.

My proposal, then: if you inherited your late brother's personal effects and do not object, would you consider sharing some items of interest with me? Though I imagine the process might be devastatingly difficult, I do hope that together we may make sense of their final days – and feel more connected to them. (I have also included an ambitiously high number of coins in this envelope to cover your potential postal expenses.)

In archival solidarity,
Sophy Cidnorghe